Amy's brown eyes were so anxious, despite the calm she appeared to radiate.

"Here. My turn to cuddle Hope and keep her happy for a bit," Josh said.

And that was definitely gratitude in her eyes as she handed the baby over.

Her hands brushed against his as they transferred the baby between them, and a frisson of desire flickered down his spine.

Inappropriate. Amy was his neighbor, and he was helping out with a tricky situation. That was it, he reminded himself. He wasn't going to hit on her and he wasn't going to let himself wonder how soft her hair was or how her skin would feel against his.

"Can I get you a drink?" she asked.

"A glass of wine would be lovely right now," he admitted. And it might distract him from all the ridiculous thoughts flickering through his head. Thoughts about how Amy's mouth was a perfect Cupid's bow and what it would feel like if he kissed her.

HER FESTIVE DOORSTEP BABY

BY
KATE HARDY

First Published in Great Britain 2016
By Mills & Boon, an imprint of HarperCollins*Publishers*
1 London Bridge Street, London, SE1 9GF

© 2016 Pamela Brooks

ISBN: 978-0-263-92041-3

23-1216

Our policy is to use papers that are natural, renewable and recyclable products and made from wood grown in sustainable forests. The logging and manufacturing processes conform to the legal environmental regulations of the country of origin.

Printed and bound in Spain
by CPI, Barcelona

Kate Hardy has always loved books and could read before she went to school. She discovered Harlequin books when she was twelve and decided this was what she wanted to do. When she isn't writing, Kate enjoys reading, cinema, ballroom dancing and the gym. You can contact her via her website, www.katehardy.com.

For Sofia-Grace, the newest baby in our family—
with lots of love on your first Christmas xxx

CHAPTER ONE

Friday 24th December

'HELLO? HELLO?'

There was no answer. It was probably a courier in the middle of a super-frantic shift, Amy thought, needing to deliver as many parcels as humanly possible on Christmas Eve and pressing every single button on the intercom in the hope of finding someone who'd buzz the front door open so they could leave a parcel in the lobby. The silence probably meant they'd stopped waiting for her to answer and were already trying someone else.

She was about to replace the receiver on her intercom system when she heard a noise.

It sounded like a baby crying.

Was it her imagination? Or maybe the courier was listening to something on the radio. An ad, perhaps.

She knew that she was being ridiculous, but something made Amy go out of her own front door and into the main lobby, just to check that everything was all right.

And there, in the corner by the front door, was a cardboard box.

Except she could still hear a baby crying, and this time she was pretty sure it wasn't on a radio.

When she drew closer, she could see that the cardboard box wasn't a parcel at all. The top of the box was open. Inside, wrapped in a soft blanket, was a baby. There were traces of blood on the baby's face and Amy had a moment of panic; but then she thought that the blood might be because the baby was very, very young.

Young enough to be a newborn.

Who on earth would leave a newborn baby in a cardboard box, in the lobby of a block of flats?

She quickly opened the front door and looked outside, but there wasn't anyone in the street who looked as if they'd just left a baby on a doorstep. Nobody running away or huddled in a hoodie, trying to hide their face.

What were you supposed to do when you found an abandoned baby? Should she take the baby straight to hospital to be checked over, or should she ring the police? If she moved the box or picked the baby up to try to soothe it, would she be disturbing forensic evidence that would help the police find the baby's mother?

Yet the baby was so tiny, and the lobby wasn't heated. She could hardly leave the poor little mite to freeze there. She was about to try the other intercoms to see if any of her neighbours was in and could ring the police for her, when the door to the lobby opened and Josh Farnham walked in.

She didn't know Josh very well; he'd moved into one of the flats on her floor about six months ago. They were on smile-and-nod terms, and she occasionally took in a parcel for him, but that was about it.

'Is everything OK?' he asked. And then he frowned as the baby cried again.

'No.' Amy gestured to the cardboard box. 'Someone's just left a baby on our doorstep.'

Josh looked utterly shocked. 'A *baby*? But—who?'

'I have no idea.'

He bent down to touch the baby's hand. Clearly he had the magic touch because the baby immediately stopped crying.

'Someone pressed my intercom but didn't speak,' Amy continued. 'I assumed it was a courier trying to find someone in so they could deliver a parcel to someone in our block, but then I thought I could hear a baby crying.' She spread her hands. 'It could've been on the radio, but something made me come out here to see, just in case. That's when I found the baby.' She bit her lip. 'There's blood on the baby's face, but I think that might be because the baby's a newborn. As in *really* newborn.'

'Have you called the police?' he asked, his blue eyes narrowing.

'I was just about to,' she said, 'but I didn't bring my phone out with me, and I'm not sure if I'm going to mess up the forensics or what have you if I take the baby into my flat.'

'You can hardly wait out here until the police arrive,' Josh said, frowning. 'Both of you would freeze. Look, let me grab some stuff from my flat so I can put up a makeshift barrier round the area where the box is now, to protect any potential evidence, then I'll check the baby over properly while you call the police.' The concern clearly showed in her expression, because he added, 'It's OK. I'm qualified. I'm a doctor in the local emergency department.'

That would explain why she hardly ever saw him. His shifts at the hospital would be very different from her own hours teaching at the local high school. But most of all Amy felt relief that she wasn't going to have to deal with this completely on her own. Where babies were concerned, she was totally clueless, and Josh seemed to know how to deal with them. 'All right. Thanks,' she said.

'I'll be quick,' he promised.

'Should I pick the baby up?' she asked when the crying started again.

'Movement usually helps settle a crying baby. If you walk up and down—obviously avoiding the area where whoever left the baby might've trodden—the baby will probably stop crying.'

That sounded like experience talking. Better and better: because Amy was very used to dealing with teenagers, but her dealings with babies had been minimal.

Especially since Michael had ended their engagement.

She pushed the thought away. *Not now.* She needed to concentrate on helping this abandoned baby, not brood over the wreckage of her past.

'What about supporting the baby's head?' she asked.

'Just hold the baby against you, like this,' Josh said, picking the baby out of the box and then holding the baby close to him to demonstrate, with one hand cradled round the baby's head so it didn't flop back.

'OK.' Carefully, Amy took the baby from him.

His hands brushed briefly against hers and it felt as if she'd been galvanised.

Oh, for pity's sake. Yes, the man was pretty—despite the fact that he needed a shave and she suspected that he'd dragged his fingers rather than a comb through his wavy dark hair—but for all she knew he could be in a serious relationship. This was so inappropriate. Even if he wasn't in a relationship, she didn't want to get involved with anyone. Because then eventually she'd have to admit to her past, and he'd walk away from her—just as Michael had. And then that would make their relationship as neighbours awkward. Amy knew she was better off on her own and keeping all her relationships platonic. Josh Farnham might be one of the most attractive men she'd ever met, but he wasn't for her.

Hoping that he'd mistake her flustered state for nerves about dealing with the baby—which was partially true in any case—Amy murmured something anodyne and started walking up and down the lobby with the baby.

Josh came back what felt like hours later but could only have been five minutes, carrying several tin cans, a pile of bandages, safety pins, a marker pen and a spiral-bound notebook.

'Are you OK to keep holding the baby?' he asked.

No. It was bringing back all kinds of emotions that Amy would much rather suppress. But she wasn't going to burden a near-stranger with her private misery. 'Sure,' she fibbed.

Josh swiftly wrote out some notes saying, *Please do not touch—waiting for police*, then marked off the area where Amy had found the cardboard box. When he'd finished, he held out his arms for the baby. 'My turn, I think,' he said.

'Thanks,' she said, grateful to be relieved of her burden. Though again her hands touched his as they transferred the baby between them, and again she felt that peculiar and inappropriate response to him, that flare of desire. She picked up the box. 'I'd better bring this.'

He nodded. 'Your flat or mine?'

'Mine, I guess,' she said.

She let them into her flat, then called the police and explained what had happened while Josh examined the baby. She couldn't help watching him while she was talking; he was so gentle and yet so sure at the same time. He checked the baby over thoroughly before wrapping the infant in the soft blanket again.

The baby wasn't wearing a nappy and had no clothes. They definitely had a problem here. And what would happen once the baby got hungry? Amy had absolutely nothing in her kitchen that was suitable for a newborn, let alone any way of feeding a baby.

'The police are on their way now. They said they'll contact Social Services and meet them here, too,' she said when she put the phone down. 'How's the baby?'

'Doing fine,' Josh said. 'Our doorstep baby's a little girl. Definitely a newborn. But I'd say she's a couple of weeks early and I'm a bit worried about the mum. She clamped the umbilical cord with one of those clips you use on packaging to keep things fresh, and my guess is she's very young and didn't tell anyone she was having the baby, and she didn't go to hospital so she had the birth somewhere on her own.'

'And then she put the baby in a box and left her in our lobby with no clothes, no nappy, no milk—just the blanket,' Amy said. She winced. 'The poor girl must've really been desperate. Do you see that kind of thing a lot at the hospital?'

'Abandoned babies, improvised cord clamps or complete lack of any baby things?' he asked. 'Not very often to any of them, let alone all three together. Though on the rare occasions the police do bring in an abandoned baby, it usually turns out that the mum's very young and very scared.'

'The police might be able to find this baby's mum and get her to hospital so she can be checked over,' Amy said.

'Let's hope so,' Josh said, sounding very far from convinced.

'I'm sorry. I rather hijacked you when you came into the lobby,' she said. 'I guess now the police are on their way I ought to let you get on.'

Josh didn't know Amy Howes very well—just that she lived in one of the other flats on his floor and she'd taken in a parcel for him a couple of times. He had no idea what she did for a living or even if she had a job.

But what he did know was that her brown eyes were sad behind her smile, and she'd looked slightly panicky at the idea of being responsible for a baby, even for the short time it would take between now and the police arriving. Especially as the baby didn't even have the basics for any kind of care.

He'd only been going to pick up some milk and bread anyway. It wasn't important. The open-all-hours shop round the corner from the hospital would probably still be open when he'd finished his shift, even though it was Christmas Eve.

Not that you'd know it was Christmas, in Amy's flat. There were a couple of cards propped up on the mantelpiece, and a few more stacked in a pile, but there wasn't a tree or any presents. Even when people were going away for Christmas, they usually displayed their cards and had some kind of decorations up. Maybe she didn't celebrate Christmas. Was that because it was too painful for her—like it was for him?

Though it wasn't any of his business.

He shouldn't get involved.

He didn't want to get involved.

And yet he found his mouth opening and the wrong words coming out. 'I'm not due at the hospital until eleven, so I can stay with you until the police get here, if you like.'

'I can't impose on you like that,' she said.

Which was his get-out clause. He ought to agree with her and leave as fast as he could. Though his mouth definitely didn't seem to be with the programme. 'It's not that much of an imposition. If I'd left my flat a couple of minutes earlier, I would've been the one to find the baby,' he said. 'And my medical knowledge might be helpful to the police.'

'True,' she said, looking relieved and grateful. 'Thank you. I have to admit I was a bit worried about looking after the baby on my own.'

'Not used to babies?'

He couldn't quite read the expression on her face before she masked it, but he knew instantly that he'd put his foot in it. Right now he had a pretty good idea that whatever had caused the sadness behind her eyes had involved a baby. A miscarriage, perhaps? Or IVF that hadn't worked and her relationship hadn't survived the strain? And maybe Christmas was the anniversary of everything going wrong for her, just as it was for him?

Not that it was any of his business. And again he reminded himself not to get involved. That pull he felt towards Amy Howes was definitely something he shouldn't act on. If she was recovering from a broken heart, the last thing she needed was to get involved with someone whose track record at relationships was as poor as his.

'I'm more used to dealing with teens,' Amy said. 'I teach maths at the local high school.'

Now that he hadn't expected. 'You don't look like a maths teacher.'

She smiled, then, and Josh's heart felt as if it had turned over. Which was anatomically impossible in the first place; and in the second place Kelly's betrayal had put him off relationships for good. Back off, he reminded himself.

'I'm definitely better at explaining surds and synthetic division than I am at changing nappies,' she said. 'Though that's not the biggest problem. The baby's going to need some nappies and some clothes. I don't know anyone in our block or nearby with a baby who could lend us anything.'

'Me neither,' he said.

'Even if the police arrive in the next five minutes, they're going to be asking questions and what have you—and I have no idea how quickly the baby's going to need a nappy.'

'The average newborn goes through ten to fifteen a day,' Josh said.

'So basically every two to three hours. I could probably make a makeshift nappy out of a towel, but that's not fair on the poor baby.' She shook her head. 'The supermarket on the corner will sell nappies and they might sell some very basic baby clothes. Toss you for it?'

'I'll go,' Josh said. 'I needed to get some bread and milk anyway. I'll pick up nappies, some clothes and some formula milk.'

The panicky look was back on Amy's face. 'What if the baby starts crying again while you're gone?'

'Pick her up and cuddle her. If all else fails, sing to her,' Josh said. 'That usually works.'

'That sounds like experience talking.'

'I'm an uncle of three,' he said. Though he was guiltily aware that he hadn't seen much of his nieces and nephew since his divorce. His family's pity had been hard enough to take, but then he'd become very aware that most of his family saw him as a failure for letting his marriage go down the tubes—and he really couldn't handle that. It had been easier to use work as an excuse to avoid them. Which was precisely why he was working at the hospital over Christmas: it meant he didn't have to spend the holiday with his family and face that peculiar mixture of pity and contempt.

'Any songs in particular?' Amy asked.

'Anything,' he said. 'The baby won't care if you're not word-perfect; she just wants a bit of comfort. I'll see you in a few minutes.' He scribbled his mobile phone number on one of the spare pieces of paper from their makeshift 'crime scene' barrier. 'Here's my number.'

'Thanks. I'll text you in a minute so you've got my number. And I'd better give you some money for the baby stuff.'

'We'll sort it out between us later,' he said. 'Is there anything you need from the supermarket?'

'Thanks, but I did all my shopping yesterday,' she said.

If Josh had done that, too, instead of feeling that he was too tired to move after a hard shift, then he wouldn't have been walking through the lobby when Amy had found the baby, and he wouldn't have been involved with any of this. Though he instantly dismissed the thought as mean. It wasn't the baby's fault that she'd been abandoned, and it wasn't the baby's fault that caring for a baby, even for a few minutes, made it feel as if someone had ripped the top off his scars.

'See you in a bit,' he said, relieved to escape.

Amy looked at the sleeping baby.

A newborn.

Eighteen months ago, this was what she'd wanted most in the world. She and Michael had tried for a baby for a year without success, and they'd been at the point of desperation when they'd walked into the doctor's office after her scan.

And then they'd learned the horrible, horrible truth.

Even though Amy hadn't had a clue and it hadn't actually been her fault that her Fallopian tubes were damaged beyond repair, Michael had blamed her for it—and he'd walked out on her. She'd hoped that maybe once he'd had time to think about it, they could talk it through and get past the shock, but he hadn't been able to do that. All he could see was that Amy had given him an STD, and because of that STD she was infertile and couldn't give him a baby. He wouldn't even consider IVF, let alone adoption or fostering. Even though Amy hadn't had any symptoms, so she'd had no idea that her ex had given her chlamydia, Michael still blamed her for being too stupid to realise it for herself.

The injustice still rankled.

But it wasn't this baby's fault.

Or the fault of the baby's mum.

'Life,' she told the baby, 'is complicated.'

And then she wished she hadn't said a word when the baby started crying.

Pick her up and cuddle her—that was Josh's advice. Except it didn't work and the baby just kept crying.

He'd also suggested singing, as a last resort. But what did you sing to a baby? Every song Amy knew had gone out of her head.

It was Christmas. Sing a carol, she told herself.

'Silent Night' turned out to be a very forlorn hope indeed. It didn't encourage the baby to be quiet in the slightest. 'Hark the Herald Angels Sing' was more like 'Hark the Little Baby Screams'.

This was terrible. She really hoped Josh came back with supplies soon. There was bound to be a massive queue at the checkouts, and what if the supermarket had run out of nappies?

Maybe a Christmas pop song would help. She tried a couple of old classics, but the baby didn't seem to like them, either.

If only Josh had let her toss a coin. As a maths teacher, she knew the probability was fifty-fifty— but she also knew that actually there was a tiny, tiny weighting in favour of heads. She would've called heads and could've been the one to go out for supplies. And Josh, who seemed far better with babies than she was, would've been able to comfort this poor little girl much more easily than Amy could. And how could someone so tiny make so much noise?

'I can't do this,' she said, trying very hard not to burst into tears herself. 'I don't know how to make everything better, baby. I can't even fix my own life, so how can I possibly fix yours?'

The baby was still crying when there was a knock on her door. To her relief, it was Josh.

'Having trouble?' he asked on seeing the red-faced, screaming baby.

'Just a bit,' Amy said dryly. Though it wasn't fair to be sarcastic to him. It wasn't his fault that she was hopelessly inexperienced with babies. 'I tried singing to her. Let's just say she doesn't like Christmas carols. Or Christmas pop songs. And I'm out of ideas.'

'OK. Let me try.' He put the bag on the floor, took the baby from her and started singing 'All I Want for Christmas is You'.

Immediately, the baby stopped crying.

'Clearly you have the knack,' Amy said.

He laughed. 'Maybe she just likes the song.'

Or his voice. He had a gorgeous singing voice, rich and deep. The kind of voice that made your knees feel as if they were melting. To cover her confusion, she asked, 'How did you get on at the supermarket?'

'Ready-mixed formula milk, a couple of bottles, a pack of newborn nappies, some baby bath stuff, three vests and three sleep suits,' he said, indicating the bag. 'Oh, and my milk and bread.'

'Do you want to put the milk in my fridge for now?' she asked.

'Thanks. That'd be good.' Then he grimaced. 'Um.

I think we're going to have to give her a bath sooner rather than later.'

Amy could see the wet patch spreading on the blanket. 'And wash that blanket?'

'Maybe leave the blanket until the police say it's OK to wash it, but we can't leave the baby wet. Is it OK to use your bathroom to clean her up?'

'Sure. I've got plenty of towels.' She found the softest ones in the airing cupboard and placed one on the radiator to keep it warm while Josh ran water into the bath. This felt oddly domestic: and it was almost exactly as she'd imagined her life being with Michael and their baby.

Except, thanks to Gavin, she couldn't have babies. And Michael was no longer part of her life. She'd heard that he'd got married and had a baby on the way, so he'd managed to make his dreams come true—because Amy was no longer holding him back.

She shook herself. This thing with the abandoned baby was only temporary. As soon as the police had taken a statement from her and from Josh, they'd take the baby to some kind of foster home and she probably wouldn't see Josh again for weeks. That frisson of desire she'd felt when his skin had brushed against hers was utterly ridiculous, and she needed to be sensible about this instead of moping for something she couldn't have.

Josh tested the temperature of the water with his elbow. 'OK. Time for your first bath, little one.'

At the first touch of the water, the baby screamed the place down. Even Josh looked fraught by the time he'd finished bathing her, and Amy's teeth were on edge.

The screams abated to grizzling once the baby was out of the bath and wrapped in the warm towel.

'She's hungry, probably,' Josh said.

Amy's heart contracted sharply. 'Poor little mite.' And how desperate the baby's mother must've been to abandon her.

Between them they managed to get the baby into the nappy and sleep suit, and Josh rocked the baby and crooned softly to her while Amy sterilised one of the bottles he'd bought and warmed the formula milk in a jug of hot water. And then it was her turn to cuddle the baby and feed her.

Sitting there, with the baby cradled on her lap, watching her drink greedily from the bottle of milk, really tugged at Amy's heart.

If she'd been less clueless about Gavin's real character—or, better still, hadn't dated him in the first place—her life could have been so different. She could've been sitting here cuddling her own baby, next to the man of her dreams. Instead, here she was, desperately trying to fill her life with work, and right now she was holding a baby she'd have to give back.

She couldn't help glancing at Josh. His expression was unreadable but, before he masked it, she saw definite pain in his eyes. He'd said that he was an uncle of three, but she had a feeling there was a bit more to it than that.

Had he lost a child?

Had someone broken his heart?

Not that it was any of her business. He was her neighbour. They knew next to nothing about each other. And that was the way things were in London. You avoided eye contact as much as you could, smiled and nodded politely if you couldn't avoid eye contact, and you most definitely didn't get involved.

The baby fell asleep almost the second after she'd finished her feed. Amy folded up a towel as a make-shift bed and placed the baby on it, covering her with another towel. She'd just tucked the baby in when her intercom buzzed.

Thankfully the noise didn't wake the baby. 'Hello?'

'It's the police. PC Graham and PC Walters.'

She buzzed them in.

One of them was carrying a sturdy metal case, which she presumed contained forensic equipment, and the other had a notebook.

'I like the scene-of-crime tape improvisation in the lobby,' the first policeman said with a smile. 'I assume you'd like the bandages back when I've finished?'

Josh smiled back. 'No. It's fine to get rid of them. Do you think you'll get anything to help you track down the baby's mother?'

'I'll go and dust the area now,' the first police-man said, 'while my colleague PC Graham here goes through everything with you.'

'Shall I put the kettle on?' Amy asked.

'That'd be lovely. Thank you,' PC Walters said, heading out of the door with his case.

'Mr and Mrs Howes, isn't it?' PC Graham asked.

'Ms Howes and Mr Farnham,' she corrected. 'We're neighbours.'

'I see.' He made a note. 'Would you mind taking me through what happened?'

Between them, Amy and Josh filled in all the de-tails of how they'd found the baby.

'I'm a doctor,' Josh said. 'I've checked the baby

over, and she's fine. I think from all the vernix on her face—that's the white stuff—she's a couple of weeks early, and I have a feeling the mum might be quite young. I'd be a lot happier if you could find the mum and get her checked over, too, because she's at a high risk of infection.'

'It might take a while to find her,' PC Graham said.

'I'm afraid we had to give the baby a bath,' Amy added. 'She didn't have a nappy or any clothes, just the blanket, and the blanket got a bit, um, messy. I haven't washed it yet, in case you need it for forensics, but I've put it in a plastic bag.'

'Thank you. So you didn't recognise the voice over the intercom?' PC Graham asked.

'Nobody spoke,' Amy said. 'I just assumed it was a courier. Then I heard what sounded like a baby's cry. I don't know why, but some instinct made me go out and see for myself.'

'Just as well you did,' the policeman said. 'And you don't know anyone who might have left the baby here?'

'I don't know anyone who's pregnant,' Amy said. Mainly because she'd distanced herself from all her friends and colleagues who'd been trying for a baby, once she'd found out that she could no longer have children herself. It had been too painful being reminded of what she'd lost.

'So what happens now?' Josh asked.

'Once the social worker's here, she'll take the baby to the hospital,' the policeman said.

Josh shook his head. 'I don't really think that's a good idea. Right now, the children's ward is stuffed full of little ones with bronchiolitis.'

'Bronchi-what?' PC Graham asked.

'Bronchiolitis. It's a virus,' Josh explained. 'If adults catch it they get a really stinking cold, but in babies the mucus gums up the tiny airways in the lungs—the bronchioles—and they can't breathe or feed properly. Usually they end up being on oxygen therapy and being tube-fed for a week. And I really wouldn't want a newborn catching it—at that age it's likely to be really serious.'

'What about the general ward?' PC Graham asked. 'Could they look after her there?'

Josh shook his head. 'At this time of year the winter vomiting virus and flu are both doing the rounds in all the wards. As a newborn, she's at high risk of picking up either or both.'

The policeman shrugged and spread his hands. 'Then I don't know. We'll see what the social worker says when she gets here.'

By the time Amy had made mugs of tea, PC Walters was back from his forensic examination of the hallway.

'Did you manage to get anything?' Amy asked.

'A smudged footprint, but no fingerprints. Hopefully we'll get something from the box she left the baby in.' PC Walters looked at Amy's pale beige carpet. 'Though I'm afraid fingerprint powder's a bit messy.'

'It doesn't matter. It won't take that long to vacuum it up afterwards,' Amy said. 'It's more important that you discover something that'll help you find the baby's mum.'

But he didn't manage to get much from the box, either. 'There's a couple of long blonde hairs, but they don't necessarily belong to the mother. Though I found an envelope under the newspaper at the bottom of the box.'

'Newspaper?' Josh asked.

'For insulation against the cold, maybe,' PC Walters said. 'There's a gold chain in there and a note—though there aren't any prints. There are a couple of fibres, so she was probably wearing gloves.'

Amy read the note and then passed it to Josh.

Please look after Hope. I'm sorry.

'So the baby's name is Hope?' Josh asked.

'Seems so.'

Amy shared a glance with Josh. *Hope.* How terribly sad, because hope was clearly the last thing the baby's mother felt right now.

'Do you recognise the handwriting at all?' PC Graham asked.

'No,' Amy said.

'Me neither,' Josh agreed.

'We can take the box back with us—and the blanket—but I don't think it's going to help much,' PC Walters said, accepting a mug of tea.

They went through the whole lot again when Jane Richards, the social worker, arrived ten minutes later.

'So what's going to happen to the baby?' Amy asked.

Jane grimaced. 'At this time of year, everyone's on leave. You're lucky if you can get anyone even to answer a phone. And with Christmas falling partly on a weekend, the chances of getting hold of someone who can offer a foster care placement are practically zero. So I guess the baby's going to have to stay in hospital for a while.'

'The local hospital's on black alert,' Josh said.

'Apart from the fact that beds are in really short supply right now, there's bronchiolitis on the children's ward, and there's flu and the winter vomiting virus in the rest of the hospital. The chances are that Hope would go down with something nasty, so they'll refuse to take her.'

Jane looked at Amy. 'As you're the one who found her, and Christmas is meant to be the season of goodwill… Would you be able to look after her for a few days?'

'Me?' Amy looked at her in shock. 'But don't you have to do all kinds of background checks on me, first?'

'You're a teacher,' Jane said, 'so you'll already have gone through most of the checks. The rest of it is just formalities and, as I'm the senior social worker on duty in this area today, I can use my discretion.'

'I'm more used to dealing with teenagers,' Amy said. 'I've not really had much to do with babies.' Much less the baby she'd so desperately wanted to have with Michael. Something that could never, ever happen for her. 'I'm not sure…' And yet Jane was right. Christmas was the season of goodwill. How could Amy possibly turn away a helpless, defenceless newborn baby?

'I could help out,' Josh said. 'I'm working today and tomorrow, but I could help out between my shifts.'

So she'd have someone to talk things over with, if she was concerned. Someone who had experience of babies—and, better still, was a doctor.

But there was one possible sticking point. Even though she knew it was intrusive, she still had to ask. 'Will your partner mind?' she asked.

'I don't have a partner,' Josh said, and for a moment she saw a flash of pain in his expression.

Did he, too, have an ex who'd let him down badly? Amy wondered. She was pretty sure that, like her, he lived alone.

'I can make decisions without having to check with anyone first,' he said. 'How about yours?'

'Same as you,' she said.

'Which makes it easy.' He turned to Jane. 'OK. We'll look after Hope between us. How long do you need us to look after her?'

She winced. 'Until New Year's Eve, maybe?'

A whole week? 'Just as well it's the school holidays,' Amy said wryly.

'I'm off for a couple of days between Christmas and New Year,' Josh said. 'I'll do as much as I can. But the baby has nothing, Jane. I just went out to get emergency milk, nappies and enough clothes to keep her going until you got here. Her mother left her wrapped in a blanket in the box, and there wasn't anything with her. Well, the police found a note and a gold chain that the mum obviously wanted the baby to have,' he amended, 'but the baby doesn't have any clothes.'

'We don't have anywhere for her to sleep—and, apart from the fact that the police have taken the box, a cardboard box really isn't a suitable bed for a baby,' Amy added.

'I can help there,' Jane said. 'We have things in the office. I can bring you a Moses basket, bedding, nappies and spare clothes, and I can organise milk. Do you have any bottles?'

'Two,' Josh said, 'and I bought a couple of cartons

of ready-mixed formula. We've muddled through with very hot water to sterilise them for now.'

'If you don't mind mixing up your own formula, I can organise more bottles and sterilising equipment,' Jane said. 'What about the baby's mum?'

'We haven't got much on the forensics side,' PC Walters said. 'The best we can do is to put out a press release and ask the local media to tell her to get in touch.'

'If she's as young as I think she might be,' Josh said, 'she'll be worried that she's in trouble—especially if she managed to hide her pregnancy.'

'Strictly speaking, it's a criminal offence to abandon a baby,' PC Graham said, 'but judges are always lenient in the case of newborns and very young, very frightened mums.'

'She really needs to get to hospital or a doctor and let them check her over,' Josh said. 'That's important because, if she's retained any of the placenta or she tore during the delivery, there's a high risk she'll develop an infection—and if it's left untreated she could become really ill.'

'We'll make sure everyone says she won't be in any trouble and we're worried about her health,' PC Graham said.

'And tell her the baby's absolutely fine and being looked after. The poor girl's probably going to be worrying about that, too,' Amy added.

Josh looked at his watch. 'Sorry. I'm going to have to leave you now. I need to be at work.' He scribbled a number on one of the spare sheets of paper. 'You've got my mobile number, Amy, and this is my direct line in the department. You can get a message to me if it's urgent. I'll be back about half-past eight this evening—unless there's a crisis in the department, in which case I'll get a message to you as early as I can.'

Amy really hoped that she wasn't going to have to use that number. 'OK. Thanks.' She paused, knowing that this probably sounded like a come-on, but hoping that he'd take it as the practical suggestion it actually was. 'Look, as you're helping me with the baby, you might as well have dinner here. It's as easy to cook for two as for one.'

'That'd be nice.'

They exchanged a glance, and another frisson of desire ran down her spine—which was completely inappropriate. OK, so they were both single, but this was all about caring for Hope, not having a wild fling with her neighbour.

She fought to keep herself sounding professional. 'Do you have any food allergies, or is there anything you don't eat?'

'No to the allergies.' He smiled. 'As for the rest, I'm a medic in the emergency department, so we tend not to be fussy. We're lucky if we get a chance to grab a chocolate bar. As long as it's food and it's hot, I'm happy.'

She smiled back. 'OK.'

Once Josh had left, PC Graham sorted out the last bits of paperwork and the police left, too.

'I'll be back later this afternoon with supplies,' Jane promised.

'We should have enough milk and nappies to last until then,' Amy said.

'Thanks.' Jane smiled at her. 'You're a life-saver—literally.'

'Not just me. My neighbour helped.' And Amy really had to remind herself that Josh was just her neighbour. They might know each other a bit better and be on friendlier terms after the next few days, but this would be a platonic relationship only.

Amy saw Jane out of the flat, then returned to watch Hope sleeping in her makeshift bed. 'It looks as if it's just you and me, baby,' she said softly. 'For the next week you're going to have complete strangers looking after you and trying to make a family for you.'

But it was Christmas, the season of miracles. With any luck Hope's mum would come forward, Jane would be able to help her, and there would be a happy ending.

CHAPTER TWO

IT WAS HOPE'S first Christmas, but Amy's flat looked just like it did on every other day of the year. She hadn't planned to be here for the festive season, so she hadn't bothered putting up a tree. When her plans had fallen through, it had felt like too much effort to get the Christmas decorations out. What was the point when she'd be here on her own?

Now, she had a reason to change that.

Even though she knew the baby wouldn't remember it or even have a clue that it was Christmas, Amy wanted to decorate her flat and make it Christmassy for Hope. Though, between feeds and nappy changes and cuddles to stop the baby crying, it took her four times as long as she'd expected. And she was panicking that she wasn't looking after Hope properly.

'I really have no idea what I'm doing,' she informed the baby, who cried a little bit more, as if agreeing with Amy. 'And I don't know who to ask. If I call Mum, she'll worry and get the next plane home from Canada—and that's not fair, because it's my parents' turn to spend Christmas with my brother Scott and his wife Rae.' Who didn't have children yet, so she couldn't ask her brother or sister-in-law for advice, either. 'Half my colleagues have teenagers, and I'm guessing they're way past remembering what the first couple of days with a newborn are like. And I'm a total cow because I distanced myself from my friends who do have babies. I can hardly ring them and ask for help when I've been so horrible and ignored their babies.'

But it had been too raw, once she'd learned that she was infertile and her dreams of having a baby were never coming true. Although she'd been genuinely pleased for her friends, she just hadn't been able to face watching them bloom through pregnancy or listening to them talk about the latest milestone their babies had reached.

But now she had a baby.

Temporarily.

And walking up and down with Hope like this, holding her close and rocking her in the hope that it would help settle her and stop her crying... This was what Amy's life could've been like, had it not been for Gavin and her own naivety. Why hadn't she even considered that, as he'd been serially unfaithful to her, in the process he might have picked up some kind of STD which didn't have any symptoms and passed it on to her? Why hadn't she got herself checked out just as a precautionary measure?

Maybe because she wasn't the suspicious sort— which was why it had taken her months in the first place to work out that Gavin was seeing other women on the side. A whole string of them. And she'd been stupidly oblivious, thinking everything was just fine between them.

'I'm an idiot,' she said with a sigh. 'But I'll do my

best to give you a decent first few days and first Christmas, Hope.'

This time, the baby gurgled.

And Amy really had to swallow the lump in her throat.

For a second the baby's dark blue eyes seemed to hold all the wisdom in the world.

How different her life could've been. But there was nothing she could do to change it now; all she could do was make the best of her situation. And, with Josh Farnham's help, do her best to make this poor baby's first few days as happy as possible.

When the baby dropped off to sleep again, Amy gently laid her on the makeshift towel bed, covered her up, and tried to work out what she needed to do next.

The intercom buzzed, and Amy rushed to get it before the noise woke the baby. 'Hello, it's Jane Richards again,' a tinny voice informed her.

'Come in,' Amy said, and buzzed her in before putting on the kettle. 'Can I make you tea or coffee?' she asked when the social worker came in laden with a Moses basket and an armful of carrier bags.

'Sorry, I can't stop for more than two minutes,' Jane said. 'I just wanted to drop these off for you, as I promised.' She put down the bags one by one, naming the contents. 'Moses basket, bedding, bottles, sterilising stuff, milk, nappies and newborn-size clothes.'

'Thanks.' The pile looked daunting, Amy thought. How could someone so tiny need so much stuff?

'The thanks are all mine,' Jane said. 'If you hadn't agreed to help out, I would've been really stuck. I did try to see if one of our foster carers could take Hope, but everyone's so busy at this time of year. In reality we're looking at the day after New Year.'

'Right.' Amy took a deep breath. Which meant she was spending the next week with a baby that she'd have to give back. It was a warning not to let herself bond too deeply with Hope.

'So how's it going?' Jane asked.

'It's a lot harder than I thought it would be,' Amy said. 'And I'm supposed to be a well-organised adult. How on earth would a young, inexperienced mum cope on her own?'

'She'd be struggling,' Jane said. 'I don't suppose the police have found Hope's mum, yet?'

'Not that I've heard,' Amy said.

'Right. So what are you struggling with most?' Jane asked. 'Is there anyone you can call on?'

'Only my neighbour,' Amy said. And she had the strongest feeling that Josh might have some issues with looking after a baby, too. Not that she could ask him without either being rude and intrusive, which might make him decide he didn't want to help, or telling him about her past—and the last thing she wanted was for him to start pitying her and seeing her in a different light. 'As for what I'm struggling with, I'm worrying that I'm doing *everything* wrong. I mean, I know I can follow the instructions with the sterilising stuff and the formula milk, and obviously I know to heat the milk in a jug of hot water rather than in the microwave, but am I feeding her enough and is she getting enough sleep?' She grimaced. 'And she cries an awful lot more than I was expecting. I'm not very good at getting her to feel secure and happy.'

'Crash course,' Jane said. 'If the baby's crying, she

either wants feeding, a nappy change or a cuddle. Sing to her, rock her, hold her, dance with her—obviously I mean more like a slow dance than break-dancing.'

That made Amy smile. 'I don't think I can break-dance on my own, let alone with a baby in my arms.'

Jane grinned back. 'I guess. OK. Make the feeds in batches that'll be enough for a day's worth and keep them in the fridge, so all you have to do in the middle of the night is heat up the milk in a jug of hot water. Keep a note of the baby's feed times and how much she takes, and write down when she sleeps and how long. That'll help you see what her routine is. And obviously try to get some sleep when Hope sleeps, or you'll be exhausted by Boxing Day.' She scribbled down a phone number. 'If you're stuck, that's my mobile.'

'You're on duty over Christmas?'

'No,' Jane admitted, 'but without you I wouldn't know what to do with Hope, so I'm happy for you to call me if you need me.'

'Thanks,' Amy said.

'Good luck.'

And then she was on her own with the baby again. She just about had time to make up the Moses basket with the bedding, sterilise the bottles Jane had brought and make up the feeds before Hope woke, crying.

Amy could definitely tell the reason for this one: Hope needed a fresh nappy.

And then the baby was hungry.

And then she wanted a cuddle.

Time was rushing away. Amy knew that Josh would be back soon, and she hadn't even looked at the inside of her fridge, let alone started preparing something to eat.

'I'm supposed to be cooking dinner tonight,' Amy told the baby. Even if the shops hadn't closed early for Christmas Eve, she wouldn't have been able to go out and pick up a pizza in any case because she couldn't leave the baby alone. It was hardly fair to ask Josh to get a takeaway on the way back from his shift. 'We're going to have to go for something that can look after itself in the oven.'

The baby gurgled.

'You have no idea how weird this is,' Amy said. 'Josh and I smile and nod at each other if we pass in the hallway, and that's it. And now he's having dinner with me tonight and helping me look after you.'

No comment from Hope.

'But it's not a date,' Amy added. 'OK, so we're both single. But my past is messy and my future would be problematic for anyone who wants to date me. In fact, I'm just rubbish at picking men. Gavin was a liar and a cheat, and when it came to a crisis Michael walked away because I wasn't enough for him. So I'm better off forgetting all about romantic relationships.'

Though maybe looking after Hope might help her finally come to terms with the fact that she wasn't going to have a child of her own. To the point where she could reconnect with her friends—OK, she'd have a bit of grovelling to do, but she had a feeling that they'd understand when she explained why she'd gone distant on them. She could enjoy babysitting her friends' children and reading stories to them, and hopefully the joy would outweigh the ache in her heart.

'Besides, there's no reason why Josh should be interested in me,' she added. She'd felt that frisson of attraction when they'd accidentally touched while caring for the baby earlier, but she had no idea whether it was mutual. 'We might become friends. Which would be nice. But that's it,' she said firmly.

Hope gurgled then, as if to say, 'How do you know what he thinks?'

She didn't. But she did need his help, so she had no intention of doing or saying anything that might make him back away. 'It's just the way it is,' she said. 'And you, Missy, are going to have to go in the Moses basket for a few minutes, to let me put something together for dinner.'

In the end, Amy had to wait for Hope to fall asleep again. And then she worked at speed to peel and chop the veg, then put them in a casserole dish with a couple of chicken breasts and half a bottle of red wine.

By the time she'd finished, Hope was crying again. Amy suppressed a sigh and went through her mental checklist. Was the baby hungry, wet or just wanted a cuddle? And why was it so hard to work out which cry meant which?

Josh headed back to his flat after his shift. Right now all he wanted to do was to fall onto the sofa and watch something on TV that didn't require him to think too much. He was bone-deep tired, and wished he hadn't offered to help with the baby; but he had a feeling that Amy had only agreed to look after the baby because he'd promised to help. It would be pretty unfair of him to bail out on her now.

And she was cooking dinner for both of them. She hadn't said anything about dessert, but he didn't ex-actly have anything in his fridge that would pass muster. A bottle of wine was the best he could offer as his contribution.

He'd told her he'd be back for half-past eight—and it was twenty-five past now, so he didn't have time for a shower. He was pretty sure he wasn't sweaty and vile, and his hair had a mind of its own anyway, so it would be sticking out at odd angles within five minutes of him putting a comb through it. No point in wasting time.

Besides, this wasn't a date. It wasn't as if he had to dress up, or was trying to impress her by being smooth, suave and charming. Amy was his neighbour and he was simply helping with the baby who'd been abandoned on their doorstep.

At Christmas.

Not that you'd know it was Christmas, looking at his flat. It was even less Christmassy than Amy's was, because he hadn't even bothered putting any cards on the mantelpiece. He wondered if she loathed Christmas as much as he did. For him, Christmas Eve would always be the anniversary of the day his life imploded. When Kelly—who had been so adamant that she wanted to concentrate on her career rather than starting a family—had told him that she was pregnant. That the baby wasn't his. And that she was leaving him for the baby's father.

Josh had been too numb to believe it at first. But while he'd been saving lives and patching up wounds, Kelly had been packing her stuff, ready to leave him. Though in some ways she'd been fair. She'd been scrupulous only to pack things that were hers and to give him first dibs on anything they'd bought together; and she'd actually asked him to divorce her on the grounds of adultery rather than trying to make out that it was his fault or from joint 'irreconcilable differences'. She'd done as much as she could to make it easy on him.

Happy Christmas. Indeed. Every single radio station had been playing Christmas heartbreak songs, and when the third station in a row had been playing a song about a man pleading with his beloved to come home for Christmas, Josh had given up and switched off the radio—because he knew that Kelly wasn't coming home to him. Not for Christmas or at any other time.

He shook himself. It wasn't Amy's fault that his ex had changed her mind about wanting a baby and then decided that she didn't want to have said baby with him.

And it definitely wasn't Amy's fault that his family had reacted in typical Farnham fashion. Josh, the baby of the family, was a big fat failure. He was the only one who hadn't managed to combine a high-flying career with a perfect marriage and family. Obviously they hadn't actually *said* the words to his face, but Josh was aware of it with every look, every raised eyebrow, every whispered aside that was cut short the second he walked into the room.

This year, Kelly would be spending her first Christmas with her new family. Including the new baby.

And Josh genuinely wanted her to be happy. Now he'd got most of the hurt and anger out of his system, he could see that he hadn't been what Kelly had needed. If she'd stayed with him out of a sense of duty, she would've grown to hate him and it would all have grown miserable and messy. As it was, their divorce had been as amicable as possible. They'd sold the house and split the proceeds, and he'd bought the flat here six months ago.

But part of him was still in limbo.

And he really wanted to blot out Christmas Eve.

Except he couldn't. He'd made a promise, and he needed to keep it. He took a deep breath and went down the corridor to Amy's flat, then knocked on the door.

She opened it, looking slightly harassed, with Hope propped up against her shoulder. Clearly looking after the baby on her own had been hard going.

He suppressed the flush of guilt—he'd spent the last nine hours working his shift at the Emergency Department, not down at the pub taking part in several Christmas parties—and handed her the bottle of wine. 'I didn't know if you preferred red or white, so I played it safe.'

'Thank you. It's very nice of you, but you didn't need to.'

'You cooked dinner, so this is my contribution,' he pointed out. 'Something smells nice.'

'It's not very exciting, I'm afraid. Just a casserole and jacket potatoes, and all the veg are mixed in with the casserole.'

But it meant that he hadn't had to cook. 'It sounds lovely.'

'It was the lowest-maintenance thing I could think of,' she admitted wryly. 'Looking after Hope took an awful lot more time and energy than I expected.'

Yes, and if things had been different he would've been celebrating his first Christmas with his daughter—except his ex-wife's baby wasn't actually his daughter. He pushed the thought away. 'So I hear from

my colleagues.' And this was his cue to play nice.
Amy's brown eyes were so anxious, despite the calm
she appeared to radiate. 'Here. My turn to cuddle Hope
and keep her happy for a bit.'

And that was definitely gratitude in her eyes as she
handed the baby over.

Though her hands brushed against his as they transferred the baby between them, and a frisson of desire
flickered down his spine.

Inappropriate. Amy was his neighbour, and he was
helping out with a tricky situation. That was it, he reminded himself. He wasn't going to hit on her and he
wasn't going to let himself wonder how soft her hair
was, or how her skin would feel against his.

'Can I get you a drink?' she asked.

'A glass of wine would be lovely right now,' he admitted. And it might distract him from all the ridiculous thoughts flickering through his head. Thoughts
about how Amy's mouth was a perfect Cupid's bow,
and wondering what it would feel like if he kissed her.

'Hard shift?'

He shrugged. 'It's always busy this time of year. Ignoring all the viruses and the elderly coming in with
breathing problems, there are the falls—especially
when it's icy like it has been tonight. And tonight the
department will be full of people who drank too much
at Christmas Eve parties and either ended up in a fight
or fell and hurt themselves.' He gave her a wry smile.
'Tomorrow will be the people who had an accident
carving the turkey, and a few more punch-ups because
people who really shouldn't be in the same room together for more than ten minutes are forced to play
nice for the whole day and it's too much for them, and

the day after that will be the people who didn't store the leftover turkey properly and gave themselves food poisoning.'

'That,' she said, 'sounds a tiny bit cynical.'

'Experience,' he said, and grimaced. 'Sorry. I guess I'm a bit tired and not the best company.'

'It's fine.' She handed him a glass of wine. 'Come and sit down. Dinner will be five minutes.'

He went into the living room and blinked in surprise. 'You have a tree.'

She smiled. 'Yes—and you wouldn't believe how long it took me to put it up.'

'But you didn't have a tree this morning.'

'That's because I wasn't intending to be here for Christmas,' she said. 'I was meant to be spending this week in Edinburgh with some of my oldest friends, but they rang yesterday to call it off because they've gone down with the flu.' Amy shrugged. 'There didn't seem much point in putting up a tree when I wasn't going to be here. But now I am, and it's Hope's first Christmas.' Her fair skin flushed. 'It might sound a bit daft, but I wanted to put up a tree for her.'

'No, it's not daft. I get what you mean.' Josh paused. 'So the lack of a tree earlier wasn't because you don't like Christmas?'

'No.' She frowned. 'I take it you don't like Christmas, then?'

'It's not my favourite time of the year,' he admitted, and was relieved when she didn't push it and ask why. Though his mouth didn't seem to want to pay her the same courtesy, because he found himself asking questions. 'So you're not spending Christmas with your family?'

Amy shook her head. 'My brother lives in Canada, so my parents spend alternate Christmases here and over in Canada.'

'And this year is Canada's turn, right?'

'Right,' she agreed.

'So luckily for Hope that means you're here.'

'Yes.' Her expression was sombre when she looked at him. 'Things could have been very different.'

'But you found her in time.' He paused. 'Is there anything I can do to help?'

'I'm about to serve dinner, so if you want to settle Hope in her Moses basket, that'd be good.'

While Amy went to the kitchen, Josh put the baby in the Moses basket. Hope grizzled for a moment and then yawned and fell asleep.

Having dinner with Amy felt weirdly intimate. Like a date—though Josh couldn't even remember the last time he'd dated. He'd had a couple of offers that he'd turned down, and some well-meaning friends had tried to match-make, but he'd taken them to one side and explained that he appreciated their effort but he wasn't ready to date again.

Was he ready now?

And why on earth was he thinking about that?

'The food's very nice,' he said, to cover his awkwardness.

'Thank you.'

He didn't have a clue what to talk about, and it made him feel slightly flustered. He was used to making polite conversation to distract his patients or get more information out of them, or being out with colleagues that he'd known for so long that he didn't have to make small talk. This was definitely outside his comfort zone. Especially as he was becoming more and more aware of how attractive Amy was: not just those huge brown eyes, but the curve of her mouth, her pretty heart-shaped face and the slight curl to her bobbed hair. It made him itch to draw her, and he hadn't felt that urge for a long time either.

'So how long have you lived here?' he asked, trying to get his thoughts back to something much more anodyne and much, much safer.

'Eighteen months. You moved here last summer, didn't you?' she replied.

'Yes. It's convenient for the hospital, just a fifteen-minute walk.'

'It's about that to school, too,' she said. 'Just in the other direction.'

He remembered that she taught maths. 'Did you always want to teach?'

'I didn't want to be an accountant, an engineer or an actuary, so teaching was my best bet for working with maths—and actually it's really rewarding when the kids have been struggling with something and it suddenly clicks for them.' She smiled. 'Did you always want to be a doctor?'

'It was pretty much expected of me—Dad's a surgeon, Mum's a lawyer, my brother Stuart's an astrophysicist and my sisters are both lecturers.' He shrugged. 'One teaches history at Oxford and the other's in London at the LSE.'

'A family of high achievers, then.'

Yes. And he hadn't quite lived up to their expectations. He'd suggested becoming a graphic designer and going to art college instead of studying for his A levels, and the resulting row had left him very aware that he'd been expected to follow in his parents' and siblings' footsteps. In the end he'd settled on medicine; at least there'd been a little bit of drawing involved. And he liked his job. He liked being able to make a difference to people's lives. And he could still sketch if he wanted to.

When he had the time.

Which wasn't often.

Pushing the thought away, he asked, 'Have you heard anything from the police?'

'Not yet. Though Jane the social worker came round with supplies this afternoon.'

'So I notice. That Moses basket looks a little more comfy than a bunch of newspaper and a cardboard box.' His smile faded. 'That poor girl. I hope she's all right.'

'Me, too. And looking after a baby is a lot harder than I expected,' Amy admitted. 'Now I know what they mean about being careful what you wish for.'

He stared at her in surprise. 'You wanted a baby?'

She looked shocked, as if she hadn't meant to admit that, then glanced away. 'It didn't work out.'

That explained some of her wariness this morning. And it was pretty obvious to him that the baby situation not working out was connected with her being single. 'I'm sorry,' he said. 'I didn't mean to bring up bad memories.'

'I know. It's OK.' She shrugged. 'There's nothing anyone can do to change it, so you make the best of the situation, don't you?'

'I guess.' It was what he'd been doing since Kelly had left him. They'd sold their house and he'd bought this flat; it was nearer to work and had no memories to haunt him with their might-have-beens. 'In the circumstances, looking after Hope must be pretty tough for you.'

'It's probably been good for me,' she said. 'And it's kind of helping me to move on.' She bit her lip. 'I've been a bit of a cow and neglected my friends who were pregnant at the time or had small children.'

He liked the fact that she wasn't blaming anyone else for her actions. 'That's understandable if you'd only just found out that option was closed to you. You're human.'

'I guess.'

More than human. What he'd seen so far of Amy Howes told him that she was genuinely nice. 'And you're not a cow. If you were, you would've just told the police and the social worker to sort out the baby between them and pushed everyone out of your flat,' he pointed out. 'So did you ring any of your friends with small children to get some advice?'

'No. I don't want them to think I'm just using them. But I'm going to call them all in the first week of the New Year,' she said, 'and apologise to them properly. Then maybe I can be the honorary auntie they all wanted me to be in the first place and I was too—well, hurting too much to do it back then.'

'That's good,' Josh said. He wondered if helping to look after Hope would help him move on, too. Right now, it didn't feel like it; and if Amy had moved here eighteen months ago, that suggested she'd had a year longer to get used to her new circumstances than he had. Maybe his head would be sorted out by this time next year, then.

He almost told Amy about Kelly and the baby; but,

then again, he didn't want her to pity him, so he knew it would be safer to change the subject. 'What did the social worker have to say?'

'She gave me a very quick crash course in looking after a baby. She said if they cry it means they're hungry, they need a fresh nappy or they just want a cuddle, though I can't actually tell the difference between any of the different cries, yet,' Amy said dryly. 'Jane also told me to write down whenever Hope has milk and how much she takes, and her nap times, so I can work out what her routine is.'

'Sounds good. How's Hope doing so far?'

'She likes a lot of cuddles and she definitely likes you talking to her. Hang on.' She went over to the sideboard and took a notebook from the top, then handed it to him. 'Here. You can see for yourself.'

He looked through the neat columns of handwriting. 'I have to admit, it doesn't mean that much to me,' he said.

'Tsk, and you an uncle of three,' she teased.

'One's in Scotland and two are in Oxford,' he explained. 'I don't see them as much as I should.' It was another failing to chalk up to his list; and he felt guilty about it.

'Hey, you're a doctor. You don't get a lot of spare time,' she reminded him.

'I know, but I ought to make more of an effort.'

'It's not always easy. I don't see much of my brother.'

'He's in Canada, thousands of miles away,' Josh pointed out. 'And I bet you video-call him.'

She nodded.

'Well, then.' Amy was clearly a good sister. Just as Josh wasn't a particularly good brother. When was the last time he'd talked to Stuart, Miranda or Rosemary? He'd used his shifts as an excuse to avoid them.

'I guess,' she said, looking awkward. 'Can I offer you some pudding? It's nothing exciting, just ice cream.'

'Ice cream is the best pudding in the universe,' he said. 'Provided it's chocolate.'

'Oh, *please*,' she said, looking pained. 'Coffee. Every single time.'

He wasn't a fan of coffee ice cream. But he wasn't going to argue with someone who'd been kind enough to make him dinner. 'Coffee's fine,' he fibbed. 'And I'll wash up.'

'That's not fair.'

'You cooked.'

'But you were at work all day.'

He coughed. 'And you've spent hours on your own looking after a baby—that's hard work, even if you're used to it.' Then he flinched, realising what he'd said and how it sounded. 'Sorry. I didn't mean it to come out like that.'

'It's OK,' she said softly. 'I know you didn't mean it like that.'

But the sadness was back in her eyes. Part of him really wanted to give her a hug.

Though that might not be such a good idea. Not when he still felt that pull towards her. He needed to start thinking of her as an extra sister or something. A sister-in-law. Someone off limits. 'Let's share the washing up,' he said instead.

Though being in a small space with her felt even more intimate than eating at her bistro table.

'So what do you usually do on Christmas Eve?' he asked, trying to make small talk.

'Last year, I had my parents staying—and I guess I was busy convincing them that I was absolutely fine and settled here.'

'Were you really absolutely fine?' he asked quietly. Back then she'd been here for six months—exactly the same position that he was in now.

'Not really,' she admitted, 'but I am now.' She paused. 'I heard a couple of months back that my ex got married and he's expecting a baby.'

'The hardest bit is trying to be happy for them when you're feeling miserable yourself.'

Her eyes widened. 'That sounds like experience talking.'

He nodded. And funny how easy it was to talk to her, now he'd started. 'I split up with my wife last Christmas Eve.'

She winced. 'There's never a good time to break up with someone, but Christmas has to be one of the roughest. And the first anniversary's always a difficult one.' She squeezed his hand briefly, but it didn't feel like pity—more like sympathy and as if she'd been there herself, which he knew she had. 'If it helps to know, it does get easier. I know everyone says that time heals. I'm not sure it does that exactly, but it does help you deal with things a bit better.'

'I'm not still in love with Kelly,' he said. 'I want her to be happy. And I'm OK now about the fact it isn't going to be with me.'

'That's good. It's the same way I feel about Michael.'

It felt as if there was some subtext going on, but

Josh didn't trust his emotional intelligence enough to try to work it out.

She shook coffee grounds into a cafetière. 'Milk? Sugar?'

'Black, no sugar, please,' he said.

'Because you're a medic and you're used to grabbing coffee as quickly as you can?' she asked.

'No. It's a hangover from my student days,' he said with a smile. 'I shared a flat with some guys who weren't that good with checking that the milk was in date. The third time you make your coffee with milk that's off, you learn it's safer to drink your coffee black.'

She smiled back. 'I knew a few people like that in my student days, too.'

It was so easy to be with Amy, Josh thought. And it felt natural to curl up on the other end of her sofa, nursing a mug of coffee and listening to music while the baby was napping in the Moses basket.

'So what do you usually do at Christmas?' she asked.

'Work,' he said. 'It feels fairer to let my colleagues who have kids spend Christmas morning with their family.'

'That's nice of you.'

'Ah, but I get to party at New Year while they have to patch up the drunks,' he said with a smile, 'so it works both ways.'

Hope woke then, and started crying softly.

'I'll go and heat the milk,' Amy said.

Josh scooped the baby onto his lap and cuddled her until Amy came back with the milk. 'My turn to feed her,' he said.

When the baby had finished, he wrote the time and millilitres on Amy's chart.

'So at the moment she's feeding every two to three hours,' he said.

'Which means I'm not going to get a lot of sleep tonight.' Amy gave a wry smile. 'It's just as well I'm not going anywhere tomorrow, or I'd be a zombie.'

The sensible bit of his brain told him to back off and keep his mouth shut. The human side said, 'We could take shifts with her.'

'But you've been at work today—and I assume from what you said that you're working tomorrow.'

'And you've been on your own with her today, which pretty much counts as a full-time job,' Josh pointed out. 'If we take turns feeding her, we'll both get a four- or five-hour chunk of sleep.'

'So, what, you take her next door after the next feed and bring her back?'

'Or, if you don't mind me sleeping on your sofa, then we don't have to move her and risk unsettling her.'

Amy frowned. 'You can't possibly sleep on my sofa. It's way too short for you.'

'Student doctors learn to sleep on anything and be fully awake within seconds. I'll be fine,' he said. 'Let me go next door and grab my duvet.'

For a moment, he thought she was going to argue with him. But then she smiled, and he could see the relief in her eyes. 'Thanks. Actually, it'll be good not having the first night with her completely on my own. I'm paranoid I'm doing everything wrong.'

'Hey—she's new at this, too. If you're doing it wrong, she doesn't know any better. And she looks pretty content to me, so I'd say you're doing just fine.'

'Even when she cried non-stop for thirty minutes this afternoon—cried herself to sleep?'

He winced. 'That's tough on you. But don't blame yourself. She would probably have done exactly the same with me.' He smiled at her. 'I'll be back in a tick.'

CHAPTER THREE

WHAT HAVE I DONE? Amy asked herself as Josh went to collect his duvet.

Two years ago, she'd been in what she'd thought was a secure relationship, trying to start a family. A year ago she'd had a broken relationship, broken dreams and a broken heart. This year, she was on an even keel; but it seemed that she was going to be spending the next week with a man she barely knew and a baby who'd been left on their doorstep. It was an odd version of what she'd wished for.

Josh came back carrying a duvet. She wasn't sure if she felt more relieved or awkward that he was still fully dressed; clearly he intended to sleep in his ordinary clothes on her sofa. Though she guessed that went with the territory of his job.

He folded the duvet neatly over the back of her sofa. 'Anything you need me to do?'

'No. Hope's milk is on the top shelf of the fridge. But help yourself to anything you want.'

He smiled. 'Fifteen years ago, that would've guaranteed you an empty fridge.'

'That's what my colleagues at school say.' She smiled back. 'The boys leave crumbs everywhere,

and the girls make chocolate mug cakes at three in
the morning and leave everything in the sink.'

'Mug cakes?' He looked blank.

'You mix everything together in a mug and then
stick it in the microwave. Three minutes later, you
have cake,' she explained. 'I haven't actually tried it.
But apparently it works perfectly when you really, really want cake at three in the morning.'

'Three minutes. Hmm. You can make a cheese
toastie in that,' he said.

She smiled. 'If you get the munchies when it's your
turn to feed Hope, feel free to make yourself a cheese
toastie.'

He grinned back. 'If I do, I promise I'll clean up
the crumbs.'

Almost on cue, Hope woke, wanting milk.

'I'll do the next feed,' Josh said when she'd finished.
'Go and get some sleep, Amy.'

Once Amy had showered and changed into her pyjamas, she lay awake in the dark, thinking that this was
the Christmas she'd never expected. It must be just as
weird for Josh, too, spending Christmas with an almost complete stranger—and tough for him, because
his wife had left him on Christmas Eve last year and
the memories had to hurt. But maybe looking after the
baby would help distract him from some of the pain.

Part of her wanted to sleep for eternity, she was so
tired—which was ridiculous, because she hadn't exactly done much all day. But looking after a newborn
baby had been fraught with worry that had unexpect-
edly worn her out. Was she doing the right thing? How
would she know if she was getting it wrong? What if
the baby was ill and she hadn't spotted the signs? Or if

she made such a mess of changing Hope that the baby ended up with nappy rash—and where would you be able to buy nappy rash cream on Christmas Day, when all the shops were shut?

The worries flickered through her head, stopping her from falling asleep. Part of her wanted to go and check that the baby was OK—but what if she woke Josh? He'd already worked a busy shift today at the hospital. Plus he was used to dealing with babies, and he'd said this was his shift; if he woke and found her checking on the baby, he might think she didn't trust him. And if that upset him enough to make him walk out on her without really discussing anything, the way Michael had walked out on her, how was she going to cope with the baby all on her own for a week?

Be careful what you wish for...

She'd longed for a baby. Now, she had exactly that. A baby to look after. For a week.

And it was terrifying.

Maybe Michael was right about her. She'd been too stupid to guess that Gavin might have given her a symptomless STD, so when she'd finally discovered the truth the treatment had been too late to prevent the damage to her Fallopian tubes. So it was her fault that she was infertile. Maybe she was too clueless to look after a baby, too. Why, why, why had she agreed to help?

She heard the baby start crying, and glanced at the clock. She hadn't even managed to sleep for five minutes. It was Josh's turn to feed the baby, but clearly he was in a deep sleep because the baby's cries grew louder.

Get up and see to the baby, she told herself sharply.

The poor little mite has nobody. Stop being so whiny and self-pitying and *get up*. You can't worry about not coping because you just *have* to. There isn't another option.

She dragged herself out of bed and stumbled into the living room. 'Shh, baby,' she whispered—but the baby just kept screaming.

Just as Amy scooped the baby out of the Moses basket, she heard Josh mumble, 'My turn. I've got this.'

'I'm awake now. I'll do it,' she said.

'We'll do it together,' Josh said. 'Cuddle the baby or do the milk?'

Amy inhaled the sweet, powdery scent of the baby.

A baby she couldn't afford to bond with. So it would be better not to get too close now.

'Milk,' she said, and handed Hope to him.

'Shh, baby,' he crooned.

On autopilot, Amy boiled the kettle and put the baby's bottle in a glass jug to heat the milk. She nearly scalded herself when she poured boiling water into the jug, and it splashed.

'Everything OK?' Josh asked, seeing her jump.

'Yes,' she fibbed. The last thing she wanted was for him to guess how stupid and useless she felt.

'Sorry I didn't wake sooner. I guess my shift took more out of me than I thought,' he said. 'I'm supposed to be helping. I've let you down.'

And then the penny dropped.

She wasn't the only one finding it hard to do this.

'You're fine,' she said. 'We're both new at this. I always tell my class, you learn more if you get it wrong first time.'

'I guess.' He sounded rueful. 'Except a baby is a

hell of a lot tougher than a page of maths problems. And, given how many babies I treat in the course of a month, I should be better at this.'

'There's a big difference between treating a baby and looking after one full time,' she reminded him. 'And didn't you say to me earlier that Hope doesn't know if we're doing it wrong?'

'Yeah. I'm glad I'm not doing this on my own,' he said.

He'd admitted it first, so it made it easier for her to say, 'Me, too. I never expected it to be this hard— you're desperate for sleep, but you're also too scared to sleep because you want to keep an eye on the baby.'

'All the *what ifs*,' he agreed. 'Being a medic is a bad thing, because you know all the worst-case scenarios and your mind goes into overdrive. You start thinking you're seeing symptoms when there aren't any. And then you're not sure if you're being ridiculously para- noid or if you really *are* seeing something.'

'And if you're not a medic, you look up stuff on the Internet and scare yourself stupid,' she said. 'Being a parent—even a stand-in—is way harder than I thought.'

'Especially the first night, when you don't have a clue what to expect,' Josh agreed.

'We're a right pair,' she said ruefully.

'No. We're a team,' Josh said.

And that spooked her even more. It was so long since she'd seen herself in a partnership that she didn't know how to react. Then she shook herself. He meant they were a team, not a couple. She was reading too much into this. To cover how flustered she felt, she shook a couple of drops of milk onto the inside of her wrist to check the temperature. 'I think it's OK for her, now.'

'Thanks. Go back to bed,' he said. 'I've got this.'

'Sure?' she checked.

'Sure.'

'OK.' And this time she felt more relaxed when she snuggled under the duvet—enough to let her drift into sleep.

The next time the baby cried, Amy got up and scooped up the Moses basket. 'Shh, baby,' she whispered. 'Two minutes.'

'OK?' Josh asked from the sofa, sounding wide awake this time.

He hadn't been joking about usually being fully awake in seconds, then.

'It's fine. It's my turn to feed her,' she said quietly. And the way they'd muddled through together earlier had given her confidence. 'Go back to sleep.'

She took the baby into the kitchen and cuddled her as she warmed the milk, then took the baby into her bedroom, kept the light down low, and cuddled the baby as she fed her.

This felt so natural, so right. But she had to re-mind herself sharply that this was only temporary and she couldn't let herself bond too closely to Hope—or start thinking about Josh as anything more than just a neighbour. By New Year, life would be back to nor-mal again. They'd be back to smiling and nodding in the corridor, maybe exchanging an extra word or two. But that would be it.

Once the baby fell asleep again, Amy laid her gently back in the Moses basket and padded into the living room. Josh was asleep on the sofa, and this time he didn't wake.

* * *

A couple of hours later, when Hope started to grizzle again, Josh was awake in seconds.

'Shh, baby,' he whispered, and jiggled her one-handed against his shoulder as he set about making up a bottle.

When it had been his turn to deal with the baby, he'd made a complete hash of it. Not being used to listening out for a newborn, he'd slept through Hope's cries. But it turned out that Amy had been having the same kind of self-doubts that he had. Given that she'd seemed so cool, calm and collected, he'd been shocked. And then relieved. Because it meant that they were in this *together*.

And they made a good team.

To the point where he actually believed that he could do this—be a stand-in parent to an abandoned baby.

Then he realised he'd been a bit overconfident when he burped Hope and she brought up all the milk she'd just drunk. All over both of them.

He really hoped Amy didn't wake and find them both in this state. 'I dare not give you a bath,' he whispered to the baby. He knew she'd scream the place down, even if he managed to put water in the bath without waking Amy. But when he stripped off her sleep suit and vest, he discovered that luckily the baby wasn't soaked to the skin. Unlike him—but he was the adult and he'd live with it. He changed the baby into clean clothes, gave her more milk, then finally settled her back into the Moses basket.

Which left him cold and wet and smelling disgusting. He could hardly have a shower right now without waking Amy, and he couldn't go back to his own flat because he didn't have a key to Amy's. Grimacing, he stripped off his T-shirt and scrubbed the worst of the milk off his skin with a baby wipe.

Was this what life would've been like if he and Kelly had had a family? Would he have made as much of a mess of being a real dad as he was making of being a stand-in dad? Or maybe Amy was right and he was being too hard on himself. But he was seriously glad he wasn't looking after the baby on his own. It helped to be able to talk to someone else and admit that you didn't know what you were doing, and for them to say the same to you. And he was pretty sure now that he'd be able to get through this week—because Amy was on his team.

The next time Amy heard Hope crying, her eyes felt gritty from lack of sleep. Either the baby had slept a bit longer between feeds this time, or Amy had been too deeply asleep to hear her crying at the last feed.

When she stumbled into the kitchen to put the kettle on and checked the top shelf of the fridge, she realised it was the latter; Josh had done the last feed. He'd left her a note propped against the kettle. His handwriting was hard to read and she smiled to herself. Josh was definitely living up to the cliché of all medics having a terrible scrawl. Eventually she deciphered the note.

On early shift this morning—back for about 5.30 this evening—Merry Christmas, J

Christmas.
Amy hadn't planned to cook the traditional turkey

dinner; she hadn't seen the point of bothering when she was going to be on her own. But now she had unexpected company for dinner. She didn't have a turkey, but she did have the ingredients to make something nice. She could wrap a couple of chicken breasts in bacon, stir fry some tenderstem broccoli with julienned strips of butternut squash and carrot in butter and chilli, and make some baked polenta chips sprinkled with Parmesan.

'I forgot how much I enjoyed cooking,' she told the baby as she fed her. 'I haven't even had people over for dinner since I moved here. I always eat out with my friends. So maybe it's time to move on a bit more and start doing the things I enjoy again.'

The baby simply drank her milk and stared at Amy with those huge dark blue eyes.

'I've spent the last eighteen months living on auto-pilot,' Amy said. 'Don't you ever make that mistake, Hope. Life's for—well, enjoying.'

Though she was pretty sure that Hope's mum was having a thoroughly miserable Christmas. 'I hope we can find your mum,' she said softly. 'And I really hope we can do something to help her. I really don't know why she left you in our lobby—whether she knew me or Josh from somewhere, or whether it was a completely random choice—but I'm glad she did, because I think you're going to help us as much as we can help you.' And she was glad that Josh had moved in on her floor, because the reason she'd got through that first night with a baby was because of him.

Once she'd showered, washed her hair and dressed, she sent Josh a text.

Hope you're having a good shift. Alternative Christmas dinner this evening. Amy

And whether Hope was responding to her sunny mood and burst of confidence, Amy had no idea, but the baby seemed content, too; she wasn't quite as fractious and unsettled as she'd been the day before. To her relief, there wasn't one of the protracted crying sessions that had left Amy feeling hopeless and frustrated and miserable.

'Merry Christmas, baby,' she said softly. 'It isn't quite the one I think your mum would've liked for you, but hopefully the police are going to find her and reunite you in the next few days.'

Amy ate yoghurt and granola for breakfast, then looked at the small stack of presents beneath the tree. It felt odd, opening her Christmas presents all on her own. But she pushed away the melancholy before it could take hold. She intended to make the best of this Christmas, and she wasn't the only one on her own. It must be much harder for Josh in the circumstances.

Most of the envelopes contained gift vouchers, but one friend had given her the latest crime novel by one of her favourite authors, another had given her some nice Christmassy scented candles and another had bought her posh chocolates.

'That's my table decorations and dessert sorted for this evening,' she told the baby. 'And in the meantime you and I are going to curl up together on the sofa and watch a pile of Christmas movies.'

CHAPTER FOUR

AFTER HIS SHIFT, Josh showered and changed before going down the corridor to Amy's flat.

He felt a bit mean; she was cooking Christmas dinner for him, but he hadn't bought her even a token present. Then again, neither of them had expected this Christmas: for a newborn to be left on their doorstep, and then to be looking after a stranger's baby together when they barely knew each other. A present probably wasn't appropriate in the circumstances. Besides, even if the shops had been open, he didn't have a clue what kind of thing Amy liked—apart from coffee ice cream, and you could hardly wrap that and leave it under a tree. The wine he was carrying came from the rack in his kitchen, and the chocolates were a kind of re-gift. Which definitely made him feel like Scrooge.

'Merry Christmas,' he said when she opened the door in answer to his knock.

'Merry Christmas,' she said. 'I thought we'd eat at about half-past six, if that's OK with you?'

'More than OK. You have no idea how much I appreciate not having to cook for myself, or be forced to munch the leftover sausage rolls people brought in to the department because I'm starving but too tired even to make a cheese toastie,' he said with a smile. He handed her the chocolates and wine. 'This is my contribution for tonight.'

'You really didn't have to, but thank you.'

'And I have to admit that the chocolates are from the Secret Santa at work, which makes me a bit of a Scrooge for kind of re-gifting them,' he confessed.

'No, it just means that you don't usually have chocolate in the house and there aren't any shops open. And they're definitely appreciated,' she said, smiling back. 'How was your shift?'

'Let's just say we've renamed one of the twelve days of Christmas. "Five Turkey Carvers",' he said ruefully. 'I've done quite a bit of stitching up today.'

'Ouch,' she said.

'So how's our little one doing?' Then he realised what he'd said and felt his eyes go wide. 'Um,' he said. 'Sorry. I didn't quite…'

'I know,' she said quietly. 'It kind of feels like being part of a new family.'

'Even though she isn't ours, and we're not…'

'…a couple. Yeah,' she said.

Josh looked at her. Amy wasn't wearing a scrap of make-up, but she was naturally beautiful. He itched to sketch her, and it had been a long while since anyone had made him feel that way.

This was dangerous.

Part of him wanted to run; but part of him was intrigued and wanted more. To cover his confusion, he asked, 'Is there anything I can do to help?'

She shook her head. 'Hope's still asleep and I haven't started cooking dinner yet, so do you want a glass of wine or a cup of tea?'

'As it's Christmas, let's go for the glass of wine,' he said.

'And, as you said you wanted to help, you can open it.'

He followed her into the kitchen. When she handed him the corkscrew, his fingers brushed against her skin and it felt weird, as if he'd been galvanised. He was shockingly aware of her, but he didn't dare look at her because he didn't want her to guess what he was thinking. Had she felt it, too? And, if so, what were they going to do about it?

He shook himself mentally. They weren't going to do anything about it. They were neighbours. Acquaintances. And that was the way it was going to stay.

He opened the wine while she took two glasses from a cupboard; then he poured the wine before lifting his own glass and clinking it against hers. 'Merry Christmas.'

'Merry Christmas,' she echoed.

'I haven't bought you a present,' he said, 'and I feel kind of bad about it.'

'I haven't bought you one, either,' she said. 'I did think about wrapping up a bottle of wine for you or something, but it didn't feel appropriate.'

'Considering we hardly know each other and don't have a clue what each other likes,' he agreed.

'We haven't bought Hope anything, either,' she said, 'but it's fine. Christmas isn't really about the presents, and perhaps what we're actually giving each other is a better Christmas than we were expecting.'

'You know,' he said, 'I think you might be right. You're a wise woman, Amy Howes.'

'It goes with the territory of being a maths teacher,' she said with a smile.

He liked her sense of humour. And, actually, the more he talked to her, the more he liked a lot of other things about her. Which again set his alarm bells ringing. He wasn't supposed to be thinking like that. He was newly divorced. Not in a place to start anything with anyone.

'Maybe,' he said, 'we can make a kind of present for Hope. A book of her days with us. Photographs, that kind of thing.'

'Add in her feed and sleep charts, too?' Amy said. 'That's a really nice idea. And then she's got something to keep.'

'So how has it been with the baby today?' he asked.

'Easier than yesterday. We've been watching Christmas movies,' she said.

'Sounds like a good plan.'

'*Love Actually* is one of my favourite films. And you really can't top the Christmas lobster.'

Then Amy remembered that one of the storylines in the movie involved an affair. Talk about rubbing salt in his wounds. How could she have forgotten that Josh's wife left him for another man, last Christmas Eve? 'Sorry. I just put my foot in it. I didn't mean to make you feel bad.'

'I'm not a fan of romcoms,' Josh said, 'and you haven't put your foot in it—even though I get what you're saying. This is way better than Christmas was last year, believe me.'

Which didn't make her feel any less guilty. Just about anything would be an improvement on his last

Christmas. 'Maybe I should start prepping dinner,' she said awkwardly.

'As the baby's asleep, is there anything I can do?'

'You can keep topping up the wine and chat to me in the kitchen, if you like,' she suggested.

'I'd like that. Funny, two days ago we were almost complete strangers,' he said, 'and now we're spending Christmas together.'

'As a kind of blended family with a baby who's a complete stranger, too,' she said.

'I still don't know anything about you,' he said, 'other than that you're a maths teacher and you have a brother who lives in Canada.'

'And you're an emergency department doctor who's the youngest of four.' She shrugged. 'OK. So what do you want to know? I'm thirty.'

'I'm thirty-two,' he said.

Amy started chopping the carrots into matchsticks.

'And you obviously enjoy cooking—or at least you're good at it,' Josh said.

She smiled. 'Thank you, and I do. Does that mean you don't?'

'I'd rather wash up than cook,' he said. 'Obviously I can cook a few basics—you wouldn't survive as a student unless you knew how to make stuff like spaghetti Bolognese and cheese toasties—but spending all that time making something that people will wolf down in two seconds flat and then forget about...' He smiled. 'Or maybe that's the medic in me talking.'

'So food's fuel rather than a pleasure?'

'At work, yes,' he admitted. 'Shamefully, I eat a chocolate bar on the run for my lunch way more often than I ought to.'

'So what sort of things do you like doing outside work?' Amy grimaced. 'I'm sorry. This sounds like a terrible speed-dating sort of grilling.'

'Speed-dating,' he said, 'is something I've never actually done.'

'Me neither,' she agreed. 'Though I guess, when you get to our age, it's probably about your only option for meeting someone, if you haven't already clicked with someone you met at work or with a friend of a friend at a party.'

'And if you're in a job with unsocial hours, work means that half the time you're not on the same shift and it's hard to find a time when you can actually do something together,' he added. 'Though I think being set up with a friend of a friend is worse than dating someone at work, because then if it doesn't work out it makes things a bit awkward with your friend. You feel a bit guilty and as if you've let your friend down.'

'That sounds like experience talking,' Amy said.

Josh wrinkled his nose. 'I did have a couple of well-meaning friends try to set me up, earlier this year, but I told them I just wasn't ready.'

She nodded. 'I know what you mean. It was a while before I could face dating after I split up with Michael; then, after that, I just didn't meet anyone I could click with.'

Though she had a feeling that she could click with Josh, given the chance. It surprised her how much she liked him and how easy he was to talk to.

'One of my friends tried speed-dating a few months back,' Josh said. 'He tried to talk me into going with him, but it sounded a bit too much like a meat market for me. He did say afterwards that all the women he'd met had had a massive list of questions they'd prepared earlier, and it felt like the worst kind of job interview.'

'I guess asking questions is a quick way of getting to know someone,' she said.

He smiled at her. 'Maybe we should look at one of those lists. It'll save us having to think up our own questions.'

'Good idea,' she said, carefully separating the tenderstem broccoli and adding it to her pile of stir-fry veg before starting on the butternut squash.

Josh took his phone from his pocket and flicked into the Internet. 'Here we go. What you do at work? Well, we already know that about each other. Where are you from?' He frowned. 'That's pretty irrelevant.' He flicked further down the list. 'OK. Let's try this one. What's the one thing about yourself that you'd like me to know?'

'I don't have a clue,' she said.

'Me, neither. Let's skip to the next one.' He grimaced. 'That's all about your last relationship. It's too intrusive. Same as whether you're looking to get married.' He shook his head. 'I can't believe you'd actually ask a complete stranger if they're looking to get married when you're thinking about maybe dating them for the first time. I mean—you might be completely incompatible. Why would you talk about marriage that early on?'

'Maybe that's the point of speed-dating. To speed everything up,' Amy said. 'If you want to settle down but the person you're thinking about dating doesn't, you're both kind of wasting each other's time.'

'That question still feels wrong.' He scrolled down

the page. 'This is a bit more like it. What do you do for fun?'

'Music,' she said promptly. 'Not clubbing—I like live music, whether it's a tiny venue where there's only enough room for a couple of dozen people listening to someone playing an acoustic guitar, or a big stadium with a massive stack of amps and a light show.'

'What kind of music?' he asked.

'All sorts—everything from pop to rock. I'm not so keen on rap,' she said, 'but I love the buzz you get from going to a concert and singing along with the rest of the audience. What about you?'

'I tend to listen to rock music when I'm running,' he said. 'Something with a strong beat that keeps me going.'

'So you're a runner?'

'Strictly outdoor. I like the fresh air, and the views,' he said, 'rather than being cooped up in a gym on a treadmill where you just see the same patch of wall for half an hour or so.'

'Park or river?' she asked.

'If it's wet, river,' he said, 'purely because you're less likely to slide on the mud and rick your ankle. If it's dry, definitely the park because it's lovely to see all that green, especially in spring when all the leaves are new and everything looks fresh. And if I worked regular hours I'd definitely have a dog to run with me.' He shrugged. 'I don't have a dog because my hours aren't regular and it wouldn't be fair to leave the dog alone for so long.'

'You look like a Labrador person,' she said.

He nodded. 'Or a spaniel. Or a Dalmatian—where I lived before, our neighbour had this amazing Dalmatian who used to smile at me. And it really was a friendly greeting rather than baring his teeth, because his tail was wagging so hard the whole time.'

Amy could see the wistfulness on his face. The breakup of his marriage had cost him more than just his relationship.

'How about you?' he asked.

'No to the running. I like spinning classes,' she said, 'because I don't have to worry about riding a bike in traffic and I don't have to drag myself outside when it's wet.'

'That's reasonable—though, actually, running in the rain is great. Dog or cat?'

'Dog,' she said. 'But, like you, I don't want to leave a dog cooped up alone in my flat all day. So I make the most of it when I go to see my parents—they've got Border terriers.'

He continued scrolling through the list of questions 'Some of these definitely sound more like the sort of thing you'd ask in a job interview. Why would you ask someone if they have a five-year plan?'

'Because you want to know if they're ambitious and would put their career before your relationship; or find out if they're the kind of person who drifts along and gets stuck in a bit of a rut,' she suggested.

'Which in turn probably means your relationship will end up in a rut, too.' He rolled his eyes. 'There have to be easier ways of getting to know what a person's like.'

'In the space of three minutes, or however long it is you have on a speed date? I don't think you have a choice but to ask intrusive questions,' she said.

'I give up on the list. What sort of thing would you ask?'

'About their interests,' she said. 'Dating someone who wanted to spend their whole weekend playing sport or watching sport would be pretty wearing.'

'Yes, because when would you get time to do other things together?' he agreed.

'In the evenings, maybe—something like the cinema?' she suggested.

'I haven't been to the cinema in way too long,' he said. 'I tend to end up waiting for things to come out on DVD, and even then I haven't caught up with all the latest releases, and I've got a pile of stuff I've been meaning to see and haven't had time for.'

'So why don't you go to the cinema?' she asked. 'Because you like the kind of things that nobody else does, so you'd have to go on your own?'

'Art-house movies in a foreign language?' he asked. 'No, it's more that my duty roster tends to get in the way and everyone's already seen the film before I get a chance. I like the big sci-fi blockbusters.'

'Ah. Now I have a question for you. Team Cap or Team Iron Man?' she asked.

'Team Cap,' he said promptly, and she gave him a high five.

'So you like the same kind of films as I do?' he asked.

'Yup. I do like romcoms as well, but I've always been a sci-fi geek. And I bought myself the one that came out last week as an early Christmas present. I know it's not strictly a Christmas movie, but maybe we could watch it tonight.'

'And we can pause or a feed. Great idea.' He smiled at her. 'So we like the same kind of films and music. How about TV?'

'Cop dramas,' she said. 'That's my guilty pleasure. All the Scandinavian noir stuff.'

'Again, I have to watch them on catch-up half the time, but me too,' he said.

'Right. Crosswords or number puzzles?'

He groaned. 'Neither. I'm assuming that you'd go for the maths problems?'

'Absolutely.' She smiled. 'Reading—fiction or non-fiction?'

'Non-fiction,' he said promptly, 'and it's usually medical journals. You?'

'Crime fiction,' she said. 'I guess it's because I like trying to solve the puzzles.'

'Beach holiday or climbing a mountain?' he asked.

'Neither—city break or road trip for me,' she said. 'I like exploring new places and seeing the sights. You?'

'I like the sound of the road trip,' he said. 'I'd love to see New England in the fall. And the hot springs and waterfalls at Yosemite.'

'I'd guessed you'd be bored on a beach, but you strike me as a mountain-climbing type,' she said.

'Not so much mountains,' he said, 'but I did do the coast-to-coast walk for charity, one year, and I loved every second of it—even the blisters.'

'I'm afraid the best I've done in the charity stakes is to make cakes and sponsor friends who do the ten-K runs,' Amy said.

'The main thing is that the money's raised. It doesn't matter who does what,' he said.

Just as Amy finished prepping dinner, Hope woke.

'Well, hello, Munchkin,' he said, and scooped the baby out of her Moses basket. 'So it's Uncle Joshy's turn to feed you.'

'I'll bring the milk in,' Amy said.

When she took the warmed milk in, Josh was sitting on the sofa, talking to the baby in a low voice and letting her wrap her tiny fist round his little finger. The sight put a lump in her throat. Josh was so warm and kind. He'd make a fabulous father one day—but that made him off limits for her, so she'd have to ignore the attraction she felt towards him. If he wanted children, she couldn't take his future away from him like that. And, given the way he was acting with the baby right now, she was pretty sure he'd want a family of his own one day.

Josh took the bottle of milk from Amy. 'Thanks.'

'No problem.'

Hope closed her eyes in bliss as she drank the milk. And it was strange how natural this felt, having a warm little weight in the crook of his arm. In another life, this could've been his baby...

He glanced at Amy. For all his scorn about the speed-dating questions, they had at least established that they had quite a few interests in common. And the more he got to know her, the more he liked her. It had been a while since he'd met someone he felt he could really be himself with.

'Hey. Smile,' she said, and held up her camera.

'For Hope's book?'

'You bet.'

'Then I ought to be sitting with the Christmas tree behind me.' He stood up, without disturbing Hope or stopping her drinking her milk, and moved so Amy could take a more Christmassy photo of them together. 'I'll take one of you with her later, too.'

'Thanks.'

She laid the table while he fed the baby. 'Sorry, it's not going to be a proper Christmas dinner, and I don't have any crackers or party hats—but I do have a Christmas scented candle.'

'Sounds good. Anything I can do to help?'

'You already are,' she said. 'And you've been at work all day. Just chill with the baby.'

This really, really felt like being part of a new little family.

Josh knew he was going to have to keep a tight grip on his imagination, because that so wasn't happening. Yes, he found Amy attractive; but the last thing he wanted to do was to have a fling with her and then for it all to go wrong and make things awkward if he bumped into her in the lobby or the corridor. They needed to keep things strictly platonic, he reminded himself.

And that was what stopped him going to chat to her in the kitchen again when the baby had finished her feed and he'd burped her.

Though sitting there watching the baby fall asleep made his fingers itch to sketch her. When he wrote all the details of the feed down in Amy's notebook, he couldn't resist flicking to the very back of the book. It didn't matter that the paper was lined and he was using a pen rather than a pencil; he gave into the urge and sketched the sleeping baby. And maybe this was something he could add to Hope's book. Something personal.

He was so wrapped up in what he was doing that he didn't notice Amy standing beside him, carrying a glass of wine.

'That's seriously good,' she said. 'Did you ever think about being an artist instead of a doctor?'

His big dream. The one that had been squashed before it had had a chance to grow. For once he answered honestly. 'Not in a family of high achievers,' he said wryly. 'Art wasn't quite academic enough for them.'

'Your parents didn't support you?' She sounded shocked. Clearly her family was the sort to encourage her to follow her dreams rather than insist that she trod the path they'd mapped out for her.

'They didn't like the idea of me going to art school,' Josh admitted. 'They said the world had changed a lot in the last generation and there weren't that many jobs in art.' At least not ones that paid well. Though he ought to be fair about it. 'I guess they had a point.'

'What made you choose medicine instead?' she asked.

'Studying biology meant I could still draw,' he said. 'Besides, art is something I can do for me.'

'Do you do much?'

That was the killer question. He smiled wryly. 'It hasn't quite worked out that way.'

'Make the time, Josh,' she said softly. 'If drawing makes you happy, make the time for it.'

Kelly had never suggested that to him.

But then again, the real him hadn't been enough for her, any more than it had been enough for his family—or Kelly would've had her baby with him instead of with another man.

He pushed the thought away. Now wasn't the time to be maudlin or filled with regrets.

'Dinner's about ready,' she said.

'Perfect timing. Munchkin here's set to sleep for

a couple of hours,' he said. 'Can I bring anything in for you?'

'No, but you can light the candle, if you want. The matches are in the top drawer of the cupboard over there.'

He lit the candle and sat down while she brought in the dishes.

'This is fabulous,' he said after the first taste of the polenta chips sprinkled with parmesan.

'Thanks. It's been a while since I've made these,' she said.

'You told me to make the time for doing something I love—that goes for you, too,' he said gently.

'I guess. I'll make more of an effort in the new year, as long as you promise to do the same.'

'I will,' he agreed. 'I've been thinking—do you reckon the baby's mother picked our block of flats at random?'

'Maybe,' Amy said. 'Are you thinking she didn't?'

'She rang your doorbell. That might've been chance—but supposing you knew her?'

Amy shook her head. 'That's unlikely. I don't know anyone who's pregnant.'

'But we think she's young and scared, right?' he asked, warming to his theory. 'The chances are, she hid her pregnancy from just about everyone. But maybe she knew you from school.'

'I didn't recognise the handwriting, so I don't think she's anyone I teach,' Amy said. She frowned. 'But then again…'

'What if she wrote the note with her non-writing hand?' Josh suggested.

'Or what if,' Amy said slowly, 'she's someone I don't

teach, so I've never really seen her handwriting properly? Now I think about it, there's a girl in my form who's gone very quiet over the last few months. I did have a confidential word with her mum, but she said Freya was being difficult because her new partner had just moved in.'

'It happens,' Josh said. 'How old is she?'

'Fifteen.'

'Then maybe, if she's unhappy at home, she's blotting it out with the help of a boyfriend.'

'I don't think she has a boyfriend,' Amy said. 'At least, not one who's at school. You normally hear the kids talking and work out who's seeing who.'

'Does she look as if she's put on weight?'

Amy thought about it. 'She always wears baggy clothes so it's hard to tell. But, now you mention it, she does look as if she's put on weight. I assumed she was comfort-eating because she was unhappy at home and I didn't want to make her feel any worse by drawing attention to it. Teens are under such pressure when it comes to body image. I didn't want to say something that would make her start starving herself. But I have noticed her dashing off to the loo in the middle of form time over the last term, and I was going to have a quiet word with her next term to check she didn't have an eating disorder.'

'Or maybe,' Josh said, 'she was dashing off to the loo because she was in the last trimester and the baby's weight was putting pressure on her bladder.'

'That's a good point. But why didn't she say anything to me?'

'In the cases I've seen at work,' Josh said, 'where the mum's under age and scared, she's either been in denial about the situation or too scared to tell anyone in case she gets into trouble.'

'That's so sad,' Amy said. 'To be young and scared and not know where to go for help.'

'She didn't say anything to you,' Josh said. 'But it would make sense that she'd leave the baby with someone she knew would help and do the right thing for the baby.'

'Agreed. But this is all speculation,' she said. 'We don't have any proof.'

'And we have to do this through the proper channels,' Josh added. 'If our theory's right, then we could do more harm than good if we go rushing over to see her.'

'Plus we don't have a car seat or anyone to keep an eye on Hope while we go and see her,' she agreed. 'Jane, the social worker, will know the right way to go about this. We can talk to her about it.'

'Tomorrow's Sunday—Boxing Day—and then Monday and Tuesday are bank holidays, so she won't be in the office for a few days,' Josh pointed out.

'She did give me her mobile number, but it was for emergencies—and, because this is a theory and we don't have any real proof, it doesn't really count as an emergency.' Amy frowned. 'I guess it'll have to wait a few days.'

'Or maybe you could text Jane tomorrow?' he suggested. 'Then she'll have the information and she can decide if she wants to take it further any earlier.'

'Good idea,' she said.

'I'm off duty tomorrow.' He gave her a wry smile. 'It would've been nice to take the baby out to the park, but as she doesn't have a coat and we don't have a pram or even a sling, and there's not going to be anywhere open tomorrow where we can buy something for her, I guess we're stuck.'

'It feels a bit like being snowbound,' Amy said, 'but without actually being snowed in.'

'And you haven't left your flat for two days.' Guilt flooded through him. She'd had the majority of the burden of worrying about the baby. 'Sorry, I should've thought of that earlier and suggested you went out to get some fresh air or something.'

'No, it's fine, but probably tomorrow I could do with some fresh air,' she admitted, 'if you don't mind looking after Hope on your own for a few minutes.'

'Sure. That's no problem.'

After dinner, they curled up on the sofa and watched the sci-fi film together. A couple of times, Josh's hand accidentally brushed against Amy's and he seriously considered letting his fingers curl round hers.

But then again, she'd said she wasn't ready for another relationship, and he knew his own head was still in a bit of a mess.

He was definitely attracted to Amy. But how could he trust that love wouldn't go wrong for him again, the way it had with Kelly? It was better to stick to just being friends. That would be safer for all of them.

'I guess it's time to get some sleep,' Amy said when she'd fed Hope and noted everything down. 'I'll do the next feed.'

'Sure?'

'Sure. Feel free to leave the TV on as long as you want, though. You won't be disturbing me.'

'OK. I'll get my duvet,' he said.

'Take my key with you,' she said. 'Merry Christmas, Josh.'

'Merry Christmas, Amy.'

For a moment he thought she was going to rise on tiptoe and kiss him, and his whole body seemed to snap to attention. What would it feel like, her lips against his skin? Would her mouth be as soft and sweet as it looked? And what if he twisted his head to the side so her mouth connected with his instead of with his cheek?

He was shocked to realise how much he wanted it to happen.

And even more shocked to realise how disappointed he was when she simply smiled and headed for the bathroom instead.

Oh, help. He really had to get a grip. He and Amy were neighbours. Maybe they were on the way to being friends. This whole thing of looking after the baby together was seriously messing with his head. He didn't want to risk his heart again. End of. So he was going to be sensible.

Completely sensible.

CHAPTER FIVE

Boxing Day—Sunday

'JOSH. *JOSH.*'

He was awake instantly, and he could hear the note of panic in Amy's voice. 'What's happened?'

'It's Hope. She feels really hot and she hardly drank any milk just now. I think there's something wrong.'

'Hold on. Where's the light? I'll take a look at her.'

She switched on one of the lamps in the living room.

Josh took the baby from Amy's arms and gently examined her. 'You're right—she does feel hot.'

'I have one of those ear thermometers. Maybe we should take her temperature and see how bad it is?' Amy suggested.

'Unfortunately, those thermometers are too big for a newborn baby's ears,' he said. 'We need a normal digital thermometer. I've got one in my bathroom— I'll go and get it.'

Amy frowned. 'But surely you can't stick a thermometer in a baby's mouth?'

'Nope—you stick it under her armpit,' he said.

'Oh.' Amy looked at him. 'Anything I can do?'

'Strip her down to her nappy and a vest while I get

the thermometer, then hold her for me and talk to her,' he said. 'And if you've got some cooled boiled water, we'll try and get her to drink some.'

When he checked the baby's temperature, he wasn't happy with the reading. 'It's thirty-eight degrees. It's a bit high, but a baby's temperature can go up and down really quickly because at this age their bodies haven't worked out yet how to control their temperature. I'm ninety-five per cent sure this is nothing serious, because the soft spot at the top of her head isn't sunken and she isn't floppy,' he reassured Amy. Though that left a five per cent chance that this was the early stages of something nasty. 'But, given that we don't really know the circumstances of her birth, there's a chance she might have a bacterial infection,' he said. And in that case she would get worse. Quickly, too, though he wasn't going to worry Amy about that now. 'The only way to find out is by a blood test and urine analysis, which I can't do here.'

'So we need to take her to hospital?' Amy asked.

He sighed. 'I'd rather not have to do that, with all the viruses going around, but babies this young can get very unwell quite quickly, so if it *is* an infection I'd want her treated for it as soon as possible. Though, at this time of the morning, the department will be relatively quiet, so we won't have to wait too long.'

'Just take our turn with the drunks who've fallen over after a party or had a punch-up?' she asked wryly.

He smiled. Clearly she'd remembered his grumpy assessment of the seasonal waiting room. 'Yes, but she'll be triaged. We prioritise when we see our patients, depending on their symptoms and how old they are. Hope will get seen really quickly because she's a newborn with a temperature.'

'We don't have a car seat or a pram. How are we going to get her to hospital?' Amy asked.

'We can't risk taking her in the back of the car in her Moses basket,' Josh said. 'Apart from the fact it's illegal and we have departmental guidelines, so we can't let anyone take a child from hospital without an appropriate seat, I also know most accidents take place within a mile of a home. We're going to have to call an ambulance.'

'OK. I'll get Hope dressed again while you call the ambulance, and then I'll throw on some clothes. Give me two minutes.'

She was as good as her word, he noticed, taking only a couple of minutes and not bothering with make-up or anything like that. Practical. He liked that.

'They'll be here in another five minutes,' he said. 'I told them we'd wait in the lobby.'

Between them, they tucked Hope into her Moses basket; Amy grabbed the notebook so they had a record of everything the baby had drunk, and they waited in the lobby until they saw the ambulance pull up outside.

'Josh! You're the last person I expected to see—nobody thought you were even dating anyone, let alone had a new baby,' the paramedic said.

Oh, help. He could really do without any gossip at work. 'The baby's not mine,' he said hastily.

The paramedic looked intrigued. 'So you're helping your...' she glanced at Amy '...friend.'

'The baby's not mine, either,' Amy said. 'We're looking after her temporarily.'

The paramedic's eyes rounded. 'Together?'

'We're neighbours,' Josh added. 'And you might have seen something about the baby in the news.'

'Oh, hang on—is this the Christmas Eve doorstep baby?'

'Yes. Her name's Hope,' Amy said, 'and she's got a temperature.'

'Thirty-eight degrees, axillary,' Josh said, 'and we stripped her off and gave her cooled boiled water, but we don't have any liquid paracetamol. I need blood tests and urine analysis to rule out a bacterial infection. She's not floppy or drowsy so I'm not panicking, but given her age and the fact that we don't know the circumstances of her birth or anything about her medical history...'

The paramedic patted his arm. 'Josh, you're off duty. Stop worrying. We'll handle it. Right now you count as a patient, not staff. Are you coming in with her?'

'We both are,' Josh said.

It was the first time Amy had ever travelled in an ambulance. And even though Josh was able to answer most of the paramedic's questions and she had the notes about Hope's feeds, it was still a worrying experience.

Especially when the paramedic put a tiny oxygen mask on the baby.

'What's wrong?' Amy asked.

'It's a precaution,' Josh said. Clearly he could tell how worried she was, because he took her hand and squeezed it to reassure her. Somehow her fingers ended up curled just as tightly round his.

The drive to hospital was short, but it felt as if it

took for ever. And when Hope was whisked into cubicles the second they arrived, with the doctor acknowledging them but asking them to wait outside, Amy's worries deepened.

'It's routine,' Josh said. 'They'll be taking blood and urine samples to check if she's got an infection.'

'But why can't we stay with her?' Amy asked. 'I mean, I know we're not her actual parents, but...'

'I know.' His fingers tightened round hers. 'As I said, it's routine and we're just going to get in the way. We need to let the team do their job.'

'You work here. Doesn't that make a difference?' Amy asked.

He shook his head.

And then a really nasty thought struck her. He'd said that new babies couldn't regulate their temperatures that well. If Hope had an infection and her temperature shot up... Could she die?

Time felt as if it had just stopped.

'Josh. Tell me she's not going to...' The word stuck in her throat.

He looked at her, and she could see her own fears reflected in his blue eyes.

'We have to wait for the test results,' he said.

The baby wasn't theirs—or at least was only theirs temporarily—but right then Amy felt like a real parent, anxious for news and trying not to think of the worst-case scenarios. Any tiredness she felt vanished under the onslaught of adrenaline. This was the only chance she might have to be a parent. And what if she lost something so precious—the baby she hadn't asked for but was beginning to fall in love with, despite her promises to herself not to let herself get involved?

'Amy,' Josh said softly. 'It's going to be all right. Alison—the doctor who is looking after her—is one of my most experienced juniors. She'll spot any problem and know how to treat it.'

'I guess.'

He must have heard the wobble in her voice, because this time he wrapped his free arm around her and held her close. 'It's going to be OK.'

She leaned back and looked at him. 'You look as worried as I feel.'

'A bit,' he admitted wryly. 'My head knows it's going to be fine. If there was anything really serious going on, Alison would've come out to see us by now.'

'But?'

'But my heart,' he continued quietly, 'is panicking. This must be what it's like to be a parent. Worrying if the baby is OK, or if you're missing something important.'

She nodded. 'I'm glad you're with me. Knowing I'm not the only one feeling like this makes it feel a bit less—well—scary.'

'Agreed.' Though she noticed he was still holding her; clearly he was taking as much comfort from her nearness as she was from his.

And then finally the curtain swished open.

'Hey, Josh. We've done bloods and urine, to rule out bacterial infections,' Alison said. 'And I gave her a proper cord clip. How on earth did you manage to change her nappy round that thing?'

'A mixture of necessity and practice,' Amy said wryly.

'Ouch,' Alison said. 'Well, you know the drill, Josh. We'll have to wait for the test results before we can tell if we need to admit her—and, given all the viruses in the hospital right now, hopefully we won't have to do that. But you can sit with the baby now while we wait for the results to come back, if you like.'

'Yes, please. And no doubt you have potential fractures in the waiting room that need looking at,' Josh said. 'Sure. We won't hold you up any longer.'

When Alison had closed the cubicle curtain behind her, Josh turned to Amy. 'We can't pick her up and hold her,' Josh said, 'because our body warmth will put her temperature up.' Which meant they had to resort to taking turns in letting Hope hold a finger in her left hand, because Hope's right hand was hooked up to a machine.

'So what does this machine do?' Amy asked.

'It's a pulse oximeter. It measures the oxygen levels in her blood,' Josh explained, 'so we know if there's a problem and we need to give her some extra oxygen through a mask, like they did in the ambulance. It's all done by light shining through her skin and it doesn't hurt her.' He was used to explaining the situation, but it felt odd to be on the other side of it, too.

'Right. Are those figures good news or bad?' she asked, gesturing to the screen.

He analysed them swiftly. 'Good. I'm happy with her oxygen sats and her pulse rate.'

Amy bit her lip. 'She's so tiny, Josh, and we're supposed to be looking after her. What if…?'

'If she has an infection, she's in the right place for us to treat it,' Josh reassured her. 'She'll be fine.'

Two hours later, the baby's temperature was down to a more normal level. The results of the blood tests had come back, and to their relief there was no sign of any bacterial infection.

'I'm pleased to say you can take her home. Just keep an eye on her and give her some liquid paracetamol every four to six hours—you know the safe dose for a baby that age,' Alison said to Josh. 'How are you getting home?'

'Ambulance, I guess,' Josh said. 'We don't have a car seat for her. The social worker obviously didn't guess we might have to rush her to hospital.'

'So you've got almost nothing for her?' Alison asked.

'Just the very basics—this Moses basket, some clothes and formula milk,' Amy confirmed.

'Poor little mite. She's lucky you found her,' Alison said. 'And that you could look after her.'

'We're neighbours,' Josh said quickly.

Alison looked at their joined hands and smiled.

Josh prised his fingers free. 'And friends. And worried sick about the baby.'

'She's going to be fine,' Alison said. 'I'll let the ambulance control know that you can go whenever they're ready.'

This time the journey wasn't as terrifying, and Hope slept through the whole thing. Though Amy felt as if she'd never, ever sleep again when she let them back into her flat. 'I'll sit up with her.'

'I'll keep you company,' he said.

'But you—' she began.

'I'm not on duty tomorrow—well, today,' he cut in. 'I'm awake now, too. And we can both catch up on our sleep later when the baby sleeps.'

'Are you sure?'

'Sure. Let's keep the light low for her, so she can sleep and we can see her.'

His duvet was still thrown over her sofa. 'Here—you might as well share the duvet with me,' he said, and tucked it over her. 'Try not to worry. We know it's not a bacterial infection, which is the important thing. Maybe it's the beginnings of a cold. Small babies tend to get temperature spikes when they get a cold. One minute they're fine, the next minute they're ill enough to worry the life out of you, and then they're absolutely fine again.' He took her hand. 'She's going to be perfectly all right, Amy. We're here and we're keeping an eye on her. And, before you say it, I'm used to not getting massive amounts of sleep. It comes with the job.'

'I guess,' she said. He was still holding her hand, and it made her feel better. She didn't pull away.

Amy woke, feeling groggy, to the sound of Hope crying.

When had she fallen asleep? How could she have neglected Hope like that? Guilt flooded through her.

But a crying baby was a good sign, right?

'OK?' Josh asked next to her, sounding much more awake than she felt.

'OK. My turn to sort her out,' she mumbled. Why had she thought it was a good idea to sit up all night on the sofa? She had a crick in her neck and her back ached. Right now she wasn't going to be a lot of use to the baby.

'It ought to be my turn,' he said, 'because she's due some more paracetamol.' He paused. 'They weighed her at hospital. Can you remember how much they said she weighed?'

'I didn't even register it,' she said. 'I was so worried that they were going to find something seriously wrong.'

'It's gone clean out of my head, too.' He blew out a breath. 'I don't want to guess at her weight and estimate the dose of paracetamol, so we're going to have to weigh her.'

'I don't actually own a pair of bathroom scales,' Amy admitted.

'How about kitchen scales, and a tray we can put her on for a moment?' Josh suggested.

She snapped the light on and gave him a wry smile. 'This has to be the strangest Boxing Day morning I've ever spent.'

'Me, too,' he said.

But at the same time it was a morning that filled her with relief—even more than the first night they'd spent with Hope, because now she knew that with Josh by her side she could face anything life threw at her.

'Give her a cuddle and I'll get the scales out,' she said.

She put a soft cloth on a baking tray, then put it on her kitchen scales and set them to zero. 'All righty.'

He set Hope on the tray and Amy peered at the display on the scales. 'Five pounds, ten ounces—or do you need it in metric?'

'Pounds and ounces are fine,' he said. 'I know how much infant paracetamol to give her now.'

He measured a dose of medicine for the baby and gave it to her through the oral syringe while Amy heated the milk.

'Sofa?' he asked.

She nodded and he carried Hope back to the sofa. This time, after he'd transferred the baby into Amy's arms so she could feed the baby, he slid one arm round Amy's shoulder.

It felt too nice for her to protest; right at that moment she felt warm, comforted and safe. After the scare that had taken them to the hospital, this was exactly what she needed. Maybe it was what he needed, too, she thought, and she tried not to overthink it. Or to start hoping that this meant Josh was starting to see her as more than just a neighbour. Yes, they could be friends. But on New Year's Day they'd have to give Hope back to the social worker—and when that part of their lives came to an end, what would happen?

Once the baby had finished drinking her milk—all sixty millilitres of it—Amy put her back in the Moses basket. Without comment, Josh put his arm round her shoulders again. Although part of Amy knew that she ought to put some distance between them, she couldn't help leaning into him, enjoying the feel of his muscular body against hers and his warmth.

They kept watch on the baby with the light turned down low, but finally Amy drifted back to sleep.

The next time Hope woke, it was a more reasonable time. Josh fed the baby while Amy showered and washed her hair, and then she took over baby duties while Josh went next door to shower and change.

She put cereals, yoghurt, jam and butter on the table, placed the bread next to the toaster, and while she waited for the kettle to boil she texted Jane Richards, the social worker.

Hope doing well. Had a bit of a temperature in the middle of the night but we checked her out at hospital and all OK. We have a theory about her mum: might be a girl from my class, but no proof. How do we check it out?

When she'd sent the text, she suddenly realised that she hadn't signed it. From the context, she was pretty sure that Jane would probably be able to work out who the text was from, but she sent a second text anyway.

This is Amy Howes btw. Not enough coffee or sleep! :)

Josh was back in her flat and they'd just finished breakfast when his phone rang.

'Do you mind if I get that?' he asked.

She spread her hands. 'It's fine.'

He returned with a smile. 'Remember Alison, the doctor who saw us last night?'

'Yes.'

'She's bringing us a pram and a snowsuit. She'll call me when she's parked and I'll go and let her in.'

Amy blinked. 'A pram and a snowsuit?'

'I'll let her explain. She's about twenty minutes away.'

True to her word, Alison called him to say that she'd just parked and had all the stuff with her.

'Feel free to ask her up for coffee,' Amy said as he headed for the door. 'It's the least I can do.'

'Thanks.'

He returned with Alison, carrying a pram, and Amy sorted out the hot drinks.

'Thank you so much for lending us the pram and snowsuit,' Amy said.

'No problem.' Alison smiled at her. 'I didn't think about it until after you'd left, but my sister was about to put her pram on eBay—it's one of those with a car seat that clips to the chassis to make a pram. She's happy to lend it to you while you're looking after Hope. And her youngest was tiny, so I've got some tiny baby clothes and a snowsuit as well. At least then you can take her out and all get some fresh air.'

'That's so kind,' Amy said.

'She didn't take much persuading,' Alison said. 'In situations like this, you always think how easily it could have been you or someone close to you. Poor little love. How's she doing?'

'Her temperature's gone down—but, when we had to give her more paracetamol this morning, I forgot how much she weighed,' Josh admitted.

'So poor little Hope had to lie on a towel on a baking tray, so we could weigh her on my kitchen scales,' Amy added.

Alison laughed. 'I can just imagine it. And, tsk, Josh, you being a consultant and forgetting something as important as a baby's weight.'

'I know. I'm totally hanging my head in shame,' Josh said, looking anything but repentant.

Amy suddenly had a very clear idea of what he was like to work with—as nice as he was as a neighbour, kind and good-humoured and compassionate, yet strong when it was necessary. Given his gorgeous blue eyes and the way his hair seemed to be messy again five minutes after he'd combed it, she'd just bet that half the female staff at the hospital had a crush on him. Not that he'd notice. Josh wasn't full of himself and aware of his good looks, the way Gavin and even Michael had been. He was genuine.

And he was off limits, she reminded herself.

Alison peered into the Moses basket. 'She's a little cutie.'

'Pick her up and give her a cuddle, if you like,' Amy said.

Alison smiled, needing no second invitation. 'I love babies. Especially when I can give them back when it comes to nappy changes.'

'Noted,' Josh said dryly.

'So she was just left in the lobby in your flats?' Alison asked.

'Yes.' Amy ran through what had happened. 'And we have a theory that her mum might be in my form group.'

'But if the mum's in your class, Amy, how come you didn't recognise her handwriting?' Alison asked.

'Because she's in my form group, not my class. I don't teach her,' Amy explained. 'It means she's there in the form room for five minutes in the morning for registration, and twenty minutes in the afternoon for registration and whatever other activities we're doing in form time—giving out letters for parents, a chance for any of them to talk to me if they're worried about something, and sometimes we do quizzes and the kind of things that help the kids bond a bit. I never see any of her written work. And it's still only a theory. If we're wrong, then we still have no clue who Hope's mum is.'

'Well, I hope they do find the poor little mite's mum.' Alison looked at Josh. 'So you two are sort of living together this week?'

'As friends,' Josh said swiftly. 'It makes sense, because otherwise we'd have to keep transferring the baby between flats and it'd unsettle her.'

Amy reminded herself that they weren't a couple. Even if they had slept on the sofa together last night and fallen asleep holding hands, and when he'd put his arm round her it had simply been comfort for both of them after their worry about the baby's health.

'It's really nice of you to look after her,' Alison said.

'What else could we do?' Amy asked. 'She's a baby. She didn't ask to be left here. The social worker couldn't get a placement because it was Christmas Eve and nobody was about, and Josh said the hospital's on black alert so the baby couldn't stay there.'

'The winter vomiting virus is everywhere,' Alison confirmed, 'and the children's ward is full of babies with bronchiolitis, something you definitely don't want a newborn to get.' She smiled at them, then handed the baby back to Amy. 'Here you go, cutie. Back to your Aunty Amy. Thanks for the coffee and biscuits. I'm heading home to bed now because I'm working the night shift again tonight and I need some sleep before I face the fractures and the ones who gave themselves food poisoning with the leftovers.'

'Thanks for bringing all this,' Josh said, 'and I owe your sister flowers and some decent chocolate. And you, too.'

Alison waved away the thanks. 'It's good to be able to do something nice for someone at Christmas. It feels as if it's putting the balance back a bit, after all the greed and rampant consumerism.'

When she'd gone, Josh turned to Amy. 'The only time you've been out of the flat since Christmas Eve morning is our middle-of-the-night trip to hospital. Do you want to go and get some fresh air?'

'That'd be good. And I could probably do with picking up something for dinner,' she said. 'I forgot to get something out of the freezer earlier.'

'I ought to be the one buying dinner,' he said. 'You've fed me two days running as it is.'

'It really doesn't matter.' Unable to resist teasing him, she added, 'But if you really want to cook for me...'

'Then you get a choice of spaghetti Bolognese or a cheese toastie,' he said promptly.

'Or maybe I should teach you how to cook something else.' She grabbed her coat and her handbag. 'I'll see you in a bit. I've got my phone with me in case you need me.'

'Great.'

It felt odd, being alone in Amy's flat, Josh thought when she'd gone. Weirdly, it felt like home; yet, at the same time, it wasn't. Everything was neat and tidy and she'd done the washing up while he was seeing Alison out of the flat, so he couldn't do anything practical to help; all he could really do was watch the baby.

He'd texted his parents and his siblings during his break at work on Christmas Day, and hadn't corrected their assumption that he was working today. Not that he really wanted to speak to any of them. If he told them how his Christmas had panned out, he knew they'd try to manage it—which drove him crazy. He was perfectly capable of managing his own life, even if he was the baby of the family and had messed up, in their eyes.

He held the baby and looked at the framed photographs on Amy's mantelpiece. The older couple were clearly her parents, and the man in one of the younger couples looked enough like her to be her brother in Canada. The other couple, he assumed, must be the friends she'd talked about staying with in Edinburgh.

'She really loves her family,' he said to the baby, 'and they clearly love her to bits, too.' He sighed. 'Maybe I should make more of an effort with mine.'

The baby gurgled, as if agreeing.

'They're not bad people. Just they have set views on what I ought to be doing with my life, and right now they feel I'm letting them down. I'm the only one in our family to get divorced. But Kelly didn't love me any more, and I couldn't expect her to stay with me just to keep my family happy. It would have made both of us really miserable, and that's not fair.'

The baby gurgled again.

'Tell you a secret,' he said. 'I think I could like Amy. More than like her.'

The baby cooed, as if to say that she liked Amy, too.

'And I would never have got to know her like this if it wasn't for you, Munchkin. We'd still just be doing the nod-and-smile thing if we saw each other in the corridor or the lobby. But this last couple of days, I've spent more time with her than I have with anyone else in a long, long time.' He paused. 'The question is, what does she think about me?'

The baby was silent.

'I'm not going to risk making things awkward while we're looking after you,' he said. 'But in the New Year I'm going to ask her out properly. Because I'm ready to move on, and I think she might be, too.'

* * *

It felt odd being out of the flat, Amy thought. It was nice to get some fresh air, but at the same time she found she couldn't stop thinking about Hope.

Or about Josh.

But what did she have to offer him?

If he wanted to settle down and have a family, then it couldn't be with her. She knew that there were other ways of having a child as well as biologically, but Michael had refused flat-out even to consider fostering or adoption. She wondered how he would've reacted to Hope; she had a nasty feeling that he would've decided it wasn't his problem and would've left it to the authorities.

Josh, on the other hand, had real compassion. He'd been instantly supportive. Even though he didn't know her well, he'd offered help when it was needed most.

She shook herself. She and Josh were neighbours, making their way towards becoming good friends. Their relationship couldn't be any more than that, so she would have to be sensible about this and damp down her burgeoning feelings towards him.

The supermarket was crowded with people looking for post-Christmas bargains. Amy avoided the clearance shelves and headed for the chiller cabinet. A few minutes later, she paid for her groceries at the checkout, and went back to the flat.

'You're back early,' he said.

'The shops were heaving.' And it hadn't felt right to go to the park without the baby. Which she knew was crazy, because Hope wasn't hers and would only be here for a couple more days. 'I thought we'd have French bread, cheese and chutney for lunch.'

'Sounds perfect. I'll prepare it, if you like, while you give our girl a cuddle.'

Her gaze met his and her heart felt as if it had just done a somersault.

'Temporary girl,' he corrected himself swiftly.

'I know what you meant.' Being with Josh and Hope felt like being part of a new family. It was so tempting, but she mustn't let herself forget that it was only temporary. Clearly Josh felt the same way. If only things were a little different. If only she'd never met Gavin, or had at least been a bit less clueless, so she'd been able to get the chlamydia treated in time…

But things were as they were, and she'd have to make the best of it instead of whining for something she knew wasn't going to happen.

'Did Jane reply to your text?' he asked.

'Not yet. And it wasn't an emergency, so I'm not expecting her to pick it up until at least tomorrow.'

'You're probably right,' he said. 'Hope's temperature has come down a lot, but it's probably too much for her to go out for a stroll in the park.' There was a definite wistfulness in his expression as he glanced at the pram.

'Maybe tomorrow,' she said.

After lunch, they spent the afternoon playing board games. 'I haven't done this for a while, either,' she admitted ruefully. 'I'd forgotten how much fun it is.'

'Remember what you said to me,' he said. 'Make the time for stuff you enjoy.'

Josh sketched Hope again in the back of the notebook after her next feed, and couldn't resist making a sneaky sketch of Amy. Though in a way that was a bad idea, because it made him really aware of the curve of her mouth and the way her hair fell—and it made him want to touch her.

He still couldn't shake how it had felt this morning to draw her into his arms and hold her close. OK, so they'd both been dog-tired and in need of comfort after their worry about Hope and a very broken night—but it had felt so right to hold her like that and fall asleep with her on the sofa.

For Hope's sake, he needed to rein himself back a bit.

'While Madam's asleep,' Amy said, thankfully oblivious to what he'd been thinking, 'maybe I can teach you how to cook something really simple and really impressive.'

'Which is?' he asked.

'Baked salmon with sweet chilli sauce, served with mangetout and crushed new potatoes.'

It sounded complicated. But clearly Amy was good at her day job, because she gave him really clear instructions and talked him through making dinner.

'I can't believe I made this,' he said, looking at the plates. After the first mouthful, he amended that to, 'I *really* can't believe I made this.'

'Healthy and impressive,' she said. 'And it's easy. Josh, what you do at work every day is way harder than cooking dinner.'

'Maybe.' But cooking for one was no fun. Which was the main reason why he lived on toasted sandwiches and takeaways.

They spent the evening curled up on the sofa, watching films. Josh was careful this time not to give in to the temptation of holding Amy's hand or drawing her into his arms.

But, after Hope's last feed of the evening, he could see the worry on Amy's face.

'Maybe we should both sleep on the sofa again tonight,' he said. 'We can still take turns at getting up for her, but it also means if you're worried you can wake me more quickly.'

She took a deep breath. 'Don't take this the wrong way,' she said, 'but I was thinking along the same lines. My bed's a double and it'll be a lot more comfortable than the sofa. We're adults and we can share a bed without...'

His mouth went dry as he finished the sentence mentally. *Without making love.*

Which was what he really wanted to do with Amy. Kiss her, discover where she liked being touched and what made her eyes go dark with pleasure.

'Fully dressed,' he said. Because lying in bed with her, with them both wearing pyjamas, might be a little too much temptation for him to resist. And he hoped she couldn't hear the slight huskiness in his voice.

'Of course.'

Her bedroom was exactly as he'd expected, all soft creams and feminine, yet without being frilly or fussy and over the top. There was a framed picture of a seascape on the wall, the curtains were floral chintz, and the whole room was restful and peaceful.

Though when he lay next to her in bed with the light off—with both of them fully dressed—he was far from feeling restful and peaceful. He was too aware of the last time he'd shared a bed with someone, just over a year ago. OK, so he'd finally got to the stage

where he could move on with his life… But could it
be with Amy? He definitely had feelings for her, and
he was fairly sure that it was mutual; but was it because they'd had this intense sharing of space over the
last few days, while they'd been looking after Hope,
or was it something real? Would he be enough for her,
the way he hadn't been for Kelly? Or would everything between them change again at New Year, once
the baby had gone?

When Hope cried, Amy got out of bed on autopilot
and scooped the baby from the Moses basket. As she
padded into the kitchen with the baby in her arms, she
woke up fully. Was it her imagination, or did Hope
feel hot again?

And then Hope only took half her usual amount
of milk.

Panic welled through her, and she switched on her
bedside light on its lowest setting. 'Josh.'

He woke immediately and sat up. 'What's wrong?'

'I might be being paranoid, but she didn't take that
much milk just now, and I think she's hot again.'

He checked the baby over, then grabbed the thermometer and took her temperature. 'Her temperature's
normal.'

'So I'm just being ridiculous.'

He settled the baby back into the Moses basket.
'No. You're being completely normal. I'd worry, too.'
He wrapped his arms round her. 'You're doing just
fine, Amy.'

For someone who was never going to be a mum?

She wasn't sure what made her lean into him—the
worry that had made her knees sag, or just the fact that

he was there, holding her and seeming to infuse his strength into her as he kept his arms round her.

And was that his mouth against her cheek, in a reassuring kiss?

Something made her tip her head back.

The next thing she knew, his mouth was against hers. Soft, reassuring, gentle.

And then it wasn't like that any more, because somehow her mouth had opened beneath his and her arms were wrapped round his neck, and he was holding her much more tightly. And the warmth turned to heat, to sheer molten desire.

Then he pulled back.

Oh, God. How embarrassing was she? Throwing herself at her neighbour. Pathetic.

'Sorry,' she mumbled, hanging her head and unable to meet his eyes. Hot shame bubbled through her. What the hell had she just done?

'I should be the one apologising to you.'

Because he'd been kind? Because he'd stopped before she'd *really* made a fool of herself?

'No,' she muttered, still not wanting to look at him and see the pity in his face.

'Maybe I should sleep on your sofa again,' he said.

And then things would be even more awkward between them in the morning. 'No, it's fine. We're neighbours—*friends*—and we're adults; and we both need to be here for Hope.' She took a deep breath. 'We can both pretend that just now didn't happen.'

'Good idea,' he said.

But she still couldn't face him when she climbed into bed and switched off the light. And she noticed that there was a very large gap in the bed between them, as if he felt as uncomfortable and embarrassed about the situation as she did.

If only she'd kept that iron control she'd prided herself on so much before today. If only she hadn't kissed him. If only she hadn't given in to temptation.

She'd just have to hope that the broken night would affect his memory and he'd forget everything about what had just happened.

And she'd really have to put out of her mind how good it had felt in those moments when he'd kissed her back.

CHAPTER SIX

Bank Holiday Monday

AMY WAS WARM and deeply, deeply comfortable.

And then she realised why.

Somehow, during the night, the large gap in the bed between her and Josh had closed. Now her head was pillowed on his shoulder, his arm was round her shoulders, her arm was wrapped round his waist, and her fingers were twined with his.

They were sleeping like lovers.

Oh, help. This was a seriously bad idea. She couldn't offer Josh a future and it wasn't fair to lead him on.

Gently, she disentangled her fingers from his. She'd just started to wriggle quietly out of his arms, hoping she wouldn't wake him, when he said, 'Good morning.'

No running away from the situation, then. They were going to have to face this head on.

'Good morning,' she muttered. 'I—um—sorry about this.'

'Me, too.' Though he didn't sound concerned or embarrassed.

'I—um—we're both tired and sleep-deprived,' she said. 'And I guess this was bound to happen as we're sharing a bed. Propinquity and all that. It doesn't mean we have…' She paused, looking for the right word. 'Intentions.'

'Absolutely,' he agreed.

Was he smiling?

She didn't dare look.

'I'll go and make us a cup of tea before Hope wakes,' she said, and wriggled out of his arms properly.

She splashed her face with cold water in the bathroom, in the hope that it would bring back her common sense. It didn't. She could still feel the warmth of Josh's arms around her, and she wanted more. So much more.

How selfish could she get?

Cross with her own stupidity, she filled the kettle with water and rummaged in the cupboard for the tea bags.

Waking with Amy in his arms was just what Josh had been dreaming about. It had taken him a moment to realise that he was awake, and she really *was* in his arms.

She'd blamed it on them both being tired and sleep-deprived, and the fact that they'd slept in the same bed. But she'd sounded distinctly flustered.

So did she feel the same way about him that he was starting to feel about her?

He'd promised himself that he'd hold back from starting a relationship with her until after the baby was settled—either with her birth mother, or with long-term foster parents. But they'd kissed, last night. They'd woken in each other's arms, as if they were meant to be there. He'd been awake before Amy and she'd stayed in his arms for a few moments after she'd woken—which she wouldn't have done if she hadn't wanted to be there.

So maybe he needed to be brave and tell her what was in his head, and see if she felt the same way.

He climbed out of bed, checked that Hope was still asleep and not overheated, and then walked into the kitchen. Amy was making the tea, dressed in rumpled clothes and with her hair all over the place—and she'd never looked more beautiful to him or more natural.

'Hey.' He walked over to her and wrapped his arms round her. 'I know I probably shouldn't be doing this, and we don't know each other very well, but we've spent a lot of time together over the last couple of days and I really like you.' He paused. 'And I think you might like me too.'

This was the moment where either she would push him away in utter shock and he'd have to avoid her for the next six months until things were back on an even keel between them, or she would tell him that she felt the same.

He really hoped it was going to be the latter.

But then an expression of pure misery crossed her face and she stepped back out of his embrace. 'I do like you,' she admitted, 'but we can't do this.'

'Because of the baby?'

She took a deep breath. 'No, not because of her.'

'Then why?' Josh asked, not understanding.

'I need to tell you something about myself.' She finished making the mugs of tea, and handed one to him. 'Let's go and sit down.'

'This sounds serious.'

'It is,' she said grimly, 'and there isn't an easy way to say it, so I'm not going to sugar-coat it.'

He followed her into the living room. She sat down at one end of the sofa; he sat next to her, wondering just what kind of bombshell she was about to drop. Was she still married to her ex? No, she couldn't be—hadn't she said something about him getting married to someone else and expecting a baby now? So what kind of thing would hold her back from starting a new relationship?

He could see her eyes fill with tears. Whatever it was, it was something really serious. Something that hurt her. And he ached for her.

Finally, she said, her voice sounding broken, 'I can't have children.'

Josh wanted to reach out and take her hand and tell her that it didn't change the way he felt, but he could see the 'hands off' signals written all over her. And as a doctor he knew the value of silence. If he let her talk, tell him exactly what was holding her back, then he might have more of a chance of being able to counter her arguments.

'That's why Michael—my ex—broke off our engagement and left,' she continued.

Josh was horrified. It must've been hard enough for Amy, finding out that she couldn't have children, but then for the man who was supposed to love her and want to marry her to walk out on her over the issue... That shocked him to the core. How could Michael have been so selfish? Why hadn't he put Amy first? And how it must've hurt her when she'd learned that his new wife was expecting a baby.

'We'd been trying for a baby for a year or so without success, so we went for investigations to find out why we couldn't conceive.' She looked away. 'I knew that the guy I'd dated before Michael had cheated on me. I found it had been more than once and with more than one other woman, and that's why I left him. I didn't want to stay with someone who didn't love me or respect me enough to be faithful. But what I didn't realise was that he'd given me chlamydia.'

Josh knew then exactly what had happened to her. 'You didn't have any symptoms?'

She shook her head. 'And obviously, because I didn't know I had it, that meant I was still infected when I started seeing Michael and we moved in together. I infected Michael. He didn't have symptoms, either.'

Quite a high percentage of people who'd been infected with chlamydia didn't have symptoms. Not that it would comfort her to know that. 'Amy, it wasn't your fault.'

She shook her head. 'I should've been more careful. Used condoms with Gavin—the one who cheated on me—instead of the Pill.'

How could she possibly blame herself? 'Before you found out that he'd cheated on you, you trusted him. How long were you together?'

'Two years.'

'So of course you'd think the Pill was a safe form of contraception. Any woman in your shoes would.' Josh shook his head, angry on her behalf. 'Gavin cheated on you, and he was the one who infected you. How could anyone possibly think it was your fault?'

'Because I should've got myself checked out. I should've realised that, because Gavin had been sleeping around, there could be consequences.'

'But you didn't have symptoms. Actually, around two thirds of women and about fifty per cent of men don't have symptoms if they're infected with chlamydia. And, if you don't have symptoms, how are you supposed to know there's a problem? It's *not* your fault,' he said again. 'I'm probably speaking out of turn, but it was totally unfair of Michael to blame you.'

'It happened. And you can't change the past, just learn from it.' She shrugged. 'So now you know. As a doctor, you've probably already guessed what the problem is, but I'll spell it out for you. The chlamydia gave me pelvic inflammatory disease and the scar tissue blocked my Fallopian tubes, so I can't have children. If you're looking to have a family in the future, then I'm not the one for you and we need to call a halt to this right now.'

And that was really what was holding her back? This time, he did reach over and take her hand. 'First of all, having children isn't the be-all and end-all of a relationship. Lots of couples can't have children or choose not to. It doesn't make their relationship and how they feel about each other any less valid. And if this thing between us works out the way I hope it might, then if we do decide in the future that we want children then we still have options. Did your specialist not mention IVF?'

She swallowed. 'Yes, but Michael didn't want to do that.'

Josh wasn't surprised. And he'd just bet the other man's reasoning was purely to do with himself, not to do with how tough the IVF process could be for a woman.

'It's not an easy option and there are no cast-iron guarantees,' he said, 'but it's still an option for tubal infertility. One of the doctors I trained with had severe endometriosis which blocked her Fallopian tubes, and she had a baby through IVF last year.'

Was that hope he saw flickering in her eyes, just then?

'And if that's not a route you want to go down—because the treatment cycle is pretty gruelling and it isn't for everyone—there's fostering or adoption.'

She blinked, as if not expecting him to have reacted that way. 'Michael wasn't prepared to even consider that.'

Because Michael was a selfish toad. Not that it was Josh's place to say so. 'I'm not Michael,' he said.

'I know.' She took a deep breath. 'But I wanted you to know the situation upfront. So, if it's a problem for you, you can walk away now and there's no damage to either of us.'

Even though they'd only got close to each other over the last couple of days, Josh had the strongest feeling that walking away from her would definitely cause damage to both of them.

'I like you,' he said again, 'and I think you might just like me back. And that's what's important here. Everything else is just details and we can work them out. Together.'

She looked at him as if she didn't quite believe him.

'If you want to work them out, that is,' he said. 'Your infertility doesn't make any difference to the way I feel about you. I still want to start dating you properly. Get to know you.'

'And it's really that easy?'

'It is for me.' He paused. 'Though, since you told me about your ex, I guess you need to know about mine.'

* * *

The woman who'd left him last Christmas Eve, pregnant with another man's child.

Amy really couldn't understand why on earth anyone would dump a man like Josh—a man who was kind and caring as well as easy on the eye. In the intense couple of days they'd spent together, she hadn't found a deal-breaking flaw in him.

'Kelly worked in advertising—so maybe if I'd gone to art college instead of med school we would've ended up working together.' He shrugged. 'But we met at a party, where we were both a friend of a friend. We fell for each other, moved in together a couple of weeks later and got married within three months.'

Alarm bells rang in the back of Amy's head. Wasn't this exactly what she and Josh were doing? Falling in love with each other a little too quickly and not thinking things through? A whirlwind romance had gone badly wrong for him before. Then again, her last two relationships had both lasted for a couple of years, so taking things slowly hadn't exactly worked for her, either.

'I assumed Kelly would want a family at some point in the future, the way I did, and she assumed that we were both ambitious and were going to put our careers first,' he said. 'We probably should have talked about that a lot more before we got married.'

He wanted a family.

Amy's heart sank.

OK, he'd said to her that her infertility didn't make a difference. But it did. As he'd said, IVF treatment could be gruelling and there were no guarantees that it would work. She'd looked into it, in the days when she'd still hoped that Michael might change his mind, and the chances of having a baby were roughly one in four. Odds which might not be good enough for Josh. Right now, they were looking after a baby together. What would happen in New Year, when life went back to normal? Would he realise then what a mistake he was making, trying to make a go of things with her?

'Kelly was working really long hours on the promise of getting a promotion. Obviously I supported her,' Josh continued, 'but then she fell in love with one of her colleagues. She said they tried to fight the attraction; but, on one project they were working on together, they went to visit a client and it meant an overnight stay. They were in rooms next to each other in the hotel; they'd had dinner out with the client and too much wine; and one thing led to another. That's when the affair started.'

Clearly Josh hadn't had a clue about it. Amy reached over and squeezed his hand. 'That's hard.'

'Yeah.' He sighed. 'She got the promotion, but she was still working crazy hours. I assumed it was because of the pressure of work in her new job, but it was actually because she was seeing the other guy.' He gave her a wry smile. 'Then she told me she was pregnant.'

'And you thought it was yours?'

'I knew it wasn't,' he said softly, 'because we'd both been working mad hours and were too tired to do anything more than fall into bed and go straight to sleep when we got home at night. We hadn't had sex for a couple of months, so there was no way the baby could possibly be mine. Though Kelly never lied to me about it. She told me it was his and she was sorry— she'd fallen in love with him and was leaving me.' He looked away. 'Funny, she ended up with the family she said she didn't want, but maybe it was really that she just didn't want to have a family with me. I wasn't enough for her.'

How could Josh possibly not be enough for someone? Amy squeezed his hand again. 'Josh, you didn't do anything wrong. It wasn't your fault.' She gave him an awkward smile. 'I guess you can't help who you fall in love with.' Hadn't she made that same mistake, falling for Mr Wrong?

'And Kelly was fair about it. She didn't try to heap the blame on me for the divorce.'

'Even when the split's amicable, it's still tough,' Amy said. 'I'm sorry you got hurt like that.'

'But?' he asked, clearly sensing that she had doubts.

'But,' she said softly, 'you said you wanted to have a family with Kelly. Even if we put IVF into the equation, there's still a very strong chance I won't be able to give you a family. So I'll understand if you want us to stay just friends.'

He shook his head. 'I want more than that from you, Amy. And in any relationship you have to make a compromise.'

'But this is one hell of a compromise. It means giving up on your plans to have a family.'

'Right now, it's still early days between you and me, and we're not making any promises to each other of happy ever after,' he said. 'But I really like you, Amy, and if it's a choice of being with you and looking at alternatives for having a family, or not being with you, then I'm on the side of alternatives.' He smiled at her. 'And we're not doing so badly with Hope. I'm beginning to think that her mum gave her exactly the right name, and also that you were right because the baby's giving us the Christmas we both need. She's brought us together and she's giving us a chance to find happiness again—together.'

Amy thought about it. 'Yes,' she said.

'So, you and me. No pressure. We'll see where things take us.'

'Sounds good to me,' Amy said. And it felt as if spring flowers had just pushed through the ground to brighten up the days after a long, long winter.

Just before lunch, Jane the social worker rang. 'How's the baby doing?' she asked.

'Fine,' Amy said. 'She's still got a bit of a temperature, but it's going down.'

'Good. So what's this theory you've got about the baby's mum?'

'Hang on—let me put you on speaker phone so Josh can hear as well and chip in,' Amy said. 'We think she might be a girl in my form. I didn't recognise the handwriting on the note because I don't actually teach her, so there's no reason for me ever to see her work or her writing.'

'We did think about maybe going round to see her for a chat,' Josh said.

'No—it's better to leave this to the authorities,' Jane said, 'especially if you don't have any proof that it's definitely her. What makes you think it's her, Amy?'

'She's gone very quiet, lately. I did bring it up with her mum, who said it was because her new partner had moved in and Freya was having trouble adjusting to the idea of someone she saw trying to take her dad's place.' She paused. 'Freya wears quite baggy clothes, not skinny trousers or anything. And because it's winter it's easier to hide a pregnancy under a baggy sweater.'

'Does she look as if she's put on weight?'

'A little bit, but body image is a really sensitive area for teens, and I guessed she might be comfort-eating if she wasn't happy at home,' Amy said. 'Drawing attention to it would only have made her feel worse, and the last thing I wanted was for her to start starving herself or taking diet pills. I was going to have a chat with her in the New Year.' She paused. 'I thought that might be why she kept rushing to the loo.'

'But that's also a symptom of late pregnancy,' Josh said.

'So how do we tackle this?' Amy asked.

'You don't. I do it,' Jane said. 'Under the safeguarding rules, Amy, I know you can give me the contact information of a student you're worried about, so can you tell me her name and address?'

Amy had accessed Freya's school records earlier, and gave Jane the relevant details.

'Thanks. I'll liaise with the police, then do a preliminary visit and see if I can get any information,' Jane said. 'And thank you.'

'Will you let me know how you get on?' Amy asked.

'I'm afraid any conversations I have will be confidential, unless I have Freya's permission to talk to you,' Jane said, sounding regretful.

'We understand. But please tell her from us that the baby's doing just fine and we'd be happy to send her a picture, or for her to come and visit Hope,' Josh said. 'And if she does turn out to be our missing mum, please persuade her to see a doctor to get checked over.

She won't be in trouble, but we need to be sure that she's all right.'

'I will,' Jane promised.

Amy looked at Josh when she'd ended the call. 'I really hope we've done the right thing.'

'We have,' he said. 'Jane's in a neutral position so, if our theory's wrong, then Freya won't be too embarrassed to walk into your form room next term. If it's right, then Jane knows all the procedures and can get Freya the help she needs.'

'I'd still rather go and see her myself,' Amy said. 'As you say, Jane's neutral and she's really nice, but she's still a stranger. Surely Freya's more likely to open up to me because she knows me?'

'If our theory's right, Freya left Hope with you because she trusted you to do the right thing and talk to the right people for her. Which you've done,' Josh pointed out.

'I guess.'

Hope woke; as soon as Amy picked her up, she could tell what the problem was. 'Nappy. Super-bad nappy,' she said.

'Oh, great,' Josh said with a sigh. 'And it's my turn to change her.'

'I'm not arguing.' Amy smiled and handed the baby over. Josh carried Hope to the bathroom. 'Come on, Munchkin. Let's sort you out.'

Josh was gone a very long time. And Amy could hear screaming, interspersed with him singing snatches of what sounded like every song that came into his head. Each one sounded slightly more desperate.

She was just about to go and see if she could do

anything to help when he came back into the kitchen carrying a red-faced, still grizzly baby.

'I was just about to come and see if you needed anything. Do I take it that it was really bad?' she asked.

'Let's just say she needed a bath,' he said grimly. 'And she doesn't like baths yet.'

'Hence the screaming and the singing?'

'Yeah.' He blew out a breath. 'I'm glad I'm not a teenager. After that nightmare in the bathroom just now, I'd be paranoid that my face was all it took to make any girl scream and run away.'

Amy couldn't help laughing. 'Hardly. You're quite pretty.'

'Pretty?' He gave her a speaking look.

'If you were a supply teacher at my school,' she said, 'you'd have gaggles of teenage girls hanging around the staff room every lunchtime in the hope of catching a glimpse of you.'

'That,' he said, 'sounds scary. I think I'd rather deal with—wait for it…' He adopted a pose and warbled to the tune of 'The Twelve Days of Christmas'. 'Five turkey carvers! Four black eyes, three throwing up, two broken ankles and a bead up a toddler's nose.'

'I ought to introduce you to our head of music,' she said, laughing. 'Between you, I can imagine you writing a panto about *The Twelve Days of ED*.'

'Better believe it.'

'So, what do you want to do this afternoon?'

'It's wet and miserable out there, and although Hope's on the mend I'd rather not take her out, even though we've got the pram and snowsuit,' Josh said.

'Festive films on the sofa, then,' she said.

He wrinkled his nose. 'I feel a bit guilty, just slobbing around on the sofa.'

'As you said, it's not the weather for going out,' she reminded him. 'And you've had tough enough shifts to justify doing nothing for a day or so. Well, nothing but alternate feeds, changing the odd really vile nappy and singing songs to stop Hope crying.'

'Well, if you put it that way...' He stole a kiss. 'Bring on the films.'

Snuggled up on the sofa with Josh and the baby, Amy had never felt more at peace. What had started off as a miserable Christmas was rapidly turning into one of the best Christmases ever.

'Do you want me to take the sofa tonight?' he asked when Hope had had her late evening feed.

'I think we go for the same deal as last night,' Amy said. 'Except maybe this time we could change into pyjamas instead of sleeping in our clothes?'

'Give me two minutes next door,' he said.

And she burst out laughing when he returned in a pair of pyjamas covered in Christmas puddings. 'That's priceless. I'm almost tempted to take a snap of you wearing them and put it in Hope's book.'

'Absolutely not. These were my best friend's wife's idea of a joke,' he said. 'I don't usually wear pyjamas. When they stayed at my flat after my housewarming, I ended up wearing a ratty old T-shirt and a pair of boxer shorts so I'd be decent, and she said I needed proper pyjamas for when I had guests. This is the only pair I own. And this is the first time I've worn them.'

Amy went hot all over at the thought of Josh, in bed with her, naked. All the words flew out of her head and she just said, flustered, 'I, um...'

He took her hand and kissed the back of each finger in turn, then turned her hand over and pressed a kiss into the palm. 'Don't be flustered. There's no pressure,' he said, his voice low and husky and sexy as anything. 'Let's go to bed. Platonically.'

And he was as good as his word. No pressure. He simply curled his body round hers, wrapped his arm round her waist, and rested his cheek against her shoulder. And, as she fell asleep, Amy felt happier than she'd been in a long, long while.

CHAPTER SEVEN

Tuesday

ON TUESDAY MORNING, Josh woke to find his arms wrapped round Amy and hers wrapped round him. And suddenly the whole world felt full of promise. He couldn't resist kissing her awake. To his relief, she didn't back away from him the way she had the previous morning; this time, she smiled and kissed him back.

'Well, happy Tuesday,' he said.

She stroked his face. 'Absolutely.'

'My turn to bring you a cup of tea in bed,' he said, kissed her lingeringly and climbed out of bed.

'Wonderful,' she said, smiling back at him.

Funny, being in her kitchen was so much better than being in his own. Even though they had similar decor, all in neutral tones, her place felt like *home*. Josh even found himself humming a happy song as he made tea.

He could hear Hope crying, and called through, 'I'll heat up some milk for Munchkin.'

'Thanks,' Amy called back.

He took the two mugs of tea and bottle of milk through to Amy's bedroom, where he found Amy cuddling the baby and crooning to her. He set the tea on her bedside table and climbed back in next to them. 'Want me to feed her?'

'Sure.' Amy transferred the baby into his arms.

Feeding the baby, cuddled up next to Amy in bed… It made Josh realise exactly what he wanted out of life—what he wanted to happen in the New Year.

To be part of a family, just like this, with Amy. Domestic bliss.

Given her fertility issues, it wasn't going to be easy. But he thought it was going to be worth the effort. The only thing was: after they gave Hope back at New Year, would Amy change her mind about him?

Amy sipped her tea and watched Josh feeding the baby. This was exactly what she wanted. To be a family, with Josh. Although part of her was still worried that her infertility was going to be an issue, he'd been very clear about being happy to look at the options of IVF treatment, adoption or fostering. So maybe it wouldn't be an issue after all.

'She's drunk a bit more than usual, this morning,' Josh said. 'That's a good sign. Maybe we can take her out this morning.'

Amy went over to the window and peeked through the curtain. 'The sun's shining.'

'How about we go for lunch in the park?' he suggested.

'And we can try out Alison's sister's pram. Great idea.' She paused. 'How often are you supposed to weigh babies?'

'I don't know.' He smiled. 'Time for the baking tray again?'

'Hey. It was being inventive,' she protested, laughing. 'And it worked, didn't it?'

Once they'd showered and dressed, Amy changed Hope's nappy and they weighed her. 'Five pounds, twelve ounces.'

'We need to write that in her book,' Josh said, and did so while Amy got the baby dressed. Between them, they got her into the snowsuit.

'It dwarfs her,' he said ruefully.

'Better too big than too small,' Amy said.

'I guess.' Josh tucked the baby into the pram underneath a blanket, and then put the apron on the pram. 'Just in case it's a bit breezy out there,' he said.

'Good idea,' Amy agreed.

Once they'd got their own coats on, they negotiated the pram out of the flat.

'This is where I'm really glad we're on the ground floor,' Amy said.

'Me, too,' Josh said. 'Even though this pram's really light, it wouldn't be much fun carrying it up or down a flight of stairs—especially if you're doing it on your own.'

They exchanged a glance, and Amy knew that he too was thinking of Hope's mum. If she was given a flat in a high-rise block, it could be tough for her to cope.

'Let's go to the park,' she said firmly. 'This is your first official trip out, Hope.'

'We ought to commemorate that for Hope's book,' Josh said. 'Time for a selfie.'

'In the lobby?'

'With the pram. You bet.' He looked at her. 'Ready?'

They crouched either side of the pram, and Josh an-

gled his phone so he could take the snap of the three
of them together.

Hope slept all the way to the park. Meanwhile Josh
slid his arm round Amy's shoulders, and they both had
one hand on the handle of the pram, pushing it together.

This felt like being part of the family Amy had always wanted. She knew it was just a fantasy, and if
the police couldn't find Hope's mother then the baby
would go formally into care, but for now she was going
to enjoy feeling this way.

The sun seemed to have brought out all the other new
parents, Josh thought. People happily strolling along
the paths, pushing prams, sometimes with a toddler in
tow as well. Slightly older children were playing on the
swings, slides and climbing frames in the park, while
their parents chatted and kept an eye on them from
benches placed around the perimeter of the play area.

Just for a moment he could imagine the three of
them here in three years' time: himself pushing Hope
on the swings as she laughed and begged to be pushed
higher, while Amy stood watching them, her face radi-
ant and her belly swollen with their new baby.

Except there were no guarantees that the IVF treatment would work, and the chances of them actually
being able to keep Hope were minimal.

He knew he was being ridiculous. Right from the
start, this had been a temporary arrangement; the baby
was theirs only for a week, and that was simply because they were the neighbours who'd found her abandoned on their doorstep on a day where none of the
official services were able to help. They couldn't be a
family with Hope.

But maybe they could help another child, through fostering or adoption.

And he knew without doubt that Amy was the one he wanted to share that family with. Thanks to Hope, he'd found that he was finally ready to move on from the wreckage of his marriage to Kelly; and because he'd been cooped up with Amy for several days he'd had the chance to get to know her properly. He could actually be himself with Amy, and it was a long time since he'd felt that.

When they stopped for a coffee and a toasted sandwich in the café in the park, the pictures were still in his head, and he found himself sketching the scene on the back of a napkin.

If only this wasn't temporary.

But for now he was going to enjoy the Christmas break he'd expected to hate.

Later that afternoon, Amy was in the middle of feeding Hope when her intercom buzzed.

'Would you mind getting that?' she asked Josh.

'Sure.' He picked up the handset. 'Hello?'

'Is that Josh? It's Jane Richards.'

'Come in,' he said, and buzzed her in. 'It's Jane,' he said to Amy as he replaced the handset. 'I'll put the kettle on.'

Had Jane talked to Freya? And was their theory right? Or was Jane just checking up on them in their role as temporary foster parents?

Josh answered the door when Jane knocked. 'The kettle's just about to boil. Tea or coffee?'

'Tea would be wonderful, thanks,' she said.

'How do you like your tea?'

'Reasonably strong, with a dash of milk and no sugar, please.' And then Jane did a double take as she saw the pram in the corner of the living room. 'Have you two been shopping or something?'

'No—it's a loan from the sister of one of my colleagues,' he said. 'She lent us a snowsuit as well, so we took Hope for a walk in the park across the road today. I think she enjoyed her first trip out.'

'And her temperature's normal again?' Jane asked.

'Yes. We wouldn't have taken her out if we'd been in the slightest bit worried about her—that's why we left it until today,' Amy said. 'She's doing fine. We weighed her this morning and she's put on two ounces.'

'You've borrowed baby scales?' Jane asked.

'Not exactly.' Josh and Amy shared a glance and grinned.

'What am I missing?' Jane asked.

'We improvised,' Josh said. 'It involved Amy's kitchen scales, a towel and a baking tray.'

Jane laughed. 'Well, clearly it worked. And you both look very comfortable with her.'

'We've had our moments,' Josh said wryly. 'She really hates having baths. You have to sing her through them.'

'But I can show you her sleep and feed charts,' Amy said. 'And we're doing a book of her first days, either for her mum or for Hope herself. We're including photos and what have you, so Hope—and her mum—don't feel they've missed anything in the future.'

'That's really sweet of you,' Jane said, accepting the mug of tea gratefully from Josh.

'Do you have any news for us?' Josh asked.

'About Freya?' She grimaced. 'I'm telling you this unofficially, because strictly speaking this should all be confidential, but I need some help—and, because it's your theory, I think you're the best ones to give me advice.'

'Why do you need help?' Amy asked, confused.

'I went to the house, but Freya's mum refused to let me in,' Jane said. 'She was quite difficult with me, so my gut feeling tells me that she has something to hide. If Freya definitely hadn't had a baby, all she had to do was call the girl down and let me see her, and I could've ticked whatever box on a form and gone away again.'

'Unless she didn't actually know that Freya had had the baby. Amy, you said she was wearing baggy clothes at school?' Josh asked.

Amy nodded.

'So she might have done the same at home. Freya could have hidden the pregnancy from her mum, had the baby—well, wherever—then gone straight home again after she'd left the baby on our doorstep. If she told her mum that she was having a really bad period, that would explain why she was bleeding so much after the birth. She's at the age where periods are still all over the place, and some girls get quite severe period pains,' Josh said thoughtfully.

'And Freya's mum did say that there were problems with the stepfather. Maybe there had been a huge row or something,' Amy suggested, 'and one of the neighbours had tried to intervene, and Freya's mum thought that someone had called you to complain about the way she was treating her daughter.'

'I still think she's hiding something. She wouldn't look me in the eye,' Jane said. 'Does Freya have a close friend she might have confided in?'

'Her best friend Alice is the most likely person,' Amy said.

'Do you have her details? And this comes under the safeguarding stuff for Freya, if you're worrying about data protection,' Jane added quickly.

Amy powered up her laptop, logged into the school system and wrote Alice's details down for Jane.

'I could have an unofficial word with her, maybe,' Amy suggested.

Jane shook her head. 'No, you need to leave this to official channels. If Alice tells me something helpful then I can do something to help Freya.' She sighed. 'Poor kid. I kind of hope your theory's wrong.'

'So do I,' Josh said, 'but I have a nasty feeling that we're right.'

'I'll be in touch, then,' Jane said. 'And thank you for everything you're doing. Obviously we'll get you financial recompense for—'

'No,' Amy cut in. 'It's nice to be able to do something practical to help. Call it a Christmas gift to Hope and her mum.'

'Seconded,' Josh said firmly. 'We're not doing this for the money.'

'OK. Well, thank you,' Jane said. 'I'll go and have a word with Alice.'

When the social worker had gone, Josh looked at Amy. 'Are you all right?'

She nodded. 'Just thinking about Freya.'

'Hopefully Jane can intervene and get her the help she needs,' Josh said. 'Hey. I could cook us dinner tonight.'

'Seriously?'

'Seriously. You've made me rethink about my cooking skills, since you taught me how to make that salmon thing.'

'OK. That'd be lovely.'

'I'll just go and get some supplies,' he said. 'I can't keep raiding your fridge.'

'You mean, I don't have anything in my kitchen that you can actually cook,' she teased.

He grinned. 'Busted.'

'I'll print out the photos we've taken of Hope and stick them in her book while you're gone,' she said.

'And label them,' he said, 'because your handwriting's a lot neater than mine.'

'Agreed.'

'Anything you need from the shops?'

'No, it's fine.' She kissed him lingeringly. 'See you later.'

In the supermarket, Josh bought ingredients for spaghetti Bolognese. Pudding would definitely have to be shop-bought, he thought, and was delighted to discover a tiramisu cheesecake in the chiller cabinet. He knew Amy liked coffee ice cream, so this looked like a safe bet.

And then he walked through the healthcare aisle and saw the condoms.

He didn't have any, and he guessed that she didn't either. It wasn't quite making an assumption; tonight wasn't going to be the night. But at some point in the future he was pretty sure that they were going to make love, and it would be sensible for them to have protection available. And he had a feeling Amy would be a lot more comfortable using condoms than any other kind of contraception, given her history.

Putting the packet of condoms in his basket felt weird. He hadn't even had to think about this for a long time; during most of their relationship, Kelly had been on the Pill. Or so he'd thought. He couldn't even remember the last time he'd bought condoms. But this made him feel like a teenager, nervous and excited all at the same time.

He shook himself and added a bottle of Pinot Grigio to his basket. And then, by the checkouts, he saw the stand of flowers. He couldn't resist buying a bunch for Amy—nothing flashy and over-the-top that would make her feel awkward and embarrassed, but some pretty gerberas and roses in shades of dark red and pink.

When he got back to the flat, she greeted him with a kiss.

'For you,' he said, handing her the flowers with a flourish.

She looked delighted. 'They're gorgeous. Thank you. That's so sweet—you didn't have to.'

'Apart from the fact that men are supposed to buy their girlfriends flowers, and you're officially my girlfriend,' he pointed out, 'I wanted to.'

She hugged him. 'And I love them. Gerberas are my favourite flowers.'

'More luck than judgement,' he said. 'And I've cheated on the pudding.'

'Need me to do anything to help after I've put these in water?'

'Nope. Though I'd better run the pudding by you, in case you hate it.'

'Oh, nice choice, Dr Farnham,' she said when he showed her the box. 'Tiramisu and cheesecake—there isn't a more perfect combination.'

He laughed. 'Just don't look at the nutritional label, OK?'

'Would that be doctor's orders?' she teased.

'It would.' He smiled at her. 'Go and sit down and carry on with whatever you were doing.'

'Reading a gory crime novel.'

'Go and sit down and I'll make dinner.'

She looked intrigued. 'So is it going to be a cheese toastie or the famous spaghetti Bolognese?'

'Wait and see.'

Except it went disastrously wrong. Not only did he burn the sauce badly enough to ruin the meal, he actually set off the smoke alarm.

And Hope took great exception to the smoke alarm. She even managed to drown it out with her screams.

Amy walked into the kitchen, jiggling the screaming baby in an attempt to calm her. 'Open the windows and flap a damp tea-towel underneath the smoke alarm,' she said. 'I set it off when I first moved in and my toaster decided not to pop the toast out again after it was done.'

It didn't make him feel any better, but he followed her instructions and eventually the smoke alarm stopped shrieking.

Hope, on the other hand, took a fair bit longer to

stop shrieking, and he'd completely run out of songs by the time Amy had warmed some milk and given the baby an unscheduled feed in an attempt to stop her screaming.

'Sorry. I don't *think* I've ruined your saucepan. But it's a close-run thing.' He grimaced. 'And there's no way I can serve up dinner.'

But Amy didn't seem fazed in the slightest. She just laughed. 'These things happen. Stick the saucepan in water and we'll soak it for a while. I'm sure it will have survived. And we'll get a takeaway for dinner. Do you fancy Indian, Chinese or pizza?'

'Pizza. And I'm buying, because dinner was supposed to be my treat tonight,' he said ruefully.

'We'll go halves,' she said, 'and you do the washing up.'

'Including the burned saucepan. Deal.' He sighed. 'It's the last time I try to impress you,' he grumbled.

She kissed him. 'Don't try to impress me. Just be yourself.'

Being himself instead of being who other people wanted him to be was what had led to a rift between himself and his family, and he was pretty sure it had also contributed a fair bit to the breakdown of his marriage.

But then again, Amy wasn't anything like Kelly or his family. Maybe it would be different with her. Maybe he'd be enough for her.

He hoped.

After the pizza—and after, to Josh's relief, he'd managed to get her saucepan perfectly clean—they spent another evening of what really felt like domestic bliss. Amy switched on her stereo and played music by some gentle singer-songwriters that had Hope snoozing comfortably, while the two of them played cards for a while and then stretched out on the sofa together, spooned together with his arms wrapped round her waist and his cheek against hers.

He couldn't remember feeling this chilled-out and happy for a long, long time. They didn't even need to talk: it was enough just to be together, relaxing and enjoying each other's warmth.

Later that evening, when Hope had had her last feed of the evening and they'd gone to bed, he found their goodnight kisses turning hotter, to the point where they were both uncovering bare skin.

He stopped. 'I don't want to rush you.'

Her skin heated. 'Sorry. You're right. We shouldn't take this too fast.'

Though he wanted to. And the expression in her gorgeous brown eyes told him that she might want to, too. He stroked her face. 'I, um, bought stuff today in the supermarket. Just in case. Not because I expect it, but… Well. Later. When we're both ready.'

She kissed him. 'We have kind of known each other for months.'

'Just not very well,' he added in fairness.

Was it his imagination, or had her pupils just gone wider?

'Maybe it's time we remedied that.'

He went very still. 'Are you sure?'

She kissed him. 'Very sure. Because the way you make me feel… I haven't felt that in a long, long time.'

'Same here,' he said.

'Then maybe we ought to seize the day.'

'Carpe diem,' he agreed.

He fetched the condoms, and checked that the baby was OK. And then there was nothing left to hold them back.

CHAPTER EIGHT

Wednesday

'SO ARE YOU back on duty today?' Amy asked.

'I'm afraid so,' Josh said. 'But I'm on a late shift, so I thought maybe we could take Hope out for a walk this morning and make the most of the sunshine.'

'Sounds good to me,' she said, smiling.

How much things had changed since Christmas Eve. Just five short days: and in that time Amy had grown much more confident with the baby.

She'd grown much more confident in herself, too. For the last eighteen months, she'd felt as if she wasn't good enough to be anyone's partner, because she couldn't offer them a family and a future. Josh had shown her just how mistaken she was. And last night, when they'd made love, he'd been so gentle with her, so tender.

Even catching his eye right now made her feel hot all over, remembering how his hands had felt against her skin, how his mouth had coaxed a response she hadn't even known she was capable of.

And Josh seemed different, too. Even though he'd told her everything about his past, she'd sensed a kind of barrier still there: as if he didn't trust anyone enough to let them see who he really was. After last night, that barrier was gone.

Walking along the riverside, hand in hand with Josh and pushing the pram, made Amy feel as if the world was full of sunshine.

And then her mobile phone rang.

'Amy Howes,' she said.

'Amy, it's Jane Richards. Where are you?'

'With Hope and Josh, by the river.' Amy went cold. The deal was that they'd be looking after Hope until New Year's Eve. There could only be two reasons why Jane was calling: either she'd found Hope's mother, or she'd found a permanent foster carer. 'Is something wrong?' she asked, knowing that the answer would be 'yes'—at least from her perspective.

'I need to see you, I'm afraid. Can I meet you at your flat?'

She took a deep breath. 'OK. We can be back in fifteen minutes.'

'Great. I'll be there,' Jane said.

Amy hung up and turned to Josh. 'You've probably already worked out that that was Jane.'

'She's found Hope's mum?'

'She didn't say. But it's either that or she's found a more permanent set of foster parents.' She held her breath for a moment in the hope that it would stop her bursting into tears.

This was ridiculous.

She'd always known that this was a temporary situation. That they'd be looking after Hope until New Year's Eve at the latest, and then they'd have to give her back.

But she'd already bonded with the baby. She'd learned the difference between a cry to say Hope was hungry, a cry to say she needed a fresh nappy, and a cry to say she wanted a cuddle. Josh, too.

Without the baby bonding them together, was this thing between them too new and too fragile to survive? Would she lose Josh as well as the baby?

'Hey. We always knew we'd have to give her back,' Josh said softly.

'I know. But I'll…' To her horror, Amy felt a tear sliding down her face.

Josh drew her into his arms and held her close. 'Miss her,' he finished. 'Me, too. It's going to be strange without Munchkin around.'

And they'd go back to living in their separate flats. Next week, term would start again and Josh would be working very different hours from hers. Would they manage to keep seeing each other? Josh himself had said how difficult it was to find time to date someone when you worked shifts.

'Amy. I take it she wants to see us?'

Amy nodded.

'When?'

'Now.' It felt as if she was forcing the word past a massive lump in her throat.

His arms tightened round her. 'Then we need to go back.'

To face the beginning of the end?

'I know,' she said softly, and made the effort to pull herself together.

Jane was waiting in the lobby by the time they got back to their block.

'I'll make tea,' Josh said. 'Strong, a dash of milk, no sugar, right?'

'Thank you,' Jane said.

Back in her flat, Amy took Hope out of the pram and her snowsuit. So this was the last time she was going to hold her. The baby Amy had promised herself she wouldn't bond with—and yet she had. This was the last cuddle. The last time she'd smell that soft powdery baby scent. The last time she'd see those beautiful dark blue eyes.

She couldn't say a word. All she could do was cuddle the baby and wish that things were different.

Jane waited until Josh was back with them and sitting next to Amy before she told them what had happened.

'This is in strictest confidence,' the social worker warned. 'I shouldn't even be telling you any of this— but without you we wouldn't have found out the full story, so I think you have a right to know. Just…' She grimaced.

'We know. And we'll keep it to ourselves,' Josh said.

'I went to see Alice, first thing this morning.' Jane bit her lip. 'She told me everything.'

'So were we right and Freya is Hope's mother?' Amy asked.

'Yes. But she doesn't have a boyfriend.' Jane took a deep breath. 'It's pretty nasty. You know you said she wasn't getting on with her mum's new partner?'

'Oh, no.' Amy felt her eyes widen as she guessed at the horrible truth. 'Please tell me he didn't interfere with her.'

Jane grimaced. 'Unfortunately, he did a lot more

than that. Freya told her mum what was happening, but she wouldn't believe the girl.'

'Surely she must've known what was going on?' Josh asked.

'Not necessarily,' Amy said. 'When I talked to her, she said that Freya was jealous and being difficult. Maybe she thought that Freya was lying about the guy to break them up and get her mother's full attention back—or even make the space to get her father back with her mother again.'

'It's easy to judge when you're outside the situation,' Jane agreed. 'She might not have known what was happening—or she might have refused to see it because she didn't want to face the truth.'

'So then Freya became pregnant?' Josh asked.

Jane nodded. 'She said she didn't know what to do when she found out.'

'I wish she'd come to me,' Amy said.

'That's what Alice's mum said, too. Between the two of you, I think you would've helped the poor child,' Jane said. 'Freya said she thought about talking to you, but she was scared you wouldn't believe her, either.'

'Poor girl. I would've listened. Why didn't Alice come and see me? She's in my form, too.'

'Freya swore Alice to secrecy,' Jane said. 'Alice agreed, but only on condition Freya promised to have the baby in hospital. She told me she thought that if Freya had the baby in hospital, someone there would get her to tell the truth and they'd help her.'

'But obviously she didn't go to hospital when she started having contractions. There's no way they would have discharged her from the ward, even with the virus situation at the hospital,' Josh said. 'Plus the baby had one of those freezer clips as a cord clamp. It looked to me as if the mum had read up about birth and was doing the best she possibly could.'

'The baby was a couple of weeks early. I guess it took her by surprise,' Jane said. 'She had the baby in the shed at home.'

Amy winced. 'In the middle of winter, all on her own, with no support. That poor child. Has she gone to hospital now?'

Jane nodded. 'I took her there myself. She's being checked over properly.'

'What about the stepfather?' Josh asked.

'I spoke to the police on the way to Freya's. They have him in custody.'

'I sincerely hope they throw the book at him and make sure he can never, ever do that to another girl,' Amy said.

'They will,' Jane reassured her.

Amy knew she had to be brave and ask the question. 'So what happens to Hope?'

'She's going to stay with Freya for a day or two, until Freya decides what she wants to do—whether she wants to keep the baby or give her up for adoption,' Jane said. 'I've got an infant seat in the car, so I can take her with me now.'

'Where are they going to stay?' Josh asked.

'Probably at the hospital—though I know there are the virus problems still, so maybe they'll go back to her mother's,' Jane said.

Amy frowned. 'Is that really a good idea? Especially if the stepfather gets out on bail?'

'Or we'll find her a safe place,' Jane said. 'It depends on what Freya wants to do.'

'I'm glad you're taking what she wants into account,' Josh said. 'It sounds to me as if the poor girl hasn't really had anyone on her side for a long time.' He looked at Amy. 'Though obviously you would've been there for her, if she'd given you the chance.'

'Yeah.' And now Freya wanted her baby back. 'I guess I'd better get Hope's stuff together,' Amy said. Keeping busy was the best way to get through this. She handed the baby to Josh, then went to bag up the sleep suits that Jane had brought, the Moses basket and bedding and bottles and sterilising equipment.

Funny, all that extra stuff should've made her flat feel cluttered. It hadn't. And, without the baby, the place was going to feel so empty.

Stupid of her to fall in love with the baby.

And equally stupid of her to fall in love with Josh.

Because there wasn't going to be a happy ending. Didn't they say be careful what you wish for? What they didn't say was that you might get what you really wanted but then have to give it back.

'I need to wash the stuff that Alison's sister lent us,' she said. 'And we've got the necklace that Freya left with Hope—she needs that. And the book we did, with her sleep chart and feed chart and weight, and pictures of her first few days and—' Her voice caught.

'I'm sorry,' Jane said. 'You've both been brilliant.'

'We're just going to miss her, that's all,' Josh said. 'We've got used to her being around.'

'Of course you have.'

Josh kissed the baby's forehead. 'Well, Munchkin, look after yourself.'

The baby grizzled, as if picking up on the dark mood in the room.

'Goodbye, Hope,' Amy whispered, unable to bear holding the baby again because she knew just how hard it would be to hand her over to the social worker.

'I'll be in touch,' Jane said.

'I'll walk you down to your car. Carry the stuff,' Josh offered.

'And I'd better start washing the things that Alison lent us,' Amy said. She didn't think she could handle watching Jane drive away with the baby.

She half expected Josh not to come back, but he knocked on her door when he'd seen Jane into her car.

'Are you OK?' he asked.

What was the point in lying? 'Not really.'

'I'll ring work and see if I can swap shifts with someone,' he said.

'No. They need you at the hospital,' Amy said.

Meaning that you don't? Josh wondered, but didn't dare to ask. Just in case that was what she said. Right now, he could see that she was hurting. He knew that when people were hurt they often said things they didn't mean but the words still caused an awful lot of damage. It would be better to back off now and regroup.

He glanced at his watch. 'Actually, I do have to go, if you're sure you don't want me to try and change my shift.'

When she said nothing, he sighed inwardly. 'I'll be home as soon as I can,' he promised.

Amy turned away. 'Sorry. I think I just need some time on my own.'

Did that mean she didn't want him to come over after work?

As if he'd spoken out loud, she said, 'I'll see you tomorrow, maybe.'

Josh went cold.

He hadn't been enough for Kelly.

And, now the baby wasn't here, Amy didn't need his help any more. She didn't need him. So he wasn't enough for her, either. What kind of delusional fool was he, to think this was going to work out?

'OK. Call me if you need me,' he said, but he knew she wouldn't.

And it was pointless trying to put his arms round her and kiss her, or tell her that everything was going to be all right. He'd seen that closed-off look with Kelly, too, and he knew what it meant.

The end.

So it was over almost as soon as it had started, Amy thought as Josh closed her front door behind him.

This morning, she'd been so happy. She'd had everything she ever wanted. A baby, and a partner who cared about her—a partner who was a decent man, one who wouldn't lie or cheat or let her down.

Except, now the baby had gone, Josh had walked away from her just as easily as Michael had. No doubt he'd been relieved when she'd said she wanted some time on her own. It meant he hadn't had to do the 'it's not you, it's me' speech.

Well, she'd pick herself up, dust herself down, and remember not to let people too close again in future.

Josh was too busy at work to get a chance to pop up to the maternity ward to see if Freya and Hope were there. When he'd finished his shift, it was too late to visit; if Freya was still on the ward, he thought, the poor girl would probably be asleep.

He walked home, and paused outside Amy's door. Should he knock and see how she was doing?

Then again, she'd said she wanted space. And she hadn't texted him, even though she knew he'd pick up any messages as soon as he'd finished his shift.

Well, he wasn't going to give up on her that easily. He knocked on the door. 'Amy? Are you there?'

She didn't answer.

He tried her mobile. A recorded voice informed him that the phone was switched off and he should leave a message or send a text.

Right.

He was pretty sure she wouldn't reply to those, either.

With a heavy heart, he carried on down the corridor to his own flat. Funny how empty the place seemed. And was it his imagination or did the place smell musty?

At least cleaning everything kept him too busy to think for a little while. He didn't bother making himself a sandwich because he just wasn't hungry. But when it came to bedtime... His double bed felt way too wide. It was worse than when he'd first moved in to the flat, because now he knew what it would feel like if the place was really home rather than simply a place to sleep and store his clothes.

But he wasn't enough for Amy, just as he hadn't been enough for Kelly. He'd just have to get used to that. And he was never going to risk his heart again.

CHAPTER NINE

Thursday

JOSH ACTUALLY TOOK his break at lunchtime, the next day, and paid a quiet visit to the maternity ward rather than heading for the canteen.

'Hey, Josh—are you coming up to see us, for a change? Usually you call us down to the Emergency Department to see a patient,' one of the obstetricians teased.

'Actually, I haven't come to see you—I've come to visit a friend of a friend during my lunch break,' he said. And that was sort of true. If you could count a week-old baby as a friend.

'Who?'

'Freya. If she's still here. I know she and the baby came in yesterday.'

His colleague frowned. 'Oh, our young missing mum? Yes, she's here. She's—' He stopped.

'Patient confidentiality,' Josh said with a sigh. 'I know. Does it help if you know I looked after the baby?'

'Downstairs?'

'Yes.' It wasn't a total stretch of the truth—he and

Amy *had* brought Hope in to the Emergency Department, and he had indeed been looking after Hope... Albeit as a stand-in parent, rather than as a doctor.

'Ah. Well, if we're talking as fellow clinicians, the baby's doing fine. Freya does have an infection, but we've put her on antibiotics and it should clear up in a couple of days. We're keeping her in for the moment to keep an eye on her.'

'Great.' Josh gave his sweetest smile. 'Can I put my head round the door for two seconds and say hello?'

'Actually, it might do the poor kid good to have a visitor,' the obstetrician said. 'Sure.'

'Thanks. Where do I find her?'

'She's in room six.'

Even better: Freya was in a room on her own, so she wouldn't be embarrassed about their conversation being overheard. 'Great. Thanks.'

He knocked on the door of room six, then went in when he heard Freya call, 'Yes?'

'Hello,' he said with a smile. 'Freya, isn't it?'

She looked at him, her eyes wide and suddenly full of fear. 'Have you come to take the baby? Are you from the police?'

'No and no,' he reassured her. The poor kid was really upset, and she could do with a bit of handholding, he thought. He knew the perfect person to do that, but right now he had a feeling that Amy's head might not be in the right place. 'And you're not in trouble. My name's Josh and I'm a doctor,' he said, indicating his white coat and his hospital identity card.

'I haven't seen you before. Are you from the maternity ward?' she asked.

'No, I'm from the Emergency Department.'

She frowned. 'But I haven't been in an accident or anything. Why do you need to see me?'

'Actually,' he said, 'I came to say hello to you and to see how Munchkin's doing.'

'Munchkin?' Freya looked confused.

'Hope,' he explained.

She frowned again. 'Why do you call her Munchkin?'

'Because she's tiny—you know, like the people in *The Wizard of Oz*.'

'Oh. And how do you know her name's Hope?'

He could understand why the poor girl was so suspicious. She'd been through a lot. Right then, he really wanted to give her a hug and tell her everything was going to work out just fine, but it wouldn't be appropriate. Plus, given what had happened to her, the contact from a strange man would probably worry her even more. 'Because,' he said quietly, 'I'm Miss Howes's neighbour and I've been helping her look after the baby for the last week.'

'Oh.' Freya bit her lip. 'Sorry. I ruined your Christmas.'

'On the contrary,' he said. 'I was planning to have a really lousy Christmas on my own, doing my shift downstairs and then eating my body weight in leftover sausage rolls that hadn't been stored properly and probably ending up with food poisoning—and because of you I had a decent Christmas dinner cooked for me and I got to spend Christmas with someone really nice.'

There was the hint of a smile, just for a moment, and then her expression switched back to gloom again.

'So can I give her a cuddle?' he asked.

'I guess.'

He picked the baby up, and settled down with her on the chair next to Freya's bed. 'Hey, Munchkin. I know you're asleep so you're not going to answer, but have you missed Uncle Joshy's terrible singing?'

Freya blinked in surprise. 'You sing to her?'

'Yup. Little tip from me—you'll need to do that a lot when she has a bath,' he said. 'She absolutely hates baths. She screams the place down.'

'What do you sing to her?'

'Anything. She doesn't care what it is, as long as you sing,' he said with a smile. And he was relieved that finally Freya seemed to be responding to him. 'So how are *you* doing?' he asked, trying to keep his voice as gentle and non-threatening as possible.

She shrugged. 'OK, I suppose.'

Well, it was probably a stupid question. He went back to safer ground. 'Hope's a really beautiful baby, you know. And her name fits her perfectly.'

A tear slid down her cheek. 'And I'm going to have to give her away.'

'Why?'

'I'm fifteen. I'm supposed to be at school.' She shook her head, looking anguished. 'I can't go to school with a baby, can I?'

'Won't your mum help?'

'No chance.' Freya gave a snort of disgust. 'She hates me—and I hate her, too.'

'Hate's a very strong word,' he said softly. 'Families can be complicated, and sometimes they can make you feel as if you've let them down. And sometimes you feel that they're the ones who let you down.'

'She thinks it's all my fault. The baby.'

He waited, giving Freya the space to find the words.

'She thinks I led him on. But I didn't.'

'I know,' he said gently.

She looked shocked. 'You believe me?'

'Yes.'

'*She* doesn't.'

'Maybe your mum just needs a bit of time to think about it,' he suggested.

'She won't change her mind.' Freya dragged in a breath. 'And I know she wants him back.'

He could understand exactly why Freya didn't want to live with her stepfather again. He didn't want the girl having to live with the man again, either. He'd quite like to rearrange the man's body parts, except he knew that violence didn't solve anything and locking the man away for a long time was a better option. 'Maybe there's another way,' he said. 'Jane, the social worker, is really nice. She might be able to find you a foster family who'll look after you and the baby.'

Freya's expression was filled with disbelief. 'Who's going to take on a fifteen-year-old and a baby? I'm going to end up in a children's home, and everyone's going to despise me.'

'There are nice people out there. People who are kind. People who help others.' He paused. 'That's why you rang Miss Howes's doorbell, isn't it?'

Freya nodded. 'She's my form teacher. Everyone loves her, because she's kind and funny.'

Yeah. And Amy had been his, for just a little while. Being without her made his heart ache.

'I knew she'd look after the baby and know what to do,' Freya continued.

'Maybe you could've talked to her when you found out you were pregnant,' he said.

'I wanted to—Alice, she's my best friend, she said I ought to, but I made her promise she wouldn't tell anyone, not even her mum.' Freya bit her lip. 'I would've told Miss Howes about *him*, but I was scared. He said if I told anyone he'd make sure nobody believed me and I'd get taken into care.'

Being taken into care probably would've been the best thing for her, Josh thought. It would have got her away from the man who'd been systematically abusing her. 'Miss Howes would've believed you. Luckily Alice did tell her mum in the end,' he said, 'because you needed antibiotics and you could've been very ill without them.' He paused. 'Would Alice's mum let you stay with them, maybe?'

Freya shook her head. 'They don't have enough room. There isn't a spare bedroom, and Alice's bedroom is too small for more than one bed, let alone another bed and a cot. So I don't know what's going to happen to me.'

'There are nice people in the world, Freya,' he said again, 'and Jane will make sure someone really nice looks after you and Hope, if you want to keep her.'

'I do.' Freya glanced down at the baby. 'Even though she's his—well, she's a girl, so she won't look like him and she won't remind me of him.'

'She's gorgeous. She's definitely got your nose and chin,' he said.

'Thank you,' she said, 'for looking after Hope for me.'

'It was a pleasure,' he said, meaning it. 'We did a notebook for her first few days—we wrote down when she slept and when she had some milk, and took some photographs.'

'I know—Miss Richards gave it to me. Thank you.'

'You've probably already worked it out for yourself, but mine's the terrible handwriting,' he said.

'Who did the drawings in the back?' she asked.

'Me,' he said.

'You're good.'

He inclined his head in acknowledgement. 'Thank you.'

'Why aren't you an artist instead of a doctor?' she asked.

'It's how things worked out,' he said. 'Sometimes, your plans don't work out quite as you thought they would, but you can still find a chance to be happy.'

'I guess,' she said, sounding unconvinced, but he hoped that she'd think about what he'd said and realise that he was telling the truth. 'Would you tell Miss Howes thanks for me?'

'Sure,' he said. Though he might have to do it by text, if she was avoiding him.

'And sorry. She's really kind. I know I shouldn't have just dumped Hope in that blanket in a cardboard box, but I just didn't know what to do.'

'Hey.' He patted her hand. 'You were having a tough time. And you knew Amy—Miss Howes—would make sure Hope was all right, so that was one thing less you had to worry about.'

'Yeah.' She sniffed.

'I've got to go back to work, now,' he said. 'But maybe I can come and see you and Hope again tomorrow?'

'I'd like that,' she said.

'And I'll bring my sketchbook. Do you a proper picture of you both together.' He stroked the baby's face. 'Nice to see you, Munchkin. Even if you weren't going

to wake up and say hello.' Gently, he transferred the
baby back to Freya's arms. 'If you need anything, get
them to call me. Josh Farnham in Emergency. They
know me up here anyway,' he said.

Freya's eyes filled with tears. 'That's so kind. Thank
you.'

And not enough people had been kind to the girl,
he thought savagely. He'd quite like a little chat with
Freya's mother about how to treat a child properly—
and she'd be squirming so much by the time he'd finished, she'd treat the girl decently for ever after. 'No
worries, Freya,' he said. 'Take care.'

He thought about it through the rest of the day.
Freya's assessment of Amy: *Everyone loves her, because she's kind and funny.*

Amy was more than that. Much more.

She made him feel as if the sun had come out after
a week of pouring rain.

And the week they'd just shared... Yes, it had been
intense, almost like being snowbound but without the
snow: but it hadn't just been the baby holding them
together. What they had was real.

She'd definitely pushed him away, yesterday. And,
now he thought about it, he realised why. She was kind
and funny and nice—and she was trying to do what
she thought was best for him. Setting him free to find
someone who could give him the family he wanted
without any complications.

Except if she'd actually said that to him, he would've
had the chance to tell her that it wasn't what he wanted.
Yes, he wanted a family; but he wanted her more. He
needed to convince her that it didn't matter if they
couldn't have children. And maybe he needed to prove

to her that he could be enough for her, the way he hadn't been enough for Kelly. What they had was too good to throw away.

He actually ran home, after his shift.

And this time he didn't knock on Amy's door; instead, he rang her buzzer on the intercom.

When she didn't answer, he wondered for a moment if she'd gone out. But something told him she was home alone, feeling as miserable as he did without her. There was only one way he could think of to make her talk to him: to lean on the buzzer, and not stop until she answered.

'Yes?' She sounded cross and miserable at the same time.

'Amy, it's Josh. We need to talk.'

'I—'

'No excuses and no refusals,' he said. 'We really do need to talk, Amy. Just give me five minutes. Please.'

She sighed. 'You didn't have to lean on the buzzer. You could've just knocked on my door.'

'And you would've ignored me, like you did last night,' he pointed out. 'Can I come in?'

She sighed again. 'I don't have any choice, do I?'

'Nope,' he said. 'We need to talk.' If she said no after she'd listened to what he had to say, then fair enough—he'd accept that. But he needed to tell her how he felt, and she needed to know what was going on in his head. The only way that was going to happen was if they talked instead of avoiding the issues.

'See you in a second,' she said.

It took him more like twenty seconds to get to her door, but at least this time she opened it when he knocked.

And she looked as if she hadn't slept. There were dark hollows under her eyes and her face was lined with misery.

'How are you doing?' he asked.

'Not brilliant,' she admitted.

Even though he'd meant to keep at arm's length until they'd talked, he couldn't just stand there and let her feel awful. He wrapped his arms round her and held her close. 'I know. Me, too. And I've missed you even more than I miss Hope.'

'Josh, I—'

'Please, just let me talk,' he said. 'If you say no when you've heard me out, I won't push you. But don't say no before you've heard what I have to say.'

'OK.' She wriggled out of his arms. 'Let's sit down. Coffee?'

'No, thanks.' He knew it was a delaying tactic, and he didn't want to wait any more. He wanted to get this sorted out right now. He followed her in to the living room and sat next to her on the sofa. 'I went to see Freya and Hope today.'

Her eyes widened. 'How are they?'

'Doing OK,' he said. 'Freya wants to keep the baby, but she doesn't want to go back to live with her mum—and she's worried about how school's going to work, with a baby.'

'We can support her,' Amy said. 'We can do a lot to help, now we know about the situation.'

He smiled. 'I knew you'd say that. And she also said she rang your doorbell because she knew you'd look after the baby and you'd know what to do.' He paused. 'She says everyone loves you, because you're kind and funny.'

Amy blinked, and he had the strongest impression that she was close to tears. 'That's nice.'

'You're more than that,' he said. 'And that's why I want to talk to you.' This time, he reached over to take her hand. 'I know this is fast and I know we both have issues from the past we'll still have to work through. But I like you—no, I more than like you, Amy.' He might as well tell her the whole lot. 'Over the last week, I've fallen in love with you. Not because of the baby, but because you're bright and you're funny and you're warm, and you have this whole aura about you that makes me feel as if the sun's just come out after a week of rain. And I know that sounds flowery and cheesy and maybe even a bit smarmy, but it's not meant to be like that.' He threw his free hand up into the air in exasperation. 'I just don't have any better words to describe it.'

'Oh, Josh.'

The expression on her face gave him hope, so he pushed on.

'I know Michael left you because you couldn't have children, but he was an idiot. He was missing the point. And I'm not Michael. Yes, I always thought I wanted a family, and spending this last week looking after Hope with you made me realise that I do still want that. But it doesn't matter that you can't have children. We did a great job as foster parents for Hope, this week, and we could do that again for another child.'

'But it's still a massive compromise,' Amy said. 'I wasn't enough for Michael.'

'And I wasn't enough for Kelly. But you're not Kelly, and I'm not Michael.' He paused. 'You're enough for me. You're everything I want. And I want you with or without a family, Amy.'

'I'm not brilliant at relationships. Not long-term,' she said. 'There was Gavin.'

'Who cheated on you. He was a snake.'

'And Michael.'

'Who was a selfish toad. I don't think your problem's with relationships, Amy—it's that you pick amphibians.'

She winced. 'Don't pull your punches.'

'There's no point in trying to sugar-coat things. You and me, we're about honesty. So we know we can trust each other. I've got my faults, just like everyone else, but I'm most definitely not a reptile,' he said. 'So do something different, this time, to make it work. Pick a man who's not a snake or a toad. Pick me.'

Could she really believe this?

Would she be enough for Josh?

Then again, she knew he had a similar issue, feeling that he hadn't been enough for his ex-wife. They were coming from the same sort of place and wanted the same sort of things.

'Pick me, Amy,' he said again, his voice soft. 'Because I choose you, too.'

'We haven't even gone out on a date together,' she said.

'Yeah—our relationship has been a bit backwards, so far. Baby first, then…' He smiled. 'Well.'

Sex. Amy's skin heated at the memories.

'Let's go out on a date tonight,' he said. 'I need a shower, but whatever I do to my hair it's going to look like this within five minutes, so I hope you'll forgive the fact that it looks a mess.'

'There's nothing wrong with your hair. It's cute.' And then, just because he looked a little bit worried and she thought he needed a bit of reassurance, she ran her fingers through his hair to smooth it slightly. 'Sexy,' she said.

'You think I'm sexy?'

'I think you're a lot of things.' And because he'd said it all first, she had the courage to say it back to him. 'You're kind and you're caring and you're reliable. You're calm in a crisis. And it scares the hell out of me that we've been on nod-and-smile terms for six months, but we've just spent a week together like a real family, and somewhere along the way I fell in love with you and I never expected anything like that to happen.'

'And you're still scared it's going to go wrong,' he said.

She nodded.

'Me, too. But we can work on that,' he said. 'Together. How long's it going to take you to get ready?'

'How dressy are we talking?'

'I know a bistro not too far from here where they do live music,' he said. 'And I patched up the chef six months ago, so I'm pretty sure they'll be able to find us a table for two.'

'Little black dress and lipstick, and do something with my hair—that'll be about twenty minutes,' she calculated swiftly.

'Deal.' He looked at her. 'And we're supposed to seal a deal, aren't we?'

In answer, she leaned forward and kissed him.

And he kissed her back until her knees went weak.

'Twenty minutes,' he said, and headed for the door. Then he leaned back round the doorframe. 'I love you,' he said, blew her another kiss, and left.

Yesterday, when Amy had had to give Hope back—even though she'd known it was going to happen—had been one of the hardest days of her life. A real emotional roller coaster that had left her miserable and lonely and aching.

Today, it felt as if she'd climbed all the way back to the top. Except this time there wasn't a sharp descent back into the shadows.

A bistro with live music. Dressy but not *too* dressy, then.

The little black dress, tights and lipstick took a couple of minutes. Her hair took slightly longer, pulled into a loose up-do with a few strands left to frame her face and soften the effect.

And then Josh rang the doorbell.

How long was it since she'd gone on a proper date? Nerves throbbed through her, but she lifted her chin and strode over to answer the door.

In a dark suit with a white shirt buttoned to the neck but without a tie, and his hair sticking up all over the place, Josh looked sexy as hell. He took her breath away.

Clearly he was just as nervous as she was, because he opened his mouth to speak and nothing came out.

Crazy. They'd spent most of the last week together, talking about practically everything in the universe.

As if he was thinking exactly the same thing, he said, 'Um, this is insane. We talked all week. But now it's our first date and I don't know what to say to you.'

'Me, too,' she said. 'You look nice.'

'You look amazing,' he said. Then he grinned. 'But actually you still look amazing when your hair's all over the place and you've slept in your clothes, so I'm not being shallow.'

'Neither was I. But thank you for the compliment.' She inclined her head in acknowledgement.

'I feel like a teenager,' he said.

'Me, too.'

'But,' he said, 'I did definitely get us a table. So hopefully this won't be the date from hell.'

'Unless the heel of my shoe gets stuck in a grate and falls off, and I knock a glass of red wine across the table and ruin your shirt.'

'Or the chef does a body swap with me and I burn the spaghetti Bolognese again…'

She laughed and took his hand. 'I think we'll be all right.'

The restaurant turned out to have a wonderful menu, and the musician that night was a singer-song-writer who alternated between the guitar and the piano. And once the food and wine had relaxed them enough that they were at ease with each other again, it turned out to be the perfect date. They didn't stop talking through the meal, and then Josh held her hand as they enjoyed the music together.

They walked home along the riverside, their arms wrapped round each other, and Josh kissed Amy under every single lamp-post. Although it had turned cold, Amy didn't care; she was simply enjoying Josh's near-ness.

He paused outside her front door. 'I guess, as this is our first date, this is where I kiss you goodnight and wish you sweet dreams?'

'And I ask you in for coffee?' She spread her hands. 'Or there's the alternative version.'

His eyes darkened. 'Which is?'

'Sweet dreams, Josh.' She kissed him.

'And now I invite you in for coffee?' he asked.

She nodded.

Josh caught his breath as he realised exactly what she meant. 'And you stay?' he asked very softly.

'You've already seen my bedroom,' she said. 'And, if this is going to be an equal relationship...'

He didn't need a second invitation. He took her hand and led her to his flat.

He made coffee, as promised; but they didn't get to drink it because he ended up carrying her to his bed instead.

Afterwards, she fell asleep in his arms. This time neither of them wore pyjamas and there were no barriers between them. And Josh thought that maybe the future was going to work.

There was just one more thing that would make life perfect—and he'd suggest that to her in the morning.

CHAPTER TEN

Friday—New Year's Eve

THE NEXT MORNING, Josh woke, warm and comfortable.

Best of all, Amy was lying asleep in his arms.

And today was New Year's Eve. A time for new beginnings. A time, he hoped, for them to make a decision together that might just change everything for both of them.

He gently moved his arm from under her shoulder, and climbed out of bed without waking her. It took just a couple of minutes to throw on some clothes and brush his teeth, and he paused to write her a note just in case she woke while he was gone.

Gone to get breakfast.
Back in five minutes. x

He stuck the note to the inside of his front door, where she couldn't possibly miss it, and headed for the bakery just down the street.

When he returned, he peeked into his bedroom and Amy was just stirring.

'Well, good morning, sleepyhead,' he teased.

She squinted at him. 'Why are you dressed? Have you got to go to work?'

'Nope. I worked Christmas, so I get New Year's off,' he said. 'I'm dressed because I just went out to get us some breakfast.' He smiled. 'I did leave you a note on the front door in case you woke while I was away, but clearly you didn't. Stay where you are and I'll bring in the goodies.'

He came back two minutes later with a tray, a plate of warm croissants, jam and butter, and two mugs of coffee.

'You made coffee that fast?' she asked.

'No. I bought it from the bakery and I just poured it out of the paper cups into mugs,' he admitted. 'I didn't want to spend any more time away from you than I had to.'

'Croissants and proper coffee. The perfect breakfast in bed. Very decadent, Dr Farnham,' she said with a smile.

'I have a much better idea for being decadent, Miss Howes,' he said. 'How about Valentine's Day in Paris—proper Parisian croissants?'

'I really like the sound of that,' she said. 'But, if it's in term-time, I won't be able to take the day off. We might have to have an unofficial Valentine's Day instead.'

'Works for me,' he said.

Once they'd finished breakfast, he asked, 'What would you like to do today?'

'I really don't mind, as long as it's with you—or is that being greedy?'

'It's what I had in mind, too,' he said. 'Maybe we can go for a walk somewhere.'

'Sounds good to me,' she said, and kissed him. 'But I can hardly go out in last night's little black dress. I need to go next door and shower and change.'

'Thirty minutes?' he asked.

'That'd be great. Though I'll do the washing up first.'

'No. I'll do that while you get ready.' He kissed her again. 'Knock for me when you're done.'

Half an hour later, Amy knocked on Josh's door—having showered, washed her hair, dried it quickly and changed into jeans, a sweater and comfortable mid-heeled boots.

'You look beautiful,' he said, and kissed her.

'So do you.' She kissed him back. 'So where are we going?' she asked.

'I was thinking, maybe we can start by visiting Freya and Hope in hospital.'

'Are you sure they haven't been discharged?' she asked.

He nodded. 'I rang the ward and checked this morning.'

'Are we actually allowed to do this?'

He shrugged. 'Give me a good reason why you can't visit one of your pupils in hospital?'

'Because we've spent most of the past week looking after her baby?' Amy suggested.

'Then you're not visiting as her form tutor. You're visiting as a friend,' he pointed out.

'I'd like to see them,' Amy said. 'But we're not going empty-handed.'

'Good idea,' Josh said. 'They told me on the ward yesterday that she hadn't had any visitors.'

Amy looked shocked. 'Not even her mum, or her best friend?'

'Nope. That's why I said I'd pop in to see her today. And I promised I'd do a sketch of her and the baby together.' He indicated his sketchbook and pencils. 'Maybe I can get it framed for her.'

'That's a really lovely idea. And I agree, we should definitely make a fuss of her,' Amy said. 'Shops, first?'

'Absolutely.'

Between them, they found a couple of cute outfits for Hope in tiny baby size, the cutest and softest little polar bear, and a board book. 'And we need to take something for Freya, too.'

'Not flowers or balloons,' Josh said. 'They're the first things that get banned as part of virus control regulations.'

'Nice smellies, then,' Amy said, and dragged him off to a small shop that specialised in cruelty-free beauty products. 'They're really popular with her year group,' Amy explained, when Josh looked mystified.

'You really do notice things, don't you?' he asked.

'I'm supposed to notice things. I'm a form tutor. And I missed Freya's pregnancy completely,' Amy said, 'so I let her down.'

He gave her a hug. 'I don't think you're the one who let her down, honey.'

She bought wrapping paper, tape, ribbon and a 'congratulations on your baby girl' card, and they stopped for a very brief coffee so Amy could wrap the presents.

'How do you do that?' Josh asked when he saw the beautifully wrapped parcels and curled ribbons. 'I wrap something and—well, I think a five-year-old could do a better job than I do.'

'It's all about angles,' she said.

'Maths teacher stuff.' He rolled his eyes.

'You got it.' She winked at him. 'But, given that you have to stitch people up without leaving scars, surely you can wrap things?'

'Wrapping,' he said, 'is way harder than suturing. Trust me on that.' He grinned. 'Let's go and see the girls.'

They learned from the midwife at the reception desk that Freya was still in room six, and Josh rapped softly on the door. 'Freya? Hello? Can we come in?'

'Josh! You said you'd come back,' she said, looking pleased to see him.

'I promised you a sketch. And I'm off duty today, so I thought now would work nicely.'

'It's so nice to see you. Thank you ever so much. It was getting a bit—well…'

'Boring, on your own?' he asked.

'A bit.' She beamed at him. 'Hope, we've got a visitor.' But then she bit her lip when she saw Amy walk into the room behind Josh. 'Oh—Miss Howes! I'm so sorry for what I did.'

'We're out of school, so you can call me Amy, and there's absolutely no need for you to apologise because you've really had a hard time,' Amy said, and gave the girl a hug. 'How are you doing?'

'I'm getting better.' A tear slid down Freya's face. 'But I ruined your Christmas.'

'No, you fixed it,' Amy said, 'because I was meant to be spending it in Edinburgh with my oldest friends—but they got the flu, so I was going to be all alone and miserable at home. Instead, I got to spend Christmas with Josh and Hope.'

'That's what he said when he came yesterday.'

Amy smiled. 'I promise we didn't confer beforehand—and how's your gorgeous baby?'

Freya indicated the crib to the side of the bed. 'She's asleep right now. Thank you for looking after her.'

'I enjoyed it,' Amy said. 'Though it was a bit of a steep learning curve— I'm more used to dealing with teenagers.' She paused and took Freya's hand. 'You could've come to talk to me, Freya, and you still can. Any time. And if you want to come back to school and do your exams, we can support you and make sure you have everything you need.'

'Really?'

'Really,' Amy said firmly.

Another tear slid down Freya's cheek. 'I wish my mum would be like you.'

'She's not been to see you yet?' Amy asked.

Freya shook her head. 'And I'm kind of glad, because I don't want to see her.'

'But you've just had a baby—surely you want your mum.'

Freya nodded, and this time she burst into tears.

Amy held her until she stopped crying.

'I don't want to give Hope away,' Freya said, 'but she'll make me. And there's nothing I can do, because who's going to let a fifteen-year-old with a baby live with them?'

Amy glanced at Josh. She could think of a solution that might work for all of them. But she couldn't say anything to Freya until she'd discussed it with Josh. Saying that you'd consider fostering someone and actually doing it were two very different things.

'Things will get better with your mum,' Amy said. 'Sometimes when you're very lonely you make wrong decisions.'

Josh looked worried, as if he thought that was a coded message to him—that she'd been lonely and agreeing to a relationship with him had been a wrong decision. She caught his eye and gave the tiniest shake of her head to reassure him, then blew him a secret kiss, and saw the tension in his shoulders relax again.

'Maybe giving each other a bit of space will help your mum make a different decision,' Amy said gently.

'She'll still choose him over me.'

Amy thought that was probably true, but it wouldn't help anything to agree with Freya right at that moment. 'It's always difficult to second-guess what someone else is going to do and right now I think you need to concentrate on yourself and the baby,' she said. 'Josh tells me you had an infection.'

Freya nodded. 'They're giving me antibiotics. And I feel a bit better than I did.'

'That's good,' Amy said.

'And we brought you both a little something,' Josh said, handing Freya the parcels and the card.

Freya opened the parcel with the sleep suits and the tiny dungarees and sweater. 'Oh, they're gorgeous,' she said. 'Look, Hope. Your first present.' She was in tears again by the time she'd unwrapped the polar bear, and sobbing openly when she opened the gift for her.

'Hey.' This time Josh was the one to give her a hug.

'It's just…'

'It's all a bit overwhelming,' Josh said, 'and you've just had a baby. Do you want me to leave the sketch until another day?'

'When my face isn't all blotchy and stuff? Yes, please.' Freya looked forlorn. 'Or is that being vain and greedy?'

'Of course it's not,' Josh reassured her.

Amy took her hand and squeezed it. 'Has Alice come to visit you yet?'

'No, even though I texted her to let her know I'm here.' Freya bit her lip. 'She probably thinks I don't want to see her because she told her mum everything when she promised me she'd keep it secret.'

'I wouldn't normally act as a go-between,' Amy said, 'but I think this is a special case. Do you want me to have a word with her?'

'Would you?'

'Of course I will.' Amy smiled at her. 'Tell you what—how about I take a photo of you and Hope on my phone to show her?'

'Even though my face is all blotchy?'

'Sweetie, you look just fine. And it's not going to be plastered all over social media, I promise. It's just so I can show Alice.'

Freya brightened, and Amy took the photograph.

She and Josh had a brief cuddle with the baby. 'We'd better let you get some rest,' Amy said, 'but we can come back and see you tomorrow, if you like?'

Freya's eyes filled with tears again, and she scrubbed them away. 'Sorry. I'm being pathetic. That'd be really nice. We'd like that, wouldn't we, Hope?'

The baby gurgled, as if in agreement.

Amy and Josh went from the hospital to Alice's house. Alice's mother opened the door to them. 'Oh, Miss Howes! Is there…?'

Amy smiled at her. 'I just wanted to say thank you for persuading Alice to talk to Jane Richards about Freya. This is my friend, Josh Farnham. And I wondered if we could see Alice for about two minutes?'

'Yes, that's fine. Come in.'

Alice's mother called the teenager down from her room.

'Miss Howes!' Alice stopped dead in the doorway.

'Hello, Alice. This is my friend, Josh,' Amy introduced him swiftly. 'We came to show you something.' Amy opened the photograph on her phone and handed it to Alice.

'Oh—Freya and her baby! But she's so tiny!' Alice said on seeing the baby. 'But how did you…?'

'Freya left the baby on our doorstep on Christmas Eve,' Amy said. 'We kind of worked out that Freya was the mum—but, without your help in confirming that so we could help her, Freya would be very ill right now. So well done for being so brave.'

'But isn't Freya angry with me for telling?' Alice asked, looking worried. 'I mean, she hasn't texted me or anything, and she hasn't been on any of the usual social media. I thought her mum had confiscated her phone and laptop but, after Miss Richards talked to me about the baby, I thought maybe Freya just didn't want to speak to me.'

'I think she's relieved you did tell, actually. She said she'd texted you to say she was in hospital,' Josh said.

'Oh, no! But I didn't get her text,' Alice said biting her lip.

'Josh and I have been her only visitors. She'd really love it if you came to see her,' Amy said gently.

'I think she's worried that you don't want anything to do with her any more.'

'But that's daft. She's my best friend. Of course I want to see her—and the baby. Can we, Mum?' Alice asked.

Alice's mum nodded. 'Of course. We'll go and buy her something nice for the baby too—I assume she's keeping the baby, Miss Howes?'

'She wants to, yes. Her little girl's called Hope.'

'That's nice.'

Amy smiled in agreement, 'And, Alice, I hope you know you can always talk to me in confidence,' she said. 'Sometimes I might have to act on what you tell me—like the social worker did, to keep Freya safe— but that's why I'm your form tutor. I'm there if you need me.'

Alice blushed, clearly not quite sure what to say. 'Thank you.'

'Anyway —we'd better go,' Amy said. 'But thanks for all your help. You did the right thing.'

Alice's mum showed them out. 'I feel better knowing there's someone like you at school keeping an eye out for the kids,' she said.

'Me? I'm just ordinary,' Amy said.

And Josh thought, no, you're not ordinary. You're really special.

Once they'd left Alice's house, Josh steered them towards the nearest coffee shop. 'I think we need to talk,' he said.

'Agreed.'

He ordered them both coffee and found a quiet table. 'Poor Freya's really been through the mill.'

'And she clearly doesn't want to go back to her

mum's, as you said yesterday. She wants to keep the baby. And she thinks she's not going to be able to do that.'

'She told me yesterday she was scared she'd end up in a children's home and everyone there would despise her.'

'Poor kid.' Amy winced. 'You know what you were saying about considering fostering?'

'Yes.' Even though he knew he was probably rushing it, Josh was pretty sure that Amy was thinking along exactly the same lines as he was. 'I think we've just found two kids who need us to be their family.'

'It's a lot to ask, Josh. Teenagers aren't easy, and neither are babies. Plus this thing between you and me—this is all really new.'

He took her hand. 'But it's also really *right*. With you, I feel as if I've found the place where I fit.'

'Me, too.' She tightened her fingers round his. 'There are probably regulations against me fostering her because I'm her form tutor.'

'There's probably a way to cut through the red tape. And we know someone who'll help,' Josh pointed out. 'Because this is a solution where we're all going to win. We all get a family. You're right in that it's not going to be plain sailing, but we can work on it together.' He paused. 'So. Your flat or mine?'

'That's a problem. Both our flats have only one bedroom, and we're going to need at least two—if not three,' Amy said.

'So either we rent out our flats and then take out a lease on a bigger place,' he said. 'Or we could sell the flats, pool our resources and buy a bigger place together.'

She took a sip of coffee. 'You know, a week ago, I was on my own and focused on my career. If someone had told me that just one week later I'd find someone who feels like my missing half and we'd be talking about house-hunting together, I would never have believed them.'

'Yeah, it's fast. Scarily fast.' He took a deep breath. 'And it was fast for me with Kelly, too, and you know that went wrong, so I'm not surprised you're having doubts. Though, just so you know, I'm not having doubts.'

'I'm not having doubts, either. Doing things fast went wrong for you last time; but doing things slowly went wrong for me the last two times. So maybe we just need to forget about the past. We're both older and wiser, and we're not going to repeat our mistakes,' she said. 'We're looking to the future. Together.'

'You, me, and a ready-made family of a teen and a baby. Works for me,' he said. 'It's not going to be perfect, and we're going to have downs as well as ups, but I'm sure this is the right thing.'

'Me, too,' Amy agreed.

'Now we just need to sort out the red tape.'

'Do you want to call Jane, or shall I?' Amy asked.

'We'll do it together,' he said. 'Just as we're going to tackle everything else.'

She took out her phone, switching it to speaker mode so Josh could hear as well, and called Jane.

'Jane? It's Amy and Josh. We were wondering—can we see you today, please?'

'Sorry, no can do. I'm afraid I'm stacked up with meetings,' Jane said.

'But you have to have a lunch break, right?' Josh asked.

'Right.' Jane sounded wary.

'If we meet you with sandwiches and coffee,' Josh said, 'can we steal the ten minutes it would've taken you to queue up to get your coffee?'

Jane gave a wry laugh. 'You obviously both really want to talk to me.'

'We do,' they said in unison.

'All right. One o'clock in the picnic bit in the park opposite my office—not because I'm trying to wriggle out of anything but, if I meet you in the office, someone's bound to drag me off into another meeting,' she said.

'The park's perfect,' Amy said.

She gave them the details; at one o'clock, Josh and Amy were waiting in the park with sandwiches, cake and coffee.

Five minutes later, Jane rushed over. 'Sorry. I couldn't get off the phone.' Her eyes widened at the array of food. 'Wow. I should let you hijack my lunch break more often.'

'We forgot to ask you what you like, so there's a variety,' Josh said.

'Fabulous. Thank you. Right. So what do you want to talk to me about?' she asked, gratefully accepting the paper cup of coffee that Amy handed to her.

'We've been to see Freya,' Amy said.

'Which is *not* what I would've advised,' Jane said.

Josh spread his hands. 'We happened to be in the area.'

Jane scoffed. 'Right.'

'She told us she doesn't want to go back to live with her mum,' Amy said.

'I don't particularly want her doing that, either,' Jane said grimly.

'But she's worried about who's going to take in a fifteen-year-old with a baby,' Josh said.

'And we have a solution,' Amy added with a smile. 'Something that means everyone wins.'

'I have no idea how you get accepted as a foster parent,' Josh said, 'but we were hoping you'd know how to cut through all the red tape and fast-track it for us.'

Jane blinked. 'Hang on. Are you telling me that you'd be prepared to foster both Freya and Hope?'

'Together,' Amy said. 'Yes.'

'But...' Jane looked confused. 'Last week, when I first met you and you agreed to look after Hope, you said you were just neighbours and barely knew each other.'

'That,' Josh said, 'was before the Christmas that changed everything. We want to be a family. And we want Freya and Hope included in that family.'

'Which is a really good start. Though you'll both have to go through an assessment process,' Jane said, 'and, if you pass—though I'm pretty sure you will—then you'll need training.'

'That's fine. School holidays won't be a problem,' Amy said, 'given that I'm a teacher.'

'You'll need a spare room,' Jane warned. 'And, with you both being in separate flats, probably one of you will have to be named as the main foster carer.'

'We've already talked about that,' Josh said, 'and we plan to go house-hunting for a place big enough for all of us.'

'It's a new year and new beginning,' Amy said. 'For all of us.'

'Then in that case,' Jane said, 'I'll do everything I can to help make this work.'

Amy and Josh lifted their paper cups of coffee in a toast. 'We'll drink to that. Our new family.'

EPILOGUE

A year later—Christmas Eve

'YOU LOOK AMAZING,' Amy's father, George, said outside the hospital chapel.

'Utterly gorgeous.' Amy's mother, Patricia, tweaked Amy's headdress and veil. 'And so do you two,' she added to Freya, who was carrying Hope in one arm and a bouquet in her free hand. 'My three girls. Look at you. And our little Hope looks so cute in that dress.'

Amy blinked back the tears. Her parents had taken Freya and Hope straight to their hearts and insisted that they were part of the family, even before the fostering had become official.

'We need a picture, George,' Patricia said.

'All four of you together. *My* girls,' he added proudly.

They posed for the photograph, and then Patricia went to sit in the front row at the chapel.

'Ready for this?' George asked softly.

'Absolutely ready,' Amy said. 'How about you, Freya?'

'Bring it on,' the teenager said with a smile.

* * *

Josh looked back down the aisle. The hospital chapel was packed with their family and friends; and his brother was standing beside him as his best man. Since Amy had been in his life, his relationship with his family had been a lot less prickly; although his family had been unnerved at first by his unconventional ready-made family, Amy had made them see that it worked and Josh was actually happy.

Amy's brother Scott was sitting at the piano; when Patricia sat down in the front row of the chapel, Scott took his cue to begin playing the largo from 'Winter' from Vivaldi's *Four Seasons*.

And then the door opened and Amy walked down the aisle towards him on her father's arm. Her short veil was held in place by a narrow crown of deep red roses, to match the ones in her bouquet, and she wore a very simple cream ankle-length dress. Behind them walked Freya as the bridesmaid, wearing a dark red version of Amy's dress, holding Hope in her arms, also wearing a dark red version of Amy's dress, but with the addition of a cream fluffy bolero to keep her warm.

My family, Josh thought.

And from today it would be that little bit more official, with Amy becoming Mrs Farnham.

Christmas Eve was the perfect day for their wedding day. A year since they'd first got to know each other properly. The anniversary of the beginning of the happiest days of their lives—and it would only get better.

'I love you, Mrs-Farnham-to-be,' he mouthed as Amy joined him at the altar.

'I love you, too,' she mouthed back.

They'd chosen to sing carols rather than hymns, picking the happiest ones that everyone knew—'Silent Night', 'Hark the Herald Angels Sing' and 'O Little Town of Bethlehem'.

And, after the ceremony, everyone in the congregation sang 'All You Need Is Love', accompanied by Scott on the piano, as Amy and Josh walked down the aisle for the first time as a married couple.

They'd booked the reception at the hotel across the road from the hospital, with a simple sit-down meal for their family and closest friends; but they'd also invited Jane the social worker and Freya's mum.

After the meal, Amy's father stood up. 'I'd like to thank everyone for coming today. Patricia and I are absolutely delighted to welcome Josh into our family—he's a lovely man, a great doctor and a fantastic artist. But, most of all, he makes my daughter happy, and as parents that's all that Patricia and I want. And I'm also delighted that we have Freya and Hope as well. So I'd like everyone to raise their glasses: I give you Josh, Amy, Freya and Hope.'

Once everyone had echoed the toast, Josh stood up. 'I'd like to thank George, Patricia, Scott and Rae for making me feel like part of their family from the first moment they met me. Today's a special day for me—it's the first Christmas Eve since my graduation where I haven't been on duty in the Emergency Department. That means this is my first real family Christmas, and I'm loving every second of it so far. Today's the first anniversary of the beginning of the happiest time in my life. So I'd like you to raise a glass to my beautiful bride, Amy, who's made me the happiest man alive, and to our beautiful bridesmaid and ring-bearer, Freya and Hope, who bring joy to our lives every day.'

'Amy, Freya and Hope,' everyone chorused.

Josh's brother Stuart stood up next. 'It's really good to see my brother so happy. And I couldn't be more thrilled to welcome Amy, Freya and Hope to our family. Because of them, my son and my two nieces are getting to see much more of their uncle. They're living proof that no matter how unconventional a family might seem, if they love each other, it'll all work out.' He smiled. 'I have a feeling the rest of the speeches aren't going to be very conventional, either. So, instead of telling you stories about Josh, I'm going to hand you over to his colleagues and Amy's to tell you what their life is like.'

The head of the music department at Amy's school stood up. 'Most of the time I get my classes to sing this as a cumulative song, but today we're doing just the last verse for you, because we'd like you to know what Christmas Eve is usually like for a maths teacher and an emergency department doctor.'

Josh took Amy's hand and squeezed it.

'Did you know about this?' she asked.

He grinned. 'Just a little bit.'

The head of music was joined by five more of Amy's colleagues and six of Josh's. Together, they sang the first line: 'On the twelfth day of Christmas, for Josh and Amy...'

Then each sang a line in turn and sat down again.

Twelve lesson-plannings,
Eleven past papers,
Ten simultaneous equations,

Nine books to mark,
Eight probabilities,
Seven bits of algebra,
Six Colles' fractures,
Five turkey carvers!
Four black eyes,
Three throwing up,
Two broken ankles,
And a bead up a toddler's nose.

Everyone applauded, and the singers all stood up again to take a bow.

Then it was Amy's turn to speak. 'I'd like to thank the Farnhams for taking us all to their hearts and making us part of their family. Thank you very much to our colleagues for their revue—absolutely spot on. And I'm afraid there's a little bit more singing now, because it's a very special person's first birthday. Without her, Josh and I might never have met properly, so please join with us in singing a very special song for Hope.'

At her signal, one of the waitresses brought out a chocolate cake in the shape of a figure one, with a single candle, and placed it on the table in front of Freya and the toddler.

Everyone sang happy birthday to Hope; Freya helped her daughter blow out the candle. When everyone cheered, Hope clapped her hands and looked thoroughly pleased with herself.

Then Freya stood up. 'I know it's not usual for the bridesmaid to make a speech, and I'm not very good at talking in public, but there's something I really want to say. Last Christmas was the worst of my life, and…' She paused, her face turning bright red, and then took a deep breath. 'And I thought I'd never see my baby again. This Christmas, life couldn't be any better. I'm thrilled to be celebrating Josh and Amy getting married, as well as Hope's first birthday. Amy's taught me so much and Josh has inspired me to become a nurse. They've both been really fantastic foster parents—and they've helped make things better with my mum, too. And Mum helped me to make something special for them.'

Freya's mother quietly took a parcel from beneath the table and handed it to Freya, who walked over to Amy and Josh and hugged them both before giving the parcel to them.

Together, they opened it to find the most beautiful frame containing a photograph of the four of them from the summer, on their first day in their new house.

Everyone clapped; Freya's face turned bright red again and she sat down again very quickly.

Josh and Amy stood up together, then. 'Thank you, Freya. It's the perfect present,' Josh said.

'And we're so glad that everyone's here today to share our special day with us,' Amy added.

'We'll cut the cake in a second,' Josh said.

'But before we start the dancing we want everyone to just chill out, relax and have a good time,' Amy finished. 'Because we really want to come and say hello to everyone and have a chat. Just have a drink while you're waiting for cake.'

Everyone clapped, and they posed for photographs before they cut the cake.

Freya's mum hugged both of them when they got to her. 'Thank you both so much. It's because of you that I'm starting to rebuild my relationship with Freya. I know it's not going to be easy, but your support means a lot to both of us. Thank you for doing for her what I was…' She grimaced. 'Well, too stupid to see. And I still can't believe you actually invited me to your wedding.'

'You're Freya's mum. That makes you part of our family,' Amy said, and hugged her.

'Everyone makes mistakes,' Josh said quietly, 'and everyone deserves a second chance. I'm really glad you came, because I think you need to be here on your granddaughter's first birthday—and it means a lot to Freya and Hope that you're here.'

Freya's mum swallowed hard. 'Thank you.'

Everyone seemed to be happy for them, Amy thought. And Jane also greeted them both with a hug. 'You two are my big success story,' she said. 'I remember last Christmas. And seeing you with Freya and Hope—well, you really make me feel my job's worthwhile. On the days when everything's going wrong, I think of you two and it makes everything a lot better.'

When they'd finally managed to have a word with everyone and were back in their seats at the top table, Josh's brother Stuart stood up.

'Ladies and gentlemen—it's time for the first dance,' he said. 'I have it on very reliable information that our Josh sings this to stop babies crying, and it actually works, so see me later if you want to hire him.'

Everyone laughed.

'But, seriously, this is the perfect song for the perfect couple at a perfect Christmas wedding. I give you Josh and Amy,' he said, and the DJ began to play 'All I Want for Christmas is You'.

Josh took his bride in his arms and danced her round

the floor. 'I love you,' he said, 'and this is the best Christmas ever.'

'I love you, too,' Amy said. 'And you're right. Today, I have everything I've ever wanted: you and our new family.'

'You and our new family,' he echoed, and kissed her.

* * * * *

THE HOLIDAY GIFT

BY
RAEANNE THAYNE

First Published in Great Britain 2016
By Mills & Boon, an imprint of HarperCollins*Publishers*
1 London Bridge Street, London, SE1 9GF

© 2016 RaeAnne Thayne

ISBN: 978-0-263-92041-3

23-1216

Our policy is to use papers that are natural, renewable and recyclable products and made from wood grown in sustainable forests. The logging and manufacturing processes conform to the legal environmental regulations of the country of origin.

Printed and bound in Spain
by CPI, Barcelona

RaeAnne Thayne finds inspiration in the beautiful northern Utah mountains, where the *New York Times* and *USA TODAY* bestselling author lives with her husband and three children. Her books have won numerous honors, including RITA® Award nominations from Romance Writers of America and a Career Achievement Award from *RT Book Reviews*. RaeAnne loves to hear from readers and can be contacted through her website, www.raeannethayne.com.

To Lisa Townsend, trainer extraordinaire,
who is gorgeous inside and out. And to Jennie, Trudy,
Karen, Becky, Jill and everyone else in our group for
your example, your encouragement, your friendship,
your laughter—and especially for making me look
forward to workouts (except the burpees—
I'll never look forward to those!).

Chapter One

Something was wrong, but Faith Dustin didn't have the first idea what.

She glanced at Chase Brannon again, behind the wheel of his pickup truck. Sunglasses shielded his eyes but his strong jaw was still flexed, his shoulders tense.

Since they had left the Idaho Falls livestock auction forty-five minutes earlier, heading back to Cold Creek Canyon, the big rancher hadn't smiled once and had answered most of her questions in monosyllables, his mind clearly a million miles away.

Faith frowned. He wasn't acting at all like himself. They were frequent travel companions, visiting various livestock auctions around the region at least once or twice a month for the last few years. They had even gone on a few buying trips to Denver together, an eight-hour drive from their little corner of eastern Idaho. He was her oldest friend—and had been since she and her sisters came to live with their aunt and uncle nearly two decades ago.

In many ways, she and Chase were really a team and comingled their ranch operations, since his ranch, Brannon Ridge, bordered the Star N on two sides.

Usually when they traveled, they never ran out of things to talk about. Her kids and their current dramas, real or imagined; his daughter, Addie, who lived with her mother in Boise; Faith's sisters and their growing families. Their ranches, the community, the price of beef, their future plans. It was all grist for their conversational mill. She valued his opinion—often she would run ideas past him—and she wanted to think he rated hers as highly.

The drive to Idaho Falls earlier that morning had seemed just like usual, filled with conversation and their usual banter. Everything had seemed normal during the auction. He had stayed right by her side, a quiet, steady support, while she engaged in—and eventually won—a fierce bidding war for a beautiful paint filly with excellent barrel racing bloodlines.

That horse, intended as a Christmas gift for her twelve-year-old daughter, Louisa, was the whole reason they had gone to the auction. Yes, she'd been a little carried away by winning the auction so that she'd hugged him hard and kissed him smack on the lips, but surely that wasn't what was bothering him. She'd kissed and hugged him tons of times.

Okay, maybe she had been careful not to be so casual

with her affection for him the last six or seven months, for reasons she didn't want to explore, but she couldn't imagine he would go all cold and cranky over something as simple as a little kiss.

No. His mood had shifted after that, but all her subtle efforts to wiggle out what was wrong had been for nothing.

His mood certainly matched the afternoon. Faith glanced out at the uniformly gray sky and the few random, hard-edged snowflakes clicking against the windshield. The weather wasn't pleasant but it wasn't horrible either. The snowflakes weren't sticking to the road yet, anyway, though she expected they would see at least a few inches on the ground by morning.

Even the familiar festive streets of Pine Gulch— wreaths hanging on the streetlamps and each downtown business decorated with lights and window dressings— didn't seem to lift his dark mood.

When he hit the edge of town and turned into Cold Creek Canyon toward home, she decided to try one last time to figure out what might be bothering him.

"Did something happen at the auction?"

He glanced away from the road briefly, the expression in his silver-blue eyes shielded by the amber lenses of his sunglasses. "Why would you think that?"

She studied his dearly familiar profile, struck by his full mouth and his tanned, chiseled features—covered now with just a hint of dark afternoon shadow. Funny, how she saw him just about every single day but was sometimes taken by surprise all over again by how great-looking he was.

With his dark, wavy hair covered by the black Stetson he wore, that slow, sexy smile, and his broad shoulders and slim hips, he looked rugged and dangerous and completely male. It was no wonder the waitresses at the café next to the auction house always fought each other to serve their table.

She shifted her attention away from such ridiculous things and back to the conversation. "I don't know. Maybe because that's the longest sentence you've given me since we left Idaho Falls. You've replied to everything else with either a grunt or a monosyllable."

Beneath that afternoon shadow, a muscle clenched in his jaw. "That doesn't mean anything happened. Maybe I'm just not in a chatty mood."

She certainly had days like that. Heaven knew she'd had her share of blue days over the last two and a half years. Through every one of them, Chase had been her rock.

"Nothing wrong with that, I guess. Are you sure that's all? Was it something Beckett McKinley said? I saw him corner you at lunch."

He glanced over at her briefly and again she wished she could see the expression behind his sunglasses. "He wanted to know how I like the new baler I bought this year and he also wanted my opinion on a…personal matter. I told him I liked the baler fine but told him the other thing wasn't any of my damn business."

She blinked at both his clipped tone and the language. Chase didn't swear very often. When he did, there was usually a good reason.

"Now you've got my curiosity going. What kind of

personal matter would Beck want your opinion about? The only thing I can think the man needs is a nanny for those hellion boys of his."

He didn't say anything for a long moment, just watched the road and those snowflakes spitting against windshield. When he finally spoke, his voice was clipped. "It was about you."

She stared. "Me?"

Chase's hands tightened on the steering wheel. "He wants to ask you out, specifically to go as his date to the stockgrowers association's Christmas party on Friday."

If he had just told her Beck wanted her to dress up like a Christmas angel and jump from his barn roof, she wouldn't have been more surprised—and likely would have been far less panicky.

"I… He…what?"

"Beck wants to take you to the Christmas party this weekend. I understand there's going to be dancing and a full dinner this year."

Beck McKinley. The idea of dating the man took her by complete surprise. Yes, he was a great guy, with a prosperous ranch on the other side of Pine Gulch. She considered him a good friend but she had never *once* thought of him in romantic terms.

The unexpected paradigm shift wasn't the only thing bothering her about what Chase had just said.

"Hold on. If he wanted to take me to the party, why wouldn't Beck just ask me himself instead of feeling like he has to go through you first?"

That muscle flexed in his jaw again. "You'll have to ask him that."

The things he wasn't saying in this conversation would fill a radio broadcast. She frowned as Chase pulled into the drive leading to his ranch. "You told him I'm already going with you, didn't you?"

He didn't answer for a long moment. "No," he finally said. "I didn't."

Unease twanged through her, the same vague sense that had haunted her at stray moments for several months. Something was off between her and Chase and, for the life of her, she couldn't put a finger on it.

"Oh. Did you already make plans?" She forced a cheerful smile. "We've gone together the last few years so I just sort of assumed we would go together again this year but I guess we should have talked about it. If you already have something going, don't worry about me. Seriously. I don't mind going by myself. I'll have plenty of other friends there I can sit with. Or I could always skip it and stay home with the kids. Jenna McRaven does a fantastic job with the food and I always enjoy the company of other grown-ups, but if you've got a hot date lined up, I'm perfectly fine."

As she said the words, she tasted the lie in them. Was this weird ache in her stomach because she had been looking forward to the evening out—or because she didn't like the idea of him with a hot date?

"I don't have a date, hot or otherwise," he growled as he pulled the pickup and trailer to a stop next to a small paddock near the barn of the Brannon Ridge Ranch.

She eased back in the bench seat, a curious relief seeping through her. "Good. That's that. We can go together, just like always. It will be a fun night out for us."

Though she knew him well enough to know something was still on his mind, he said nothing as he pulled off his sunglasses and hooked them on the rearview mirror. What did his silence mean? Didn't he *want* to go with her?

"Faith," he began, but suddenly she didn't want to hear what he had to say.

"We'd better get the beautiful girl in your trailer unloaded before the kids get home."

She opened her door and jumped out before he could answer her. Yes, sometimes she was like her son, Barrett, who would rather hide out in his room all day and miss dinner than be scolded for something he'd done. She didn't like to face bad things. It was a normal reaction, she told herself. Hadn't she already had to face enough bad things in her life?

After a moment, Chase climbed out after her and came around to unhook the back of the trailer. The striking black-and-white paint yearling whinnied as he led her out into the patchy snow.

"She's a beauty, isn't she?" Faith said, struck all over again by the horse's elegant lines.

"Yeah," Chase said. Again with the monosyllables. She sighed.

"Thanks for letting me keep her here for a couple of weeks. Louisa will be so shocked on Christmas morning."

"Shouldn't be a problem."

He guided the horse into the pasture, where his own favorite horse, Tor, immediately trotted over as Faith closed the gate behind them. As soon as Chase unhooked the young horse from her lead line, she raced to the other side of the pasture, mane and tail flying out behind her.

She was fast. That was the truth. Grateful for her own cowboy hat that shielded her face from the worst of the frost-tipped snowflakes, Faith watched the horse race to the other corner of the pasture and back, obviously overflowing with energy after the stress of a day at the auction and then a trailer ride with strangers.

"Do you think she's too much horse for Lou?" she asked while Chase patted Tor beside her.

He looked at the paint and then down at Faith. "She comes from prime barrel racing stock. That's what Lou wants to do. For twelve, she's a strong rider. Yeah, the horse is only green broke but Seth Dalton can train a horse to do just about anything but recite its ABCs."

"I guess that's true. It was nice of him to agree to take her, with his crazy training schedule."

"He's a good friend."

"He is," she agreed. "Though I know he only agreed to do it as a favor to you."

"Maybe it was a favor to you," he commented as he pulled a bale of hay over and opened it inside the pasture for the horses.

"Maybe," she answered. All three Dalton brothers had been wonderful neighbors and good friends to her. They and others in the close-knit ranching community in Cold Creek Canyon and around Pine Gulch had stepped up in a hundred different ways over the last two and a half years since Travis died.

She would have been lost without any of them, but especially without Chase.

That vague unease slithered through her again. What was wrong between them? And how could she fix it?

She didn't have the first clue.

What was a guy supposed to do?

Ever since Beck McKinley cornered him at the diner to talk about taking Faith to the stockgrowers' holiday party, Chase hadn't been able to think straight. He felt like the other guy had grabbed his face and dunked it in an ice-cold water trough, then kicked him in the gut for good measure.

For a full ten seconds, he had stared at Beck as a host of emotions galloped through him faster than a pack of wild horses spooked by a thunderstorm.

Beckett McKinley wanted to date Faith. *Chase's* Faith.

"She's great. That's all," Beck had said into the suddenly tense silence. "It's been more than two years since Travis died, right? I just thought maybe she'd be ready to start getting out there."

Chase had thought for a minute his whole face had turned numb, especially his tongue. It made it tough for him to get any words out at all—or maybe that was the ice-cold coating around his brain.

"Why are you asking me?" he had finally managed to say.

If possible, Beck had looked even more uncomfortable. "The two of you are always together. Here at the auction, at the feed store, at the diner in town. I know you're neighbors and you've been friends for a long time. But if there's something more than that, I don't want to be an ass and step on toes. You don't have to tell me what happens to bulls who wander into somebody else's pen."

It was all he could do not to haul off and deck the guy for the implied comparison that Faith was just some lonely heifer, waiting for some smooth-talking bull to wander by.

Instead, he had managed to grip his hands into fists, all while one thought kept echoing through his head.

Not again.

He thought he was giving her time to grieve, to make room in her heart for someone else besides Travis Dustin, the man she had loved since she was a traumatized girl trying to carve out a new home for her and her sisters.

Chase had been too slow once before. He had been a steady friend and confidant from the beginning. He figured he had all the time in the world as he waited for her to heal and to settle into life in Pine Gulch. She had been so young, barely sixteen. He wasn't much older, not yet nineteen, and had been busy with his own struggles. Even then, he had been running his family's ranch on his own while his father lay dying.

For six months, he offered friendship to Faith, fully expecting that one day when both of them were in a better place, he could start moving things to a different level.

And then Travis Dustin came home for the summer

to help out Claude and Mary, the distant relatives who had raised him his last few years of high school.

Chase's father was in his last few agonizing weeks of life from lung cancer that summer. While he was busy coping with that and accepting his new responsibilities on the ranch, Travis had wasted no time sweeping in and stealing Faith's heart. By the time Chase woke up and realized what was happening, it was too late. His two closest friends were in love with each other and he couldn't do a damn thing about it.

He could have fought for her, he supposed, but it was clear from the beginning that Travis made her happy. After everything she and her sisters had been through, she deserved to find a little peace.

Instead, he had managed to put his feelings away and maintain his friendship with both of them. He had even tried to move on himself and date other women, with disastrous consequences.

Beck McKinley was a good guy. A solid rancher, a devoted father, a pillar of the community. Any woman would probably be very lucky to have him, as long as she could get past those hellion boys of his.

Maybe McKinley was exactly the kind of guy she wanted. The thought gnawed at him, but he took some small solace in remembering that she hadn't seemed all that enthusiastic at the idea of going out with him.

Didn't matter. He knew damn well it was only a matter of time before she found someone she *did* want to go out with. If not Beck, some other smooth-talking cowboy would sweep in.

He hadn't fought for her last time. Instead, he had

stood by like a damn statue and watched her fall in love with his best friend.

He wouldn't go through that again. It was time he made a move—but what if he made the wrong one and ruined everything between them?

He felt like a man given a choice between a hangman's noose and a firing squad. He was damned either way.

He was still trying to figure out what to do when she shifted from watching the young horse dance around the pasture in the cold December air. Faith gazed up at the overcast sky, still dribbling out the occasional stray snowflake.

"I probably should get back. The kids will be out of school soon and I'm sure you have plenty of things of your own to do. You don't have to walk me back," she said when he started to head in that direction behind her. "Stay and unhitch the horse trailer if you need to."

"It can keep. I'll walk you back up to your truck. I've got to plug in my phone anyway."

A couple of his ranch dogs came out from the barn to say hello as they walked the short distance to his house. He reached down and petted them both, in total sympathy. He felt like a ranch dog to her: a constant, steady companion with a few useful skills that came in handy once in a while.

Would she ever be able to see him as anything more?

"Thanks again, Chase," Faith said when they reached her own pickup truck—the one she had insisted on driving over that morning, even though he told her he could easily pick her up and drop her back off at the Star N.

"You're welcome," he said.

"Seriously, I was out of my depth. Horses aren't exactly my area of expertise. Who knows, I might have brought home a nag. As always, I don't know what I would do without you."

He could feel tension clutch at his shoulders again. "Not true," he said, his voice more abrupt than he intended. "You didn't need me. Not really. You'd already done your research and knew what you wanted in a barrel racer. You just needed somebody to back you up."

She smiled as they reached her pickup truck and a pale shaft of sunlight somehow managed to pierce the cloud cover and land right on her delicate features, so soft and lovely it made his heart hurt.

"I'm so lucky that somebody is always you," she said.

He let out a breath, fighting the urge to pull her into his arms. He didn't have that right—nor could he let things go on as they were.

"About the stockgrowers' party," he began.

If he hadn't been looking, he might have missed the leap of something that looked suspiciously like fear in her green eyes before she shifted her gaze away from him.

"Really, it doesn't bother me to skip it this year if you want to make other plans."

"I don't want to skip it," he growled. "I want to go. With you. On a date."

He intended to stress the last word, to make it plain this wouldn't be two buddies just hanging out together, like they always did. As a result, the word took on unnatural proportions and he nearly snapped it out until it arced between them like an arrow twanged from a crossbow.

Eyes wide, she gazed at him for a long moment, clearly startled by his vehemence. After a moment, she nodded. "Okay. That's settled, then. We can figure out the details later."

Nothing was settled. He needed to tell her *date* was the operative word here, that he didn't want to take her to the party as her neighbor and friend who gave her random advice on a barrel racing horse for her daughter or helped her with the hay season.

He wanted the right to hold her—to dance with her and flirt and whisper soft, sexy words in her ear.

How the hell could he tell her that, after all this time, when he had so carefully cultivated a safe, casual relationship that was the exact opposite of what he really wanted? Before he could figure that out, an SUV he didn't recognize drove up the lane toward his house.

"Were you expecting company?" she asked.

"Don't think so." He frowned as the car pulled up beside them—and his frown intensified when the passenger door opened and a girl jumped out, then raced toward him. "Daddy!"

Chapter Two

He stared at his eleven-year-old daughter, dressed to the nines in an outfit more suited to a photo shoot for a children's clothing store than for a working cattle ranch.

"Adaline! What are you doing here? I didn't expect to see you until next weekend."

"I know, Dad! Isn't it great? We get extra time together—maybe even two whole weeks! Mom pulled me out of school until after Christmas. Isn't that awesome? My teachers are going to email me all my homework so I don't miss too much—not that they ever do anything the last few weeks before Christmas vacation anyway but waste time showing movies and doing busywork and stuff."

That sounded like a direct quote from her mother, who had little respect for the educational system, even the expensive private school she insisted on sending their daughter to.

As if on cue, his ex-wife climbed out of the driver's side of what must be a new vehicle, judging by the temporary license plates in the window.

She looked uncharacteristically disordered, with her sweater askew and her hair a little messy in back where she must have been leaning against the headrest as she drove.

"I'm so glad you're home," she said. "We took a chance. I've been trying to call you all afternoon. Why didn't you answer?"

"My phone ran out of juice and I forgot to take the charger to the auction with us. What's going on?"

He knew it had to be something dramatic for her to bring Addie all this way on an unscheduled midweek visit.

Cindy frowned. "My mother had a stroke early this morning and she's in the hospital in Idaho Falls."

"Oh, no! I hadn't heard. I'm so sorry."

He had tried very hard to earn the approval of his in-laws but the president of the Pine Gulch bank and his wife had been very slow to warm up to him. He didn't know if they had disliked him because Cindy had been pregnant when they married or because they didn't think a cattle rancher with cow manure on his boots was good enough for their precious only child.

They had reached a peace accord of sorts after Addie came along. Still, he almost thought his and Cindy's divorce had been a relief to them—and he had no doubt they had been thrilled at her second marriage to an eminently successful oral surgeon in Boise.

"The doctors say it appears to be a mini stroke. They suspect it's not the first one so they want to keep her for observation for a few days. My dad said I didn't have to come down but it seemed like the right thing to do," Cindy said. "Considering I was coming this way anyway, I didn't think you would mind having extra visitation with Addie, especially since she won't be here over the holidays."

He was aware of a familiar pang in his chest, probably no different from what most part-time divorced fathers felt at not being able to live with their children all the time. Holidays were the worst.

"Sure. Extra time is always great."

Cindy turned to Faith with that hard look she always wore when she saw the two of them together. His ex-wife had never said anything but he suspected she had long guessed the feelings he had tried to bury after Faith and Travis got married.

"We're interrupting," she said. "I'm sorry."

"Not at all," Faith assured her. "Please don't be sorry. I'm the one who's sorry about your mother."

"Thanks," Cindy said, her voice cool. "We spent an hour at the hospital before we came out here and she seems in good spirits. Doctors just want to keep her for observation to see if they can figure out what's going on. Dad is kind of a mess right now, which is why I thought it would be a good idea for me to stay with him, at least for the first few days."

"That sounds like a good idea."

"Thanks for taking Addie. Sorry to drop her off without calling first. I did try."

"It's no problem at all. I'm thrilled to have her."

The sad truth was, they got along and seemed to parent together better now that they were divorced than during the difficult five years of their marriage, though things still weren't perfect.

"I packed enough for a week. To be honest, I don't know what I grabbed, since I was kind of a mess this morning. Keith was worried about me driving alone but he had three surgeries scheduled today and couldn't come with me. His patients needed him."

"He's a busy man," Chase said. What else *could* he say? It would have been terribly hypocritical to lambast another man in the husband department when Chase had been so very lousy at it.

"I should get back to the hospital. Thanks, Chase. You're a lifesaver."

"No problem."

"I'm so sorry about your mother," Faith said.

"Thank you. I appreciate that."

Cindy opened the hatchback of the SUV and pulled out Addie's familiar pink suitcase. He hated the tangible reminder that his daughter had to live out of a suitcase half her life.

After setting the suitcase on the sidewalk, Cindy went through her usual drawn-out farewell routine with Addie that ended in a big hug and a sloppy kiss, then climbed into her SUV and drove away.

"My feet are cold," Addie announced calmly, apparently not fazed at all to watch her mother leave, despite the requisite drama. "I'm going to take my suitcase to my room and change my clothes."

She headed to the house without waiting for him to answer, leaving him alone with Faith.

"That was a curveball I wasn't expecting this afternoon,"

"Strokes can be scary," Faith said. "It sounds like Carol's was a mild one, though, which I'm sure is a relief to everyone. At least you'll get to spend a little extra time with Addie."

"True. Always a bonus."

He had plenty of regrets about his life but his wise, funny, kind daughter was the one amazing thing his lousy marriage had produced.

"I know this was a busy week for you," Faith said. "If you need help with her, she's welcome to spend time at the Star N. Louisa would be completely thrilled."

He had appointments all week with suppliers, the vet and his accountant, but he could take her with him. She was a remarkably adaptable child.

"The only time I might need help is Friday night. Think Aunt Mary would mind if she stayed at your place with Lou and Barrett while we're at the party?"

Her forehead briefly furrowed in confusion. "Oh. I almost forgot about that. Look, the situation has changed. If you'd rather stay home with Addie, I completely understand. I can tag along with Wade and Caroline Dalton or Justin and Ashley Hartford. Or, again, I can always just skip it."

Was she looking for excuses not to go with him? He didn't want to believe that. "I asked you out. I want to go, as long as Mary doesn't mind one more at your place."

"Addie's never any trouble. I'm sure Mary will be fine with it. I'll talk to her," she promised. "If she can't do it, I'm sure all the kids could hang out with Hope or Celeste for the evening."

Her sisters and their husbands lived close to the Star N and often helped with Barrett and Louisa, just as Faith helped out with their respective children.

"I'll be in touch later in the week to work out the details."

"Sounds good." She glanced at her watch. "I really do need to go. Thanks again for your help with the horse."

"You're welcome."

As she climbed into the Star N king-cab pickup, he was struck by how small and delicate she looked compared to the big truck.

Physically, she might be slight—barely five-four and slender—but she was tough as nails. Over the last two and a half years, she had worked tirelessly to drag the ranch from the brink. He had tried to take some of the burden from her but there was only so much she would let him do.

He stepped forward so she couldn't close the door yet.

"One last thing."

"What's that?"

Heart pounding, he leaned in to face her. He wanted her to see his expression. He wanted no ambiguity about his intentions.

"You need to be clear on one thing before Friday. I said it earlier but in all the confusion with Addie showing up, I'm not sure it registered completely. As far as I'm concerned, this is a date."

"Sure. We're going together. What else would it be?"

"I mean a date-date. I want to go out with you where we're not only good friends hanging out on a Friday night or two neighboring ranchers carpooling to the same event. I want you to be my date, with everything that goes along with that."

There. She couldn't mistake *that*.

He saw a host of emotions quickly cross her features—shock, uncertainty and a wild flare of panic. "Chase, I—"

He could see she wasn't even going to give him a chance. She was ready to throw up barriers to the idea before he even had a chance. Frustration coiled through him, sharp as barbed wire fencing.

"It's been two and a half years since Travis died."

Her hands clamped tight onto the steering wheel as if it were a bull rider's strap and she had to hang on or she would fall off and be trampled. "Yes. I believe I'm fully aware of that."

"You're going to have to enter the dating scene at some point. You've already got cowboys clamoring to ask you out. McKinley is just the first one to step up, but he won't be the last. Why not ease into it by going out with somebody you already know?"

"You."

"Why not?"

Instead of answering, she turned the tables on him.

"You and Cindy have been divorced for years. Why are you suddenly interested in dating again?"

"Maybe I'm tired of being alone." That, at least, was the truth, just not the whole truth.

"So this would be like a...trial run for both of us? A way to dip our toes into the water without jumping in headfirst?"

No. He had jumped in a long, long time ago and had just been treading water, waiting for her.

He couldn't tell her that. Not yet.

"Sure, if you want to look at it that way," he said instead.

He knew her well enough that he could almost watch her brain whir as she tried to think through all the ramifications. She overthought everything. It was by turns endearing and endlessly frustrating.

Finally she seemed to have sifted through the possibilities and come up with a scenario she could live with. "You're such a good friend, Chase. You've always got my back. You want to help make this easier for me, just like you helped me buy the horse for Louisa. Thank you."

He opened his mouth to say that wasn't at all his intention but he could see by the stubborn set of her jaw that she wasn't ready to hear that yet.

"I'll talk to Aunt Mary about keeping an eye on the kids on Friday. We can work out the details later. I really do have to go. Thanks again."

Her tone was clearly dismissive. Left with no real choice, he stepped back so she could close the vehicle door.

She was deliberately misunderstanding him and he

didn't know how to argue with her. After all these years of being her friend and so carefully hiding his feelings, how did he convince her he wanted to be more than that?

He had no idea. He only knew he had to try.

Faith refused to let herself panic.

I want you to be my date, with everything that goes along with that.

Despite her best efforts, fear seemed to curl around her insides, coating everything with a thin layer of ice.

She couldn't let things change. End of story. Chase had been her rock for two years, her best friend, the one constant in her crazy, tumultuous life. He had been the first one she had called when she had gone looking for Travis after he didn't answer his cell and found him unconscious and near death, with severe internal injuries and a shattered spine, next to his overturned ATV.

Chase had been there within five minutes and had taken charge of the scene, had called the medics and the helicopter, had been there at the hospital and had held her after the doctors came out with their solemn faces and their sad eyes.

While she had been numb and broken, Chase had stepped in, organizing all the neighbors to bring in the fall harvest. He had helped her clean up and streamline the Star N operation and sell off all the unnecessary stock to keep their head above water those first few months.

Now the ranch was in the black again—thanks in large part to the crash course in smart ranch practices

Chase had given her. She knew perfectly well that without him, there wouldn't *be* a Star N right now or The Christmas Ranch. She and her sisters would have had to sell off the land, the cattle, *everything* to pay their debts.

Travis hadn't been a very good businessman. At his death, she'd found the ranch was seriously overextended with creditors and had been operating under a system of gross inefficiencies for years.

She winced with the guilt the disloyal thought always stirred in her, but it was nothing less than the truth. If her husband hadn't died and things had continued on the same course, the ranch would have gone bankrupt within a few years. Through Chase's extensive help, she had been able to turn things around.

The ranch was doing so much better. The Christmas Ranch—the seasonal attraction started by her uncle and aunt after she and her sisters came to live with them—was finally in the black, too. Hope and her husband, Rafe, had done an amazing job revitalizing it and making it a powerful draw. That success had only been augmented by the wild viral popularity of the charming children's book Celeste had written and Hope had illustrated featuring the ranch's starring attraction, Sparkle the Reindeer.

She couldn't be more proud of her sisters—though she did find it funny that, of the three of them, *Faith* seemed the one most excited that Celeste and Hope had signed an agreement to allow a production company to make an animated movie out of the first Sparkle book.

Despite a few preproduction problems, the process

was currently under way, though the animated movie wouldn't come out for another year. The buzz around it only heightened interest in The Christmas Ranch and led to increased revenue.

The book had helped push The Christmas Ranch to self-sufficiency. Without that steady drain on the Star N side of the family operation, Faith had been able to plow profits back into the cattle ranch operation.

As she drove past the Saint Nicholas Lodge on the way to the ranch house, she spotted both of her sisters' vehicles in the parking lot.

After taking up most of the day at the auction, she had a hundred things to do. As she had told Chase, Barrett and Louisa would be home from school soon. When she could swing it, she liked being there to greet them, to ask about their day and help manage their homework and chore responsibilities.

On a whim, though, she pulled into the parking lot and hurriedly texted both of her children as well as Aunt Mary to tell them she was stopping at the lodge for a moment and would be home soon.

The urge to talk to her sisters was suddenly overwhelming. Hope and Celeste weren't just her sisters, they were her best friends.

She had to park three rows back, which she considered a great sign for a Tuesday afternoon in mid-December.

Tourists from as far away as Boise and Salt Lake City were making the trek here to visit their quaint little Christmas attraction, with its sleigh rides, the reindeer herd, the village—and especially because this was the home of Sparkle.

As far as she was concerned, this was just home.

The familiar scents inside the lodge encircled her the moment she walked inside—cinnamon and vanilla and pine, mixed with old logs and the musty smell of a building that stood empty most of the year.

She heard her younger sisters bickering in the office before she saw them.

"Cry your sad song to someone else," Celeste was saying. "I told you I wasn't going to do it again this year and I won't let you guilt me into it."

"But you did such a great job last year," Hope protested.

"Yes I did," their youngest sister said. "And I swore I wouldn't ever do it again."

Faith poked her head into the office in time to see Hope pout. She was nearly three months pregnant and only just beginning to show.

"It didn't turn out so badly," Hope pointed out. "You ended up with a fabulous husband and a new stepdaughter out of the deal, didn't you?"

"Seriously? You're giving the children's show credit for my marriage to Flynn?"

"Think about it. Would you be married to your hunky contractor right now and deliriously happy if you hadn't directed the show for me last year—and if his daughter hadn't begged to participate?"

It was an excellent point, Faith thought with inward amusement that Celeste didn't appear to share.

"Why can't you do it?" Celeste demanded.

"We are booked solid with tour groups at the ranch until Christmas Eve. I won't have a minute to breathe from now until the New Year—and that's with Rafe making me cut down my hours."

"You knew you were going to be slammed," Celeste said, not at all persuaded. "Talk about procrastination. I can't believe you didn't find somebody to organize the variety show weeks ago!"

"I *had* somebody. Linda Keller told me clear back in September she would do it. I thought we were set, but she fell this morning and broke her arm, which leaves me back at square one. The kids are going to be coming to practice a week from today and I've got absolutely no one to lead them."

Hope shifted her attention to Faith with a considering look that struck fear in her heart.

"Oh, no," she exclaimed. "You can forget that idea right now."

"Why?" Hope pouted. "You love kids and senior citizens both, plus you sing like a dream. You even used to direct the choir at church, which I say makes you the perfect one to run the Christmas show."

She rolled her eyes. Hope knew better than to seriously consider that idea. "Right. Because you know I've got absolutely nothing else going on right now."

"Everyone is busy. That's the problem. Whose idea was it to put on a show at Christmas, the busiest time of the year?"

"Yours." Faith and Celeste answered simultaneously.

Hope sighed. "I know. It just seemed natural for The Christmas Ranch to throw a holiday celebration for the senior citizens. Maybe next year we'll do a Christmas in July kind of thing."

"Except you'll be having a baby in July," Faith pointed out. "And I'll be even more busy during the summer."

"You're right." She looked glum. "Do you have any suggestions for someone else who might be interested in directing it? I would hate to see the pageant fade out, especially after last year was such a smash success, thanks to CeCe. You wouldn't believe how many people have stopped me in town during the past year to tell me how much they enjoyed it and hoped we were doing another one."

"I believe it," Celeste said. "I've had my share of people telling me the same thing. That still doesn't mean I want to run it again."

"I wasn't even involved with the show and I still have people stop me in town to tell me they hope we're doing it again," Faith offered.

"That's because you're a Nichols," Hope said.

"Right. Which to some people automatically means I burp tinsel and have eggnog running through my veins."

Celeste laughed. "You don't?"

"Nope. Hope inherited all the Christmas spirit from Uncle Claude and Aunt Mary."

The sister in question made a face. "That may be true, but it still doesn't give me someone to run the show this year. But never fear. I've got a few ideas up my sleeves."

"I can help," Celeste said. "I just don't want to be the one in charge."

Faith couldn't let her younger sister be the only generous one in the family. She sighed. "Okay. I'll help again, too. But only behind the scenes—and only because you're pregnant and I don't want you to overdo."

Hope's eyes glittered and her smile wobbled. "Oh. You're both going to make me cry and Rafe tells me I've already hit my tear quota for the day. Quick, talk about something else. How did the auction go today?"

At the question, all her angst about Chase flooded back.

She suddenly desperately wanted to confide in her sisters. That was the whole reason she'd stopped at the lodge, she realized, because she yearned to share this startling development with them and obtain their advice.

I want you to be my date, with everything that goes along with that.

What was she going to do?

She wanted to ask them but they both adored Chase and it suddenly seemed wrong to talk about him with Hope and Celeste. If she had to guess, she expected they would probably take his side. They wouldn't understand how he had just upended everything safe and secure she had come to depend upon.

When she didn't answer right away, both of her sisters looked at her with concern. "Did something go wrong with the horse you wanted to buy?" Celeste asked. "You weren't outbid, were you? If you were, I'm sure you'll be able to find another one."

She shook her head. "No. We bought the horse for about five percent under what I was expecting to pay and she's beautiful. Mostly white with black spots and lovely black boot markings on her legs. I can't wait for Louisa to see her."

"I want to see her!" Hope said. "You took her to Chase's pasture?"

"Yes, and a few moments after we unloaded her, Cindy pulled up with Addie. Apparently Carol Johnson had a small stroke this morning and she's in the hospital in Idaho Falls so Cindy came home to be with her and help her father."

At the mention of Chase's ex-wife, both of her sisters' mouths tightened in almost exactly the same way. There had been no love lost between any of them, especially after Cindy's affair with the oral surgeon who eventually became her husband.

"So Cindy just dropped off Addie like UPS delivering a surprise package?" Hope asked, disgust clear in her voice.

"What about school?" ever-practical Celeste asked. "Surely she's not out for Christmas break yet."

"No. She's going to do her homework from here." She paused, remembering the one other complication. "I haven't asked Mary yet if she's available but in case she's not, would either of you like a couple of extra kids on Friday night? Three, actually—my two and Addie. Chase and I have a…a thing and it might run late."

"Oh, I wish I could," Hope exclaimed. "Rafe and I promised Joey we would take him to Boise to see his mom. We're staying overnight and doing some shopping while we're there."

"How is Cami doing?" Faith asked. "She's been out of prison, what, three months now?"

"Ten weeks. She's doing so well. Much better than Rafe expected, really. The court-ordered drug rehab she had in prison worked in her case and the halfway house is really helping her get back on her feet. Another six months and she's hoping she can have her own place and be ready to take Joey back. Maybe even by the time the baby comes."

Hope tried to smile but it didn't quite reach her eyes and Faith couldn't resist giving her sister's hand a squeeze. Celeste did the same to the other hand. Hope and her husband had cared for Rafe's nephew Joey since before their marriage after his sister's conviction on drug and robbery charges. They loved him and would both be sad to see him go.

Joey seemed like a different kid than he'd been when he first showed up at The Christmas Ranch with Rafe, two years earlier, sullen and confused and angry...

"We're trying to convince her to come back to Pine Gulch," Hope said, trying to smile. "It might help her stay out of trouble, and that way we can remain part of Joey's life. So far it's an uphill battle, as she feels like this is where all her troubles started."

Her sister's turmoil was a sharp reminder to Faith. Hope might be losing the boy she considered a son, and Celeste's stepdaughter, Olivia, still struggled to recover from both physical injuries and the emotional trauma of witnessing her mother's murder at the hands of her mentally ill and suicidal boyfriend.

In contrast, the problem of trying to figure out what to do with Chase seemed much more manageable.

"Anyway," Hope said, "that's why I won't be around Friday to help you with the kids. Sorry again."

"Don't give it another thought. That's exactly where you need to be."

"The kids are more than welcome at our place," Celeste said. "Flynn and Olivia are having a movie marathon and watching *Miracle on 34th Street* and *White Christmas*. I'll be writing during most of it, but hope to sneak in and watch the dancing in *White Christmas*."

She used to love those movies, Faith remembered. When she was young, her parents had a handful of very old, very worn VCR tapes of several holiday classics and would drag them from place to place, sometimes even showing them at social events for people in whatever small village they had set their latest medical clinic in at the time.

She probably had been just as baffled as the villagers at the world shown in the movies, which seemed so completely foreign to her own life experience, with the handsomely dressed people and the luxurious train rides and the children surrounded by toys she could only imagine.

"That sounds like the perfect evening," she said now. "Maybe I'll join the movie night instead of going to a boring Christmas party with Chase. I can bring the popcorn."

"You can't skip the stockgrowers' party," Celeste said. "It's the big social event of the year, isn't it? Jenna McRaven always caters that gala so you know the food will be fantastic, plus you'll be going with Chase. How can any party be boring with him around?"

Again, she wanted to blurt out to her sisters how strangely he was acting. She even opened her mouth to do it but before she could force the words out, she heard familiar young voices outside in the hallway just an instant before Barrett and Louisa poked their heads in, followed in short order by Celeste's stepdaughter, Olivia, and Joey. Liv went straight to Celeste while Joey practically jumped into Hope's outstretched arms.

It warmed her heart so much to see her sisters being such loving mother figures to children who needed them desperately.

"Joey and Olivia were coming to the house to hang out when I got your text," Louisa said. "We saw all your cars so decided to stop here to say hi before we walk up to the house from the bus stop."

"I'm so glad you did," Faith said.

She hugged them both, her heart aching with love. "Good day?" she asked.

Louisa nodded. "Pretty good. I had a substitute for science and she was way nicer than Mr. Lewis."

"Guess who got a hundred-ten percent on his math test?" Barrett said with a huge grin "Go on. Guess."

She made a big show of looking confused and glancing in the other boy's direction. "You did, Joey? Good job, kid!"

Rafe's nephew giggled. "I only got a hundred percent. I missed the extra credit but Barrett didn't."

Her son preened. "I was the only one in the class who got it right."

"I'm proud of both of you. What a smart family we have!"

Except for her, the one who couldn't figure out how to protect the friendship that meant the world to her.

Chapter Three

As he drove up to the Star N ranch house four days after the auction, Chase couldn't remember the last time he'd been so on edge. He wasn't nervous—or at least he would never admit to it. He was just unsettled.

So many things seemed to hinge on this night. How was he supposed to make Faith ever view him as more than just her neighbor and best friend? She had to see him for himself, a man who had spent nearly half his life waiting for her.

He didn't like the way that made him sound weak, like some kind of mongrel hanging on the fringes of her life, content for whatever scraps she threw out the kitchen door at him. It hadn't been like that. He had genuinely tried to put his unrequited feelings behind him after she and Travis got married. For the most part, he had succeeded.

He had dated a great deal and had genuinely liked several of the women he dated. In the beginning, he had liked Cindy, too. She had been funny and smart and beautiful. He was a man and had been flattered—and susceptible—when she aggressively pursued him.

When she told him she was pregnant, he decided marrying her and making a home for their child was the right thing to do. He really had tried to make their marriage work but he and Cindy were a horrible mismatch from the beginning. He could see now that they would never have suited each other, even if that little dusty corner of his heart hadn't belonged to the wife of another man.

"This is going to be so fun," Addie declared beside him. She was just about dancing out of her seat belt with excitement. "Seems like it's been forever since I've had a chance to hang out with Louisa and Olivia. It's going to be awesome."

The plan for the evening had changed at the last minute, Faith had told him in a quick, rather awkward conversation earlier that day. Celeste and Flynn decided to move their movie party to the Star N ranch house and the three girls were going to stay overnight after the movie.

If Lou and Olivia were as excited as Addie, Celeste and Mary were in for a night full of giggling girls.

His daughter let out a little shriek when he pulled up and turned off the engine.

"This is going to be *so fun*!" she repeated.

He had to smile as he climbed out and walked around to open the door. He never got tired of seeing the joy his daughter found in the simple things in life.

"Hand me your suitcase."

"Here. You don't have to carry everything, though. I can take the rest."

After pulling her suitcase from behind the seat, she hopped out with her pillow and sleeping bag.

"Careful. It's icy," he said as they headed up the sidewalk to the sprawling ranch house.

She sent him an appraising look as they reached the front door. "You look really good, Dad," she declared. "Like, Nick Jonas good."

"That's quite a compliment." Or it would be if he had more than the vaguest idea who Nick Jonas was.

"It's true. I bet you'll be the hottest guy at the party, especially since everyone else will be a bunch of married old dudes, right?"

He wasn't sure about that. Justin Hartford was a famous—though retired—movie star and Seth Dalton had once been quite a lady's man in these parts.

"You're sweet, kiddo," he said, kissing the top of her head that smelled like grape-scented shampoo.

Man, he loved this kid and missed her like crazy when she was staying with her mother.

"Doesn't their house look pretty?" she said cheerfully as she rang the doorbell.

The Star N ranch house was ablaze with multicolored Christmas lights around the windows and along the roofline, and their Christmas tree glowed merrily in the front bay window.

It was warm and welcoming against the cold, starry night.

The first year after Travis died, Faith had refused to hang any outside Christmas lights on the house and had only had a Christmas tree because Chase had decorated her Christmas tree with the kids and Aunt Mary. Faith hadn't been up to it and had claimed ranch business elsewhere while they did it.

Last year, he and Rafe had hung the outside Christmas lights.

This year, Faith herself had hung the lights, with Barrett and Lou helping her.

He wanted to think there was some symbolism in that, one more example that she was moving forward with her life.

Addie was about to ring the doorbell again when it suddenly opened. Faith's aunt stood on the other side and at the sight of him, Mary gave a low, appreciative whistle that made him feel extremely self-conscious.

"I should yell at you for ringing the doorbell when I've told you a hundred times you're family, but you look so good, I was about to ask Miss Addie what handsome stranger brought her to our door."

His daughter giggled and kissed the wrinkled cheek Mary offered. "Hi, Aunt Mary. It's just my dad. But I told him on the way that he looked super hot. For an old guy, anyway."

He *felt* hot in his suit and tie, but probably not the way she meant. Mary grinned. "You're absolutely right," she said. "Nice to see you dressed up for once."

"Thanks," he answered.

Before he could say more, Louisa burst into the room and started dancing around Addie. "You're here! You're here! I've been dying to see you and do more than just talk on the phone and text and stuff. It feels like *forever* since you've been here."

The girls hugged as if they had been separated for months.

"Need me to carry your stuff to your room?" he asked.

"It's just a suitcase and sleeping bag, Dad. I think we can handle it."

"Let's hurry, before Barrett finds out you're here and starts bugging us," Louisa said.

Poor Barrett, who until recently had been completely outnumbered by all the women in his life. At least now he had a couple of uncles and an honorary cousin in Rafe's nephew, Joey.

"Faith only came in from the barn about half an hour ago so she's still getting ready," Mary said, her plump features tight with disapproval for a moment before she wiped the expression away and gave him a smile instead. "I heard the shower turn off a few minutes ago so it shouldn't be long now."

He tried not to picture Faith climbing out of the shower, all creamy skin with her tight, slender body covered in water droplets. Once the image bloomed there, it was tough to get it out of his head again to focus on anything else.

"It's fine," he answered. "We've got plenty of time."

"You're too patient," Mary said. Her voice had an unusually barbed tone to it that made him think she wasn't necessarily talking about him waiting for Faith to get dressed for their night out.

"Maybe I just don't want to make anybody feel rushed," he answered carefully—also talking about more than just that evening.

Mary sniffed. "That's all well and good, but sometimes time can be your worst enemy, son. People get set in their ways and can't see the world is still brimming over with possibilities. Sometimes they need a sharp boot in the keister to point them in the right direction."

Well, that was clear enough. Mary *definitely* wasn't talking about the time Faith was taking to get ready. He gave her a searching look. Maybe he hadn't been as careful as he thought about not wearing his heart on his sleeve.

He loved Faith's aunt, who had opened her home and her heart to Faith and her sisters after the horrible events before they came to Pine Gulch. She and Claude had offered a safe haven for three grieving girls but they had provided much more than that. Through steady love and care, the couple had helped the girls begin to heal.

Mary had truly been a lifesaver after Travis's death, as well. She had moved back into the ranch house and stepped up to help with the children while Faith struggled to juggle widowhood and single motherhood while suddenly saddled with the responsibilities of running a big cattle ranch on her own.

"I'm just saying," Mary went on, "maybe it's time to get off your duff and make a move."

He could feel tension spread out from his head to

his shoulders. "That's the plan. What do you think to-night is about?"

"I was hoping."

She frowned, blue eyes troubled. "Just between me and you and that Christmas tree, I've got a feeling that might be the reason why a certain person just came in from the barn only a half hour ago, even though she knew all day you were on the way and exactly what time she would need to start getting ready."

Did that mean Mary thought Faith was avoiding the idea of going on a real date with him? He couldn't tell and before he had the chance to ask for clarification, Flynn Delaney came into the living room.

The other man did a double take when he spotted Chase talking to Mary. "Wow. A tie and everything."

Chase shrugged, though he could feel his skin prickle. "A Christmas party for the local stockgrowers association might not be a red-carpet Hollywood affair, but it's still a pretty big deal around here."

"Take it from me—it will be much more enjoyable for everyone involved."

He wasn't so sure about that, especially if Faith was showing reluctance about the evening.

"Sometime this week, Rafe and I are planning to spruce up the set we used last year for the Christmas show. If you want to lend a hand, we'll pay you in beer."

He had come to truly enjoy the company of both of Faith's brothers-in-law. They were both decent men who, as far as he was concerned, were almost good enough for her sisters.

"Addie's in town right now and I feel bad enough

about leaving her tonight when our time together is limited. I'll have to see what she wants to do but I'm sure she wouldn't mind coming out again and riding horses with Lou."

"I get it. Believe me."

Flynn had been a divorced father, too. He and his famous actress wife had been divorced several years before she was eventually killed so tragically.

The other man looked down the hallway, apparently to make sure none of the kids were in earshot. "I hear a certain *H-O-R-S-E* is safely ensconced at your place now."

"Lou is twelve years old and can spell, you know," Mary said with a snort.

Flynn grinned at the older woman. "Yeah. But will she slow down long enough to bother taking time to do it? That's the question."

Chase had to laugh. The horse and Louisa would be perfect for each other. "Yeah. She's a beauty. Louisa is going to be thrilled, I think. You all are in for a fun Christmas morning."

"You'll come over for breakfast like you usually do, won't you?" Mary asked.

He wasn't so sure about that. Maybe he would have to see how that evening went first. He hoped like hell that he wasn't about to ruin all his most important relationships with Faith's family by muddying the water with her.

"I hope so," he started to say, but the words died when he heard a commotion on the stairs and a moment later, Faith hurried down them wearing a silver-and-blue dress that made her look like a snow princess.

"Sorry. I'm so sorry I'm late," Faith exclaimed as she fastened a dangly silver earring.

He couldn't have responded, since his brain seemed to have shut down.

She looked absolutely stunning, with her hair piled on top of her head in a messy, sexy bun, strands artfully escaping in delectable ways. She wore a rosy lipstick and more eye makeup than usual, with mascara and eyeliner that made her eyes look huge and exotically slanted.

The dress hugged her shape, with a neckline that revealed just a hint of cleavage. She wore strappy sandals that made him wonder if he was going to have to scoop her up and carry her through the snow.

He was so used to seeing her in jeans and a T-shirt and boots, wearing a ponytail and little makeup except lip balm.

She was beautiful either way.

He swallowed, realizing he had to say something and not just stand there like an idiot.

"You're worth the wait," he said.

His voice came out rough and she flashed him a startled look before he saw color climb her cheeks.

"I don't know about that. It's been a crazy day and I feel like I've been running since five a.m. I'll probably fall asleep the moment I get into your truck."

He would love to have her curl up beside him and sleep. It certainly wouldn't be the first time.

"I'll have to see what I can do to keep you awake," he murmured.

"Driving with the windows down and the music cranked always helps me," Flynn offered.

"I spent too long fixing that hair for you to mess it up with a wind tunnel," Celeste Nichols Delaney said as she followed her sister down the stairs.

Her words brought Chase to his senses and he realized he had been standing in the entryway, gaping at her like he'd never seen a beautiful woman before.

He cleared his throat and forced himself to smile at Celeste. "We can't have that. You did a great job."

"I did, especially with Faith trying to send three emails, put on her makeup and help Barrett with his English homework at the same time."

"I appreciate your hard work," Faith said. "I think I'm finally ready. I just need my coat."

She made it the rest of the way down the stairs on the high heels and reached inside the closet in the entryway, but before she could pull off the serviceable ranch coat she always wore, Celeste slapped her hand away. "Oh, no you don't."

Faith frowned at her sister. "Why not? This is a stockgrowers' dinner. You think they've never seen a ranch coat before?"

"Not with that dress, they haven't. That's why I brought over this."

She pulled a soft fawn coat reverently from the arm of the sofa. "I bought this last month in New York when Hope and I were there meeting with our publisher."

"I don't want to wear your fancy coat."

"Too bad. You're going to."

Celeste could be as stubborn as the other sisters. "Fine," Faith finally sighed, reaching for the coat that looked cashmere and expensive. With a subtle wink, Celeste ignored her sister's outstretched hand and gave it to Chase instead. It was soft as a newborn kitten. He felt inordinately breathless as he moved behind Faith and helped her into it.

She smelled…different. Usually she smelled of vanilla and oranges from her favorite soap but this was a little more intense, with a low, flowery note that made him want to bury his face in her neck and inhale.

"There you go," he said gruffly.

"Thanks." It was obvious she wasn't comfortable dressing up, perhaps because so much of her childhood was spent with parents who gave away most of their material possessions to the people they worked with in impoverished countries.

"Are you happy now?" Faith said to her sister.

"Yes. You're beautiful." Celeste's eyes were soft and a little teary. "Sometimes you look so much like Mom."

"She must have been stunning," Flynn said, kissing his sister-in-law on the cheek.

Chase cleared away the little catch in his throat. "Breathtaking," he agreed.

Her cheeks turned pink at the attention. "I still think we'd have much more fun staying home and watching Christmas movies with the kids," she said. She smiled at the three of them but he was almost certain he saw a flicker of nervousness in her eyes again.

"Now, there's absolutely no reason for the two of

you to rush back," Celeste assured them. "The three of us have got this covered. The kids will all be fine. Go and have a great time."

"That's right," Mary said. She gave Chase a pointed look, as if to remind him of their conversation earlier. "You ask me, these parties end way too soon. I suppose that's what you get when you hang out with people who have to wake up early to feed their livestock. So don't feel like you have to come straight home when it's over. You could even go catch a movie in town if you wanted or grab drinks at that fancy new bar that opened up on the outskirts of town."

"The only trouble is we both *also* have to wake up early to take care of our livestock," Faith said with a laugh that sounded slightly strained.

"Louisa. Barrett," she called. "I'm leaving. Come give me a hug."

All the children, not only her two, hurried down the stairs to join them.

"You look beautiful, Faith," Addie exclaimed. "What a cute couple you guys are. Wait. Let me get a picture so I can show my friends."

She pulled out the smartphone he didn't think she needed yet and snapped a picture.

"Oh! What a good idea," Celeste said. "I want a picture, too."

"We're just going to a Christmas party. It's not the prom," Faith said. Her color ratcheted up a notch, especially when Aunt Mary pulled out her phone as well and started clicking away taking pictures.

"I'm posting this one," her aunt declared. "You both

look so good. In fact, you better watch it, Chase, or you'll have about a hundred marriage proposals before the night is over. My friends on social media can be a wild bunch."

Faith's cheeks by now were as red as the ornaments on the tree. This was distressing her, and though he didn't quite understand why, it didn't matter. His job was to protect her—even from loving relatives with cell phone cameras.

"Okay, that's enough paparazzi for tonight. We'll really be late if this keeps up."

"You don't want that. You'll miss all of Jenna McRaven's good food," Mary said.

"Exactly." He hugged his daughter. "Be good, Ads. I imagine you'll still be up when I bring Faith back but if you're not, I'll see you in the morning."

"Bye, Dad. Have fun."

He waited for Faith to hug and kiss her kids and admonish them to behave for Aunt Mary and the Delaneys, then he held the door open for her and they headed out into the cold air that felt refreshing on his overheated skin.

Neither of them said anything as he led her to his pickup and helped her inside. He wished he had some kind of luxury sedan to take her to the party but that kind of vehicle wasn't very practical on an eastern Idaho ranch. At least he'd taken the truck for a wash and had vacuumed up any dried mud and straw bits out of the inside.

It took a little effort to tuck the soft length of her coat inside. "Better make sure I don't shut the door on

Celeste's coat," he joked. "She would probably never forgive me."

He went around and climbed inside, then turned his pickup truck around and started heading toward the canyon road that would take them to Pine Gulch and the party.

"My family. Ugh. You'd think I never went to a Christmas party before, the way they carry on." Faith didn't look at him as she fiddled with the air vent. "I don't know what's gotten into them all. I mean, we went together last year to the exact same party and nobody gave it a second thought."

A wise man would probably keep his mouth shut, just go with the flow.

Maybe he was tired of keeping his mouth shut.

"If I had to guess," he said, after giving her a long look, "they're making a fuss because they know this is different, that we're finally going out on a real date."

Chapter Four

At his words, tension seemed to clamp around her spine with icy fingers.

We're finally going out on a real date.

She had really been hoping he had forgotten all that nonsense by now and they could go to the party as they always had done things, as dear friends.

She didn't know what to say. She couldn't stop thinking about that moment when she had started down the stairs and had seen him standing there, looking tall and rugged and gorgeous, freshly shaved and wearing a dark Western-cut suit and tie.

He had looked like he should be going to a country music awards show with a beautiful starlet on his arm or something, not the silly local stockgrowers association party with *her*.

She had barely been able to think straight and literally had felt so weak-kneed she considered it a minor miracle that she hadn't stumbled down the stairs right at his feet.

Then he had spotted her and the heat in his eyes had sent an entire flock of butterflies swarming through her insides.

"Every time I bring up that this is a date, you go silent as dirt," he murmured. "Why is that?"

She drew in a breath. "I don't know what to say."

He shot her a quick look across the bench seat of his truck. "Is the idea of dating me so incomprehensible?"

"Not incomprehensible. Just…disconcerting," she answered honestly.

"Why?" he pressed.

How was she supposed to answer that? He was her best friend and knew all her weaknesses and faults. Surely he knew she was a giant coward at heart, that she didn't *want* these new and terrifying feelings.

She had no idea how to answer him so she opted to change the subject. "I haven't had a chance to ask you. How's Louisa's new horse?"

He shifted his gaze from the road, this time to give her a long look. She thought for a moment he would call her on it and press for an answer. To her relief, he turned back to the road and, after a long pause, finally answered her.

"Settling in, I guess. She seems to have really taken to Tor—and vice versa."

"I hope they won't be too upset at being separated

when we send the new horse to Seth Dalton's after Christmas."

"I'm sure they'll survive. If not, we can always arrange visitation."

That word inevitably reminded her of his ex-wife.

"How is Cindy's mother doing?" she asked.

He shrugged. "Fine, from what I hear. She's probably going to be in the hospital another week."

"Does that mean the cruise is off?"

"Cindy insists they don't want to cancel the cruise unless it's absolutely necessary. I'm still planning my Christmas celebration with Addie on December 20."

"It's just another day on the calendar," she said.

"Don't let Hope hear you say that or she might ban you from The Christmas Ranch," he joked.

They spoke of the upcoming children's Christmas show and the crowds at the ranch and the progress of her sisters' movie for the remainder of the short drive to the reception hall where the annual dinner and party was always held.

He found a parking space not far from the building and climbed out to walk around the vehicle to her side. While she waited for him to open her door, Faith took a deep breath.

She could do this. Tonight was no different from dozens of other social events they had attended together. Weddings, birthday parties, Fourth of July barbecues. Things had never been awkward between them until now.

We're finally going out on a real date.

When she thought of those words, little starbursts of panic flared inside her.

She couldn't give in. Chase was her dear friend and she cared about him deeply. As long as she kept that in mind, everything would be just fine.

She wasn't certain she completely believed that but she refused to consider the alternative right now.

The party was in full swing when they arrived. The reception hall had been decorated with an abundance of twinkling fairy lights strung end to end and Christmas trees stood in each corner. Delectable smells wafted out of the kitchen and her stomach growled, almost in time to the band playing a bluegrass version of "Good King Wenceslas." A few couples were even dancing and she watched them with no small amount of envy. She missed dancing.

"You'd better give me Celeste's New York City coat so I can hang it up," Chase said from beside her.

She gave him a rueful smile. "I'm a little afraid to let it out of my sight but I guess I can't wear it all night."

"No, you can't. Go on inside. I'll hang this and be there in a moment."

She nodded and stepped into the reception room. Her good friend Jennie Dalton—Seth Dalton's wife and principal of the elementary school—stood just inside. Jennie was talking with Ashley Hartford, who taught kindergarten at the elementary school.

While their husbands were lost in conversation, the two women were speaking with a young, lovely woman she didn't recognize—which was odd, since she knew just about everyone who came to these events.

Jennie held out a hand when she spotted her. "Hello, my dear. You look gorgeous, as always."

Faith made a face, wishing she didn't feel like a frazzled, overburdened rancher and single mother.

She held a hand out to the woman she didn't know. "Hi. I'm Faith Dustin."

The woman had pretty features and a sweet smile. "Hello. I'm Ella Baker. You may know my father, Curt."

"Yes, of course. Hello. Lovely to meet you."

Curt Baker had a ranch on the other side of town. She didn't know him well but she had heard he had a daughter he didn't know well who had spent most of her life living with her mother back East somewhere. From what she understood, his daughter had returned to help him through a health scare.

"Your dad is looking well."

Ella glanced at her father with a troubled look, then forced a smile. "He's doing better, I suppose."

"Ella is a music therapist and she just agreed to take the job of music teacher at the school for the rest of the school year," Jennie said, looking thrilled at the prospect.

"That's a long time coming."

"Right. We've had the funding for it but haven't been able to find someone suitable since Linda Keller retired two years ago. We've been relying on parent volunteers, who have been wonderful, but can only take the program so far. I'm a firm believer that children learn better when we can incorporate the arts in the classroom."

"I completely agree," Faith said, then was suddenly struck by a small moment of brilliance. "Hey, I've got a terrific way for you to get to know some of the young people in the community."

"Oh?"

"My family runs The Christmas Ranch. You may have seen signs for it around town."

"Absolutely. I haven't had time to stop yet but it looks utterly delightful."

"It is." She didn't bother telling the woman she had very little to do with the actual operations of The Christmas Ranch. It was always too complicated explaining that she ran the cattle side of things—hence her presence at this particular holiday party.

"Last year we started a new tradition of offering a children's Christmas variety show and dinner for the senior citizens in town. It's nothing grand, more for fun than anything else. The children only practice for the week leading up to the show, since everyone is so busy this time of year. Linda Keller, the woman who retired a few years ago from the school district, had offered to help us this year but apparently she just broke her arm."

"That's as good an excuse as any," Ashley said.

"I suppose. The point is my sisters are desperate for someone to help them organize the show. I don't suppose there's any chance you might be interested."

It seemed a nervy thing to ask a woman she had only met five minutes earlier. To Faith's relief, Ella Baker didn't seem offended.

"That sounds like a blast," Ella exclaimed. "I've been looking for something to keep me busy until the New Year when I start at the school part-time."

Hope was going to owe her *big-time*—so much that Faith might even claim naming rights over the new baby.

"Great! You'll have fun, I promise. The kids are so cute and we've got some real talent."

"This is true," Ashley said. "Especially Faith's niece, Olivia. She sings like an angel. Last year the show was so wonderful."

"The senior citizens in the area really ate it up," Jennie affirmed. "My dad couldn't stop talking about it. The Nichols family has started a wonderful thing for the community."

"This sounds like a great thing. I'm excited you asked me."

"If you give me your contact info, I can forward it to my sister Hope. She's really the one in charge."

"Your name is Faith and you have a sister named Hope. Let me guess, do you have another one named Charity?"

"That would be logical, wouldn't it? But my parents never did what was expected. They named our youngest sister Celeste."

"Celeste is the children's librarian in town and she's also an author," Ashley said. "And Hope is an illustrator."

"Oh! Of course! Celeste and Hope Nichols. They wrote 'Sparkle and the Magic Snowball'! The kids at the developmental skills center where I used to work loved that story. They even wrote a song about Sparkle."

Faith smiled. "You'll have to share it with Celeste and Hope. They'll be thrilled."

She and Ella were sending contact information to each other's phones when she felt a subtle ripple in the air and a moment later Chase joined them.

Speaking with the women had begun to push out some of the butterflies inside her but they suddenly returned in full force.

"Sorry I was gone so long. I got cornered by Pete Jeppeson at the coatrack and just barely managed to get away."

"No worries. I've been meeting someone who is about to make my sisters very, very happy. Chase Brannon, this is Ella Baker. She's Curt's daughter and she's a music therapist who has just agreed to help out with the second annual Christmas Ranch holiday show."

Chase gave Ella a warm smile. "That's very kind of you—not to mention extremely brave."

The woman returned his smile and Faith didn't miss the sudden appreciative light in her eyes, along with a slightly regretful look, the sort a woman might wear while shopping when someone else in line at the checkout just ahead of her picks out the exact one-of-a-kind piece of jewelry she would have chosen for herself.

"Brave or crazy," Ella said. "I'm not sure which yet."

"You said it. I didn't," Chase said.

Both of them laughed and as she saw them together, a strange thought lodged in her brain.

The two of them could be perfect for each other.

She didn't want to admit it but Ella Baker seemed on the surface just the sort of woman Chase needed. She had only just met the woman but she trusted her instincts. Ella seemed smart and pretty, funny and kind.

Exactly the sort of woman Chase deserved.

He said he was ready to date again and here was a perfect candidate. Wouldn't a truehearted friend do everything in her power to push the two of them together—at least give Chase the chance to get to know the other woman?

She hated the very idea of it, but she wanted Chase to be happy. "Will you both excuse me for a moment? I just spotted Jenna McRaven and remembered I need to talk to her about a slight change in the menu for the dinner next week."

She aimed a bright smile at them. "You two should dance or something. Go ahead! I won't be long."

She caught a glimpse of Ella's startled features and the beginnings of a thundercloud forming on Chase's but she hurried away before he could respond.

He would thank her later, she told herself, especially if Ella turned out to be absolutely perfect for him.

He only needed to spend a little time with her to realize the lovely young woman who had put her life on hold to help her ailing father was a much better option than a prickly widow who didn't have anything left in her heart to give him.

She found Jenna in the kitchen, up to her eyeballs in appetizers.

This was the absolute worst time to bug her about a catering job, when she was busy at a different one. Faith couldn't bother her with a small change in salad dressing—especially when she was only using this as an excuse to leave Chase alone with Ella Baker. She would call Jenna later and tell her about the change at a better time.

"Hi, Faith! Don't you look beautiful tonight!"

She almost gave an inelegant snort. Jenna's blond curls were piled on her head in an adorable messy bun and her cheeks looked rosy from the heat of the kitchen and probably from the exertion of preparing a meal for so many people, while Faith had split ends and hands desperately in need of a manicure.

"I was just going to say the same to you," she said. "Seriously, you're the only person I know who can be neck-deep in making canapés and still manage to look like a model."

Jenna rolled her eyes as she continued setting out appetizers on the tray. "You're sweet but delusional. Did you need something?"

Faith glanced through the open doorway, where she could see Chase bending down to listen more closely to something Ella was saying. The sight made her stomach hurt—but maybe that was just hunger.

"Not at all. I was just wondering if you need any help back here."

Jenna looked startled at her question but not ungrateful. "That's very sweet but I'm being paid to hang out here in the kitchen. You're not. You should be out there enjoying the party."

"I can hear the music from here, plus helping you out in the kitchen would give me the chance to talk to a dear friend I don't see often enough. Need me to carry out a tray or two?"

Jenna blew out a breath. "I should say no. You're a

guest at the party. I hate to admit it, but I could really use some help for a minute. It's a two-person job but my assistant has the flu so I'm a little frantic here. Carson will be here to help me as soon as he can, but his flight from San Francisco was delayed because of weather so he's running about an hour behind."

Faith found it unbearably sweet that Jenna's billionaire husband—who commuted back and forth between Silicon Valley and Pine Gulch—was ready to help the wife he adored with a catering job. "I can help you until he gets here. No problem."

Jenna lifted her head from her task long enough to frown. "Didn't I see you come in with Chase when I was out replenishing the Parmesan smashed potatoes? I can't let you just ditch him."

She glanced at the door where he was now smiling at something Ella said.

"We drove here together, yes," she answered. "But I'm hoping he'll be dancing with Curt Baker's daughter in a moment."

"Oh. Ella. Jolie just started taking piano lessons from her. She's a delight."

"I think she would be great for Chase so I'm trying to give them a chance to get to know each other. Let nature take its course and all."

Jenna's busy hands paused in her work and she gave Faith a careful look. "You might want to ask Chase his opinion on that idea," she said mildly.

"I don't need to ask him. He's my best friend. I know what he needs probably better than he knows himself."

Jenna opened her mouth to answer, then appeared to think better of it.

She was right, Faith told herself. Chase would thank her later; she was almost certain of it.

Chapter Five

Faith was trying to ditch him.

He knew exactly what she was doing as she moved in and out of the kitchen carrying trays of food for Jenna McRaven's catering company. It wasn't completely unusual for her to help out behind the scenes, but he knew in this case she was just looking for an excuse to avoid him.

He curled his hands into fists, trying to decide if he was more annoyed or hurt. Either way, he still wanted to punch something.

The woman beside him hummed along with the bluegrass version of "Silver Bells." Ella Baker had a pretty voice and kind eyes. He felt like a jerk for ignoring her while he glowered after Faith, even though Ella wasn't the date he had walked in with.

"What were you doing before you came back to Pine Gulch to stay with your father?" he asked.

"I was the music instructor at a residential school for developmentally delayed children in Upstate New York, the same town where you can find the boarding school I attended myself from the age of eight, actually."

Boarding school? What was the story there? He wouldn't have taken Curt Baker as the sort of guy to send his kid to boarding school to be raised by someone else most of the year. He couldn't imagine it—it was hard enough packing Addie off to live with her mother half the time.

"Sounds like you were doing good work."

"I found it very rewarding. Some of my students have made remarkable progress. Music can be a comfort and a joy, as well as open doors to language and auditory processing skills I wouldn't have imagined before I started in this field."

"That sounds interesting."

She made a face. "To me, anyway. Sorry. I tend to get a little passionate when I talk about my job."

"I admire that in a person."

"It's not all I do, I promise. I did play piano and I sing in a jazz trio on the weekends."

"That's great! Maybe you ought to perform at the holiday show yourself."

She made a face. "I probably would be a little out of place, since it sounds like this is mostly a show featuring children. I'm happy enough behind the scenes."

The band changed to a slower song, a wistful holiday tune about regret and lost loves.

"Oh, I love this song," she exclaimed, swaying a little in time to the music.

What was the etiquette here? He had come to the party with a woman who was doing her best to stay away from him. Meanwhile another one was making it clear she wanted to dance.

He didn't know the social conventions but he figured simple politeness trumped the rules anyway.

"Would you like to dance?" he finally asked. If Faith would rather hide out in the kitchen than spend time in conversation with him, he probably wasn't committing some grave faux pas by asking another woman for a simple dance.

Ella's smile was soft with delight. "I would, actually. Thanks."

How weird was this night turning out? Chase wondered as he led the woman out to the dance floor with about a dozen other couples. He had come to the party hoping to end up with Faith in his arms. Instead, she was currently busy carrying out a pot of soup while he was dancing with a woman he had only just met.

Ella was a good conversationalist. She asked him about his ranch and Pine Gulch and the surroundings. He told her about Addie and the cruise she was going on with her mother and stepfather over the holidays and his plans to have their own Christmas celebration a few days before the twenty-fifth.

He actually enjoyed himself more than he might have expected, though beneath the enjoyment he was aware of a simmering frustration at Faith.

When the song ended, he spotted Ella's father on

the edge of the dance floor speaking with a ranching couple he knew who lived up near Driggs. He led her there, visited with the group for a moment, then made his excuses and headed straight for the kitchen.

He found Faith plating pieces of apple pie. She was talking to Jenna McRaven but her words seemed to stall when she spotted him.

"Are you going to hide out in here all night?"

Her gaze shifted away from his but not before he saw the shadow of nervousness there. "I'm not hiding out," she protested. "I was just giving Jen a hand for a minute. Anyway, you've been busy dancing with Ella Baker."

Only because his real date was as slippery as a newborn calf.

"You've done more than enough," Jenna assured her. "I'm grateful for your help but I'm finally caught up in here. Carson's plane just landed and he's on his way here to help me with the rest of the night. You really need to go out and enjoy the party."

Faith opened her mouth to protest but Jenna gave her a stern look. "I'm serious, sweetie. Go out and enjoy all this delicious food I've been slaving over for a week. Now hand over the apron and back away slowly and nobody will get hurt."

"Fine. If you insist." Faith huffed out a little breath but untied her apron and set it on an empty space on the counter. Chase wasn't about to let her wriggle away again. He hooked his hand in the crook of her elbow and steered her out into the reception hall and over to the buffet line.

They grabbed their food, which all appeared delicious, then Faith scanned the room. "I see a couple of chairs over by Em and Ashley. Why don't we go sit with them?"

He enjoyed hanging out with their neighbors but right now he would rather find a secluded corner and have this out. Barring that, he would rather just go home and get the hell out of this suit and tie.

Nothing was working out as he planned and he felt stupid and shortsighted for thinking it might.

"Sure. Sounds good," he lied.

She led the way and as soon as they were seated, she immediately launched into a long conversation with the other couples.

By the time dinner was over, he was more than ready to throw up his hands and declare the evening a disaster, convinced she was too stubborn to ever consider they could be anything but friends.

Sitting at this table with their neighbors and friends filled him with a deep-seated envy that left him feeling small. They were all long-married yet still obviously enamored with each other, with casual little touches and private smiles that left him feeling more lonely than ever.

The band had begun to move away from strictly playing holiday songs and began a cover of a popular upbeat pop song, adding a bluegrass flair, of course. Ashley Hartford lit up. "Oh! I love this song. Come dance with me, darling."

Though they had four children and had been married for years, Justin gave her the sort of smoldering look Chase guessed women enjoyed, since the man had made millions on the big screen, before he walked away from it all to come to Pine Gulch.

"Let's do it," he said.

"We can't let them show us up," Emery declared to her husband. "I know you hate to dance but will you, just this once?"

Nate Cavazos, former army Special Forces and tough as nails, sighed but obediently rose to follow his petite wife out to the dance floor. Their departure left him alone at the table with Faith, along with an awkward silence.

He gestured to the floor. "Do you want to dance?"

Panic flickered in her eyes and his gut ached. She had been his friend for nearly two decades. They had laughed together, cried together, confided secrets to each other.

Why the hell couldn't she see they were perfect for each other?

"Forget it," he said. "You're not enjoying this. Why don't I just go get Celeste's fabulous coat and we can take off?"

Her lush mouth twisted into a frown. "That's not fair to you."

She looked at the dance floor for a moment, then back at him. "Actually, let's go dance. I would like it very much."

He wanted to call her out for the lie but it seemed stupid to argue. Instead, Chase scraped his chair back, then reached a hand out. She placed her slim, cool, working-rancher hand in his and he led her out to the dance floor.

Just as they reached it, the music shifted to a song

he didn't know, something slow and dreamy, jazzy and soft. He pulled her into his arms—finally!—and they began to move in time to the music.

"This is nice," she murmured, and he took that as encouragement to pull her a little closer. She smelled delicious, that subtle scent he had picked up earlier, and he closed his eyes and tried to burn the moment into his memory.

She stumbled a little and when he glanced down, she was blushing. "Sorry. I'm not very good at this. I never learned to dance, unless you count some of the native dances we did in South America and Papua New Guinea."

"I'd like to see some of those."

She laughed. "I doubt I could remember a single one. Hope probably can. She was always more into them than I was. You're a very good dancer. Why didn't I know that?"

"I guess we haven't had much call to dance together."

His mother had taught him, he remembered, when he was about fourteen or fifteen, before his father's diagnosis and his family fell apart.

His mother had told him he needed to learn so he wouldn't be embarrassed at school dances. Turns out, he hadn't needed the lessons. His father's cancer and the toll the treatment had taken on him had left Chase little time for frivolous things like proms. It was all he could do to keep the ranch running while his mother ran his dad back and forth to the cancer center in Salt Lake City.

Despite the long, difficult fight, his father had lost

the battle. After he died, things had been worse. His mother had completely fallen apart that first year and had slipped into a deep, soul-crushing depression that lasted for a tough four years, until she finally went to visit a sister in Seattle, fell in love with a restaurant owner she met there and moved there permanently.

Sometimes he wondered what might have happened if his father hadn't died, if Chase hadn't been forced to put his own plans for college on the back burner.

If he had been in a better place to pursue Faith first.

If.

It was a word he really hated.

A few more turns around the dance floor and she appeared to relax and seemed to be enjoying the music and the moment. He even made her laugh a few times. The music shifted into another slow dance and she didn't seem in a hurry to stop dancing so he decided to just go with it.

If he had his choice, he would have frozen that moment forever in time, just savoring the scent of her hair and the way her curves brushed against him and the way she fit so perfectly in his arms.

Too quickly, the music ended and she pulled away.

"That was nice," she said. "Thanks."

Dancing with him had been a big step for her, he knew.

"They're about to serve dessert," he said on impulse. "What do you say we grab a couple slices of that apple pie in a couple of to-go boxes and take off somewhere to enjoy it where we can look at Christmas lights?"

"We don't have to leave if you're enjoying yourself."

"I just want to be with you. I really don't care where."

He probably shouldn't have been that blunt. She nibbled on her lip, clearly mulling her options, then smiled. "Let's go."

She hated being a coward.

Her sister Hope plowed through life, exploring the world as their parents had, experiencing life and collecting friends everywhere she went. Celeste, the youngest, was shy and timid and could be socially awkward. That seemed to have changed significantly since her marriage to Flynn and since her literary career took off, requiring more public appearances and radio interviews. Celeste seemed to be far more comfortable in her own skin these days.

Now Faith was the timid one.

Losing her husband and becoming a widow at thirty-two had changed her in substantial ways. Sometimes she wasn't even sure who she was anymore.

She had never considered herself particularly brave, though she had tried to put on a strong front for Hope and Celeste after their parents died. They had needed her and while she wanted to curl up into herself, she had tried to set an example of courage for her sisters.

After Travis died, she had wanted to do the same. That time, her children had needed her. She had to show them that even in the midst of overwhelming grief they could survive and even thrive.

Right now, that facade of strength seemed about to crumble to dust. In her heart, she was terrified and it seemed to be growing worse. She was so afraid of shaking up the status quo, setting herself up for more pain.

More than that, she was afraid of hurting Chase.

She wouldn't worry about that now. Once they were alone, just the two of them, they could forget all this date nonsense and just be Chase and Faith again, like always.

Jenna McRaven didn't ask questions when they asked if she had any to-go boxes. She pulled out a cardboard container that she loaded with two pieces of caramel-topped apple pie.

A moment later, without giving explanations to anyone, they grabbed Celeste's luxurious coat and hurried outside into the December night.

Her breath puffed out as they made their way to his pickup but she wasn't cold. She wanted to give credit to the fine cashmere wool but in truth she was still overheated from the warm dance floor and her own ridiculous nerves.

"Where should we go for dessert?" he asked. "What do you think about Orchard Park? It offers a nice view of town."

She would rather go back to the Star N and change into jeans and a T-shirt. Barring that, Orchard Park would have to do. "Sounds good," she answered.

He turned on a Christmas station and soft, jazzy music filled the interior of his pickup truck as he drove the short distance from the reception hall to an area of new development in Pine Gulch.

A small subdivision of single-family homes was being built here on land that had once been filled with fruit trees. The streets had names like Apple Blossom Drive, Jubilee Lane and McIntosh Court and only about half the lots had new houses.

Chase pulled above the last row of houses to a clearing at the end of the road, probably where the developer planned to add more houses eventually.

He put the vehicle in Park but left the engine running. Warm air poured out of the vents from the heater, wrapping them in a cozy embrace.

"I'm sorry I didn't think to get a bottle of wine but I should have some water in my emergency stash."

He climbed out and rummaged in a cargo box in the backseat before emerging with a couple of water bottles.

Given the harsh winters in the region, most people she knew kept kits in their vehicles with water bottles, granola bars and foil emergency blankets in case they were stranded in a blizzard.

"Don't forget to replenish your supply," she said when he slid back in the front seat.

"I won't. Nothing worse than being stuck in four-foot-high drifts somewhere with nothing to drink but melted snow."

That had never happened to her, thankfully. She unscrewed the cap and took a drink of the water, which was remarkably cold and refreshing, then handed him the to-go carton of pie Jenna had given them along with the fork her friend had provided.

"I guess it's fitting we should eat an apple pie here," she said.

His teeth gleamed in the darkness as he smiled. "Anything else wouldn't seem as appropriate, would it?"

With the glittery stars above them and the colorful lights of town below, she took a bite of her pie and nearly swooned from the sheer sensory overload.

"Wow. That's fantastic," she breathed. It was flaky and crusty and buttery, with just the right hint of caramel. "Jenna is a master of the simple apple pie. I've got her recipe but I can never make it just like this. I don't know what she does differently from me or Aunt Mary or my sisters but it's so fantastic."

"Even without ice cream."

She laughed. "I was thinking that but didn't want to say it."

It seemed a perfect moment, so much better away from the public social pressure of the party. She took a deep breath and realized she hadn't fully filled her lungs all evening. Stupid nerves.

"I love the view from this area," she said. "Pine Gulch seems so peaceful and quiet."

"I suppose it looks so peaceful because you can't see from up here how old Doris Packer is such a bitter old hag or how Ben Tillman has a habit of shortchanging his customers at the tavern or how Wilma Rivera is probably talking trash about her sister-in-law."

He was so right. "It's easy to simply look at the surface and think you know a place, isn't it?"

"Right." He sent her a sidelong look. "People are much the same. You have to dig beneath the nice clothes and the polite polish to find the essence of a person."

She knew the essence of Chase Brannon. He was a kind, decent, *good* man who so deserved to be happy.

She sighed and could feel the heat of his gaze.

"That sounded heavy. What's on your mind?"

She had a million things racing through her thoughts and didn't know how to talk to him about any of it. She couldn't tell him that she felt like she stood on the edge of a precipice, toes tingling from the vast, unknown chasm below her, and she just didn't know how much courage she had left inside her to jump.

"I'm feeling bad about taking you away from the party," she lied.

"You didn't take me away. Leaving was my idea, remember?"

He reached up to loosen his tie. Funny how that simple act seemed to help her remember this was Chase, her best friend. She wanted him to be happy, no matter what.

"It was a good idea. Still, if we had stayed, maybe you could have danced with Ella Baker again."

He said nothing but annoyance suddenly seemed to radiate out of him in pointed rays.

"She seems very nice," Faith pressed.

"Yes."

"And she's musical, too."

"Yes."

"Not to mention beautiful, don't you think?"

"She's lovely."

"You should ask her out, since you suddenly want to start dating again."

He made a low sound in the back of his throat, the kind of noise he made when his tractor broke down or one of his ranch hands called in sick too many times.

"Who said I wanted to start dating again?" he said, his voice clipped.

"You did. You're the one who insisted this was a *date-date*. You made a big deal that it wasn't just two friends carpooling to the stockgrowers' party together, remember?"

"That doesn't mean I'm ready to start dating again, at least not in general terms. It only means I'm ready to start dating *you*."

There it was.

Out in the open.

The reality she had been trying so desperately to avoid. He wanted more from her than friendship and she was scared out of her ever-loving mind at the possibility.

The air in the vehicle suddenly seemed charged, crackling with tension. She had to say something but had no idea what.

"I… Chase—"

"Don't. Don't say it."

His voice was low, intense, with an edge to it she rarely heard. She had so hoped they could return to the easy friendship they had always known. Was that gone forever, replaced by this jagged uneasiness?

"Say…what?"

"Whatever the hell you were gearing up for in that tone of voice like you were knocking on the door to tell me you just ran over my favorite dog."

"What do you want me to say?" she whispered.

"I sure as hell don't want you trying to set me up with another woman when you're the only one I want."

She stared at him, the heat in his voice rippling down

her spine. She swallowed hard, not knowing what to say as awareness seemed to spread out to her fingertips, her shoulder blades, the muscles of her thighs.

He was so gorgeous and she couldn't help wondering what it would be like to taste that mouth that was only a few feet away.

He gazed down at her for a long, charged moment, then with a muffled curse, he leaned forward on the bench seat and lowered his mouth to hers.

Given the heat of his voice and the hunger she thought she glimpsed in his eyes, she might have expected the kiss to be intense, fierce.

She might have been able to resist that.

Instead, it was much, much worse.

It was soft and unbearably sweet, with a tenderness that completely overwhelmed her. His mouth tasted of caramel and apples and the wine he'd had at dinner—delectable and enticing—and she was astonished by the urge she had to throw her arms around him and never let go.

Chapter Six

For nearly fifteen years, he had been trying *not* to imagine this moment.

When she was married to one of his closest friends, he had no idea she tasted of apples and cinnamon, that she smelled like oranges and vanilla sprinkled across a meadow of wildflowers.

He hadn't wanted to know she made tiny little sounds of arousal, little breathy sighs he wanted to capture inside his mouth and hold there forever.

It was easier *not* knowing those things. He could see that now.

He had hugged her many times and already knew how perfectly she fit against him. Sometimes when they would come back from traveling out of town together— Idaho Falls for the livestock auction or points farther away to pick up ranch equipment or parts—she would fall asleep, lulled by the motion of the vehicle and the rare chance to sit in one place for longer than five minutes.

He loved those times. Invariably, she would end up curled against him, her head on his shoulder. It would always take every ounce of strength he possessed not to pull her close, tuck her against him and drive off into the sunset.

He had always tried to remember his place as her friend, her support system.

Aching and wistful, he would spend those drives wishing he could keep driving a little extra or that when they arrived at their destination, he could gently turn her face to his and wake her with a kiss.

It was a damn good thing he hadn't ever risked something so stupid. If he had, he would never have been able to let her go.

He had her now, though, and he wasn't about to let this moment go to waste. She needed to see that she was still a lovely, sensual woman who couldn't spend the rest of her life hidden away at the Star N, afraid to let anybody else inside.

If he couldn't talk her into giving him a chance, perhaps he could seduce her into it.

It wasn't the most honorable thought he'd ever had, but right now, with her mouth warm and open against his and her silky hair under his fingertips, he didn't care.

He deepened the kiss and she froze for a second, and then her lips parted and she welcomed him inside, her tongue tangling with his and her hands clutching his shirt.

She might never be able to love him as he wanted but at least she should know she was a beautiful, desirable woman who had an entire life ahead of her.

He wasn't sure how long they spent wrapped around each other. What guy could possibly pay attention to insignificant little details like that when the woman he loved was kissing him with abandon?

He only knew he had never been so grateful for his decision to get a bench seat in his pickup instead of two buckets. Without a console in the way, she was nearly in his lap, exactly where he wanted her...

This was the dumbest thing he had ever done.

Even as he tried to lose himself in the kiss, the thought seemed to slither across his mind like a rattlesnake across his boot.

He was only setting himself up for more heartache. He should have thought this through, looked ahead past the moment and what he wanted right now.

How could he ever go back to being friends with her, trying like hell to be respectful of the subtle distance she so carefully maintained between them? He couldn't scrub these moments from his mind. Every time he looked at her now, he would remember this cold, star-filled night with the glittering holiday lights of Pine Gulch spread out below them and her warm, delicious mouth tangling with his.

Some small but powerful instinct for self-preservation clamored at him that maybe he better stop this while he still could, before all these years of pent-up desire burst through his control like irrigation water through a busted wheel line. He couldn't completely lose his head here.

He drew in a sharp breath and eased away from her. Her features were a pale blur in the moonlight but her lips were swollen from his kiss, her eyes half-closed. Her hair was tousled from his hands and she looked completely luscious.

He nearly groaned aloud at the effort it took to slide away from her when his entire body was yelling at him to pull her closer.

She opened her eyes and gazed at him, pupils dilated and her ragged breathing just about the most erotic sound he'd ever heard.

He saw the instant awareness returned to her eyes. They widened with shock and something else, then color soaked her cheeks.

She untangled her hands from around his neck and eased away from him.

"It's been a long time since I made out with a pretty girl in a pickup truck," he said into the suddenly heavy silence. "I forgot how awkward it could be."

She swallowed hard. "Right," she said slowly. "It's the pickup truck making things awkward."

They both knew it was much more than that. It was the years of history between them and the weight of a friendship that was important to both of them.

"I so wish you hadn't done that," she said in a small voice.

Her words carved out another little slice of his heart. "Which? Kissed you? Or stopped?"

She shifted farther away from him and turned her face to look out at the town below them.

Instead of answering him directly, she offered up what seemed to him like a completely random change of topic.

"Do you remember the first time we met?"

Of course he remembered. Most guys remembered the days that left them feeling as if they had been run over by a tractor.

"Yes. You and your sisters had only been here with Mary and Claude a day or two."

"It was February 18, a week after our mother's funeral. We had been in Idaho exactly forty-eight hours."

She remembered it so exactly? He wasn't sure what to think about that. He only remembered that he had been sent by his mother to drop off a meal for "Mary's poor nieces."

The whole community knew what had happened to her and her sisters—that their parents had been providing medical care in a poor jungle town in Colombia when the entire family had been kidnapped by rebels looking for a healthy ransom.

After all these years, he still didn't know everything that had happened to her in that rebel camp. She didn't talk about it and he didn't ask. He did know her father had been shot and killed by rebels during a daring rescue mission orchestrated by US Navy SEALs, including a very young Rafe Santiago, now Hope's husband.

He didn't know much more now than he had that first time he met her. When the news broke a few months earlier and her family returned to the US, it had been big news in town. How could it be otherwise, given that her father had grown up in Pine Gulch and everyone knew the family's connection to Claude and Mary?

Unfortunately, the family's tragedy hadn't ended with her father's death. After their rescue, her mother had been diagnosed with an aggressive cancer that might have been treatable if she hadn't been living in primitive conditions for years—and if she hadn't spent the last month as a hostage in a rebel camp.

That had been Chase's mother's opinion, anyway. She had been on her way out of town to his own father's cancer treatment but had told him to drop off a chicken rice casserole and a plate of brownies to the Nichols family.

He remembered being frustrated at the order. Why couldn't she have dropped it off on her way out of town? Didn't he have enough to do on the ranch, since he was basically running things single-handedly?

Claude had answered the door, with the phone held to his ear, and told him Mary was in the kitchen and to go on back. He had complied, not knowing the next few moments would change his life.

He vividly remembered that moment when he had seen Faith standing at the sink with Mary, peeling potatoes.

She had been slim and pretty and fragile, with huge green eyes, that sweet, soft mouth and short, choppy blond hair—which she later told him she had cut herself with a butter knife sharpened on a brick, because of lice in the rebel camp.

He also suspected it had been an effort to avoid unwanted attention from the rebels, though she had never told him that. He couldn't imagine they couldn't see past her choppy hair to the rare beauty beneath.

Yeah, a guy tended to remember the moment he lost his heart.

"I gave you a ride into town," he said now. "Mary needed a gallon of milk or something."

"That's what she said, anyway," Faith said, her mouth tilted up a little. "I think she only wanted me to get out of the house and have a look at our new community and also give me a chance to talk to someone around my own age."

Not *that* close in age. He had been eighteen and had felt a million years older.

She had been so serious, he remembered, her eyes solemn and watchful and filled with a pain that had touched his heart.

"Whatever the reason, I was happy to help out."

"Everyone else treated us like we were going to crack apart at any moment. You were simply kind. You weren't overly solicitous and you didn't treat me like I had some kind of contagious disease."

She turned to face him, still smiling softly at the memories. "That was the best afternoon I'd had in *forever*. You told me jokes and you showed me the bus stop and the high school and the places where the kids in Pine Gulch liked to hang out. At the grocery store, you introduced me to everyone we met and made sure cranky Mr. Gibbons didn't cheat me, since I didn't have a lot of experience with American money."

She had been an instant object of attention everywhere they went, partly because she was new to town and partly because she looked so exotic, with a half-dozen woven bracelets on each wrist, the choppy hair, her wide, interested eyes.

"A few days later, you came back and said you were heading into town and asked if Aunt Mary needed you to come with me to pick anything else up."

That had basically been a transparent ploy to spend more time with her, which everyone else had figured out but Faith.

"That meant so much to me," she said. "Your own father was dying but that didn't stop you from reaching out and trying to help me acclimatize. I've never forgotten how kind you were to me."

Was it truly kindness, when he was the one who had benefited most? "It couldn't have been easy to find yourself settled in a small Idaho town, after spending most of your childhood wandering around the world."

"It was easier for me than it was for Hope and Celeste, I think. All I ever wanted was to stay in one place for a while, to have the chance to make friends finally. Friends like you."

She gave him a long, steady look. "You are my oldest and dearest friend, Chase. Our friendship is one of the most important things in my life."

He wanted to squeeze her hand, to tell her he agreed with her sentiments completely, but he didn't dare touch her again right now.

"Ditto," he said gruffly.

She drew in a breath that seemed to hitch a little. She looked out the windshield, where a few clouds had begun to gather, spitting out stray snowflakes that spiraled down and caught the light of the stars.

"That's why I have to ask you not to kiss me again."

Chapter Seven

Though she didn't raise her voice, her hard-edged words seemed to echo through his pickup truck.

I have to ask you not to kiss me again.

She meant what she said. He knew that tone of voice. It was the same one she used with the kids when meting out punishment for behavioral infractions or with cattle buyers when they tried to negotiate and offered a price below market value.

Her mind was made up and she wouldn't be swayed by anything he had to say.

Tension gripped his shoulders and he didn't know what the hell to say.

"That's blunt enough, I guess," he finally answered. "Funny, but you seemed to be into it at the moment. I guess I misread the signs."

Her mouth tightened. "It's a strange night. Neither of us is acting like ourselves. Can we just...leave it at that?"

That was the last thing he wanted to do. He wanted to kiss her again until she couldn't think straight.

He hadn't misread *any* signs and they both knew it. After that first moment of shock, she returned the kiss with an enthusiasm and eagerness that had left him stunned and hungry.

"Can you just take me home?" she asked in a low voice.

"If that's what you want," he said.

"It is," she answered tersely.

A few moments ago she had wanted *him*.

She was attracted to him. Lately he had been almost sure of it but some part of him had worried his own feelings for her were clouding his judgment. That kiss and her response told him the sexual spark hadn't been one-sided.

Nice to know he was right about that, at least.

She was attracted to him but she didn't want to be. How did a guy work past that conundrum?

The task suddenly seemed insurmountable.

He put the pickup in gear and focused on driving instead of on the growing realization that she might never be willing to accept him as anything more than her oldest and dearest friend.

Maybe, just maybe, it was time he accepted that and moved on with his life.

Though his features remained set and hard as he drove her back to the Star N, Chase carried on a casual con-

versation with her about the new horse, about a bit of
gossip he heard about cattle futures at the stockgrowers'
party, about Addie's Christmas presents that still needed
to be wrapped.

Under other circumstances, she might have been
quite proud of her halfway intelligent responses—
especially when she really wanted to collapse into a
boneless, quivering heap on the truck seat.

She couldn't stop remembering that kiss—the heat
and the magic and the wild intensity of it.

Her heartbeat still seemed unnaturally loud in her
ears and she hadn't quite managed to catch her breath,
though she could almost manage to string two thoughts
together now.

She felt very much like a tiny island in the middle
of a vast arctic river just beginning the spring thaw,
with chunks of ice and fast-flowing water buffeting
against it in equal parts, bringing life back to the frozen landscape.

She didn't *want* to come to life again. She wanted
that river of need to stay submerged under a hard layer
of impenetrable ice forever.

Knowing that hollow ache was still there, that her
sexuality hadn't shriveled up and died with Travis, completely terrified her.

She was a little angry about it, too, if she were honest. Why couldn't she just resume the state of affairs
of the last thirty months, that sense of suspended animation?

This was *Chase*. Her best friend. The man she relied on for a hundred different things. How could she

possibly laugh and joke with him like always when she would now be remembering just how his mouth had slid across hers, the glide of his tongue, the heat of his muscles against her chest.

She didn't want that river of need to come to churning, seething life again.

Yes, her world had been cold and sterile since Travis died, but it was *safe*.

She felt like she was suffocating suddenly, as if that wild flare of heat between them had consumed all the oxygen.

She rolled her window down a crack and closed her eyes at the welcome blast of cold air.

"Too warm?" he asked.

Oh, yes. He didn't know the half of it. "A little," she answered in a grave understatement.

He turned the fan down on the heating system just as her phone buzzed. She pulled it from the small beaded handbag Celeste had offered for the occasion.

It was a text from her sister: Girls are asleep. Don't rush home. Have fun.

She glanced at the message, then slid her phone back into the totally impractical bag.

"Problem?" he asked.

"Not really. I think Celeste was just checking in. She said the girls are asleep."

"I hope Addie was good."

"She's never any trouble. Really, we love having her around. She always seems to set a good example for my kids."

"Even Barrett?"

She relaxed a little. Talking about their children was much easier than discussing everything else.

"He can be such a rascal when Addie's there. I don't get it. He teases both of them mercilessly. I try to tell him to cut it out but the truth is I think he has a little crush on her."

"Older women. They're nothing but trouble. I had the worst crush on Maggie Cruz but she never paid me the slightest bit of attention. Why would she? I was in fifth grade and she was in eighth and we were on totally different planets."

The only crush she could remember having was the son of the butcher in the last village where they'd lived in Colombia. He had dark, soulful eyes and curly dark hair and always gave her all the best cuts when she went to the market for her family.

That seemed another lifetime ago. She couldn't even remember being that girl who once smiled at a cute boy.

By the time Chase pulled up to the Star N a few moments later, her hormones had almost stopped zinging around.

He put the truck in Park and opened his door.

"Since Addie's asleep, you don't have to come in," she said quickly, before he could climb out. "You don't really have to walk me to the door like this was a real date."

Why did she have to say that? The words seemed to slip out from nowhere and she wanted to wince. She didn't need to remind him of the awkwardness of the evening.

He said nothing, though she didn't miss the way his

mouth tightened and his eyes cooled a fraction before he completely ignored what she said and climbed out anyway.

Everything between them had changed and it made her chest ache with regret.

"Thanks, Chase," she said as they walked side by side through the cold night. "I had a really great time."

"You don't have to lie. It was a disaster from start to finish."

The grim note in his voice made her sad all over again. She sighed. "None of that was your fault. Only mine."

"The old, *it's not you, it's me* line?" he asked as they reached the door. "Really, Faith? You can't be more original than that?"

"It *is* me," she whispered, knowing he deserved the truth no matter how painful. "I'm such a coward and I always have been."

He made a low sound of disbelief. "A coward. You."

"I am!"

"This is the same woman who woke up the day after her husband's funeral, put on her boots and went to work—and who hasn't stopped since?"

"What choice did I have? The ranch was our livelihood. Someone had to run it."

"Right. Just like somebody jumped into a river to save a villager in Guatemala while everybody else was standing on the shore wringing their hands."

She stared at him. "How did you... Where did you hear that?"

"Hope told me once. I think it was after Travis died.

She also told me how you took more than one beating while you were all being held hostage because you stepped up to take responsibility for something she or Celeste had done."

She was the oldest. It had been her job to protect her sisters. What else could she do especially since it was her fault they had all been taken hostage to begin with?

She had told that cute boy she had a crush on the day they were supposed to go to Bogota so her mother could see a doctor and that they would probably be leaving for good in a few weeks.

She had hoped maybe he might want to write to her. Instead, he must have told the psychotic rebel leader their plans. The next time she saw that boy, he had been proudly wearing ragged army fatigues and carrying a Russian-made submachine gun.

"You're not a coward, Faith," Chase said now. "No matter how much you might try to convince yourself of that."

A stray snowflake landed on her cheek and she brushed it away. "You are my best friend, Chase. I'm so afraid of destroying that friendship, like I've screwed up everything else."

He gave her a careful look that made her wish she hadn't said anything, had just told him good-night and slipped into the house.

"Can we... More than anything, I would like to go back to the way things were a few weeks ago. Without all this...awkwardness. When we were just Faith and Chase."

He raised an eyebrow. "You really think we can do that, after that kiss?"

She shivered a little, from more than simply the cold night. "I would like to try. Please, Chase."

"How do two people take a step backward? Something is always lost."

"Can't we at least give it a shot? At least until after the holidays?"

She hoped he couldn't hear the begging tone of her voice that seemed so loud to her.

"I won't wait forever, Faith."

"I know," she whispered.

"Fine. We can talk again after the New Year."

Her relief was so fierce that she wanted to weep. At least she would have his friendship through the holidays. Maybe in a few more weeks, she would be able to find the courage to face a future without his constant presence.

"Thank you. That's the best gift anyone could give me this year."

She reached up to give him a casual kiss on the cheek, the kind she had given him dozens of times before. At the last minute, he turned his head, surprise in his eyes, and her kiss landed on the corner of his mouth.

Instantly, the mood shifted between them and once more she was aware of the heat of him and the coiled muscles and the ache deep within her for him and only him.

He kissed her fully, his mouth a warm, delicious refuge against the cold night. His scent surrounded her— leather and pine and sexy, masculine cowboy—and she desperately wanted to lean into his strength and surrender to the delicious heat that stirred instantly to life again.

Too soon, he stepped away.

"Good night," he said, his eyes dark in the glow from the porch light. He opened the door for her and waited until she managed to force her wobbly knees to carry her inside, then he turned around and walked to his pickup truck.

She really wanted nothing more than to shrug out of Celeste's luxurious coat, kick off her high heels, slip away to her room and climb into bed for the next week or two.

Unfortunately, a welcoming party waited for her inside. Celeste, Flynn and Aunt Mary were at the table with mugs of hot chocolate steaming into the air and what looked like a fierce game of Scrabble scattered around the table—which hardly seemed a fair battle since Celeste was a librarian and an author with a freaky-vast vocabulary.

All three looked up when she walked into the kitchen.

"Chase didn't come in?" Mary asked, clear disappointment on her wrinkled face.

Sometimes Faith thought her great-aunt had a little crush on Chase herself. What other reason did she have for always inviting him over?

"No," she said abruptly.

How on earth was she going to face him, again, now that they had kissed twice?

"How was your date?" Celeste asked. Though the question was casual enough, her sister gave her a searching look and she suddenly wanted desperately to confide in her.

She couldn't do it, at least not with Flynn and Mary listening in. "Fine," she answered.

"Only fine?" Mary asked, clearly surprised.

"Fun," she amended quickly. "Dinner was delicious, of course, and we danced a bit."

"Chase is a great dancer," Mary said, her eyes lighting up. "I could have danced with him all night at Celeste's wedding, except Agatha Lindley kept trying to cut in. I don't think he wanted to dance with her at all but he was just too nice."

"She was there tonight, though she didn't cut in. Unless she tried it when he was busy dancing with Ella Baker."

"Ella Baker?" Celeste frowned. "I don't think I know her."

"She's Curt Baker's daughter. She's moved to Pine Gulch to look after her father."

"The girls at the salon were talking about her when I went for my color this week," Mary said. "She teaches music or something, doesn't she?"

With a jolt, Faith suddenly remembered her conversation with the woman at the beginning of the party, which seemed like a dozen lifetimes ago. "Oh! I have news. Big news! I can't believe I almost forgot."

"You probably had other things on your mind," Flynn murmured, his voice so dry that she shot him a quick look.

Did her lips look as swollen as they felt, tight and achy and full? She really hoped not.

"You owe me so big," she said. "I begged Ella Baker to help out with the Christmas program. I told her my sisters were desperate and she totally agreed to do it!"

Celeste's eyes widened. "Are you kidding? What's wrong with the woman?"

"Nothing. She was very gracious about it and even said it sounded like fun."

"Right. Fun," Celeste said with a shake of her head.

"You had fun, don't deny it," Mary said. "Look how it ended up for you. Married to a hot contractor, tool belt and all."

"Thanks, my dear." Flynn gave a slow grin and picked up Mary's hand and kissed the back of it in a totally un-Flynn-like gesture that made Celeste laugh and Mary blush and pull her hand away.

"That was a definite side benefit," Celeste murmured, and Flynn gave her a private smile that made the temperature in the room shoot up a dozen degrees or so.

"Well, I'm afraid we don't exactly have more hot contractors to go around for Ella Baker," Faith said. "Though I do think she would be absolutely perfect for Chase. I told him so, but for some reason, he didn't seem to want to hear it."

All three of them stared at Faith as if she had just unleashed a rabid squirrel in the kitchen.

"You told Chase you think this Ella Baker would be perfect for him," Celeste repeated, with such disbelief in her voice that Faith squirmed.

"Yes. She seems like a lovely person," she said, more than a little defensive.

"I'm sure she is," Celeste said. "That doesn't mean

you should have tried to set Chase up with her while the two of you were out together on a date. I'll admit I didn't have a lot of experience before I met Flynn but even I know most guys in general probably wouldn't appreciate that kind of thing. Chase in particular probably didn't want to hear you suggest other women you think he ought to date."

Why Chase in particular? She frowned, though she was aware she had botched the entire evening from the get-go. How was she possibly going to fix things between them?

"We're friends," she retorted. "That's the kind of things friends do for each other, pick out potential dating prospects."

None of them seemed particularly convinced and she was too exhausted to press the point. It was none of their business anyway.

She pulled off Celeste's coat and hung it over one of the empty chairs and also pulled all her personal things out of the little evening bag.

"Thanks for letting me use your coat and bag."

"You're welcome. Anytime."

Right. She wasn't going to another stockgrowers' party. *Ever.*

"I'm going to go change into something comfortable."

"I'll come help you with the zipper. That one sticks, if I remember correctly."

"I don't need help," she said.

"That, my dear, is a matter of opinion."

Celeste rose and followed her up the stairs. As she

helped Faith out of the dress, her sister talked of the children and what they had done that evening and about the latest controversy at the library.

Beneath the light conversation, she sensed Celeste had something more to say. She wasn't sure she wanted to hear it but she couldn't stand the charged subtext either.

After she changed into her favorite comfy pajamas, she sat on the edge of her bed and finally braced herself. "Okay. Out with it."

Celeste deliberately avoided her gaze, confirming Faith's suspicions. "Out with what?" she asked, her tone vague.

"Whatever is lurking there on your tongue, dying to spill out. I can tell you have something to say. You might as well get it over with, for both our sakes. What did I do wrong?"

After a pause, Celeste sat down next to her on the bed.

"I'm trying to figure out if you're being deliberately obtuse or if you honestly don't know—all while I'm debating whether it's any of my business anyway."

"Remember what mom used to say? Better to keep your nose in a book than in someone else's business. Most of your life, you've had a pretty good track record in that department. Don't ruin it now."

Celeste sighed. "Fine. Deliberately obtuse it is, then."

She pulled her favorite sweatshirt over her head. This was more like it, in her favorite soft pajama bottoms and a comfortable hoodie. She felt much more at ease dressed like this than she ever would in the fancy clothes she had been wearing all evening.

"I don't know about *deliberate* but I'll admit I must be obtuse, since I have no idea what you're trying to dance around here."

"Really? No idea?"

The skepticism in her sister's voice burned. "None. What did I do wrong? I was careful with your coat, I promise."

"For heaven's sake, this isn't about the stupid coat."

"I'm not in the mood to play twenty questions with you. If you don't want to tell me, don't."

Celeste's mouth tightened. "Fine. I'll come out and say it, then. Can you honestly tell me you have no idea Chase is in love with you?"

At her sister's blunt words, all the blood seemed to rush away from her brain and she was very glad she was sitting down. Her skin felt hot for an instant and then icy, icy cold.

"Shut up. He is not."

Celeste made a disgusted sound. "Of course he is, Faith! Open your eyes! He's been in love with you *forever.* You had to have known!"

Whatever might be left of the apple pie and the small amount she had eaten at dinner seemed to congeal into a hard, greasy lump in her stomach.

She didn't know whether to laugh at the ridiculous joke that wasn't really funny at all or to tell her sister she was absolutely insane to make such an outrageous accusation. Underneath both those reactions was a tangled surge of emotion and the sudden burn of tears.

"He's not. He *can't* be," she whispered.

It couldn't be true. Could it?

Celeste squeezed her fingers gently, looking as if she regretted saying anything. "Use your head, honey. He's a good neighbor, yes, and a true friend. But can you really not see that his concern for you goes way beyond simple friendship?"

Chase was always there, a true and loyal friend. The one constant, unshakable force in her world.

"I don't want him to be." Her chest felt tight now and she could feel one of those tears slip free. "What am I going to do?"

Celeste squeezed her fingers. "You could try being honest with yourself and admit that you have feelings for him, too."

"As a friend. That's all," she insisted.

Celeste's eyes were full of compassion and exasperation in equal measures. "I love you dearly, Faith. You know I do. You've been my second mother since the day I was born, and from the time I was twelve years old you helped Aunt Mary and Uncle Claude raise me. You're kind and loving, a fantastic mom to Barrett and Lou, a ferociously hard worker. You've taught me so much about what it is to be a good person."

She tugged her hand away, sensing her sister had plenty more to say, and steeled herself to hear the rest.

"But?"

Celeste huffed out a breath. "But when it comes to Chase Brannon, you are being completely stupid and, as much as I hate to say it, more than a little cruel."

"That's a harsh word."

"The man is in love with you and when you sit there pretending you didn't know, you are lying to me, yourself and especially to Chase."

"He has never *once* said anything." She still couldn't make herself believe it.

"The last two years, he has shown you in a thousand different ways. You think he comes over three or four times a week to help Barrett with his homework because he loves fourth grade arithmetic? Can anyone really be naive enough to think he adores cleaning out the rain gutters in the spring and autumn because it's his favorite outdoor activity? Does he check the knock in your pickup's engine or help you figure out the ranch accounts or take a look at any sick cattle you might have because he wants to? No! He does all of those things because of *you*."

Faith could come up with a hundred other things he did for her or for the kids or Aunt Mary. That didn't necessary mean he was in *love* with her, only that he was a good, caring man trying to step up and help them after Travis's death.

The nausea inside her now had an element of panic. Had she been ignoring the truth all this time because she simply hadn't wanted to see it? What kind of horrible person was she? It made her feel like the worst kind of user.

"He's my best friend," she whispered. "What would I do without him?"

"I'm afraid you might have to figure that out sooner than you'd like, especially if you can't admit that you might have feelings for him, too."

With that, her sister rose, gave her a quick hug. "We all loved Travis. He was like the big brother I never had. He was a great guy and a good father. But he's gone, honey. You're not. I'll give you the benefit of the doubt and accept that maybe you didn't want to see that Chase is in love with you so you have avoided facing the truth. But now that you know, what are you going to do about it?"

Her sister slipped from the room before she could come up with a response—which was probably a good thing since Faith had no idea how to answer her.

Chapter Eight

"Why couldn't Lou come with us to take me home?" Addie asked Faith as they pulled out of the Star N driveway to head toward Chase's place.

Faith tried to smile but it ended in a yawn. She was completely wrung out after a fragmented, tortured night spent mostly staring up at her ceiling, reliving the evening—those kisses!—and her conversation with Celeste and wondering what she should do.

She must have slept for a few hours, on and off. When she awoke at her five-thirty alarm, all she wanted to do was pull the covers over her head, curl up and block out the world for a week or two.

Faith blinked away the yawn and tried to smile at Chase's daughter again. "She had a few chores to do this morning and I decided it was better for her to finish them as soon as she could. Sorry about that."

Addie gave her a sudden grin. "Oh. I thought it was maybe because you didn't want her to see her Christmas present in the pasture."

She winced. She should have known Addie would figure it out. The girl was too smart for her own britches. She only hoped she could also keep a secret. "How did you know about that?"

"My dad didn't tell me, in case you're wondering. It wasn't that hard to figure it out, though, especially since Lou hasn't stopped talking about the new barrel racing horse she wants. It seemed like too much of a coincidence when I saw a new horse suddenly had shown up in my dad's pasture."

Faith didn't see any point in dissembling. Christmas was only a few weeks away and the secret would be out anyway. "It wasn't a coincidence," she confirmed. "Your dad helped me pick her out and offered to keep her at Brannon Ridge until after Christmas, when we take her to the Dalton ranch to be trained."

"Louisa is going to be so excited!"

"I think so." Her daughter was a smart, kind, *good* girl. Louisa worked hard in school, did her chores when asked and was generally kind to her brother. She had channeled her grief over losing her father at such a young age into a passion for horse riding and Faith wanted to encourage that.

"I won't tell. I promise," Addie said.

"Thank you, honey."

Addie was a good girl, as well. Some children of divorce became troubled and angry—sometimes even manipulative and sly, pitting one parent against the other for their own gain as they tried to navigate the difficult waters of living in two separate households. Addie was the sweetest girl—which seemed a minor miracle, considering her situation.

"Maybe once she's trained, Lou might let me ride her once in a while," the girl said.

Faith didn't miss the wistful note in Addie's voice. "You know, if you want a horse of your own, you could probably talk your dad into it."

Quite frankly, Faith was surprised Chase hadn't already bought a horse for his daughter.

"I know. Dad has offered to get me one since I was like five. It would be nice, but it doesn't seem very fair to have a horse of my own when I could only see it and ride it once or twice a month. My dad would have to take care of it the rest of the time without me."

"I'm sure he wouldn't mind. He already has Tor. It wouldn't be any trouble at all for him to take care of two horses instead of only one."

"Maybe if I lived here all the time," Addie said in a matter-of-fact tone. "It's hard enough, only seeing my dad a few times a month. I hate when I have to go back to Boise. It would be even harder if I had to leave a horse I loved, too."

Faith swallowed around the sudden lump in her throat. The girl's sad wisdom just about broke her heart. "I can understand that. But you do usually spend summers on the ranch," she pointed out. "That's the best time for riding horses anyway."

"I guess." Addie didn't seem convinced. "I just wish I could stay here longer. Maybe come for the whole school year sometime, even if I wouldn't be in the same grade with Louisa."

"Do you think you might come here to go to school at some point?"

"I wish," she said with a sigh. "My mom always says she would miss me too much. I guess she thinks it's okay for Dad to miss me the rest of the time, when I'm with her."

If she hadn't been driving, Faith would have hugged her hard at the forlorn note in her voice. Poor girl, torn between two parents who loved and wanted her. It was an impossible situation for all of them.

She and Addie talked about the girl's upcoming cruise over the holidays with her mother until they arrived at Chase's ranch. When she pulled up to the ranch, she spotted him throwing a bale of hay into the back of his pickup truck like it weighed no more than a basketball.

She shivered, remembering the heat of his mouth on hers, the solid strength of those muscles against her.

On the heels of that thought came the far more disconcerting one born out of her conversation with Celeste.

The man is in love with you and when you sit there pretending you didn't know, you are lying to me, yourself and especially to Chase.

Butterflies jumped around in her stomach and she realized her fingers on the steering wheel were trembling.

Oh. This would never do. This was *Chase*, her best

friend. She *couldn't* let things get funky between them. That was exactly what she worried about most.

Celeste had to be wrong. Faith couldn't accept any other possibility.

The moment she turned off the vehicle, Addie opened the door and raced to hug her dad.

Could she just take off now? Faith wondered. She was half-serious, until she remembered Addie's things were still in the back of the pickup truck.

In an effort to push away all the weirdness, she drew in a couple of cleansing breaths. It didn't work as well as she hoped but the extra oxygen made her realize she had probably been taking nervous, shallow breaths all morning, knowing she was going to have to face him again.

She pulled Addie's sleeping bag out from behind the seat and pasted on a casual smile, knowing even as she did it that he would be able to spot it instantly as fake.

When she turned around, she found him and Addie just a few feet away from her. His eyes were shaded by his black Stetson and she couldn't read the expression there but his features were still, his mouth unsmiling.

"Looks like we caught you going somewhere," she said.

"Just down to the horse pasture to check on, uh, things there."

If she hadn't been fighting against the weight of this terrible awkwardness, she might have managed a genuine smile at his attempt be vague.

"You don't need to use code. Your daughter is too smart for either of us."

"You don't have to tell me that." He smiled down at

Addie and something seemed to unfurl inside Faith's chest. He was an excellent father—and not only to his daughter.

Since Travis died, he had become the de facto father figure for Louisa and Barrett. Oh, Rafe and Flynn did an admirable job as uncles and showed her children how good, decent men took care of their families. But Louisa and Barrett turned to Chase for guidance most. They saw him nearly every day. He was the one Louisa had invited when her class at school had a father-daughter dance and that Barrett had taken along to the Doughnuts with Dad reading hour at school.

They loved him—and he loved them in return. That had nothing to do with any of the nonsense Celeste had talked about the night before.

"Did you have fun last night?" Chase asked Addie now.

"Tons," she declared. "We popped popcorn and watched movies and played games. I beat everybody at UNO like three times in a row and Barrett said I was cheating only I wasn't. And then we all opened our sleeping bags under the Christmas tree and put on another movie and I fell asleep. This morning we had hot chocolate with marshmallows and pancakes shaped like snowmen. It was awesome."

"I'm so glad. Here, I can take that stuff."

He reached to grab the sleeping bag and backpack from Faith. As he did, his hand brushed her chest. It was a touch that barely connected through the multiple layers she wore—coat, a fleece pullover and her silk long underwear—but she could hardly hold back a shiver anyway.

"I'll just take it all into the house now," Addie said. "Thanks for the ride, Faith."

"You're very welcome," she said.

After she strapped the bag over her shoulder and Chase handed her the sleeping bag, she waved at Faith and skipped into the house, humming a Christmas carol.

What a sweet girl, Faith thought again. She didn't let her somewhat chaotic circumstances impact her enjoyment of the world around her. Faith could learn a great deal from the girl's example.

"I'll add my thanks to you for bringing her home," Chase said. "I appreciate it, though I could have driven over to get her."

"I really didn't mind. I've got to run into Pine Gulch for a few things anyway. Can I bring you back anything from the grocery store?"

They did this sort of thing all the time. He would call her on his way to the feed store and ask if she needed anything. She would bring back a part from the implement store in Idaho Falls if she had to go for any reason.

She really hoped the easy, casual give-and-take didn't change now that everything seemed so different.

"We could use paper towels, I guess," he said, after a pause. "Oh, and dishwasher detergent and dish soap."

"Sure. I can drop it off on my way home."

"No rush. I'll pick it up next time I come over."

"Sounds good," she answered. At his words, her smile turned more genuine. This seemed much like their normal interactions—and if he was talking about coming to the ranch again, at least he wasn't so upset at her that he was going to penalize the kids by staying away.

"Did you hear Jim Laird messed up his knee?" he asked. "Apparently he slipped on ice and wrenched things and Doc Dalton sent him over to Idaho Falls for surgery yesterday. I wondered why he wasn't at the party last night. I was hoping Mary Beth wasn't in the middle of a relapse or something."

She didn't like hearing when bad things happened to their neighbors. Jim was a sweet older man in his seventies whose wife had multiple sclerosis. They ran a small herd of about fifty head and he often bought alfalfa from her.

"As if he didn't have enough on his plate! What is Mary Beth going to do? She can't possibly do the feedings in the winter by herself."

"Wade Dalton, Justin Hartford and I are going to split the load for a few weeks, until he can get around again."

He was always doing things like that for others in the community.

"I want into the rotation. I can take a turn."

"Not necessary. The three of us have it covered."

She narrowed her gaze. "For six months after Travis died, ranchers up and down the Cold Creek stepped up to help us at the Star N. I'm in a good place now, finally, and want to give back when I can."

The ranch wouldn't have survived without help from her neighbors and friends—especially Chase. She had been completely clueless about running a cattle ranch and would have been lost.

Now that she had stronger footing under her, she wanted to start doing her best to pay it forward.

Chase looked as if he wanted to argue but he must have seen the determination in her expression. After a moment, he gave an exasperated sigh.

"Fine. I'll have Wade give you a call to work out the details."

She smiled. "Thanks. I don't mind the early-morning feedings either."

"I'll let Wade know."

There. That was much more like normal. Celeste had to be wrong. Yes, Chase loved her—just as she loved him. They were dear friends. That was all.

"I better run to the store before the shelves are empty. You know how Saturdays get in town."

"I do."

"So paper towels, dish soap and dish detergent. You can pick up everything tomorrow when you come for dinner," she said.

"That would work."

She felt a little more of the tension trickle away. At least he was still planning to come for dinner.

She loved their Sunday night tradition, when she and her sisters and Aunt Mary always fixed a big family meal and invited any neighbors or friends who would care to join them. Chase invariably made it, unless he was driving Addie back to Boise after a weekend visitation.

"Great. I'll see you tomorrow."

He looked as if he wanted to say something more but she didn't give him the chance. Instead, she jumped into her pickup and pulled away, trying her best not to look at him in the rearview mirror, standing lean-hipped and gorgeous and watching after her.

They had survived their first encounter post-kiss. Yes, it had been tense, but not unbearably so. After this, things between them would become more comfortable each time until they were back to the easy friendship they had always enjoyed.

She cared about him far too much to accept any other alternative.

He stood and watched her drive away, fighting the urge to rub the ache in his chest.

The entire time they talked about groceries and hot chocolate and Jim Laird's bum knee, his damn imagination had been back in a starlit wintry night, steaming up the windows of his pickup truck.

That kiss seemed to be all he could think about. No matter what else he might be trying to focus on, his brain kept going back to those moments when he had held her and she had kissed him back with an enthusiasm he had only dreamed about.

Hot on the heels of those delicious memories, though, came the cold, hard slap of reality.

I have to ask you not to kiss me again.

She was so stubborn, fighting her feelings with every bit of her. How was he supposed to win against that?

He pondered his dwindling options as he headed inside to find Addie so she could put on her winter clothes and help him feed the horses.

He found her just finishing a call on her cell phone with a look of resignation.

"Who was that?" he asked, though he was fairly sure he knew the answer. He and Cindy were just about the only ones Addie ever talked to on the phone.

"Mom," she said, confirming his suspicion. "She said Grandma is doing better and Grandpa says he doesn't really need her help anymore. She decided to take me back tomorrow so I can finish the last week of school."

Why didn't she call him first to work out the details?

He was surrounded by frustrating women.

"That's too bad. I know you were looking forward to practicing for the show with Louisa."

Her face fell further. "I forgot about that!" she wailed. "If I don't go to practice, I don't know if I can be in the show."

"I'm sure we can talk to Celeste and Hope and get special permission for you to practice at home. You'll be here next weekend and the first part of next week so you'll be able to be at the last few practices."

"I hope they'll let me. I really, really, *really* wanted to be in the Christmas show."

"We'll work something out," he assured her, hoping he wasn't giving her unrealistic expectations. "Meanwhile, why don't you grab your coat and boots. Since you're so smart and already figured out the new horse is for Lou, do you want to meet her for real so you can tell me what you think?"

"Yes!" she exclaimed.

"You'll have to work hard to keep it a secret."

"I know. I would never ruin the surprise."

With that promise, his daughter raced for the mudroom and her winter gear and Chase leaned a hip against the kitchen island to wait for her and tried not to let his mind wander back to those moments in his pickup that were now permanently imprinted on his brain.

Chase headed up the porch steps of the Star N ranch house with a bag of chips in one hand and a bottle of his own homemade salsa in the other, the same thing he brought along to dinner nearly every Sunday.

The lights of the house were blazing a warm welcome against the cold and snowy Sunday evening but his instincts were still urging him to forget the whole thing and head back home, where he could glower and stomp around in private.

He was in a sour mood and had been since Cindy showed up three hours earlier than planned to pick up Addie, right as they were on their way out the door to go to their favorite lunch place.

It was always tough saying goodbye to his daughter. This parting seemed especially poignant, probably because Addie so clearly hadn't wanted to go. She had dragged her feet about packing up her things, had asked if they could wait to leave until after she and Chase had lunch, had begged to say goodbye to the horses.

Cindy, annoyed at the delays, had turned sharp-tongued and hard, which in turn made Addie more pouty than normal. Addie had finally gone out to her mother's new SUV with tears in her eyes that broke his heart.

Being a divorced father seriously sucked sometimes.

In his crazier moments, he thought about selling the ranch and moving to Boise to be closer to her, though he didn't know what the hell he would do for a living. Ranching was all he knew, all he had ever known. But he would do whatever it took—work in a shoe factory if he had to—if his daughter needed him.

He wasn't sure that was the answer, though. She loved her time here and seemed to relish ranch life, in a way Cindy never had.

With a sigh, he rang the doorbell, grimly aware that much of his sour mood had roots that had nothing to do with Cindy or Addie.

He had been restless and edgy since the last time he rang this doorbell, when he had shown up at this same ranch to pick up Faith for that disaster of a date two nights earlier.

How many mistakes could one man make in a single evening? Part of him wished he could go back and start the whole stupid week over again and just let his relationship with Faith naturally evolve from friendship to something more.

How long would that take, though? He had a feeling he could have given her five years—ten—and she would still have the same arguments.

Despite all his mistakes, he had to hope he hadn't completely screwed up their friendship for good, that things weren't completely wrecked between them now.

As she had a few nights earlier, Aunt Mary was the one who finally answered the doorbell.

"It's about time," she said, planting hands on her hips. "Faith needs a man in the worst way."

He blinked at that, his imagination suddenly on fire. "O-kay."

Mary looked amused and he guessed she could tell immediately what detour his brain had taken.

"She needs your grilling skills," she informed him.

He told himself that wasn't disappointment coursing through him. "Grilling skills. Ah. You're grilling tonight."

"We *would* be, but Faith is having trouble again with that stupid gas grill. I swear that thing has it out for us."

He gestured behind him to the elements just beyond the porch. "You do know it's starting to snow, right?"

Aunt Mary shrugged. "You hardly notice out there, with the patio heater and that cover Flynn built us for the deck. Steaks sounded like a great idea at the time, better than roast or chicken tonight, but now the grill is being troublesome. Rafe and Hope aren't back yet from visiting Joey's mom, and Flynn had to fly out to California to finish a project there. That leaves Celeste, Faith and me. We could really use somebody with a little more testosterone to figure out what we're doing wrong."

"I'm not an expert on gas grills but I'll see what I can do."

"Thanks, honey."

He followed Mary inside, where they were greeted by delectable smells of roasting potatoes and yeasty rolls. No place on earth smelled better than this old ranch house on Sunday evenings.

"I've got to finish the salad. Go on ahead," Mary said.

He walked through the kitchen to the door that led to the covered deck. Faith didn't see him at first; she was too busy swearing and fiddling with the controls of the huge, fancy silver grill Travis had splurged on a few months before his death.

She was dressed in a fleece jacket, jeans and boots, with her hair loose and curling around her shoulders. His chest ached at the sight of her, like it always did. He wished, more than anything, that he had the right to go up behind her, brush her hair out of the way and kiss the back of that slender neck.

Little multicolored twinkly Christmas lights covered all the shrubs around the deck and had been draped around the edges of the roof. He didn't remember seeing Christmas lights back here and wondered if Hope had done it to make the rear of the house look more festive. It did look over The Christmas Ranch, after all.

Faith wasn't the biggest fan of Christmas, which he found quite ironic, considering she was part owner of the largest seasonal attraction in these parts.

She fiddled with the knobs again, then smacked the front of the grill. "Why won't you light, you stupid thing?"

"Yelling at it probably won't help much."

She whirled around at his comment and he watched as delectable color soaked her cheeks. "Chase! Oh, I'm so glad to see you!"

He was aware of a fierce, deep-seated need to have her say those words because she wanted to see *him*, not because she had a problem for him to solve.

"Mary said you're having grill trouble."

"The darn thing won't ignite, no matter what I do. It's not getting propane, for some reason. I've been out here for ten minutes trying to figure it out. It's a brand-new tank that Flynn got for us a few weeks ago and we haven't used it since. I checked the propane tank. I tried dropping a match in case it was the ignition. I tried all the knobs about a thousand times. I just think this grill hates me."

He found it more than a little amusing that she had learned to drive every piece of complicated farm machinery on the place over the last two years and could round up a hundred head of cattle on her own, with only the dogs for help, but she was intimidated by a barbecue grill.

"This one can be finicky, that's for sure."

She frowned at the thing. "Travis had to buy the biggest, most expensive grill he could order—forget that the controls on it are more confusing than the space shuttle."

She didn't say disparaging things about her late husband very often. In this case, he had to agree with her. He had loved the guy, but she was absolutely right. Travis Dustin always had to have the best, even when they couldn't afford it. His poor management and expensive tastes in equipment—and his gross negligence in not leaving her with proper life insurance—had all contributed to the big financial hole he had left his family when he died.

"I'll take a look," he said.

She stepped aside and he knelt down to peer at the connection. It only took him a moment to figure out why the grill wouldn't work.

"Here's your trouble. Looks like the gas hose isn't connected tightly. It's come loose from the tank."

He made the necessary adjustment, then stood, turned on the propane and hit the ignition. The grill ignited with a whoosh of instant heat.

She made a face. "Now I feel like an idiot. I swear I checked that already."

"It's easy to overlook."

"I guess my mind must have been on something else."

He had to wonder what. Was she remembering that kiss, too? He cast her a sidelong look and found a pink tinge on her cheeks again that might have been a blush—or just as easily might have been from the cold.

"Thank you for figuring it out," she said.

"No problem. You'll need to let the grill heat up for about ten minutes, then I can come back and take care of the steaks."

"Thank you. No matter how well I think I know my way around all the appliances in my kitchen, apparently this finicky grill remains my bugaboo. Or maybe it's outdoor cookery in general."

"I can't agree with that. I seem to remember some mean Dutch oven meals where you acted as camp cook when Trav and I would combine forces for roundup in the fall."

"That seems like a long time ago."

"Not that long. I still dream about your peach cobbler." Usually his dreams involved her kissing him between thick, gooey spoonfuls, but he decided it would probably be wise not to add that part.

Still, something of his thoughts must have appeared on his face because she seemed to catch her breath and gazed wide-eyed at him in the multicolored glow from the Christmas lights.

"I didn't know you liked it that much," she said after a moment, her voice a little husky. "Dutch oven cooking is easy compared to working this complicated grill. I'll be happy to make you a peach cobbler this summer, when the fruit is in season."

"Sounds delicious," he answered, his own voice a little more gruff than usual, which he told himself was because of the cold—though right now he was much warmer than he might have expected.

She swallowed hard and he was almost positive her gaze drifted to his mouth and then quickly away again. He *was* sure the color on her cheeks intensified, which had to be from more than the cold.

Was she remembering that kiss, too? He wanted to ask her—or better yet, to step forward and steal another one, but the door from the house opened and Louisa popped her head out.

"Hey, Chase! Where's Addie? Didn't she come with you?"

He took a subtle step back. "No. She went back to Boise with her mom this afternoon. Didn't she tell you?"

Her face fell. "Oh, no! Does that mean she won't be able to do the show with us? She thought she could! She and I and Olivia were going to sing a song together!"

"She still wants to. She'll have to miss the first few rehearsals, but she should be here next week for the actual show. We'll do our best to get her back here for rehearsal by Thursday. I might have to run into Boise to make it happen."

"Isn't that your day to help out at Jim Laird's place?"

Rats. He had forgotten all about that. "Yes. I'll figure out a way to swing it."

"I'll help," she said promptly. "I can either run to Boise for you or take your day at Jim's house. Either way, we will get Addie here."

His heart twisted a little that with everything she had to do here at the Star N, she would even consider driving six hours round-trip to pick up his daughter.

"Thank you, but I think I can manage both. If I take off as soon as I finish feeding my stock and his, I should be able to have Addie back in time for practice. It's important to her so I'll figure out a way to make it happen."

Both Faith and her daughter gave him matching warm looks that made him forget all about the snow just beyond their little covered patio.

"Thanks, Chase. You're the *best*," Lou said. Despite the cold, she padded out to the deck in her stocking feet and threw her arms around his waist. He smiled a little and hugged her back, thinking how much he loved both Louisa and her brother. They were great kids, always thinking of others. They were like their mother in that respect.

"Better head back inside. It's cold out here and you don't have shoes or a coat."

"I do have to go back in. I have to finish dessert. I made it myself. Aunt Mary hardly helped at all."

"I can't wait," he assured her.

She grinned and skipped back into the house, leaving him alone again with Faith. When he turned away from the doorway, he found her watching him with an expression he couldn't read.

"What did I say?" he asked.

"I... Nothing," she mumbled. "I'll go get the steaks."

She hurried past him before he could press her, leaving him standing alone in the cold.

Chapter Nine

Faith couldn't leave the intimacy of the covered deck quickly enough.

She felt rattled and unsettled and she hated it. With a deep sense of longing, she remembered dinner just the previous Sunday, when they had laughed and joked and teased like always. He had stayed to watch a movie and she had thrown popcorn into his mouth and teased him about not shaving for a few days.

There had been none of this tension, this awareness that seemed to hiss and flare between them like that stupid grill coming to life.

She had wanted him to kiss her. It was all she could seem to think about, that wondrous feeling of being alive, desired.

Another few moments and she would have been the one to kiss him.

She forced herself to move away from the door and into the kitchen, where Aunt Mary looked up from the rolls she was pulling apart.

"Tell me Chase saved the day again."

"We're in business. It was all about the gas connection. I feel stupid I didn't look there first."

"Sometimes it takes an outside set of eyes to identify the problem and find the solution."

Could someone outside her particular situation help her figure out how to go back in time and fix what felt so very wrong between her and Chase?

"Where are the steaks?" she asked her aunt.

"Over there, by the microwave."

"Whoa," she exclaimed when she spotted them. "That's a lot of steak for just us."

"I took out a few extras in case we had company or so we could use the leftovers for fajitas one day this week. Good thing, because Rafe and Hope said they're only about fifteen minutes out. I'm sure glad they'll beat the worst of the snow. I feel a big storm coming on."

"The weather forecast said most of the storm will clip us."

"Weather forecasts can be wrong. Don't be surprised if we get hit with heavy winds, too."

She had learned not to doubt her great-aunt's intuition when it came to winter storms. After a lifetime of living in this particular corner of Idaho, Mary could read the weather like some people read stock reports.

Sure enough, the wind had already picked up a little

when she carried the tray of steaks out to the covered deck. Chase stood near the propane heater, frowning as he checked something on his phone.

"Trouble?" she asked, nodding at the phone.

"Just Cindy," he answered, his voice terse.

"I'm sorry."

He made a face as he took the tray from her and used the tongs to transfer the steaks onto the grill.

"Nothing new," he said as the air filled with sizzle and scent. "Apparently Addie sulked all the way to Boise about having to go back when she was expecting to stay through the week with me and practice for the show with Olivia and Lou. Of course Cindy blames me. I shouldn't have gotten her hopes up, etc. etc.—even though *she* was the one who changed her mind from her original plan."

Faith wanted to smack the woman. Why did she have to be so difficult?

"Maybe you should petition again for primary custody."

He sighed. "She would never agree. I don't know if that would be the best thing for Addie anyway. Her mom and stepfather have given her a good life in Boise. I just wish she could be closer."

She decided not to tell him about her conversation with Addie the previous morning. What a difficult situation for everyone involved. Her heart ached and she wished, more than anything, that she could give him more time with his daughter for Christmas.

He was such a good man, kind and generous. He

deserved to be happy—which was yet another reason she needed to help him find someone like Ella Baker.

That was what a true friend would do, help him find someone whose heart was whole and undamaged, who could cherish all the wonderful things about him.

Some of her emotions must have appeared on her features because he gave her an apologetic look. "Sorry. I didn't mean to bring you down."

She mustered a smile. "You didn't. What are friends for, if you can't complain about your ex once in a while?"

"I shouldn't complain about her at all. She's my child's mother and overall she takes excellent care of her. She loves her, too. I have to keep reminding myself of that." He shrugged. "I'm not going to worry about it more tonight. For now, let's just enjoy dinner. And speaking of which, I can handle the steaks from here, if you want to go back inside. That wind is really picking up."

"I was planning on grilling," she protested. "You should be the one to go inside. I can take over, as long as you've got the grill working."

"I don't mind."

"If you go inside now, I bet you could nab a hot roll from Aunt Mary."

"Tempting. But no." He wiggled the utensil in his hand. "I've got the tongs, which gives me all the power."

She gave him a mock glare. "Hand them over."

"Come get them, if you think you're worthy."

He held them over his head, which was way over *her* head.

Despite the cold wind, relief wrapped around her like a warm blanket. He was teasing her, just like normal and for a ridiculous moment, she wanted to weep.

Perhaps they *could* find an even footing, return to their easy, dependable friendship.

"Come on. Give," she demanded. She stretched on tiptoe but the tongs were still completely out of reach.

He grinned. "Is that the best you can do?"

Never one to back down from a challenge, she hopped up and her fingers managed to brush the tongs. So close! She tried again but she forgot the wooden planks of the deck were a bit slippery with cold and condensation. This time when she came down, one boot slid and she stumbled a little.

She might have fallen but before she could, his arms instantly came around her, tongs and all.

They froze that way, with his arms around her and her curves pressed against his hard chest. Their smiles both seemed to freeze and crack apart. Her gaze met his and all the heat and tension she had been carefully shoving down seemed to burst to the surface all over again. His mouth was *right there*. She only had to stand on tiptoe again and press her lips to his.

Yearning, wild and sweet, gushed through her and she was aware of the thick churn of her blood, a low flutter in her stomach.

She hitched in a breath and coiled her muscles to do just that when she heard the creak of the door hinges.

She froze for half a second, then quickly stepped away an instant before Rafe tromped out to the deck.

Her brother-in-law paused and gave them a long, considering look, eyebrows raised nearly to his hairline. He hesitated briefly before he moved farther onto the deck.

"You people are crazy. Don't you know December in Idaho isn't the time to be firing up the grill?"

Something was definitely fired up out here. The grill was only part of it. Her face felt hot, her skin itchy, and she could only hope she had moved away before Rafe saw anything—*not* that there had been anything to see.

"Steaks just don't taste the same when you try to cook them under the broiler," Chase said. "Though the purist in me would prefer to be cooking them over hot coals instead of a gas flame."

"You ever tried any of that specialty charcoal?" Rafe asked. "When I was stationed out of Hawaii, I tried the Ono coals they use for luaus. Man, that's some good stuff. Burns hot and gives a nice crisp crust."

"I'll have to try it," Chase said.

"I came to see if you needed help but it looks like you don't need me. You two appear to have things well in hand," he said.

Was his phrasing deliberate? Faith wondered, feeling her face heat even more.

"Doing our best," Chase replied blandly.

She decided it would be wise to take the chance to leave while she could. "Thanks for offering, Rafe. I actually have a few things I just remembered I have to do before dinner. It would great if you two could finish up out here."

She rushed into the house and tried to tell herself she was grateful for the narrow escape.

* * *

Chase took another taste of Aunt Mary's delicious mashed potatoes dripping with creamy, rich gravy, and listened to the conversation ebb and flow around him.

He loved listening to the interactions of Faith and her family. With no siblings of his own, he had always envied the close relationships among them all. They never seemed to run out of things to talk about, from current events to Celeste's recent visit to New York to the progress of Hope's pregnancy.

The conversation was lively, at times intense and heated, and never boring. The sisters might disagree with each other or Mary about a particular topic but they always did so with respect and affection.

It was obvious this was a family that loved each other. The girls' itinerant childhood—and especially the tragedy that had followed—seemed to have forged deep, lasting bonds between Faith and her sisters.

Sometimes they opened their circle to include others. Rafe and his nephew Joey. Flynn and Olivia. Chase.

He could lose this.

If this gamble he was taking—trying to force Faith to let things move to the next level between them— didn't pay off, he highly doubted whether Mary would continue to welcome him to these Sunday dinners he treasured.

Things very well might become irreparably broken between them. His jaw tightened. Some part of him wondered if he might be better off backing down and keeping the status quo, this friendship he treasured.

But then he would see Rafe touch Hope's hand as he

made a point or watch Celeste's features soften when she talked about Flynn and he knew he couldn't let it ride. He wanted to have that with Faith. It was possible; he knew it was. That evening on the deck had only reinforced that she was attracted to him but was fighting it with everything she had.

They could be as happy as Rafe and Hope, Celeste and Flynn. Couldn't she see that?

He had told her he would give her time but even though it had only been a few days, he could feel his patience trickling away. He had waited so long already.

"Who's ready for dessert?" Louisa asked eagerly, as the meal was drawing to a close.

Barrett rolled his eyes. "I haven't even finished my steak. You're just in a hurry because you made it."

"So? I never made a whole cheesecake by myself before. Mom or Aunt Mary always helped me, but I made this one all by myself. I even made the crust."

"I saw it in the kitchen and it looks delicious," Chase assured her. "I can't wait to dig in."

She beamed at him and his heart gave a sharp little ache. This was another reason he didn't want to remain on the edge of Faith's life forever. Louisa and Barrett were amazing kids, despite everything they had been through. He wanted so much to be able to help Faith raise them into the good, kind people they were becoming.

He had no idea what he would do next if she was so afraid to take a chance on a relationship with him that she ended up pushing him out of all of their lives.

He would be lost without them.

He set his fork down, the last piece of delicious steak he had been chewing suddenly losing all its flavor.

He had to keep trying to make her see how good they could all be together, even when the risks of this all-or-nothing roll of the dice scared the hell out of him.

"Okay, do you want chocolate sauce or raspberry?" Lou asked.

He managed a smile. "How about a little of both?"

"Great idea," Mary said. "Think I'll have both, too."

Louisa went around the table taking orders like a server in a fancy restaurant, then she and Olivia headed for the kitchen. When Faith rose to go with them to help, Louisa made her sit back down.

"We can do it," she insisted.

The girls left just as another gust of wind rattled the windows and howled beneath the eaves of the old house. The electricity flickered but didn't go out and he couldn't help thinking how cozy it was in here.

They talked about the record-breaking crowd at The Christmas Ranch that weekend until the girls came back with a tray loaded with slices of cheesecake. They were cut a little crooked and the presentation was a bit messy but nobody seemed to mind.

"This is delicious. The best cheesecake I think I've ever had," Chase said after his first bite, which earned him a huge grin from Louisa.

"It is really excellent," Celeste said. "And I've had cheesecake in New York City, where they know cheesecake."

Louisa couldn't have looked happier. "Thanks. I'm going to try an apple pie next week."

He couldn't resist darting a glance at Faith and wondered if he would ever be able to eat apple pie again without remembering the cinnamon-sugar taste of her mouth.

She licked her lips, then caught his eyes and her cheeks turned an instant pink that made him suddenly certain she was thinking about the kiss, too.

"That wind is sure blowing up a storm," Rafe commented.

"The last update I heard on the weather said we're supposed to have another half foot of snow before morning," Hope said.

"Yay!" all of the children exclaimed together.

"Maybe we won't have school," Joey said with an unmistakably hopeful note in his voice.

"Yeah!" Barrett exclaimed. "That would be awesome!"

"I wouldn't plan on it," Mary said. "I hate to be a downer but I've lived here most of my life and can tell you they hardly ever close school on account of snow. As long as the buses can run, you'll have school."

"It really depends on the timing of the storm and the kind of snowdrifts it leaves behind," Chase said, not wanting the kids to completely give up hope. "If it's early in the morning before the plows can make it around, you might be in luck."

"We should probably head home before the worst of it hits," Rafe said.

"Same here," Celeste said. "I'm so glad Flynn put new storm windows in that old house this summer."

Flynn had spent six months renovating and adding

on to his late grandmother's old house down the road, a project which had been done just days before their wedding in August.

Chase remembered that lovely ceremony on the banks of the Cold Creek, when the two of them—so very perfect for each other—had both glowed with happiness.

Watching them together had only reinforced his determination to forge his own happy ending with Faith, no matter what it took. He had spent the past few months touching her more in their regular interactions, teasing her, trying anything he could think of to convince her to think of him as more than just her friend and confidant.

Right now he felt further from that goal than ever.

Sometimes their Sunday evening dinners would stretch long into the night when they would watch a movie or play games at the kitchen table, but with the storm, everyone seemed in a hurry to leave. They stayed only long enough to clean up the kitchen and then only he, Mary, Faith and her children were left.

"How's the homework situation?" Faith asked from her spot at the kitchen sink drying dishes, a general question aimed at both of her children.

"I had a math work sheet but I finished it on the bus on the way home from school Friday," Louisa said. Chase wasn't really surprised. She was a conscientious student who rarely left schoolwork until Sunday evening.

"How about you, Barrett?"

"I'm almost done. I just had a few problems in math

and they're *hard*. I can ask my teacher tomorrow. We might not even have school anyway so maybe I won't have to turn them in until Tuesday."

"Let's take a look at them," Chase said.

Barrett groaned a little but went to his room for his backpack.

"You don't have to do that," Faith said.

"I don't mind," he assured her.

They sat together at the desk in the great room while the Christmas lights glowed on the tree and a fire flickered in the fireplace. It wasn't a bad way to spend a Sunday night.

After only three or four problems, a lightbulb seemed to switch on in the boy's head—as it usually did.

"Oh! I get it now. That's easy."

"I told you it was."

"It wasn't easy the way my teacher explained it. Why can't you be my teacher?"

He tried not to shudder at the suggestion. "I'm afraid I've already got a job."

"And you're good at it," Mary offered from the chair where she sat knitting.

"Thanks, Mary. I do my best," he answered humbly. He loved being a rancher and wanted to think he was a responsible one.

Now that the boy seemed to be in the groove with his homework, Chase lifted his head from the book and suddenly spotted Faith in the mudroom, putting on her winter gear. He had been so busy helping Barrett, he hadn't noticed.

"Where are you off to? Not out into that wind, I hope."

"I just need to make sure the tarp over the outside haystack is secure. Oh, and check on Rosie," she said, referring to one of her border collies. "She was acting strangely this morning, which makes me think she might be close to having her puppies. I've been trying to keep her in the barn but she wanders off. Before the storm front moves in, I want to be sure she's warm and safe."

Chase scraped his chair back. "I'll come with you."

"You don't need to. You just spent a half hour working on Barrett's homework. I'm sure you've got things to worry about at your place."

He couldn't think of anything. He generally tried to keep things in good order, addressing problems when they came up. He always figured he couldn't go wrong following his father's favorite adage: an ounce of prevention was worth a pound of cure. Better to stop trouble before it could start.

"I'll help," he said. "I'll check the hay cover while you focus on Rosie."

Her mouth tightened for an instant but she finally nodded and waited while he threw his coat on, then together they walked out into the storm.

Darkness came early this time of year near the winter solstice but a few high-wattage electric lights on poles lit their way. The wind howled viciously already and puffed out random snowflakes at them, hard as sharp pebbles.

Below the ranch house, he could see that the parking lot of The Christmas Ranch—which had been full when he pulled up—was mostly cleared out now, with a horse-drawn sleigh on what was probably its last go-round of the evening making its way back to the barn near the lodge.

He would really like to find time before Christmas to take Addie on a ride, along with Faith and her children.

The Saint Nicholas Lodge glowed cheerily against the cold night. Beyond it, the cluster of small structures that made up the life-size Christmas village—complete with indoor animatronic scenes of elves hammering and Santa eating from a plate of cookies—looked like something from a Christmas card.

Her family had created a celebration of the holidays here, unlike anything else in the region. People came from miles around, eager to enhance their holiday spirit.

"It's nice that Hope has hired enough staff now that she doesn't have to do everything on her own," he said.

"With the baby coming, Rafe insisted she cut back her hours. No more fourteen-hour days, seven days a week from Thanksgiving to New Year's."

Those hours were probably not unlike what Faith did year-round on the Star N—at least during calving and haying season and roundup. In other words, most of the year.

She worked so hard and never complained about the burden that had fallen onto her shoulders after Travis died.

When they reached the haystack, tucked beneath a huge open-sided structure with a metal roof, he heard the problem before he saw it, the thwack of a loose tarp cover flapping in the wind. Each time the wind dug underneath the tarp, it pulled it loose a little further. If they didn't tie it down, it would eventually pull the whole thing loose and she would not only lose an expensive tarp but potentially the whole haystack to the storm.

"That's gotten a lot worse, just in the last few hours," she said, pitching her voice louder to be heard over the wind. "I should have taken time to fix it earlier when I first spotted the problem, but I was doing about a hundred other things at the time. I was going to fix it in the morning, but I didn't take into account the storm."

"It's fine," he said. "We'll have it safe and secure in no time. It might take both of us, though—one to hold the flap down and hold the flashlight while the other ties it."

They went to work together, as they had done a hundred times before. He wrestled the tarp down, which wasn't easy amid the increasing wind, then held it while she tied multiple knots to keep it in place.

"That should do it," she said.

"While we're out here, let's tighten the other corners," he suggested.

When he was satisfied the tarp was secure—and when the bite of the wind was close to becoming uncomfortable—he tightened the last knot.

"Thanks, Chase," she said.

"No problem. Let's go see if Rosie is smart enough to stay in from the cold."

She clutched at her hat to keep the wind from tugging it away and they made their way into the relative warmth and safety of her large, clean barn.

The wind still howled outside but it was muted, more like a low, angry buzz, making the barn feel like a refuge.

"That wind has to be thirty or forty miles an hour," she said, shaking her head as she turned on the lights inside the barn.

"At least this storm isn't supposed to bring bitter cold along with it," he said. "Where's Rosie?"

"I set her up in the back stall but who knows if she decided to stay put? I really hope she's not out in that wind somewhere."

Apparently the dog knew this cozy spot was best for her and her pups. They found her lying on her side on an old horse blanket with five brand-new white-and-black puppies nuzzling at her.

"Oh. Will you look at that?" Faith breathed. Her eyes looked bright and happy in the fluorescent barn lights. "Hi there, Rosie. Look at you! What a good girl. Five babies. Good job, little mama!"

She leaned on the top railing of the stall and he joined her. "The kids will be excited," he observed.

"Are you kidding? *Excited* is an understatement. Puppies for Christmas. They'll be thrilled. If I let her, Louisa probably would be down here in a minute and want to spend the night right there in the straw with Rosie."

The dog flapped her tail at the sound of her name and they watched for a moment before he noticed her water bowl was getting low. He slipped inside the stall and picked up the food and the water bowls and filled them each before returning them to the cozy little pen.

For his trouble, he earned another tail wag from Rosie and a smile from Faith.

"Thank you. Do you think they'll be warm enough out here? I can take them into the house."

"They should be okay. She might not appreciate being moved now. They're warm enough in here and they're out of the wind. If you're really worried about it, I can bring over a warming lamp."

"That's a good idea, at least for the first few days. I've got one here. I should have thought of that."

She headed to another corner of the barn and returned a moment later with the large lamp and they spent a few moments hanging it from the top beam of the stall.

"Perfect. That should do the trick."

While the wind howled outside, they stood for a while watching the dog and her pups beneath the glow of the heat lamp. He wasn't in a big hurry to leave this quiet little scene and he sensed Faith wasn't either.

"Seems like just a minute ago that she was a pup herself," she said in a soft voice. "I guess it's been a while, though. Three years. She was in the last litter we had out of Lillybelle, so she would have been born just a few months before Travis…"

Her voice broke off and she gazed down at the puppies with her mouth trembling a little.

"Life rolls on," he said quietly.

"Like it or not, I guess," she answered after a moment. "Thanks for your help tonight, first with Barrett's homework and then with storm preparation. You're too good to us."

"You know I'm always happy to help."

"You shouldn't be," she whispered.

He frowned. "Shouldn't be what?"

She kept her attention fixed on the wriggling puppies. "Celeste gave me a lecture the other night. She told me I'm not being fair to you. She said I take you for granted."

"We're friends. Friends help each other. You feed me every Sunday and usually more often than that. Addie practically lives over here when I have visitation and also ranch work I can't avoid. And you bought my groceries the other day, right?"

"Don't forget to take them home when you go." She released a heavy sigh. "We both know the ledger will never be balanced, no matter how many groceries I buy for you. The Star N wouldn't have survived without you. I don't know why you are so generous with your time and energy on our behalf but I hope you know how very grateful we are. How very grateful *I* am. Thank you. And I hope you know how…how much we all love you."

He looked down at her, wondering at the murky subtext he couldn't quite read here.

"I'm happy to help out," he answered again.

She swallowed hard, avoiding his gaze. "I guess what I wanted to tell you is that things are better now. The Star N is back in the black, thanks in large part to you and to The Christmas Ranch finally being self-sustaining. I'll never been an expert at ranching but I kind of feel like

I know a little more what I'm doing now. If you…want
to ease away a bit so you can focus more on your own
ranch, I would completely understand. Don't worry. We'll
be fine."

It took about two seconds for him to go from confusion to being seriously annoyed.

"So you're basically telling me you don't want me
hanging around anymore."

She looked instantly horrified. "No! That's not what
I'm saying at all. I just…don't want you to feel obligated
to do as much as you have for us. For me. I needed help
and would have been lost without you the last two years
but you can't prop us up forever. At some point, I have
to stand on my own."

"Would you be saying this if I hadn't kissed you the
other night?"

Her eyes widened and she looked startled that he had
brought the kiss up when they both had been so carefully avoiding the subject.

Finally she sighed. "I don't know," she said, her voice
low again and her gaze fixed on the five little border
collie puppies. "It feels like everything has changed."

She sounded so miserable, he wanted to pull her into
his arms and tell her he was sorry, that he would do his
best to make sure things returned to the way they were
a week ago.

"Life has a way of doing that, whether we always
like it or not," he said, knowing full well he wouldn't
go back, even if he could. "Nobody escapes it. The trick
is figuring out how to roll with the changes."

She was silent for a long time and he would have given anything to know what she was thinking.

When she spoke, her voice was low. "I can't stop thinking about that kiss."

Chapter Ten

At first he wasn't sure he heard her correctly or if his own subconscious had conjured the words out of nowhere.

But then he looked at her and her eyes were solemn, intense and more than a little nervous.

He swallowed hard. "Same here. It's all I could think about during dinner. I would like, more than anything, to kiss you again."

She opened her mouth as if she wanted to object. He waited for it, bracing himself for yet one more disappointment. To his utter shock, she took a step forward instead, placed her hands against his chest and lifted her face in clear invitation.

He didn't hesitate for an instant. How could he? He wasn't a stupid man. He framed her face with his hands, then lowered his mouth, brushing against hers once, twice. Her mouth was cool, her lips trembling, and she tasted of raspberry and chocolate from Louisa's cheesecake—rich, heady. Irresistible.

At first she seemed nervous, unsure, but after only a moment, her hands slid around his neck and she pressed against him, surrendering to the heat swirling between them.

He was awash in tenderness, completely enamored with the courageous woman in his arms.

Optimism bubbled up inside him, a tiny trickle at first, then growing stronger as she sighed against his mouth and returned his kiss with a renewed enthusiasm that took his breath away. For the first time in days, he began to think that maybe, just maybe, she was beginning to see that this was real, that they were perfect together.

They kissed for several delicious moments, until his breathing was ragged and he wanted nothing more than to find a soft pile of straw somewhere, lower her down and show her exactly how amazing things could be between them.

A particularly fierce gust of wind rattled the windows of the barn, distracting him enough to realize a cold, drafty barn that smelled of animals and hay might not be the most romantic of spots.

With supreme effort, he forced his mouth to slide away from hers, pressing his forehead to hers and giving them both a chance to collect their breath and their thoughts.

Her eyes were dazed, aroused. "I feel like I've been

asleep for nearly three years and now…I'm not," she admitted.

He pressed a soft kiss on her mouth again. "Welcome back."

She smiled a little but it slid away too soon, replaced by an anxious expression, and she took another step away. He wanted to tug her back into his arms but he knew he couldn't kiss her into accepting the possibilities between them, as tempting as he found that idea.

"I'm afraid," she admitted.

His growing optimism cooled like the air that rushed between them. "Of what? I hope you know I would rather stab myself in the foot with a pitchfork than ever hurt you."

"Maybe I don't want to hurt *you*," she whispered, her features distressed. "You're the best man I know, Chase. When I think about…about not having you in my life, I feel like I'm going to throw up. But I'm not sure I'm ready for this again—or that I ever will be."

Well. That was honest enough. He had to respect it, even if he didn't like it. It took him a moment to grab his scrambled thoughts and formulate them into something he hoped came out coherently.

"That's a decision you'll have to make," he said, choosing his words with care. "But think about those puppies. We can keep them here under that heat lamp forever where it's safe and warm and dry. That's the best place for them right now, I agree, while they're tiny and vulnerable. But they won't always be the way they are right now, and what kind of existence would those puppies have if they could never really have the chance to experience the world? They're meant to run across fields and chase birds and lie stretched out in the summer sunshine. To live."

She let out a breath. "You're comparing me to those puppies."

"I'm only saying I understand you've suffered a terrible loss. I know how hard you've fought to work through the grief. It's only natural to want to protect yourself, to be afraid of moving out of the safe place you've created for yourself out of that grief."

"Terrified," she admitted.

His heart ached for her and the struggle he had forced on her. He wanted to reach for her hands but didn't trust himself to touch her right now. "I can tell you this, Faith. You have too much love inside you to spend the rest of your life hiding inside that safe haven while the world moves on without you."

Her gaze narrowed. "That's easy for you to say. You never lost someone you loved with all your heart."

He wanted to tell her he *had*, only in a different way. He had lost her over and over again—though could a guy really lose what he'd never had?

"You're right. I can only imagine," he lied.

As tempting as it was to tell her everything in his heart—that he had loved her since that afternoon he took her shopping for Aunt Mary—he didn't dare. Not yet. Something told him that would send her running away even faster.

She would have to be the one to make the decision about whether she was ready to open her heart again.

The storm rattled the window again, fierce and de-

manding, and she shivered suddenly, though he couldn't
tell if it was from the cold or from the emotional winds
battering them. Either way, he didn't want her to suffer.

"Let's get you back to the house. Mary will be wondering where we are."

She nodded. After one more check of the puppies,
she tugged her gloves back on and headed out into the
night.

Faith was fiercely aware of him as they walked from
the barn to the ranch house with the wind and snow
howling around them.

She felt as if all the progress she had made toward
rebuilding her world had been tossed out into this storm.
She had been so proud of herself these last few months.
The kids were doing well, the ranch was prospering, she
had finally developed a new routine and had begun to
be more confident in what she was doing.

While she wouldn't say she had been particularly
happy, at least she had found some kind of acceptance
with her new role as a widow. She was more comfortable in her own skin.

Now she felt as if everything had changed again.
Once more she was confused, off balance, not sure how
to put one more step in front of the other and forge a
new path.

She didn't like it.

Even in the midst of her turmoil, she couldn't miss
the way he placed his body in the path of the wind to
protect her from the worst of it. That was so much like

Chase, always looking out for her. It warmed her heart, even as it made her ache.

"You still need your groceries," she said when they reached the house. "Come in and I'll grab them."

He looked as if he had something more to say but he finally nodded and followed her inside.

Though she could hear the television playing down the hall in the den, the kitchen was dark and empty. A clean, vacant kitchen on Sunday night after the big family party always left her feeling a little bereft, for some strange reason.

She flipped on the light and discovered a brown paper bag on the counter with his name on it. She couldn't resist peeking inside and discovered it contained a half dozen of the dinner rolls. Knowing Aunt Mary and her habits, she pulled open the refrigerator and found another bag with his name on it.

"It looks like Mary saved some leftovers for you."

"Excellent. It will be nice not having to worry about dinner tomorrow."

She knew he rarely cooked when Addie was with her mother, subsisting on frozen meals, sandwiches and the occasional steaks he grilled in a batch. Mary knew it, too, which might be another reason she invited him over so often.

Faith headed to the walk-in pantry where she had left the things she bought at the store for him.

"Here you go. Dishwashing detergent, dish soap and paper towels."

"That should do it. Thanks for picking them up for me."

"It was no trouble at all."

"I'll check in with you first thing in the morning to see if you had any storm damage."

If she were stronger, she would tell him thank you but it wasn't necessary. At some point in a woman's life, she had to figure out how to clean up her own messes. Instead, she did her best to muster a smile. "Be careful driving home."

He nodded. Still looking as if he had something more to say, he headed for the door. He put a hand on the knob but before he could turn it, he whirled back around, stalked over to her and kissed her hard with a ferocity and intensity that made her knees so weak she had to clutch at his coat to keep from falling.

She could only be grateful none of her family members came into the kitchen just then and stumbled over them.

When he pulled away, a muscle in his jaw worked but he only looked at her out of solemn, intense eyes.

"Good night," he said.

She didn't have the breath to speak, even if she trusted herself to say anything, so she only nodded.

The moment he left, she pulled her ranch coat off with slow, painstaking effort, hung it in the mudroom, then sank down into a kitchen chair, fighting the urge to bury her face in her hands and weep.

She felt like the world's biggest idiot.

She knew she relied on him, that he had become her rock and the core of her support system since Travis died. He made her laugh and think, he challenged her, he praised her when things went well and held her when they didn't.

All this time, when she considered him her dearest friend, some part of her already knew the feelings she had for him ran deeper than that.

She felt so stupid that it had taken her this long to figure it out. She had always known she loved him, just as she had told him earlier.

She had just never realized she was also *in love* with him.

How had it happened? How could she have *let* it happen?

She should have known something had shifted over the last few months when she started anticipating the times she knew she would see him with a new sort of intensity, when she became more aware of the way other women looked at him when they were together, as she started noticing a ripple of muscle, the solid strength of him as he did some ordinary task in the barn.

She should have realized, but it all just seemed so... natural.

She was still sitting there trying to come to terms with the shock when Mary came into the kitchen wearing her favorite flannel nightgown over long underwear and thick socks.

"Did Chase take off? I had leftovers for him."

She summoned a smile that felt a little wobbly at the edges. "He took them. Don't worry."

"Oh, you know me. Worrying is what I do best." Mary looked out the window where the snow lashed in hard pellets. "I'll tell you, I don't like him driving into the teeth of that nasty wind. All it would take would be one tree limb to fall on his pickup truck."

Her heart clutched at the unbearable thought.

This. This was why she couldn't let herself love him. She would not survive losing a man she loved a second time.

She pushed the grim fear away, choosing instead to focus on something positive.

"Rosie had her puppies. Five of them."

"Is that right?" Mary looked pleased.

"They're adorable. I'm sure the kids will want to see them first thing."

"I made them take their showers for the night. Barrett isn't very happy with me right now but I'm sure he'll get over it. They're both in their rooms, reading."

She would go read to them in a moment. It was her favorite part of the day, those quiet moments when she could cuddle her children and explore literary worlds with them. "Thank you," she said to her aunt. "I don't tell you enough how much I appreciate your help."

Mary sat down across from her at the table. "Are you okay? You seem upset."

For a moment, she desperately wanted to confide in her beloved great-aunt, who was just about the wisest person she knew. The words wouldn't come, though. Mary wouldn't be an unbiased observer in this particular case as Mary adored Chase and always had.

"I'm just feeling a little down tonight."

Mary took Faith's hands in her own wrinkled, age-spotted ones. "I get that way sometimes. The holidays sure make me feel alone."

A hard nugget of guilt lodged in her chest. She wasn't the only one in the world who had ever suffered heartache. Uncle Claude had died five years earlier and they all still missed him desperately.

"You're not alone," she told her aunt. "You've got us, as long as you want us."

"I know that, my dear, and I can't tell you how grateful I am for that." Mary squeezed her fingers. "It's not quite the same. I miss my Claude."

She thought of her big, burly, white-haired great-uncle, who had adored Christmas so much that he had started The Christmas Ranch with one small herd of reindeer to share his love of the holiday with the community.

"I'm thinking about dating again," Mary announced. "What do you think?"

She blinked at that completely unexpected piece of information. "Really?"

"Why not? Your uncle's been gone for years and I'm not getting any younger."

"I... No. You're not. I think it's great. Really great."

Her aunt made a face. "I don't know about *great*. More like a necessary evil. I'd like to get married again, have a companion in my old age, and unfortunately you usually have to go through the motions and go on a few dates first in order to get there."

Her seventy-year-old great-aunt was braver than she was. It was another humbling realization. "Do you have someone in mind?"

Her aunt shrugged. "A couple of widowers at the senior citizens center have asked me out. They're nice enough, but I was thinking about asking Pat Walters out to dinner."

She tried not to visibly react to yet another stunner. For years, Pat had been one of the men who played Santa Claus at The Christmas Ranch. His wife had died just a few months after Uncle Claude.

She digested the information and the odd *rightness* of the idea.

"You absolutely should," she finally said. "He's a great guy."

"He is. Truth is, we went out a few times three years ago when I was living in town and we had a lot of fun together. I didn't tell you girls because it was early days yet and there was nothing much to tell."

She shrugged her ample shoulders. "But then Travis died and I moved back in here to help you with the kids. I just didn't feel like the time was right to complicate things so Pat and I put things on the back burner for a while."

Oh, the guilt. The nugget turned into a full-on boulder. Had she really been so wrapped up in her own pain that she hadn't noticed a romance simmering right under her nose?

What else had she missed?

"I wish you had told me," she said. "I hate that you put your life on hold for me. I would have been okay. Celeste was here to help me out in the evenings and I could have hired someone to help me with Lou and Barrett when I was busy on the ranch and couldn't take them with me."

Mary frowned. "I didn't tell you about Pat to make you feel guilty. You didn't force me to move in after

Travis died. You didn't even *ask* me. I did it because I needed to, because that's what family does for each other."

Mary and Claude had been helping her and her sisters for eighteen years, since they had been three traumatized, frightened, grieving girls.

Her aunt, with her quiet strength, support and wisdom, had been a lifesaver to her after her parents died and even more of one after Travis died.

"I can never repay you for everything you've done," she said, her throat tight and the hot burn of tears behind her eyes.

Mary sat back in her chair and skewered her with a stern look. "Is that what you think I want? For you to repay me?"

"Of course! I wish I could."

"Well, you're right. I do."

She blinked. "Okay."

"You can do that by showing me I taught you a thing or two over the years about surviving and thriving, even when the going is tough."

She stared at her aunt, wondering where this was coming from. "I… What do you mean?"

"Life isn't meant to be lived in fear, honey," Mary said.

It was so similar to her recent conversation with Chase that she had to swallow. "I know."

"Do you?" Mary pressed. "I'm just saying. Chase won't wait around for you forever, you know."

Faith pulled her hands from her aunt's and curled

them into fists on her lap. "I don't know what you mean."

Mary snorted. "Of the three of you, you were always the worst liar. You know exactly what I mean. That boy is in love with you and has been forever."

She felt hot and then ice-cold. First Celeste, now Aunt Mary. What had they seen that she had missed all this time?

She wanted to protest but even in her head, any counterargument she tried to formulate sounded stupid and trite. Was it true? Had he been in love with her and had she been so preoccupied with life that she hadn't realized?

Or worse, much worse, had she realized it on some subconscious level and simply taken it for granted all this time?

"Chase is my best friend, Mary. He's been like a father to the kids since Travis died. And you and I both know we would have had to sell the ranch if he hadn't helped me pull it back from the brink."

Her aunt gave her a hard look. "Seems to me there are worse things to base a relationship on. Not to mention, he's one good-looking son of a gun."

She couldn't deny that. And he kissed like a dream.

"I'm so scared," she whispered.

Mary made that snorting noise again. "Who isn't, honey? If you're not scared sometimes, you're just plain stupid. The trick is to decide how much of your life you're willing to sacrifice for those fears."

Before she could come up with an answer, her aunt

rose. "I'm going to turn in and you've got kids waiting for you to read to them."

She rose, as well. "Thank you, Mary."

She didn't know if she was thanking her for the advice or the last eighteen years of wisdom. She supposed it didn't really matter.

Her aunt hugged her. "Don't worry. You'll figure it out. Good night, honey. Sleep well."

She would have laughed if she thought she could pull it off without sounding hysterical.

Something told her more than the wind would be keeping her up that night.

She didn't see Chase at all the next week. Maybe he was only giving her space, as she had asked, or maybe he was as busy at his place as she was at the Star N, trying to finish up random jobs before the holidays.

Or maybe he was finally fed up with her cowardice and indecision.

Though she didn't see him, she did talk to him on the phone twice.

He called her once on Monday morning, the day after the storm and that stunning kiss in the barn, to make sure her ranch hadn't sustained significant damage from the winds and snows.

On Thursday afternoon, he called to tell her he was driving to Boise to pick up Addie a day earlier than planned and asked if she needed him to bring anything back from Boise for the kids' stockings.

He had sounded distant and frazzled. She knew how tough it was for him to be separated from Addie over the holidays, which made his thoughtfulness in worrying about Louisa and Barrett even more touching.

Again, she wanted to smack Cindy for her selfishness in booking a cruise over the holidays without consulting him.

He could have withheld permission and the court would have sided with him. After Cindy sprang the news on him, though, he had told Faith he hadn't wanted to drag Addie into a war between her parents.

As a result, he was planning their own Christmas celebration a few days before the actual holiday, complete with Christmas Eve dinner, presents and all.

"I think we're covered," she told him, her heart aching. "Be careful driving back. Oh, and let Addie know she's still on to sing with Louisa and Olivia. Ella is planning on it."

"I'll tell her. She'll be thrilled. Thanks."

She wanted to tell him so many other things. That she hadn't stopped thinking about him. That their kisses seemed to play through her head on an endless loop. That she just needed a little more time. She couldn't find the courage to say any of it so he ended up telling her goodbye rather abruptly and severing the connection.

There had been times when they stayed on the phone the entire time he drove to Boise to pick up his daughter, never running out of things to talk about.

Were those days gone forever?

She sighed now and headed toward Saint Nicholas Lodge with a couple of letters that had been delivered to the main house by accident, probably because the post office had temporary help handling the holiday mail volume.

Though she waved at the longtime clerk at the gift store, she didn't stop to chat, heading straight for the office instead, where she found Hope sitting behind her desk.

"Mail delivery," Faith announced, setting the letters on the desk. "It looks like a bill for reindeer food and one for candy canes. I might have a tough time convincing my accountant those are legitimate expenses for a cattle ranch."

When Hope didn't reply, Faith's gaze sharpened on her sister. Fear suddenly clutched her when she registered her sister's pale features, her pinched mouth, the haunted eyes. "What is it, honey? What's wrong?"

"Oh, Faith. I... I was just about to call you."

Her sister's last word ended in a sob that she tried to hide but Faith wasn't fooled. She also suddenly realized her sister's arms were crossed protectively across her abdomen.

"What's wrong? Is it the baby?"

Hope nodded, tears dripping down the corners of her eyes. "I've been having crampy aches all day and I... I just don't feel good. I was just in the bathroom and...had some spotting. Oh, Faith. I'm afraid I'm losing the baby."

She burst into tears and Faith instantly went to her side and wrapped her arms around her. Her younger sister was normally so controlled in any crisis. Even when they had been kidnapped, Hope had been calm and cool.

Seeing her lose it like this broke Faith's heart in two.

"What do you need me to do? I can call Rafe. I can run you into the doctor's. Whatever you need."

"I just called Rafe." Hope wiped at her eyes, though she continued to weep. "He's on his way and we're running into Jake Dalton's office. It might be nothing. I might be overreacting. I hope so."

"I do, too." She whispered a prayer that her sister could endure whatever outcome.

She wouldn't let herself focus on the worst, thinking instead about what a wonderful mother Hope would be. She was made for it. She loved children and had spent much of her adult life following their parents' examples and trying to help those in need around the world in her own way.

Really, coming home and running The Christmas Ranch had been one more way Hope wanted to help people, by giving them a little bit of holiday spirit in a frazzled word.

"It's the worst possible time," Hope said, her eyes distressed. "Within the hour, I've got forty kids showing up to practice for the play."

"That is absolutely the least of your concerns," Faith said, going into big sister mode. "I forbid you to worry about a single thing at The Christmas Ranch. You've got an excellent staff, not to mention a family ready to step in and cover whatever else you might need. Focus on yourself and on the baby. That's an order."

Hope managed a wobbly smile that did nothing to conceal the fear beneath it. "You're always so bossy."

"That's right." She squeezed her sister's fingers.

"And right now I'm ordering you to lie down and wait for your husband, this instant."

Hope went to the low sofa in the office and complied. While she rested, Faith found her sister's coat and her voluminous tote bag and carried them both to her, then sat holding her hand for a few more moments, until Rafe arrived.

He looked as pale as his wife and hugged her tightly, green eyes murky with worry. "Whatever happens, we'll be okay," he assured her.

It took all her strength not to sob at the gentleness of the big, tough former navy SEAL as he all but carried Hope out to his SUV and settled her into the passenger side. Faith handed her the tote bag she had carried along.

"Call me the minute you know anything," she ordered.

"I will. I promise. Faith, can you stay during rehearsals to make sure Ella has everything she needs?"

"Of course."

"Don't tell Barrett and Lou yet. I don't want them to worry."

"Nothing to tell," she said. "Because you and that baby are going to be absolutely fine."

If she kept saying that, perhaps she could make it true.

She watched them drive away, shivering a little until she realized she had left her own coat in Hope's office. Before she could go inside for it, she spotted Chase's familiar pickup truck.

How did he always know when she needed him? she

wondered, then realized he must be dropping Addie off for rehearsal.

She didn't care why he had come. Only that he was there.

She moved across the parking lot without even thinking it through. Desperate for the strength and comfort of his embrace, she barely gave him time to climb out of his vehicle before she was at his side, wrapping her arms tightly around him.

She saw shock and concern flash in his eyes for just an instant before he held her tight against him. "What's going on? What's wrong?" he asked, his voice urgent.

Addie was with him, Faith realized with some dismay. She couldn't burst into tears, not without the girl wondering about it and then telling Lou and Barrett, contrary to Hope's wishes.

"It's Hope," she whispered in his ear. "She's threatening a miscarriage."

He growled a curse that made Addie blink.

"It's too early to know for sure yet," Faith said quietly. "Rafe just took her to the doctor."

"What can I do?"

It was so like him to want to fix everything. The thought would have made her smile if she weren't so very worried. "I don't think we can do anything yet. Just hope and pray she and the baby will both be okay."

"Will she need extra help here at The Christmas Ranch? I can cover you at the Star N if you need to step in here until the New Year."

Oh, the dear man. He was already doing extra work

for their neighbor and now he wanted to add Faith's workload to his pile, as well.

"I hope I don't have to take you up on that but it's too early to say right now."

"Keep me posted."

"I will. I… Thank you, Chase."

"You're welcome."

She would have said more but other children started to arrive and the moment was gone.

Chapter Eleven

Chase ended up staying to watch the rehearsal, figuring he could help corral kids if need be.

He had plenty of other things he should be doing but nothing else seemed as important as being here if Faith or her family needed him.

A few minutes after the rehearsal started, Celeste showed up. She went immediately to the office, where Faith was staring into space. The two of them embraced, both wiping tears. Not long after, Mary showed up, too, and the three of them sat together, not saying much.

He wanted to go in there but didn't quite feel it was his place so he stayed where he was and watched the children sing about Silver Bells and Holly Jolly Christmases and Silent Nights.

About an hour into rehearsal—when he felt more

antsy than he ever remembered—Faith took a call on her cell phone. The anxiety and fear on her features cut through him and he couldn't resist rising to his feet and going to the doorway.

"Are they sure? Yes. Yes. I understand." Her features softened and she gave a tremulous smile. "That's the best news, Rafe. The absolute best. Thank you for calling. I'll tell them. Yes. Give her all our love and tell her to take care of herself and not to worry about a thing. That's an order. Same goes for you. We love you, too, you know."

She hung up, her smile incandescent, then she gave a little cry that ended on a sob. "Dr. Dalton says for now everything seems okay with the baby. The heartbeat is strong and all indications are good for a healthy pregnancy."

"Oh, thank the Lord," Mary exclaimed.

She nodded and they all spent a silent moment doing just that.

"Jake wants to put her on strict bed rest for the next few weeks to be safe," Faith said after a moment. "That means the rest of us will have to step up here."

"I'm available for whatever you need," Chase offered once more.

She gave him a distracted smile. "I know but, again, you have plenty to do at your own place. We can handle it."

"I want to help." He tried to tamp down his annoyance that she was immediately pushing aside his help.

"We actually could use him tomorrow," Celeste said thoughtfully.

Faith didn't look convinced. "We'll just have to cancel that part of the party, under the circumstances. The kids will have to understand."

"They're kids," her sister pointed out. "They won't understand anything but disappointment."

"I'll just do it, then," Faith said.

"How, when you're supposed to be helping me with everything else?"

He looked from one to the other without the first idea what they were talking about. "What do you need me to do?"

"I've been running a holiday reading contest at the library for the last two months and the children who have read enough pages earned a special party tomorrow at the ranch," Celeste said. "Sparkle is supposed to make an appearance and we also promised the children wagon rides around the ranch. Our regular driver will be busy taking the regular customers to see the lights so Rafe has been practicing with our backup team so he could help out at the party. Obviously, he needs to be with Hope now. Flynn is coming back tomorrow but he won't be here in time to help, even if he learns overnight how to drive a team of draft horses."

Why hadn't they just asked him in the first place? Was it because things with him and Faith had become so damn complicated?

"I can do it, no problem—as long as you don't mind if Addie comes along."

Celeste gave him a grateful smile. "Oh, thank you! And Addie would be more than welcome. She's such a reader she probably would have earned the party anyway. Olivia, Lou and Faith are my volunteer helpers and I'm sure they would love Addie's help."

"Great. I'll plan on it, then. Just let me know what time."

They worked out a few more details, all while he was aware of Faith's stiff expression.

At least he would get to see her the next day, even if she clearly didn't want him there.

She lived in the most beautiful place on earth.

Faith lifted her face to the sky, pale lavender with the deepening twilight. As she drove the backup team of draft horses around the Star N barn so she could take them down to the lodge late Sunday afternoon, the moon was a slender crescent above the jagged Teton mountain range to the east and the entire landscape looked still and peaceful.

Sometimes she had to pinch herself to believe she really lived here.

When she was a girl, she had desperately wanted a place to call her own.

She had spent her entire childhood moving around the world while her parents tried to make a difference. She had loved and respected her parents and understood, even then, that they genuinely wanted to help people as they moved around to impoverished villages setting up medical clinics and providing the training to run them after they left.

She wasn't sure *they* understood the toll their self-ordained missionary efforts were taking on their daughters, even before the terrifying events shortly before their deaths.

Faith hadn't known anything other than their transitory lifestyle. She hadn't blinked an eye at the primitive conditions, the language barriers, making friends only to have to tearfully leave them a few months later.

Still, some part of her had yearned for *this*, though she never had a specific spot in mind. All she had really wanted was a place to call her own, anywhere. A loft in the city, a split-level house in the suburbs, a double-wide mobile home somewhere. She hadn't cared what. She just wanted roots somewhere.

For nearly sixteen years, that had been her secret dream, the one she hadn't dared share with her parents. That dream had become reality only after a series of traumas and tragedies. The kidnapping. The unspeakable ordeal of their month spent in the rebel camp. Her father's shocking death during the rescue attempt, then her mother's cancer diagnosis immediately afterward.

She had been shell-shocked, grieving, frightened out of her mind but trying to put on a brave front for her younger sisters as they traveled to their new home in Idaho to live with relatives they barely knew.

When Claude picked them up at the airport in Boise and drove them here, everything had seemed so strange and new, like they had been thrust into an alien landscape.

Until they drove onto the Star N, anyway.

Faith still remembered the moment they arrived at the ranch and the instant, fierce sense of belonging she had felt.

In the years since, it had never left her. She felt the same way every time she returned to the ranch after spending any amount of time away from it. This was home, each beautiful inch of it. She loved ranching more than she could have dreamed. Whoever would have guessed that she would one day become so comfortable at this life that she could not only hitch up a team of draft horses but drive them, too?

The bells on the horses jingled a festive song as she guided the team toward the shortcut to the Saint Nicholas Lodge. Before she could go twenty feet, she spotted a big, gorgeous man in a black Stetson blocking their way.

"I thought I was the hired driver for the night," Chase called out.

She pulled the horses to a stop and fought down the butterflies suddenly swarming through her on fragile wings.

"I figured I could get them down there for you. Anyway, we just bought new sleigh bells for the backup sleigh and I wanted to try them out."

"They sound good to me."

"I think they'll do. Where's Addie?"

"Down at the lodge, helping Olivia and Lou set things up for the party. We stopped there first and Celeste sent me up here to see if you needed help with the team."

Faith fought a frown. She had a feeling her sister sent him out here as yet another matchmaking ploy. Her family was going to drive her crazy. "I've got things under control," she lied. She was only recently coming to see it wasn't true, in any aspect of her life.

"That's good," he said as he greeted the horses, who were old friends of his. "How's Hope?"

"I checked on her a few hours ago and she is feeling fine. She had a good night and has had no further symptoms today. Looks like the crisis has passed."

In the fading light, she saw stark relief on his chiseled features. "I'm so glad. I've been worried all day. And how is your other little mama?"

It took her a moment to realize he meant Rosie. "All the pups are great. They opened their eyes yesterday. The kids have had so much fun watching them. You'll have to bring Addie over."

"I'll try to do that before she leaves on Wednesday but our schedule's pretty packed between now and then. I don't think we'll even have time for Sunday dinner tomorrow."

"Oh. That's too bad," she said, as he moved away from the horses toward the driver's seat of the sleigh. "The family will miss you."

"What about you?" he asked, his voice low and his expression intense.

She swallowed, not knowing what to say. "Yes," she finally said. "Good thing we're not having steak or we wouldn't know how to light the grill."

"Good thing." He tipped his hat back. "Is there room for me up there or are you going to make me walk back to the lodge?"

She slid over and he jumped up and took the reins she handed him.

Though there was plenty of space on the bench, she immediately felt crowded, fiercely aware of the heat of him beside her.

Maybe *she* ought to walk back to the lodge.

The thought hardly had time to register before he whistled to the horses and they obediently took off down the drive toward the lodge, bells jingling.

After a moment, she forced herself to relax and enjoy the evening. She could think of worse ways to spend an evening than driving across her beautiful land in the company of her best friend, who just happened to be a gorgeous cowboy.

"Wow, what a beautiful night," he said after a few moments. "Hard to believe that less than a week ago we were gearing up for that nasty storm."

"We're not supposed to have any more snow until Christmas Eve."

"With what we already have on the ground, I don't think there's any question that we'll have a white Christmas."

"Who knows? It's Idaho. We could have a heat wave between now and then."

"Don't break out your swimming suit yet," he advised. "Unless you want to take a dip in Carson and Jenna McRaven's pool at their annual party this week."

"Not me. I'm content watching the kids have fun in the pool."

The McRavens' holiday party, which would be the night *after* the show for the senior citizens, had become legendary around these parts, yet another tradition she cherished.

"I don't think I'll be able to make it to that one this year," he said. "It's my last day with Addie."

"You're still doing Christmas Eve the night of the show?"

"That's the plan."

It made her heart ache to think of him getting everything ready for his daughter on his own, hanging out stockings and scattering her presents under the tree.

"You're a wonderful father, Chase," she said softly.

He frowned as the sleigh's movement jostled her against him. "Not really. If I were, I might have tried harder to stay married to her mother. Instead, I've given my daughter a childhood where she feels constantly torn between the both of us."

"You did your best to make things work."

"Did I?"

"It looked that way from the outside."

"I should never have married her. If she hadn't been pregnant with Addie, I wouldn't have."

He was so rarely open about his marriage and divorce that she was momentarily shocked. The cheery jingle bells seemed discordant and wrong, given his serious tone.

"It was a mistake," he went on. "We both knew it. I just hate that Addie is the one who has suffered the most."

"She has a mother and stepfather who love her and a father who adores her. She's a sweet, kind, good-hearted girl. You're doing okay. Better than okay. You're a wonderful father and I won't let you beat yourself up."

He looked touched and amused at the same time as

he pulled the sleigh to a stop in front of the lodge. "I've been warned, I guess."

"You have," she said firmly. "Addie is lucky to have you for a father. Any child would be."

His expression warmed and he gazed down at her long enough that she started wondering if he might kiss her again. Instead, he climbed down from the sleigh, then held a hand up to help her out.

She hesitated, thinking she would probably be wise to make her way down by herself on the complete opposite side of the sleigh from him. But for the last ten minutes, they had been interacting with none of the recent awkwardness and she didn't want to destroy this fragile peace.

She took his hand and stepped gingerly over the side of the sleigh.

"Careful. It's icy right there," he said.

The words were no sooner out of his mouth when her boot slipped out from under her. She reached for the closest handhold, which just happened to be the shearling coat covering the muscled chest of a six-foot-two-inch male. At the same moment, he reacted instinctively, grabbing her close to keep her on her feet.

She froze, aware of his mouth just inches from hers. It would be easy, so easy, to step on tiptoe for more of those delicious kisses.

His gaze locked with hers and she saw a raw hunger there that stirred answering heat inside her.

The moment stretched between them, thick and rich like Aunt Mary's hot cocoa and just as sweet.

Why was she fighting this, again? In this moment,

as desire fluttered through her, she couldn't have given a single reason.

She was in love with him and according to two of her relatives, he might feel the same. It seemed stupid to deny both of them what they ached to find together.

"Chase," she murmured.

He inched closer, his breath warm on her skin. Just before she gathered her muscles to stand on tiptoe and meet him, one of the horses stamped in the cold, sending a cascade of jingles through the air.

Oh. What was she doing? This wasn't the time or the place to indulge herself, when a lodge full of young readers would descend on them at any moment.

With great effort, she stepped away. "Hang out here and I'll go check with Celeste to see when she'll be ready for the kids to go on the sleigh."

He tipped his hat back but not before she saw frustration on his features that completely matched her own.

Chapter Twelve

"Wow," Chase said as his daughter rushed down the stairs so they could leave for the Saint Nicholas Lodge. "Who is this strange young lady in my house who suddenly looks all grown-up?"

Addie grinned and swirled around in the fancy red-and-gold velvet dress she was wearing to perform her musical selection with Olivia and Louisa. "Thanks, Dad," she said. "I love this dress *so much*! I wish I could keep it but I have to give it back after the show tonight so maybe someone else can wear it for next year's Christmas show."

"Those are the breaks in show business, I guess," he said. "You've got clothes to change into, right?"

She held up a bag.

"Good. Are you're sure you don't need me to braid your hair or something?"

He was awful with hair but had forced himself to learn how to braid, since it was the easiest way to tame Addie's curls.

"No. Faith said she would help me fix it like Louisa and Olivia have theirs. That's why I have to hurry."

"Yes, my lady. Your carriage awaits." He gave an exaggerated bow and held out her coat, which earned him some of Addie's giggles.

"You're so weird," she said, with nothing but affection in her voice.

"That's what I hear. Merry Christmas, by the way."

She beamed. "I'm so glad we're having our pretend Christmas Eve on the same night as the show. It's perfect."

He buttoned up her coat, humbled by the way she always tried to find a silver lining. "Even though we can't spend the whole evening playing games and opening presents, like we usually do?"

"You only let me open one present on Christmas Eve," she reminded him. "We can still do that after the show, and then tomorrow we'll open the rest of them on our fake Christmas morning."

"True enough."

"Presents are fun and everything. I love them. Who doesn't?"

"I can't think of anyone," he replied, amused by her serious expression.

"But that's not what Christmas is really about. Christmas is about making other people happy—and our show will make a lot of lonely older people very happy. That's what Faith said, anyway."

His heart gave a sharp little jolt at her name, as it always did. "Faith is right," he answered.

About the show, anyway. She wasn't right about him, about them, about the fear that was holding her back from giving him a chance. He couldn't share that with his child so he merely smiled and held open the door for her.

"Let's go make some people happy," he said.

Her smile made her look wiser than her eleven years, then she hurried out into the December evening.

Three hours later, he stood and clapped with the delighted audience as the children walked out onto the small stage at the Saint Nicholas Lodge to take their final bow.

"That was amazing, wasn't it?" Next to him, Flynn beamed at his own daughter, Olivia, whose red-and-gold dress was a perfect match to those worn by Louisa and Addie.

"Even better than last year, which I didn't think was possible," Chase said.

"Those kids have truly outdone themselves this year," Flynn said, gazing out at the smiles on all the wrinkled and weathered faces in the audience as they applauded energetically. "Like it or not, I have a feeling this show for the senior citizens of Pine Gulch has now officially entered into the realm of annual traditions."

Chase had to agree. He had suspected as much after seeing the show the previous year. Though far from an

elaborate production—the cast only started rehears-
ing the week before, after all—the performance was
sweet and heartfelt, the music and dancing and dramatic performances a perfect mix of traditional and
new favorites.

Of course the community would love it. How could
they do otherwise?

"I'm a little biased, but our girls were the best,"
Flynn said.

Again, Chase couldn't disagree. Olivia had a pure,
beautiful voice that never failed to give him chills, while
Lou and Addie had done a more than adequate job of
backing her up on a stirring rendition of "Angels We
Have Heard on High" that had brought the audience
to its feet.

"I overheard more than one person saying that was
the highlight of the show," Chase said.

He knew Flynn had become more used to his daughter onstage over the last year as she came out of her
shell a little more after witnessing the tragedy of her
mother's death. While Flynn would probably never love
it, he appeared to be resigned to the fact that Olivia,
like her mother and grandmother before her, loved per-
forming and making people happy.

Almost without conscious intention, his gaze strayed
to Faith, who was hugging the children as they came
offstage. She wore a silky red blouse that caught the
light and she had her hair up again in a soft, romantic
style that made him want to pull out every single pin.

She must have felt his attention. She looked up from
laughing at something cute little Jolie Wheeler said and

her gaze connected with his. Heat instantly sparked between them and he watched her smile slip away and her color rise.

They gazed at each other for a long moment. Neither of them seemed in a hurry to look away.

He missed her.

He hadn't really spoken with her since that sleigh ride the other night. She had seemed to avoid him for the rest of that evening, and he and Addie hadn't made it to Sunday dinner that week.

When he dropped Addie off earlier in the evening, he had greeted Faith, of course, but she had seemed frazzled and distracted as she hurried around helping the children with hair and makeup.

He hadn't had time to linger then anyway, as Rafe had sent him out to pick up some of the senior citizen guests who didn't feel comfortable driving at night amid icy conditions.

Now Jolie asked her a question and Faith was forced to look down to answer the girl, severing the connection between them and leaving him with the hollow ache that had become entirely too familiar over the last few weeks.

More than anything, he wished he knew what was in her head.

Addie came offstage and waved at him with an energy and enthusiasm that made Flynn laugh.

"I think someone is trying to get your attention," his friend said to Chase in a broad understatement.

"You think?" With a smile, Chase headed toward his daughter.

"Did you see me, Dad?" she exclaimed.

"It was my very favorite part of the show," he told her honestly.

"Lots of other people have told us that, too. We *were* good, but everyone else was, too. I'm so glad I got to do it, even though I missed the first rehearsals."

"So am I."

She hugged him and he felt a rush of love for his sweet-natured daughter.

"What now?" he asked.

"I need to change out of the dress and give it back, I guess," she said, her voice forlorn.

"You sound so sad about that," Faith said from behind him.

He hadn't seen her approach and the sound of her voice so near rippled down his spine as if she had kissed the back of his neck.

Addie sighed. "I just love this dress. I wish I could keep it. But I understand. They need to keep it nice for someone else to wear next year."

Faith hugged her. "Sorry, honey. I took a thousand pictures of you three girls, though. You did such a great job."

Addie grinned. "Thanks, Faith. I *love* my hair. Thank you for doing it. I wish it could be like this every day."

"You are so welcome, my dear," she said with a smile that sent a lump rising in his throat. These were the two females he loved most in the world, with Louisa, Mary and Faith's sisters filling in the other slots, and he loved seeing them interact.

"I guess I should be wishing you a Merry Christmas Eve," Faith said.

"It's the best Christmas Eve on December 20 I ever had," Addie said with a grin, which made Faith laugh.

The sound tightened the vise around his chest. She hadn't laughed nearly enough over the last three years.

What would everyone in the Saint Nicholas Lodge do if he suddenly tugged her to him and kissed her firmly on the mouth for all to see?

"What's for Christmas Eve dinner?" Faith asked him before he could think about acting on the impulse.

He managed to wrench his mind away from impossible fantasies. "You know what a genius I am in the kitchen. I bought a couple of takeout dinners from the café in town. We *are* having a big breakfast tomorrow, though. I can handle waffles and bacon."

"Why don't you eat your Christmas Eve dinner here? We have so much food left over. I think Jenna always overestimates the crowd. Once the crowd clears, we're going to pull some of it out. Everyone is starving, since we were all too busy for dinner before the show to take time for food. You're more than welcome to stay— though I completely understand if you have plans at home for your Christmas Eve celebration."

"Can we, Dad?" Addie begged. "I won't see my friends for three weeks after this."

She wouldn't see *him* for that amount of time either— a miserable thought.

He shrugged, already missing her. "We don't have any plans that are set in stone. I think the only other thing we talked about, besides the show, was playing a couple of games."

"And reading the Christmas story," she pointed out.

"Right. We can't forget that," he answered. "I don't mind if we stay, as long as you promise to go straight to bed when we're done. Santa can't come if you're not asleep."

She rolled her eyes but grinned at the same time. At eleven, she was too old for Santa but that didn't stop either of them from carrying on the pretense a little longer.

"I'm going to go change and tell Lou and Livvie that we're having dinner here," she announced.

She hurried away, leaving him alone with Faith—or as alone as they could be in a vast holiday-themed lodge still filled with about twenty other people.

"It really was a wonderful show," he said.

"I can't take any of the credit."

He had to smile, remembering how busy she had been before and during the show. The previous year had been the same. She claimed she wanted nothing to do with the holiday show, then pitched in and did whatever was necessary to pull it off.

His smile slid away when he realized she was gazing at his mouth again.

Yeah. He decided he didn't much care what people would think if he kissed her again right now.

She swallowed and looked away. "I need to, um, probably take Sparkle back to the barn for the night."

Besides the musical number with Addie and her friends, the other highlight of the show had been when

Celeste, under duress, read from her famous story "Sparkle and the Magic Snowball" to the captivated audience while the *real* Sparkle stood next to her, looking for all the world as if he were reading the story over her shoulder.

"I'll help," he offered.

Both of them knew she didn't need his help but after a moment, she shrugged and headed toward the front door and the enclosure where Sparkle hung out when he made appearances at the lodge.

Faith paused long enough to grab her coat off the rack by the door and toss his to him, then the two of them walked outside into the night.

The reindeer wandered over to greet them like old friends, the bells on his harness jingling merrily.

"Hey, Sparkle. How are you, pal?"

The reindeer lipped at his outstretched hand, making Chase wish he'd brought along an apple or something.

"I really don't need your help," Faith said. "He's so easygoing this is a one-person job—if that. I could probably tell him to go to bed and he would wander over to the barn, flip the latch and head straight for his stall. He might even turn off the lights on his way."

He had to smile at the whimsical image. "I'm here. Let's do this so we can eat, too."

With a sigh, she reached to unlatch the gate. Before she could, Ella Baker came out of the lodge, bundled against the cold and carrying an armload of sheet music.

"You're not staying for dinner?" Faith asked after they exchanged greetings.

"I can't. My dad is having a rough time right now so

I need to take off. But thank you again for asking me to do this. I had so much fun. If you do it again next year and I'm still in town, I would love to help out."

"That's terrific!" Faith exclaimed. "I'll let Hope know. I can guarantee she'll be thrilled to hear this. Thank you!"

"I'm so sorry your sister couldn't be here to see it," Ella said. "I hope the live video worked so she could watch it at home."

Hope was still taking it easy, Chase knew, though she'd had no other problems since that frightening day the week before.

"She saw it," Faith assured her. "I talked to her right afterward and she absolutely loved it, just like everyone else did."

"Oh, I'm so glad." Ella smiled, then turned to him. "Chase, it's really good to see you again. I didn't have the chance to tell you this the other night but I had such a great time dancing with you. I'd love to do it again sometime."

It was clearly an invitation and for a moment, he didn't know what to say. Any other single guy in Pine Gulch would probably think he'd just won the lottery. Ella was lovely and seemed very nice. A relationship with her would probably be easy and uncomplicated— unlike certain other women he could mention.

The only trouble was, that particular woman in question had him so wrapped up in knots, he couldn't untangle even a tiny thread of interest in Ella.

"I'm afraid opportunities to dance are few and far

between around here," he said, in what he hoped was a polite but clear message.

"You two could always go to the Renegade," Faith suggested blithely. "They have a live band with dancing just about every Saturday night."

For a moment, he could only stare at her. Seriously? She was pimping him out to take another woman dancing?

"That would be fun," Ella said, obviously taking Faith's suggestion as encouragement. "Maybe we could go after the holidays."

Chase didn't want to hurt her but he was not about to take her up on the invitation to go out dancing while he was standing in front of the woman he loved.

Even if it had been Faith's suggestion in the first place.

"I don't know," he said, in what he hoped was a noncommittal but clear voice. "I have my daughter a couple weekends a month and it's tough for me to get away."

Understanding flashed in her eyes along with a shadow of pained rejection. He hated that he had planted it there—and hated more that Faith had put him in the position in the first place.

"No problem," she said, some of the animation leaving her features. "Let me know if you have a free night. I've got to run. Good night. And Merry Christmas in advance."

She gave a smile that was only a degree or two shy of genuine and headed out into the parking lot toward her car.

He wasn't sure how, exactly, but Chase managed to

hold on to the slippery, fraying ends of his temper as they led the reindeer the short distance across the snowy landscape to The Christmas Ranch barn.

It coiled through him as they worked together to take off Sparkle's harness and bells, gave him a good brushing, then made sure he had food and water.

He should just let it go, he told himself after they stepped out of the stall and closed the gate.

The evening had been wonderful and he didn't want to ruin it by fighting with her.

He almost had himself convinced of that but somehow as he looked at her, his anger slipped free and the words rolled out anyway.

"Why the hell would you do that?"

Chapter Thirteen

Faith stared at him, stunned by the anger that seemed to seethe around them like storm-tossed sea waves.

"Do...what?"

"You know. You just tried to set me up with Ella Baker again."

Her face flamed even as she shivered at his hard tone. Oh. That.

"All I did was mention that the Renegade has dancing on Saturday nights. I only thought it would be fun for the two of you."

His jaw worked as he continued to stare down at her. "Is that right?"

"Ella is really great," she said. She might as well double down on her own stupidity. "I've seen her with the kids this week and she's amazing—so patient and kind and talented. You heard her sing. Any single guy would have to be crazy not to want to go out with her."

"Really, Faith. *Really?*" The words came at her like a whip snapping through the cold air.

He was furious, she realized. More angry than she had ever seen him. She could see it in every rigid line of his body, from his flexed jaw to his clenched fists.

"After everything that's happened between us these last few weeks, you seriously want to stand there and pretend you think I might have the slightest interest in someone else?"

She let out a breath, ashamed of herself for dragging an innocent—and very nice—woman into this. She didn't even know why she had. The words had just sort of come out. She certainly didn't *want* Chase dating Ella Baker but maybe on some level she was still hanging on to the hope that they could somehow return to the easy friendship of a few weeks ago and forget the rest of this.

"I can't help it if I want you to be happy," she said, her voice low. "You're my dearest friend."

"I don't want to be your friend." He growled an oath that had her blinking. "After everything, can you really not understand that? Fine. You want me to be clear, I'll be clear. I don't want to be your buddy and I don't want to date Ella Baker. She is very nice but I don't have the slightest flicker of interest in her."

"Okay," she whispered. She shouldn't be relieved about that but she couldn't seem to help it.

He gazed down at her, features hard and implacable. "There is only one woman I want in my life and it's you,

Faith. You have to know that. I'm in love with you. It's you. It has *always* been you."

She caught her breath at his words as joy burst through her like someone had switched on a thousand Christmas trees. She wanted to savor it, to simply close her eyes and soak it in.

I love you, too. So, so much.

The words crowded in her throat, jostling with each other to get out.

Over the last few weeks, she had come to accept that unalterable truth. She was in love with him and had been for a long time.

Perhaps some little part of her had loved him since that day he drove her into town when she was a frightened girl of fifteen.

What might have happened between them if his father hadn't been dying, if Travis hadn't come back to the Star N and she hadn't been overwhelmed by the sweet, kind safety he offered, the anchor she had so desperately needed?

She didn't know. She only knew that Chase had always been so very important in her world—more than she could ever have imagined after Travis died so suddenly.

The reminder slammed into her and she reached out for the rough planks of Sparkle's enclosure for support.

Travis.

The images of that awful moment when she had found him lying under his overturned ATV—covered in blood, so terribly still—seemed to flash through her mind in a grim, horrible slide show. She hadn't been able to save him, no matter how desperately she had tried as she begged him not to leave her like her father, her mother.

She had barely survived losing Travis. How could she find the strength to let herself be vulnerable to that sort of raw, all-consuming, soul-destroying pain again?

She couldn't. She had been a coward so many years ago as a helpless girl caught up in events beyond her control and she was still a coward.

Faith opened her mouth to speak but the words wouldn't come.

The silence dragged between them. She was afraid to meet his gaze but when she forced herself to do it, she found his eyes murky with sadness and what she thought might be disappointment.

"You don't have to say anything." All the anger seemed to have seeped out of him, leaving his features as bleak as the snow-covered mountains above the tree line. "I get it."

How could he, when *she* didn't understand? She had the chance for indescribable happiness here with the man she loved. Why couldn't she just take that step, find enough strength inside herself to try again?

"It doesn't matter how much time I give you. You've made up your mind not to let yourself see me as anything more than your *dearest friend* and nothing I do can change that."

She wanted to tell him that wasn't true. She saw him for exactly what he was. The strong, decent, wonderful man she loved with all her heart.

Fear held both her heart and her words in a tight, icy grip. "Chase, I—" she managed, but he shook his head.

"Don't," he said. "I pushed you too hard. I thought you might be ready to move forward but I can see now I only complicated things between us and wasted both of our time. It was a mistake and I'm sorry."

"I'm the one who's sorry," she said softly, but he had turned around and headed for the door and she wasn't sure he heard her.

The moment he left, she pressed a hand to her chest and the sharp, cold ache there, as if someone had pierced her skin with an icicle.

She wanted so badly to go after him but told herself maybe it was better this way.

Wasn't it better to lose a friendship than to risk having her heart cut out of her body?

Chase didn't know how he made it through the next few days.

The hardest thing had been walking back inside the Saint Nicholas Lodge and trying to pretend everything was fine, with his emotions a raw, tangled mess.

He was pretty sure he fooled nobody. Celeste and Mary seemed especially watchful and alert as he and Addie dined with the family. As for Faith, she had come in about fifteen minutes after he did with her eyes red and her features subdued. She sat on the exact opposite side of the room from him and picked at her food, her features tight and set.

He was aware of a small, selfish hope that perhaps

she was suffering a tiny portion of the vast pain that seemed to have taken over every thought.

She had left early, ostensibly with the excuse of taking some of the leftovers to Rafe and Hope, though he was fairly certain it was another effort to avoid him.

He did his best to put his pain on the back burner, focusing instead on making his remaining few hours with his daughter until after the New Year memorable for her.

Their premature Christmas Eve went off without a hitch. When they returned home, she changed into her pajamas and they played games and watched a favorite holiday movie, then she opened the one early present he allowed her—a carved ornament he had made from a pretty aspen burl on a downed tree he found in the mountains. In the morning she opened the rest of her presents from him and he fixed her breakfast, then she helped him take care of a few chores.

Too soon, her mother showed up after visiting her parents at the care center where Cindy's mother was still recovering from her stroke.

Chase tried to put on a smile for Cindy, sorry all over again for the mess he had made of his marriage.

He had tried so hard to love her. Those early days had been happy, getting ready for the baby and then their early days with Addie, but their shared love of their daughter hadn't provided strong enough glue to keep them together.

It hadn't been Cindy's fault that his heart hadn't been completely free. Despite his best efforts, she somehow had sensed it all along and he regretted that now.

He understood why disappointment and hurt turned her bitter and cold toward him and he resolved to do his best to be kinder.

Addie had decided to leave some of the gifts he had given her at the ranch so she could enjoy them during her time with him there, but she still had several she wanted to take home. After he loaded them into her mom's SUV, he hugged his daughter and kissed the top of her head. "Have a fun cruise, Addie-bug, and at Disney World. I want to hear every detail when you get back."

"Okay," she said, her arms tight around his neck. "You won't be by yourself on Christmas, will you, Dad? You'll go open presents at the Star N with Louisa and Barrett, right?"

His heart seemed to give a sharp little spasm. That's what he had done for several years, even before Travis died, but that was looking unlikely this year.

"I'm not sure," he lied. "I'll be fine, whatever I do. Merry Christmas, kiddo."

As they drove away, he caught sight of the lights of the Star N and The Christmas Ranch below the Brannon Ridge.

How was he going to make it through the remainder of his life without her—and without Lou and Barrett and the rest of her family he loved so much?

He didn't have the first idea.

"Why isn't Chase coming for dinner tonight?" Louisa asked as she and Barrett decorated Christmas cookie angels on the kitchen island.

"Yeah. He always comes over on Christmas Eve," Barrett said.

"And on Christmas morning when we open presents," Louisa added.

Faith had no idea how to answer her children. It made her chest ache all over again, just thinking about it.

That morning she had gathered her nerve and called to invite him for dinner and to make arrangements for transferring Louisa's Christmas present from Brannon Ridge to the Star N. She had been so anxious about talking to him again after four days of deafening silence, but the call went straight to voice mail.

He was avoiding her.

That was fairly obvious, especially when he texted just moments later declining her invitation but telling her that he already had a plan to take care of the other matter and she didn't need to worry about it.

The terse note after days of no contact hurt more than she could have imagined, even though she knew it was her own fault. She wanted so much to jump in her truck and drive to his ranch, to tell him she was sorry for all the pain she had put them both through.

"I guess he must have made other plans this year," she said now in answer to her daughter.

Mary made a harrumphing sort of noise from her side of the island but said nothing else in front of the children, much to Faith's relief.

Though her aunt didn't know what had transpired between Faith and Chase, Mary knew *something* had. She blamed Faith for it and had made no secret that she wasn't happy about it.

"Addie texted me a while ago. She's worried he'll be all by himself for the holidays," Louisa said. Her daughter made it sound like that was the worst possible fate anyone could endure and the guilty knot under Faith's rib cage seemed to expand.

Her children loved Chase—and vice versa. She hated being the cause of a rift between them.

"We should take him some of our cookies," Barrett suggested.

"That's a great idea," Mary said, with a pointed look at her. "Faith, why don't you take him some cookies? You could be there and back before everybody shows up for dinner."

He didn't want cookies from her. He didn't want *anything*—except the one thing she wasn't sure she had the strength to give.

"Maybe we can all take them over later," she said.

The three looked as if they wanted to argue but she made an impromptu excuse, desperate to escape the guilt and uncertainty. "I need to go. I've got a few things I need to do out in the barn before tonight."

"Now?" Mary asked doubtfully.

"If I finish the chores now, I won't have to go out to take care of them in the middle of our Christmas Eve party with Hope and Celeste," she said.

It was a flimsy excuse but not unreasonable. She did have chores—and she had plans to hang a big red ribbon she had already hidden away in the barn across the stall where she planned to put Lou's new horse. She could do that now, since Louisa had no reason to go out to the barn between now and Christmas morning.

She grabbed her coat and hurried out before any of them could argue with her.

Outside, a cold wind blew down off Brannon Ridge and she shivered at the same time she yawned.

She hadn't been sleeping much the last few weeks, which was probably why her head ached and her eyes felt as if they were coated with gritty sandpaper.

Maybe she could just go to bed and wake up when Christmas was over.

She sighed. However tempting, that was completely impossible. She had hours to go before she could sleep. It was not yet sunset on Christmas Eve—she still had to make it through dinner with her sisters and their families. Both of them were coming, since Hope had been cleared to return to her normal activities.

They would want to know where Chase was and she didn't know how to answer them.

Not only that but her kids would likely be awake for hours yet, jacked up on excitement and anticipation—not to mention copious amounts of sugar from the treats they had been making and sampling all day.

She should take sugar cookies to Chase. He loved them and probably hadn't made any for himself.

How could she possibly face him after their last encounter?

Tears burned behind her eyes. She wanted to tell herself it was from the wind and the lack of sleep but she knew better. This was the season of hope, joy, yet she felt as if all the color and light had been sucked away, leaving only uniform, lifeless gray.

She was in love with him and she didn't know what to do about it.

The worst part was knowing that even if she could find the strength and courage to admit she loved him, she was afraid it was too late.

He had looked so bleak the last time she saw him, so distant. Remembering the finality in that scene, the tears she had been fighting for days slipped past her defenses.

She looked out at the beautiful landscape—the snow-covered mountains and the orange and yellows of the sunset—and gave in to the torment of her emotions here, where no one could see her.

After a few moments, she forced herself to stop, wiping at the tears with her leather gloves. None of this maudlin stuff was helping her take care of her chores and now she would have to finish quickly so she could hurry back to the house to fix her makeup before her sisters saw evidence of her tears and pressed her about what was wrong.

How could she tell them what a mess she had made of things?

With another sigh, she forced herself to focus on the job at hand. She walked through the snow to the barn and pushed the door open but only made it a few steps before she faltered, her gaze searching the interior.

Something was wrong.

Over the past two and a half years, she had come to know the inside of this barn as well as she did her own bedroom. She knew it in all seasons, all weather, all moods.

She knew the scents and the sounds and the shifting light—and right now she could tell something was different.

Someone was here.

She moved quietly into the barn, reaching for the pitchfork that was usually there. It was missing but she found a shovel instead and decided that would have to do.

No one else should be here.

She had two part-time ranch hands but neither was scheduled to be here on Christmas Eve. She had given both time off for the holidays and didn't expect to see them until the twenty-seventh. Anyway, if it had been Bill or Jose, wouldn't she have seen their vehicles parked out front?

With the shovel in hand, she headed farther into the interior of the big barn, eyes scanning the dim interior. Seconds later she spotted it—a beautiful paint mare in one of the stalls near the far end of the barn.

At almost that exact moment, she heard a noise coming from above her. She whirled toward the hayloft that took up one half of the barn and spotted him there, his back to her, along with the missing pitchfork.

"Chase!" she exclaimed. "What are you doing here?"

He swiveled around, and for an arrested moment, he looked at her with so much love and longing, she almost wept again.

Too quickly, he veiled his features. "Feeding Lou's new horse. While I was at it, I figured I could take care of the rest of your stock in the barn so you wouldn't have to worry about it tonight. I was hoping to get out of here before you came down from the house but obviously I'm not fast enough."

He had done that for her, even though he was furious with her. She wanted to cry all over again.

Happiness seemed to bloom through her like springtime and the old barn had never looked so beautiful.

She swallowed, focusing on the least important thought running through her head. "How did you get the new horse down here? I never saw your trailer."

"I didn't want Lou to see it and wonder what was going on so I came in the back way, down the hill. I rode Tor and tied the mare's lead line to his saddle."

"You came down through all that snow?" she exclaimed. "How on earth did you manage that?" There were drifts at least four feet deep in places on that ridgeline.

"It was slow going but Tor is tough and so's the new little mare. She's going to be a great horse for Lou."

She felt completely overwhelmed suddenly, humbled and astonished that he would go to such lengths for her daughter.

And for her, she realized.

This was only one of a million other acts over the last few years that provided all the evidence anyone could need that he loved her.

"I can't believe you would do that."

"Don't make a big deal out of it," he said, his tone distant.

"It is a big deal to me. It's huge. Oh, Chase."

The tears from earlier broke free again and a small

sob escaped before she could cover her mouth with her fingers.

"Cut it out. Right now."

She almost laughed at the alarm in his voice, despite the tears that continued to trickle down her cheeks.

"I can't. I'm sorry. When the man I love shows me all over again how wonderful he is, I tend to get emotional. You're just going to have to deal with that."

Her words seemed to hang in the air of the barn like dust motes floating in the last pale shafts of Christmas Eve sunlight. He stared at her for a second, then lurched toward the ladder. Before he reached it, his boot heel caught on something. He staggered for just a moment and tried to regain his balance but he didn't have anything to hold on to.

He fell in what felt like slow motion, landing with a hard thud that sounded almost as loud as her instinctive scream.

He couldn't breathe—and not because her words had stunned him. No. He literally couldn't breathe.

For a good five seconds, his lungs were frozen, the wind knocked hard out of him. He was aware on some level of her running toward him to kneel next to him, of her panicked, tearstained features and her hands on his face and her cries of "breathe, breathe, *breathe*."

He wasn't sure if the advice was for him or herself but then, just as abruptly, the spasm in his diaphragm eased and he could inhale again, a small breath and then increasingly deeper until he dared talk again.

"I'm…okay."

She was reaching for her phone when he spoke. At his voice, she gasped, dropping it to the concrete floor of the barn and throwing herself across him with an impact that made him grunt.

She immediately eased away. "Where does it hurt? I need to call an ambulance. It will probably take them a while to get here so it might be faster for me to just drive you."

The panic in her voice seeped through his discomfort and he reached out a hand to cover hers.

"I don't...need an ambulance. The breath...was knocked out of me...but I'm okay."

The alfalfa he had been forking down for the animals had cushioned most of the impact and he knew there was no serious damage, even though everything still ached. He might have a broken rib in there, but he wasn't about to tell her that.

"Are you sure? That was a hard fall."

"I'm sure."

Her hand fluttered in his and he suddenly remembered what she had said and his complete shock that had made him lose his footing.

He sat up and wiped at her tears.

"Faith. What were you saying just before I fell?"

She looked down, her cheeks turning pink. "I... Nothing."

It was the exact antithesis of *nothing*. "You said you loved me," he murmured.

She rubbed her cheek on her shoulder as if trying to hide evidence of the tears trickling down. "That was a pretty hard fall," she said again. "Are you sure you didn't bump your head, too?"

"Positive. I know what I heard. Why do you think I fell? You shocked me so much I forgot I was ten feet up in the air. Say it again."

Her hand fluttered in his again but he held it tight. He wasn't going to let her wriggle away this time. After a moment, she stopped and everything about her seemed to sigh.

"I love you," she whispered. "I've known it for a while now. I just... I've been so afraid."

"I know. I'm sorry."

He hadn't wanted to make her suffer more than she already had. But maybe they both had to pass through this tough time to know they could make it through to the other side.

He pulled her toward him and his breath seemed to catch all over again—and not at all from the pain—when she wrapped her arms around his waist and rested her cheek against his chest.

Joy began to stir inside him, tentative at first and then stronger.

She belonged exactly here. Surely she had to know that by now.

"After Travis died, I never wanted to fall in love again. Ever," she said, her voice low. "I guess it's a good thing I didn't."

He frowned in confusion, nearly groaning at the possibility of more mixed signals from her.

And then she kissed him. Just like that. She lifted her head, found his mouth and kissed him with a fierce emotion that sent joy rushing through him like the Cold Creek swollen with runoff.

"I didn't need to fall in love," she said, her beautiful eyes bright with more tears and a tenderness that made *him* want to weep. "I was already there, in love with my best friend. That love surrounded me every moment of every day. I just had to find the strength to open my heart to it."

"And have you?"

She kissed him again in answer and he decided he wanted to spend every Christmas Eve right here with her in her barn, surrounded by animals and hay and possibilities.

He had no idea how all his Christmas wishes had come true but he wasn't about to question it.

"I love you, Chase Brannon," she murmured against his mouth.

He didn't want to ask but he had to know. "What changed?"

"Why am I not afraid to admit I love you?" She smiled a little. "Who said I'm not? But I have been thinking about something my dad told us over and over when we were held prisoner in Colombia. *Remember, girls*, he would say in that firm voice. *Faith is always stronger than fear.* He was talking about faith in the abstract, not me in particular, but I have decided to listen to his words and apply them to me. I can't let my fear control me. I *am* stronger than this—and during the times when I'm not, I've got your strength to lean on."

He kissed her, humbled and overwhelmed and incredibly grateful for this amazing woman in his arms, who had been through incredible pain but came through with grace, dignity and a beautiful courage.

He wiped a tear away with his thumb, grateful beyond words that such a woman was willing to face her completely justifiable fears for *him*.

"I thought I was going to have a heart attack just now when you fell. For an instant, it was like Travis all over again—but it also confirmed something I had already been thinking."

"Oh?"

She pressed her cheek against his hand. "I've been worried that I'm not strong enough to open my heart to you. The real question is whether I'm strong enough to live without you. When I saw you fall, in those horrible few seconds when you weren't breathing, I realized the answer to that is an unequivocal, emphatic no. I can't bear the idea of not being with you."

He couldn't promise nothing would ever happen to him—but he could promise he would love her fiercely every single day of his life.

"I love you, Chase. I love you, my kids love you, my entire family loves you. I need you. You are my oldest and dearest friend—and my oldest and dearest love."

He framed her face in his hands and kissed her with all the pent-up need from all these years of standing on the sidelines, waiting for their moment to be right. He almost couldn't believe this was real. Maybe he was simply hallucinating after having the wind knocked out of him. But his senses seemed even more acute than usual, alive and invigorated, and the joy expanding in his chest was too bright and wild and beautiful to be imaginary.

People said Christmas was a time for miracles.

He would never doubt that again.

Epilogue

Christmas Eve, one year later

"Okay, help me out, Mary. Where do you keep the salad tongs since you and Pat have renovated the kitchen?"

With whitewashed cabinets and new stainless steel appliances, the new Star N kitchen was beautiful, Faith had to admit—almost as pretty as the renovated kitchen at the Brannon Ridge that had been her wedding present from Chase. But after two months, she still couldn't seem to figure out how to find things here now.

Mary headed to a large drawer on the island. "It made more sense to keep all the utensils in the biggest drawer here where they can all fit instead of scattered throughout the kitchen. I don't know why it took me

fifty years to figure that out. Is this what you're looking for?"

"Yes! Thank you."

She added the dressing to the rest of the ingredients
in her favorite walnut cranberry salad and tossed it with
the tongs. "There. That should do it. Everything looks
great, Mary."

"Thanks." Her aunt beamed and Faith thought, not
for the first time, that Mary seemed years younger since
her marriage to Pat.

"Thank you for hosting the party here at the Star N."

"Christmas is about home and this old house is home
to you girls," Mary said simply. "It seemed right, even
though all of you have bigger places now. Your kitchen
up at Brannon Ridge is twice the size as this one."

As they were discussing how they would merge their
lives after they were married, she and Chase had looked
at both houses and decided to run both ranches from
Brannon Ridge. The house was bigger for all three of
their kids and assorted horses, dogs and barn cats.

It had been a good decision, confirmed just a few
months after Faith and Chase's wedding, when Mary
announced she and her beau were getting married and
wanted to renovate the Star N—a process now in the
final phases.

"Anything else I can carry out to the dining room?"
she asked.

"I made a fruit salad, too. It's in the refrigerator,"
Mary said.

Faith grabbed it and, with one bowl under each arm,

headed for the two long tables that had been set up in the great room to hold the growing family.

She was arranging the bowls when Hope wandered over. "Hey, do you have any idea where I can find tape? I've still got one present to wrap."

"Let me get this straight. You run the most famous Christmas attraction in the Intermountain West *and* you've illustrated a holiday book that was turned into a movie currently ranked number one at the box office for the fourth consecutive week. Yet here it is five p.m. on Christmas Eve and you're still not finished wrapping your presents?"

"Oh, give me a break. I've had a little bit on my plate. You would not *believe* how much of my day this little creature takes up."

Faith smiled. "I think I would. I've had two of my own, remember? Here. Give."

Her sister held up the wriggling adorableness that was her six-month-old son, Samuel, born healthy and full-term, with no complications whatsoever from that early scare more than a year ago.

"You can have him if you tell me where I can find tape."

"The desk drawer in the office." She grinned and admitted the truth. "That's where I put it a half hour ago, anyway, when I finished wrapping my last present."

Hope snorted but fulfilled her part of the deal by handing over the boy.

After she left, Faith nuzzled his neck. Oh, he smelled delicious. Her heart seemed to burst with happiness. "Hey, Sammy. How's my favorite guy?"

"Wow. I guess that puts us in our place, right, Barrett?"

She looked up to find Chase and her son in the doorway, stomping snow off their boots after coming in from shoveling the driveway.

He was smiling but she didn't miss the light in his gaze as he watched her cuddle Hope's cute little boy.

How was it possible that, even after a year, she loved Chase more every single time she saw him?

"My favorite *little* guy," she amended. "You two are my favorite bigger guys. How's the snow out there?"

"Still coming down," Chase said. "Mary said she thinks we'll get another six or seven inches out of the storm. Perfect for cuddling in by the fire and hanging out with the family on Christmas morning."

"I hope Celeste and Flynn make it."

"They pulled in right as we were finishing the driveway," he assured her.

"That's good," Mary said from the kitchen. "Everything's ready and I'm *starving*."

"Sorry we're late," Celeste said as she, Flynn and Olivia came in with their arms loaded down with gifts.

"We still had to wrap a couple of presents," Olivia explained.

Hope paused in the act of setting her hastily wrapped final present under the big tree in the window. "Seriously, CeCe? On Christmas Eve? Maybe next year you should plan ahead a little better," she said virtuously.

Faith had to laugh, which ended up startling Sammy. "Sorry, kiddo."

"Here, I'll take him back."

She didn't want to surrender the soft little bundle

but Mary came in just then. "Great. Everybody's here. Find your places."

After handing Sammy back to his mother, she found a place beside Chase. Addie and Louisa sat at her other side while Barrett sat on Chase's other side.

When they were all settled, Celeste looked around at their family.

"I have an announcement to make. *We* do, actually."

Olivia, Faith noticed, was just about jumping out of her chair in excitement.

"Is this about *Sparkle and the Magic Snowball* being number one again at the box office?" Addie asked.

"Everybody knows that already," Olivia said.

"Is it about the new Sparkle book that's coming out next summer or the movie sequel they're already making?" Louisa asked.

"No," Flynn said. "Though that's all very exciting."

He reached for Celeste's hand and Faith held her breath, sensing what was coming next before her sister even said it.

"We're having a baby."

The table erupted into squeals of excitement and hearty congratulations.

"Another baby. What wonderful news—and the perfect time to find out, on Christmas Eve," Mary exclaimed, her features soft with delight. "When are you due?"

"June. Right around the book launch, which isn't the greatest of timing, I know."

"We'll figure it out," Hope said. "This is so great!

Maybe you'll have a boy, too, and he and Sammy can be best friends!"

Faith felt a big, strong hand reach out and grip hers. She glanced at her husband and saw a secret little smile there, the same one exploding in her heart. The two new cousins would soon become three, but she and Chase were the only ones at the table who knew that, for now.

They wouldn't share their news yet. Faith was only eight weeks along and they had decided to wait until after the New Year to tell anyone. Even Barrett, Lou and Addie didn't know yet.

It was tough to keep the news under wraps but there would be time enough to let the family know even more joy would soon be on the way.

For now, she would celebrate her sister's happiness.

Her heart seemed filled to overflowing and tears welled up as she looked around the table at her family, these people she loved so much.

Pregnancy hormones were making her *crazy*. She cried at everything these days. This, the chance to spend Christmas Eve with all the people she loved most in the world, was worth a few tears, she decided.

Chase's strong, callused fingers threaded through hers and more tears leaked out. He nudged her shoulder with his, and then her oldest and dearest friend—and the man she loved with all her heart—handed her his napkin so she could dry her tears.

"What's wrong? Why are you crying, Mom?" Louisa asked, concern in her eyes that could look so fierce and determined when she and the horse she adored galloped through a barrel course.

Faith sniffled a little more. "I'm happy. That's all."

"Cut it out or you'll set me off," Celeste said.

"And me," Hope said. "Since I had Sammy, I cry if the wind blows at me from the wrong direction."

Faith gave her sisters a watery smile. Their father's words certainly held true for his daughters. Each of them had proved that faith *was* stronger than fear, that they could move past the tough experiences in their past and let love help them heal.

She tightened her fingers around Chase's, the joy in her heart blazing as brightly as the lights on Aunt Mary's big Christmas tree that sent out warmth and color and hope across the snowy night.

* * * * *

Don't miss the other Nichols sisters' stories
of love and Christmas, part of
THE COWBOYS OF COLD CREEK *series:*

A COLD CREEK CHRISTMAS STORY
THE CHRISTMAS RANCH

Available now from Mills & Boon Cherish!

MILLS & BOON®

Cherish™

EXPERIENCE THE ULTIMATE RUSH OF FALLING IN LOVE

MILLS & BOON®

EXCLUSIVE EXTRACT

When Eloise Miller finds herself thrown into the role of maid of honour at the wedding of the year, her plans to stay away from the gorgeous best man are scuppered!

Read on for a sneak preview of
SLOW DANCE WITH THE BEST MAN
by Sophie Pembroke

Maid of honour for Melissa Sommers. How on earth had this happened? And the worst part was—

'Sounds like we'll be spending even more time together.' Noah's voice was warm, deep and far too close to her ear.

Eloise sighed. That. That was the worst thing. Because the maid of honour was *expected* to pair up with the best man, and that would not make her resolution to stay away from Noah Cross any easier at all.

She turned and found him standing directly behind her, close enough that if she'd stepped back a centimetre or two she'd have been in his arms. Suddenly she was glad he'd alerted her to his presence with his words.

She shifted further away and tried to look like a professional, instead of a teenager with a crush. Looking up at him, she felt the strange heat flush over her skin again at his gorgeousness. Then she focused, and realised he was frowning.

'Apparently so,' she agreed. 'But I'm sure I'll be far too busy with all the wedding arrangements—'

'Oh, I doubt it,' Noah interrupted, but he still didn't sound entirely happy about the idea, which surprised her. Perhaps she'd misread his flirting earlier. Maybe he really was like that with everyone and, now the reality of having to spend time with her had set in, he was less keen on the idea. 'Melissa has quite the packed schedule for the wedding party, you know. She's right—you're going to have to find someone to take over most of your job here.'

Eloise sighed. She *did* know. She'd helped Laurel plan it, after all.

And, now she thought about it, every last bit of the schedule involved the maid of honour and the best man being together.

Noah smiled, a hint of the charm he'd exhibited earlier showing through despite the frown, and Eloise's heart beat twice in one moment as she accepted the inevitable.

She was doomed.

She had the most ridiculous crush on a man who clearly found her a minor inconvenience.

And—even worse—the whole world was going to be watching, laughing at her pretending that she could live in this world of celebrities, mocking her for thinking she could ever be pretty enough, funny enough…just *enough* for Noah Cross.

Don't miss
SLOW DANCE WITH THE BEST MAN
by Sophie Pembroke

Available January 2017
www.millsandboon.co.uk

Give a 12 month subscription to a friend today!

Call Customer Services
0844 844 1358*

or visit
millsandboon.co.uk/subscriptions

MILLS & BOON®

Why shop at millsandboon.co.uk?

Each year, thousands of romance readers find their perfect read at millsandboon.co.uk. That's because we're passionate about bringing you the very best romantic fiction. Here are some of the advantages of shopping at www.millsandboon.co.uk:

* **Get new books first**—you'll be able to buy your favourite books one month before they hit the shops

* **Get exclusive discounts**—you'll also be able to buy our specially created monthly collections, with up to 50% off the RRP

* **Find your favourite authors**—latest news, interviews and new releases for all your favourite authors and series on our website, plus ideas for what to try next

* **Join in**—once you've bought your favourite books, don't forget to register with us to rate, review and join in the discussions

Visit **www.millsandboon.co.uk**
for all this and more today!